Smacking her hands o[...] the bed. Then she tipped him onto it. [...] civiously.

"You know what?" she asked in a dreamy voice. "I think I'm starting to feel the wonder of Christmas already."

"I think that's my line," Reid told her, grinning. "You're supposed to be teaching *me* about Christmas, remember?"

"Oh yeah?" Karina asked. "Well, get ready to learn, then."

The two of them smiled at each other, entirely in sync.

Then Karina jumped on the bed and lost herself in the moment, knowing that forever after she would associate the mingled fragrances of mistletoe, bayberry, and dog biscuits with the single most sexually gratifying night of her life.

She hoped.

Almost half an hour later, she knew.

Fa la la. Fa la la. *Fa la LAAAA!*

Wiggling her bare toes with utter satisfaction, Karina shot a smug smile at Reid. He panted beside her, lying sideways on the bed, half tangled in the snowman-print flannel sheets. At the wonderful, amazing, hot-hot-hot sight of him, she sighed.

"So . . . how do you like Christmas now?" she asked.

"I'm not sure." He rolled over and kissed her, then ran his hands along the length of her naked torso. "I think I need another lesson to find out. I might need *several* more lessons."

"Do you really think you're up for it?"

Saucily, Reid raised his eyebrows. He aimed his gaze lower. Much lower. All the way down to his . . . mischief maker.

"Oh, I'm up for it," he confirmed. Then he pulled her into his arms again, gave her a smile, and proceeded to prove it.

Naughty or nice is way overrated, Karina decided as she felt Reid's body cover hers, igniting a new burst of giddiness and heat in her midsection. *Naughty wins, all the way. . . .*

Books by Lisa Plumley

MAKING OVER MIKE

FALLING FOR APRIL

RECONSIDERING RILEY

PERFECT TOGETHER

PERFECT SWITCH

JOSIE DAY IS COMING HOME

ONCE UPON A CHRISTMAS

MAD ABOUT MAX

SANTA, BABY
(anthology with Lisa Jackson,
Elaine Coffman, and Kylie Adams)

I SHAVED MY LEGS FOR THIS?!
(anthology with Theresa Alan,
Holly Chamberlin, and Marcia Evanick)

LET'S MISBEHAVE

HOME FOR THE HOLIDAYS

MY FAVORITE WITCH

Published by Kensington Publishing Corporation

Holiday Affair

Lisa Plumley

WITHDRAWN

ZEBRA BOOKS
KENSINGTON PUBLISHING CORP.
http://www.kensingtonbooks.com

ZEBRA BOOKS are published by

Kensington Publishing Corp.
119 West 40th Street
New York, NY 10018

All Kensington titles, imprints, and distributed lines are available at special quantity discounts for bulk purchases for sales promotion, premiums, fund-raising, educational or institutional use.

Special book excerpts or customized printings can also be created to fit specific needs. For details, write or phone the office of the Kensington Special Sales Manager: Kensington Publishing Corp., 119 West 40th Street, New York, NY 10018. Attn. Special Sales Department. Phone: 1-800-221-2647.

Zebra and the Z logo Reg. U.S. Pat. & TM Off.

ISBN-13: 978-1-4201-0569-8
ISBN-10: 1-4201-0569-8

First Printing: October 2010
10 9 8 7 6 5 4 3 2 1

Printed in the United States of America

For John Plumley, the undisputed king of gifts that make me cry with happiness. Merry Christmas, honey! I love you!

Chapter One

December 15th
San Diego, California

"Michael, wait. Let me help you with that."

With a hasty glance in her rearview mirror, Karina Barrett scrambled out of her old Corolla. On the sidewalk just beyond her parked car, her children stopped to wait for her. Olivia patted her blond bangs, preparing for another day of fifth grade at Marsden Elementary School. Josh clutched a plastic tray of supermarket-baked cupcakes for his third grade class and shifted from foot to foot beside his sister. Michael, in first grade now and proud of it, blithely kept on walking. His backpack nearly dwarfed him. The poster board in his hands wobbled and bowed, making it almost impossible for him to see where he was going.

"No, thanks!" He shook his head. "I don't need any help."

"Oh, yes, you do." Karina reached him seconds before he careened into another student. With deft fingers, she plucked the poster board from Michael's hands. At the sight of the copious cotton ball "snow" glued to the front, she smiled. "This poster is so cute, Michael. But it's almost as big as you are!"

"No, it's not," her son protested. "I'm *way* bigger!"

He wasn't. Not yet. Thank goodness. But Karina had already parented one boy through this superhero-loving, wanting-to-be-big stage. She knew better than to disagree outright. While she weighed her options, other students swarmed past them, talking and laughing and occasionally skateboarding toward the building.

Only in California. Or at least, *not* in Minnesota or another state where December brought snowstorms and icicles instead of sunny days at the beach and afternoons spent shopping for surfboards and flip-flops. After today, it would officially be winter break—the run-up to Christmas and all its festivities.

But despite the plastic "evergreen" wreath wired to the grille of the Ford Explorer parked behind her car and the poinsettia-printed, sequin-bedecked blouse worn by Michael's teacher as she motioned for her students to line up at the edge of the playground, it didn't feel much like Christmas to Karina.

Maybe because she wasn't ready for Christmas yet. Not this year. Or possibly ever again. The whole idea of confronting the holidays made her feel downright woozy. She'd been avoiding it for as long as she could. But now—on the last full day of school—she couldn't sidestep the issue any longer.

It wasn't the weather that bothered her. Or the lack of traditional wintery ambiance. As a lifelong Californian, she was used to seventy-six-degree Christmases and spray-on snow. She was even used to wearing shorts while gift shopping. What she *wasn't* used to was being solely responsible for managing all the holiday activities herself—for giving her kids a Christmas to remember, no matter what. This year, it would be up to Karina to play Santa, wrap all the gifts, wrestle an enormous Douglas fir into its three-legged, red and green stand, decorate that tree (even the very highest branches), hang multicolored chaser lights on the eaves, bake cookies and gingerbread. . . .

Just thinking about it made her want to crawl back into bed. She'd never handled all those activities on her own. How was she supposed to manage it this year? Especially with scarcely enough money to pay the bills? And a secret fear of ruining everything?

She *had* to do a good job of it, though. For her kids' sakes. Olivia, Michael, and Josh deserved it, especially after all the turmoil they'd been through over the past year.

With effort—and a deliberately cheerful smile—Karina forced her attention away from her worries. Instead, she examined the "winter celebration" poster her youngest son had scissored, crayoned, and lavishly glued at the kitchen table last night. At Marsden Elementary School, even secular Christmas activities were out. Benign, nonsectarian "seasonal celebration" activities were in. That was why Karina had donated her entire cache of makeup-removing cotton balls to Michael's poster, upon which not a single Santa or Rudolph or glittery angel could be seen.

Encouraging anything remotely Christmassy would have meant breaking the rules. And Karina was not a rule breaker at heart. She believed in sticking to the playbook, cooperating as much as possible, and—most of all—doing right by her children. Even when those children—like Michael—might feel they didn't need her.

"Well," she said, "even big guys need help sometimes."

Michael scoffed at that. "That's not what Dad says. He says a man should be a man. He lets me do *everything* by myself."

Her six-year-old "man" spread his arms like wings. His expansive gesture suggested *everything* from pouring his own apple juice to playing Xbox until four A.M. to putting down a cool fifty on the Chargers versus the Seahawks, with a ten-point spread and the Seahawks favored.

Karina didn't doubt Michael's story was true—at least

partly. Concerned, she cast a questioning glance at Olivia and Josh. In response, they only lifted their gazes to the cloudless California sky, eyebrows arched in elaborate, unified—and entirely unlikely—innocence. *We don't know nothin',* their mulish, pint-sized expressions said. *You can't make us talk.*

Any second now, she half expected them to come out with a nonchalant whistle. *Nothing to see here. Move along, Mom.*

Hmmm. She'd have to discuss this with her ex-husband. Eric wouldn't like her "butting in" again, but it couldn't be helped. After their weekends with Eric at his new beachside condo, their children always came home wired, rebellious, and—most alarming of all—secretive. Karina needed to investigate why that was.

Until now, she hadn't wanted to push for details about the kids' visits with their dad. She hadn't wanted to be one of "those" divorcées—the ones who put their children in the middle, used them to spy on their exes, or tried to make them choose sides. Above all else, she'd striven to be fair and aboveboard—even when Eric had made her want to strangle him with one of those skinny "euro-chic" scarves he'd started wearing recently.

She'd burst out laughing the first time she'd dropped off Michael, Olivia, and Josh and gotten an eyeful of Eric sporting skintight hipster jeans, a V-necked T-shirt, and three yards of gnarly linen around his neck. He'd flashed her a double-gun salute and told her he "rocked that look"!

Karina hadn't had the heart to tell him how idiotic he appeared—less "rockin'" and more "delusional Pete Wentz wannabe who's way too old to pull off that eyeliner."

Yep. *Eyeliner.* On her thirty-six-year-old aerospace engineer ex-husband, who—as far as she knew—still commuted to work and kept a scale model of a P-51 Mustang in his cubicle.

Thinking back on the incident, Karina figured she probably deserved a medal of some sort, just for keeping quiet. And for stifling her laughter too. The awful truth was, she might want to nut punch her cheating ex, but that didn't mean she wanted to hurt his feelings. She didn't want to be *mean* or anything.

On the other hand, there must be some serious rules infractions going on at Eric's playhouse of a condo, if the resulting freedom was appealing enough to make Olivia and Josh band together to protect it. Most of the time, the two of them were poster children for sibling rivalry. Once you added Michael to the mix, things could get out of hand pretty quickly.

But her children's "rambunctiousness" (as a few teachers, some of the PTO parents, and their own grandmother called it) was a problem for another day. So was her ex-husband's new life and all its Hot Topic accoutrements. Right now, Karina had a grade-school drop-off to accomplish, and not much time to do it in. Even now, suburban SUVs choked the parking lot behind her, snaking along the curb like overgrown Hot Wheels sets.

Or maybe like regular *vehicles*. Period.

Karina shook her head. She'd obviously been spending way too much time at the toy store. Her ex-husband was living it up Hugh-Hefner-with-his-Bunnies style, and she was keeping an eagle eye on the arrival of new Tonka trucks and updated Bratz dolls.

As a substitute for a social life went, haunting the toy store was pretty lame. But it *had* made her popular with her children's friends. *And* it had given her an encyclopedic knowledge of Bionicles, Power Miners, and Creator sets too.

Who knew where that could take her? Heck, she was well on her way to dating again. She'd be irresistible . . . to one of those geeks who flooded San Diego every summer during Comic-Con.

Yikes. Karina shuddered at the thought. She might be a little lonely right now, but not lonely enough to take a chance on another equation-spouting, scarf-wearing, smarty-pants man-child like Eric. The next man she dated would be as far from dorkdom as she could manage—just as insurance against another broken heart. It was for her own good. After all, everyone knew she had a weakness for intelligence. A fondness for technical expertise. And—*oh yeah*—a total, paralyzing, realized-it-too-late inability to protect her heart when it came to relationships.

The last thing she needed was a man. For at least a decade or two. Maybe longer. How long could she go before her libido quit nagging at her? Karina wondered. As it was, she still experienced the occasional inconvenient heat wave—particularly when confronted with, say, an unexpectedly sexy man stocking up on salsa, chips, and honey in the grocery store checkout lane last Tuesday. Just to name a totally nonspecific example.

She still wondered what all that honey had been for . . . and would have offered a few risqué ideas if asked nicely, too.

Eric had cheated on her and abandoned her, Karina reminded herself indignantly; he hadn't neutered her. But surely those urges would go away if she just ignored them long enough. Right?

She had to focus on something else. *Anything* else.

"Come on, you guys." She waved the poster board toward the school's sleek entryway. Built when defense contractors had first swarmed San Diego's balmy coastline more than fifty years ago, the building was red brick, low slung, retro, and painstakingly restored, just like all the houses in the adjacent neighborhood Karina couldn't *quite* afford to live in anymore.

Despite the meager support payments Eric made, her standard of living had definitely taken a nosedive after her divorce. She refused to give up and move to a cheaper place, though. She hated to upset the kids any more than she and Eric had done already. If she had to, she could always take a temp job to make ends meet. "Let's get you three settled in, okay?"

Olivia rolled her eyes. "Mom, *stop.*" She swiped her hand across her throat, mimicking a director's "cut" sign. Her gaze slid past Karina's sunglasses, chin-length blond curly hair, and hastily pulled on T-shirt. "You're wearing *pajamas,*" she hissed.

Oh. Yeah. "So? Only the bottoms, that's all." Karina gestured at her perfectly respectable T-shirt. "Let's go."

"And fuzzy slippers." Josh sighed . . . just like his dad.

"Big deal." Affecting a light tone, Karina hustled them forward. She glanced back at the other parents—all of whom were undoubtedly wearing actual pants at that moment, as they perched appropriately behind the wheels of their SUVs. "Wearing pajama pants around town is cool these days, right? With Uggs?"

"Uggs?" This time, it was Olivia's turn to snort. She cast a despairing glance at her mother's non-Ugged, beslippered feet. "Sure, Mom. Maybe if you're a college student, like Chelsea, who's studying for finals or something, so you don't care how you look. *Or* if you're a complete social recluse. *Uggs?* Really?"

Josh gave her a somber shake of his head. Michael cast a longing glance at the jungle gym. Karina only stifled a sigh.

Chelsea. She didn't want to think about her ex-husband's new girlfriend, much less be compared (unfavorably) to her by her own daughter. Chelsea was busty, tattooed, and pierced. She was good at surfing. She was studying to be a veterinarian. She was twenty-two, giggly, and pretty, and she was even relatively *nice,* particularly to the kids, whenever they visited.

But that didn't mean Karina had to devote precious brain space to Chelsea. Or to her colorful collection of skimpy bikini tops. Or to whatever she and Eric were probably doing together most nights—potentially with some organic buckwheat honey thrown into the mix to add a little novelty.

Mmmm . . . honey. The things you could do with a little—

Or maybe not. Honey-Buying Man was *her* fantasy. Her never-to-be-fulfilled, time-wasting, impossible fantasy. Argh.

Thankfully, one of the other parents honked just then, yanking Karina from the brink of a full-on pity party *and* giving her a chance to think about something else besides her arrested sense of fashion and her stalled desirability. Evidently, her aura of coolness had atrophied right along with her sex appeal—at least if Eric's tearful, posterectile dysfunction–prompted, I'm-leaving-you midnight confessionals could be believed.

Jerk. With a determined effort, Karina straightened her spine, then smiled at Josh, Michael, and Olivia.

Her priority was her children. Period. Whatever it took, she intended to make sure they were happy. Happy happy happy.

"Hey! I just had a genius idea!" Karina said. "Why don't I spend the day volunteering here at school? I think I can help out in all three of your classes, if I try hard enough."

Michael gave her a quizzical look. Olivia and Josh merely groaned. "Mom, that's okay," her daughter said. "You *really* don't have to volunteer anymore. It's the last day before winter break! We're just going to have parties and stuff anyway, so—"

"So that's all the more reason to be here, I'd say. Your teachers are bound to appreciate the extra help." Beaming, Karina gave each of her children a warmhearted hug. She felt better already. "I'll just go park the car in the visitor's lot. I'll be back in a sec."

Raring to go (now that she had a mission), Karina headed for her Corolla. The sun sparkled off its dented roof. The other parents smiled at her. Her slippers bopped along merrily.

Maybe she *could* handle Christmas all on her own this year, she decided with a burst of optimism. Right after she helped out here at the school for a while. And right after she shopped for some much-needed groceries later (there was always the outside chance she'd see Honey-Buying Man at Ralph's again). And of *course* she'd have to change her outgoing voice mail message at the office sometime today too, Karina remembered. She'd forgotten to do that earlier in the week. All faculty members were supposed to change their message at the end of each semester at the college where she worked as an academic advisor. But *immediately* after that—

"Mom?" Olivia called.

Cheerily, Karina wheeled around.

Her daughter grabbed her own pants. In an exasperated pantomime, Olivia waggled the legs of her jeans. Then she spread her arms and pointed both index fingers at Karina, looking a little too "gangsta" for comfort. "Hell-*o*. Pajamas?"

"Don't worry. I was planning to go home and change first."

Change of plans. She definitely had to go home and change first.

Feeling flustered but purposeful, Karina swiveled again. She returned Michael's poster board to him, gave each of her children a kiss on the tops of their heads, then scooted them off toward the school building. "I'll be back! See you soon!"

She watched as they trooped dutifully away.

"Have a nice day!" She blew a kiss. "Love you!"

The three of them just kept going, with Michael in the lead. A little crestfallen, Karina crossed her arms over her chest. Were they simply going to go straight inside without another word? Without even waving good-bye?

At the last instant, Josh glanced over his shoulder. He adjusted his cupcakes, then gave her a tiny, barely perceptible, flicking-a-bug-off-his-shoulder-style wave. "Love you too, Mom."

Awww. At his gesture, Karina turned to mush all over again.

Then she rushed to her Corolla, hell-bent on a mission to get dressed, get organized, and get cracking on creating the very best Christmas her children had ever seen. Right after she volunteered at school, shopped for groceries, voice mailed, and tackled all those other must-do items on her mental to-do list.

She'd swear those tasks were multiplying somehow . . . kind of like the love she felt for her children had done, when she'd become almost solely responsible for their well-being after her divorce. The plain truth was, however much Eric loved his children (and he did), he'd become way too preoccupied with reliving his misspent youth to be counted on for anything. Which reminded her: She needed to get Santas and stockings, gifts and carols, traditions and eggnog, wrapping paper and ornaments. . . .

And candy canes. Candy canes! She'd forgotten how much Olivia, Michael, and Josh loved hunting in the Christmas tree to find them hidden among the branches. How could she have a not-to-be-missed Christmas without candy canes? Oh God oh God oh—

Stopping at the curb, Karina inhaled deeply to ward off the sudden sensation that she was about to hyperventilate. In. Out. In. Out. Just the way that *Oprah* guru had recommended on TV last month. She felt serene. She felt calm. She felt at peace.

She felt as though she was staring straight at an unmistakably flat tire on her Corolla.

She was. Well, it was a good thing she *wasn't* wearing real pants, cute high heels, and a fashionable, flirty top, like the other moms were, she decided as she wrenched open the trunk, hauled out the jack, and examined her spare tire. Because tire grime was hell on those two-hundred-dollar jeans that were so popular among the PTO elite. And trendy stilettos made it hard to balance while unscrewing lug nuts. And

the only person Karina could really depend on was herself—
a lesson she'd forget at her own peril, whether she was wearing
baggy flannel PJs or not.

Resolute, she gave an apologetic wave to the other parents
for bollixing up the school drop-off line, then got down to
work changing her flat tire. If only she could change her life
just as easily as she could change her poor squashed-looking
tire, Karina thought as she hunkered beside her old car.

No, scratch that. She'd had enough unwanted change for a
lifetime already. The only thing on *her* holiday wish list this
year was a nice, old-fashioned Christmas—one that was free
of turmoil and blissfully free of unreliable men like Eric.

*Please, Santa. Just give me that much. I promise I'll
be good.*

It wouldn't be tough. After all, Karina was always good.
Determinedly, tirelessly . . . *boringly* good.

Chapter Two

Tuesday (or maybe Thursday)
Inland Australia: The Outback

Muscles flexing with exertion, Reid Sullivan belly crawled over a slab of unforgiving rock. At the top, he peered over it. Bright daylight struck his face. Squinting, he tried to focus on the next ridge—the next target. It looked a long way off. And if the sun had already risen, time was running out. Damn.

After a glance at the bulky cast on his left leg, Reid kept going. He crawled a few more meters. Underbrush scraped his chest. Red dust filled his nostrils. Branches poked painfully through his T-shirt. Rocks jabbed his knees, even through the protective covering of his tough canvas trail pants.

At least he was properly equipped and appropriately dressed for the rough trail ahead, though. That was more than he could say for the hapless people behind him.

Straightening atop the next hunk of rock, he glanced back at them. There were four of them, all men who'd paid Reid to lead them through the desolate landscape. They were counting on him—and they were struggling. Even now, one of the men—a middle-aged CEO with one of those prissy, prep-school nicknames like Biff or Binky or Buster—flopped on his backside. He sat beside a clump of spiky mulga, panting like a Labrador.

"Keep moving!" Reid gave a military-style "go ahead" sign. "It's only a few more kilometers till we reach the next zone."

"A few more *kilometers?*" Binky's eyes bulged. "Jesus, dude! You never said we had several kilometers ahead of us!"

"How far is that for real?" Binky's cohort, Booster, asked. "You know, in American?" He panted even harder, pulling up a figurative chair as he squatted on a boulder. "How many miles?"

"Not many. Do the math." It wasn't exactly rocket science to convert kilometers into miles. These four brainiacs ought to be up for the task. Possibly by counting on their fingers. Half expecting them to do just that, Reid idly examined a jagged scrape on his bare bicep. He didn't know where he'd gotten it. But he'd been cut up, bruised up, and hurt plenty of times in his life. He could take it. Experimentally, he flexed his arm.

It felt fine. Drawn by the gesture, his companions' gazes traveled to his biceps, then moved across his broad chest and muscular shoulders. In unison, the men frowned. Deeply.

Uh-oh. Reid recognized that look. It expressed admiration and belligerence in equal measure. Yes, he was big. Yes, he was fit. Yes, he could probably bench-press Binky, if he tried to.

But he wasn't going to. For one thing, the big crybaby would probably start howling if Reid so much as looked at him sideways. Binky was not exactly a tough guy. His reaction to their trek had proven that already. For another, Reid had quit performing those kinds of stupid macho stunts *years* ago.

Okay. He'd quit doing the bench-press one a few months ago. But the plain fact was, Reid stayed in shape because, in his line of work, his life depended on it. So did his companions'.

That meant he couldn't let up on them. No matter what.

"Get off your asses and scale that outcropping. Now."

"Hey!" The third man widened his eyes beneath his wide-brimmed, khaki bush hat. His nose glowed with a thick stripe of sunscreen. "Watch your tone. I didn't get up at dawn this morning just to be treated like some kind of flunky, you know."

"Yeah," Booster said hotly. "Me neither. Do you understand exactly how many thousands of people across the globe depend on *important* men like us for their livelihoods? Do you?"

"At least one person is depending on us for his next paycheck." Binky's tone was snide. "And that's you, Sullivan!"

He had a point. But Reid didn't care. "A paycheck would be nice. But a dead man can't spend a dime. So keep moving."

He compressed his mouth, then turned away. After a few tense seconds, he heard telltale lumbering footfalls behind him.

Good. It was about damn time this bunch fell in line. Ordinarily, Reid was a patient man. But this particular group—

A bloodcurdling, girlish scream rent the morning air.

Reid twisted around. His leg cast dislodged stones and dust, making them ping away. Down the trail, Booster stood with his mouth agape, legs stiff as he pointed at something nearby.

"A—" He moistened his dry mouth with a dart of his tongue. Clearly, he'd ignored Reid's hydration instructions. "A rat!"

The other three men skittered behind him, their gazes wary.

"It's *huge!*" Binky swore, cowering, as he spied it. "Huge!"

"It's probably poisonous." Binky gave a dour, knowing nod. "*Everything* is poisonous around here. *Super* poisonous."

"Just like that big-ass spider we saw." One of the other men gestured wildly. "Australia is trying to murder us!"

Asshat number four picked up a stick. "Hundred bucks says I can kill it. Freaking rat." He gave an ineffectual swing. "Ha!"

Make that asshat *numero uno.* Reid shook his head, then

strode purposefully in their direction. He cast a long, sharply angled shadow over the men as he plucked away the stick.

"Oh good." Booster gave him a bloodthirsty gaze. "It's about time you manned up and started living up to that badass reputation of yours, Sullivan. *You're* going to kill it!"

"Nobody's killing it." Reid hurled the stick across the sun-baked terrain, his scowl deepening with disapproval. Why was everyone's first impulse to squash what they didn't understand? "And it's not a rat. It's a wombat." To be fair, most creatures out here in the Outback looked ratlike. A surprising number of them sported pink hairless tails. But he wasn't in the mood to cut this pea-brained quartet any slack. "It's *not* poisonous. But if that had been an Inland Taipan"—a snake that lived in remote areas like this—"it would have bitten you. In the time it took you to squeal, partial paralysis would have begun setting in."

The four men's mouths gaped in shock. Fear. And surprise.

Those doltish looks could mean only one thing. Reid swore. "You didn't read *any* of the pretravel materials I sent you?"

Beneath his stern gaze, Binky looked away first. "I had my admin prepare a summary. But it was on my BlackBerry, and it—"

"It was confiscated by your goddamn staff! All of our BlackBerrys were! I haven't checked the market for days. Days!" Shuddering, Booster cast an accusing glance at the third man. Rover. Gopher. No, *Topher*. "We're completely out of the loop. Nobody told me about *that* part of this team-building event."

Asshat crossed his arms over his chest. He appeared to be sulking over losing his wombat-bashing stick. "Didn't you get the memo? Corporate thinks it's a good idea to be unplugged."

Beside him, Topher gave a vigorous nod. "During strictly designated intervals only, of course. It's all part of the official

Qualifying Your Quality initiative we're launching. My department came up with a totally kick-ass slogan. Get this—"

"Get moving." Reid turned. "We're burning daylight."

"No, that's not it. It's—"

"This area is prone to flash flooding." Reid tromped onward—more awkwardly and less athletically than he was used to, thanks to the leg cast that hampered his stride. "Remember what I told you: If you see water coming, stay away from the banks. Don't try to beat the flood—you can't. Get to higher ground."

Binky, Topher, Booster, and Asshat plodded along.

"But there isn't a cloud in the sky," Binky pointed out.

"Doesn't matter." Pausing at the edge of a dry creek bed, Reid adjusted his pack. He'd taken on this job as a favor to his longtime friend Shane Evans, who ran an adventure travel business out of Perth. Shane's remote base of operations—the site from which Reid had begun this trip—felt a million miles away. "Out here, a flash flood will kill you."

He should have expected it: The four men scoffed.

Right on cue, a wall of water roared down the creek bed. Moving fast, it swirled directly into their path. Tautly, Reid looked at the muddy eddies headed straight for them.

Against all reason, he grinned. He just couldn't help it.

There was a lot to be said for karmic justice. In Reid's experience, that variety of justice usually came in with a bang— and left men like this clueless crew whimpering in its wake.

If nothing else, this day was about to get a lot more interesting.

Karina, sweaty and dust covered and exasperated, was standing hip deep among several cardboard storage boxes when her cell phone rang. Stooped in the hot, poorly lit area the Realtor had euphemistically described as an "attic" twelve years ago when she and Eric had bought their house as newlyweds, she scrambled to answer the call. It was probably one of the community college students she advised. Technically, she was off duty until mid-January. But she liked to make herself available between semesters, just in case someone needed her.

"Karina Barrett. How can I help?" she asked crisply.

There was a pause. Then her younger sister Stephanie's voice came over the line. She sounded weary. And befuddled. "Karina? Did I call you at work? What time is it anyway?"

Karina took the cell phone from her ear and squinted at the glowing display. Watches were so 2002. She put it in place again. "It's just after seven. And no, I'm at home. What's up?"

"Hmmm. I thought you were going to stop making yourself available to your students at all hours."

"I was." Still cradling her cell phone, Karina dropped to her knees in front of the next box. "I am."

"Then why did you answer your phone that way?"

"What way?"

"Like the secret love child of Miss Manners and a Marine."

Karina laughed. "Takes one to know one."

"Guilty. At least I get compensated appropriately for it."

"That's true." Stephanie worked as an expert risk-assessment evaluator for Edgware Consulting, a global hospitality management company. She and her husband, Justin, were the epitome of dual-career coupledom. Both of them worked hard, played hard, and still found the time to indulge in creative, "enriching" hobbies with their four-year-old son, Blake Whitmore Dodger Taylor. They were always jetting off to preschool yoga or Classical French Cooking for Families or artsy indie films and documentaries. "Listen: If you were Eric—"

"I'd hate myself, because I'd be a loser."

"—where would you put four boxes of Christmas decorations?"

"Four boxes?" Stephanie offered a succinct, unprintable

suggestion. "I'd shove them straight up his no-good, cheating—"

"Never mind. I'll just keep looking."

"You can't find any of your Christmas stuff?"

"No." Before Karina could stop herself, her worst suspicion slipped out. "I think Eric took everything when he moved out."

"That dirtbag *stole* your Christmas decorations?"

"Well . . . legally speaking, they're his decorations too. California *is* a community-property state." *Thank God.* Otherwise Karina would've been left with nothing when her husband left. Balanced on her knees, she opened the flaps on another box. It contained baby clothes—things she'd boxed up when Michael had grown too big for them. At the time, she'd thought she and Eric might have another child. She sighed. "I should have expected this, I guess. I just wish he'd told me he wanted them first."

This put a new wrinkle in her never-ending Christmas to-do list, she realized. Now, not only did she have to handle everything (impeccably!) by herself, she also had to start over from scratch, without so much as a piece of tinsel. Ho ho ho.

Hoping to shore up her spirits, Karina inhaled deeply. Then she smiled into her cell phone. "It's all right," she told her sister. "I can manage without our old Christmas decorations. Some of them were getting pretty ratty anyway."

Because we loved them so much, Velveteen Rabbit style.

Back in the day, she and the kids had loved reading that story together. It had made regular appearances as part of their bedtime routine. Lately, though, that formerly dependable routine had gone through some changes.

Okay, that routine had been demolished, plain and simple. Despite Karina's efforts, it turned out their routine *hadn't* been so dependable, after all. Partly that was because preteen Olivia could scarcely be pried away from texting her friends on her cell phone at all hours. Partly it was because Josh insisted on being the one to read, rather than being read to (something Olivia tended to take exception to). Partly it was because the whole endeavor still felt weird without Eric participating. Now, only Michael was willing to snuggle after a nighttime bath, with a stuffed animal in the crook of his elbow, as he listened to Karina read.

Pretty soon, her littlest boy was bound to take a stand against "stupid" bedtime rituals too, just like his brother and sister had. It was just the way things were going these days.

With a sigh, Karina gazed around the attic. First her husband. Then the kids' bedtime routine. Now her Christmas decorations. What next?

She couldn't believe something *else* was gone from her life . . . just like that. It felt as though her entire existence was being sneaked away in increasingly smaller increments, and there was nothing she could do about it.

Except go with the flow. So that's what she'd do.

Determinedly, Karina put away the box of onesies and tiny shorts. She would have liked to have had more children. She absolutely had love to spare. But a ginormous family wasn't in the cards for her, apparently. Eric had made sure of that when he'd decided to play Dream House with Beach Bunny Chelsea.

"This way, the kids and I can have things exactly the way we want them. I'll get all new decorations. It'll be better than ever, probably! So Eric is doing me a favor. Sort of."

"Nice call, Mother Teresa," Stephanie deadpanned. "You're too kind—as usual."

"Well, what's done is done, right? There's no point freaking out now." Through the opening that led to the "attic" came the sounds of something thumping. Then a high-pitched shriek. Olivia. Then another retaliatory thump and a subsequent howl. Possibly Josh. Uh-oh. She'd have to get downstairs soon. "Listen, I think the kids are getting into something they shouldn't. I've got to run, Steph, so—"

"Wait." Stephanie sounded harried. All lightheartedness vanished from her tone. "Please. I need your help."

"With what?"

"Well . . . It's complicated."

Complicated? It wasn't like Stephanie to be so hesitant. Feeling concerned, Karina gripped her cell phone more tightly.

"Complicated like, 'The coq au vin for my supper club isn't Julia Child worthy'?" she asked, striving for the breeziness her sister lacked. "Or complicated like, 'I just found Justin licking the banisters and singing a Lady Gaga song'?"

"Um, *not* the coq au vin. Or the licking."

"Just the singing?"

"Actually, he has a very nice voice."

Stephanie's admiring tone made Karina smile, despite everything. Her sister and Justin gave her hope. They proved two people *could* be genuinely happy together. Stephanie and Justin respected one another. They trusted one another. They helped one another in ways that Karina had always wanted to help Eric.

Unfortunately, Eric hadn't wanted her help. Or *her.*

But Stephanie still needed her. So much so that Karina could have sworn she heard a faint crackling sound travel across the phone line, followed by a harsh, relieved exhalation.

"Are you smoking again?" she demanded.

Silence. Guilty silence. Then, "Only one. It's been a long day. I hardly know my own name at this point. I'm in trouble!"

"Whatever you need," Karina said, "I'll do it."

"Don't you want to know what it is first?"

"You can fill me in later." Hearing another thump, Karina peered through the "attic" opening. "In the meantime . . . Any ideas how to remove glitter from an eight-year-old boy's hair?"

* * *

It didn't take long for the creek bed to fill. Or for Reid's travel companions to eyeball the frothy rushing water, stare across it at the sudden, glittering mirage of the Evans Adventure Travel campsite—their ultimate destination, which hadn't been visible until they'd reached the crest of the ridge—and foolishly decide they could probably make it across.

"We can probably make it across!" Binky shouted.

"Hell yeah!" Booster agreed. "Let's go."

"Hundred bucks says I'm first to make it," Asshat put in.

The rest of them clamored to get in on that action.

Disappointed, Reid shook his head. He consulted his watch. He'd hoped things would go differently today. On the other hand, he usually hoped things would go differently . . . and was generally disappointed. As though in blatant proof of that trend, his charges continued to lay bets on their odds of surviving the flash-flood waters, in direct defiance of Reid's instructions.

"So long, suckers!" Topher yelled gleefully. He took off his pack, held it over his head, then waded in. Wearing a smug smile, he turned to face them all. "See? Water's fine."

Oh hell. The overconfident ones were always the worst— the loudest, the lamest, and the biggest pains in Reid's ass. Swearing, he plucked at the Velcro straps encasing his leg cast. Just to be on the safe side. If worse came to worst—and it probably would—the unwieldy thing would only slow him down.

"Oh no, you didn't!" Binky shouted. He waded in too.

Oh boy. The stupidity was contagious. Even as Reid doubled his efforts to free himself of his leg cast, the crunch of footsteps on rocks alerted him that someone was approaching.

Reid glanced up. A little girl stopped a short distance from him. Her brow furrowed as she examined the flood.

Then she shrugged and stuffed her hands in her pockets. "Dad, would you please tell Alexis to give me back my stuffed dingo puppy? She hid it, and she won't tell me where it is."

"Nicole, honey, I'm a little busy right now."

"I know, Dad. But you're the only one who can help, 'cause you're the smartest and the strongest. And Alexis—"

"Nuh-uh! Don't listen to her, Dad!" His other daughter— one year older than Nicole's ten—scrambled over the ridge. Down the slope behind her stood an official Evans Adventure Travel Jeep, parked crookedly in the dirt. "Whatever she said, I didn't do it!" Alexis shouted. "I swear. I hate her stupid dingo."

"It's *not* stupid!" Nicole shrieked, lips trembling.

"Is too." Alexis crossed her arms. "Stupid like you."

"No name-calling." Reid scowled at his daughters. Then, with that parental edict automatically delivered, he jabbed his chin toward his group of foundering travelers. "As soon as I'm done with this bunch, I'll help you look for your dingo, Nicole. And Lex . . . Don't tell me you drove the Jeep again?"

Casually, his daughter quirked one skinny shoulder. "It's not my fault the garage here doesn't have better security."

"They have an alarm, infrared sensors, keyless entry—"

"Like I said." Clearly relishing the fact that she'd defeated all those high-tech measures, Alexis grinned. "They need better security. Besides, I'm old enough to drive."

"No, you're not," Nicole disagreed. "You only look like you're old enough to drive if you're wearing enough eye shadow."

Eye shadow? On his little girl? His multilingual, tomboy-ish, sweet little girl? Reid must have heard wrong.

"So? You're just mad because you can't reach the pedals."

Nicole's cheeks pinkened—a dead giveaway that she'd tried. And failed. And hadn't wanted her dad to know about it.

"The two of you should quit stealing Jeeps." Reid issued the statement distractedly, the way he performed most parental duties that involved rules and restrictions and pointless niceties. As far as he was concerned, kids should be kids—not tiny, obedient adults. "I draw the line at breaking the law."

"Since when?" Alexis asked. "That one time in Istanbul—"

"Seriously. *Later.*" Reid worked more diligently at his leg cast coverings. Near the creek, Booster and Asshat struggled just as mightily with their backpack straps. They both waded in.

Nicole noticed. "Um, Dad? Those guys don't look so smart."

"Yeah." Alexis made a face. "They're about as sure-footed as that guide we had in the Himalayas last year. The drunk one."

Reid remembered him. He'd had to haul up their "sherpa" from the edges of snowy drop-offs more than once. That would teach him to mentor enthusiastic newbies. More and more, though, it seemed as though newbies were the only ones who wanted to go into the adventure travel business. Except they wanted to do their work in comfort, with high-def TVs in their roomy tents, 24/7 Internet access, and magically retouched souvenir photos of their "adventures" to show for their troubles afterward. Sort of like the corporate crew currently flailing away in the creek.

Business definitely wasn't what it used to be. Sometimes Reid wondered if he'd be happier in another line of work.

Usually those glum thoughts occurred at times like these, though, when his inconvenient sense of duty forced him to do something unpleasant . . . like dive into a cold, muddy undertow.

A strangled cry came from the creek bed. Topher sank.

"Dad . . ." Nicole bit her lip. "That guy just went under."

"I know, honey. I'm going."

Reid ripped off the remainder of his leg cast, took off his

boots, then stood. His cast and its engineered coverings landed in a neat pile at Alexis's feet. They drew her attention.

"Ah. The old 'fake cast' maneuver." She nodded, probably remembering the other times Reid had employed the same strategy with his clients. Certain clients relied on him too much—to the extent that it made them reckless. Reid had begun wearing the leg cast on trial runs—especially with arrogant types like Binky, Asshat, Booster, and Topher—several years ago. It forced clients to take their own welfare more seriously . . . at least in theory. "Nice one, Dad. I'll bet they didn't even spot the trick fastenings." She picked it up. "I did a good job on this."

That was true. Alexis was handy in that way. She always had been. At five, she'd dismantled Reid's compass and trail watch—and then reassembled them. At eight, she'd reprogrammed his GPS units and hacked his satellite phone. Now, at eleven, she had yet to meet the device, technology, or ordinary, old-school lock and key that could defeat her talents.

"You did, Alexis," Nicole said. "You're smart like that."

"Ha. Nice try, stupidhead. Flattery will *not* get you your stuffed dingo back."

"Then you *do* have it!" Nicole muttered a French swearword—one Reid should have disapproved of. "I knew it! Give it back!"

"Why don't you make me? I'd like to see you try."

Ahead in the creek, Asshat and Binky fell to their knees with an enormous splash. Their packs fell too. Booster gawked at them, then tried to pull Topher to his feet. He dropped like a stone, splattering his expensive designer "safari gear" with mud.

This bunch really was hopeless.

There was no help for it. Reid would have to go in after them. Squaring his shoulders, he faced his bickering preteen daughters. "You two play nicely together. I'll be right back."

With renewed agility, he waded into the rushing waters.

Chapter Three

Staring into the campfire that night, Reid rested his forearms on his thighs. In the darkness surrounding him, Outback creatures skittered and cried, carrying on their simple lives.

Eat. Sleep. Fuck. Hunt. Lather, rinse, repeat.

He tried to keep his own life just as simple. Lately, though, things had begun to feel increasingly complicated.

Take today's test run, for instance. After he'd fished Topher from the drink, he'd dragged Binky and Booster safely to the creek bank. He'd signaled the Evans Adventure Travel remote engineer to cut the water supply that had artificially caused the flood and drain it into the base camp's reclaimed water holding tank. Then Reid had rescued Asshat, chewed out the man for kicking off the whole sorry mess with his idiotic crossing-the-creek bet, and told them all he was out as their assigned guide.

Out. Period. End of story. They'd failed Reid's obligatory pretrip test run, performed in a safe, relatively controllable circuit around the base campsite. There was no way he'd chance taking them on a real trek across the Outback. He knew better.

As Reid should have expected, though, the privileged foursome had reacted to his decision with about as much maturity as they did everything else—meaning, none at all. Even now, the sounds of Binky and Booster haranguing Shane drifted across the campsite's grounds, stirring the cooling air with ugly obscenities and an even uglier aura of I-want-that entitlement.

Frowning, Reid turned his attention to Nicole and Alexis. Their tent, well lighted by a pair of solar-powered lanterns and decorated with the tribal rugs they'd helped barter for in Marakesh, stood a few meters away with its flaps open.

Inside, his daughters perched cross-legged on hi-tech sleeping bags, heads bowed over their homeschooling textbooks. Nicole hugged her stuffed dingo. Nearby, their nanny/tutor, Amanda, flopped on another bedroll with a jar of Marmite and a pack of crackers by her side, a battered paperback clutched in her hands. Knowing Amanda, it was probably a travel memoir.

She was obsessed with them. She was also obsessed with trying every local delicacy they encountered in their journeys. She'd eagerly sampled fermented herring in Sweden, *jibachi senbei*—crunchy wasp crackers—in Japan, and Ugli fruit straight from the tree in Jamaica. Amanda loved to travel, which only made her an even more ideal companion for Alexis and Nicole.

Reid had hired Amanda on an old friend's recommendation, when she still was a fresh-faced graduate of Vrije Universiteit in Amsterdam. In the two years since, he hadn't had cause to regret his decision. Although Amanda was only twenty-four now, she was responsible, smart, resourceful, and irreplaceable.

Not as irreplaceable as his daughters. But important.

Remembering the way Alexis had boosted that old Jeep

earlier today, Reid smiled. That girl had a lot of her mother in her, starting with her red hair, freckles, and tall, gangly figure—and ending with her utter imperviousness to rules or traditions. In a few years, Alexis would be drawing boys like butterflies to sugarcane. She was just that pretty—and that unique.

Inevitably, he knew, there would be crushes and flirting, first dates and curfews, breakups and heartache. Reid only hoped he'd have the wisdom to cope with it all. Failing that, he figured if any unruly boys came to call on his daughter, he'd bench-press them until they agreed to behave.

And Nicole . . . She *really* worried him. Or she would have if Reid were the worrying kind. Mostly, he took things as they came. But Nicole might change that. She had a natural gift for charming people—from nomadic sheepherders in Lhasa to salty-tongued net fishermen in Norway. Everyone who met her liked her.

Her charisma was as inexplicable as it was undeniable. *Like father, like daughter,* his ex-wife would have said. At least Gabby might have said that, had she dragged herself away from her academic research career long enough to pay attention to something (or someone) that couldn't be put under a microscope.

Gabby Foster-Sullivan was never short on theories, Reid knew, whether the topic under discussion was the potential genetic inheritability of charisma or the proper way to eat *injera* with *wat.* At first, Reid had loved that about her. He'd loved her verve, her long legs, and her agile mind with equal enthusiasm. When they'd met near a research site just outside Kazakhstan, Gabby had theorized that their similarly no-madic approaches to life would make them perfect for one another. Reid had agreed.

When they'd married and then had Alexis and Nicole, Gabby had theorized that there'd be nothing more satisfying than combining parenthood, marriage, and itinerant botanical research. Reid had agreed with that too. But later, when he and Gabby had found themselves pulled in two different directions—on two separate continents—his (now ex-) wife had come up with other, less complimentary theories to describe their life together.

One had been that Reid was selfish for not settling down near Gabby's research sites. Another had been that Reid should have grown out of his wanderlust, the same way their children had grown out of diapers. Reid hadn't agreed with those theories. Frankly, he'd been pissed to have his life's passion—exploring the world—equated to potty training. But he *had* agreed, sadly, with Gabby's final theory: Sometimes love wasn't enough.

Most times love wasn't enough, Reid had learned since then. His bachelor existence here in the Outback was proof of that.

But at least he had his children with him. Reid was grateful for that—which brought him back to Nicole. Charisma like his daughter's came with a price, he knew. And although at the moment Nicole used her persuasive abilities harmlessly—to wheedle extra treats from local grandmotherly types or to stall on doing her history homework—soon she was likely to discover other, riskier uses for her skills. Or to use those skills on unscrupulous outsiders—people who couldn't see the tenderhearted girl beneath the smiles. People who might hurt her.

Hell. Being a father was the hardest thing Reid had ever done. Given the adventuresome life he'd led so far, that was saying something, too. Over the past two decades, he'd faced down grizzlies, brush fires, and semidelirious clients in the grips of dengue fever. He'd hung zip lines from skyscraper heights in Costa Rica. He'd endured volcanic eruptions and arctic frostbite. He'd even survived freeze-dried pinto bean chili. In the end, he'd come through all those experiences with one sure bit of knowledge: The only way to survive was to put one foot in front of the other, keep moving, and refuse to quit.

That was exactly what he intended to do with his kids.

"Ooh! That scrape doesn't look so good."

Pulled from his thoughts by that feminine voice, Reid glanced up to see the camp's medic, Helene, standing in front of him. She pursed her lips as she examined his arm, then leaned closer, treating him to a cleavage-filled view down her partly unbuttoned shirt. Knowing Helene and her Scandinavian-style sexual directness, the view was wholly intentional. Given half a chance, Helene would have preferred to be naked at all times.

"You should come to my tent." Helene lifted her gaze to his. She licked her lips. "I could . . . tend to this for you?"

"It's only a scratch. I can hardly feel it."

"Mmm. Interesting. Tell me something." She dropped her hand to his thigh, unsubtly caressing him. "Can you feel . . . this?"

Reid grinned. He covered her hand with his, stopping her ascent toward his groin. In the firelight, Helene pouted.

"A dead man could feel that. You have talented hands."

"That's what they told me in medical school."

Reid raised his eyebrows. "Interesting school. But I'm going to have to pass." Regretfully, he squeezed her hand. He softened his voice. "By morning, I'll probably be headed for another campsite, with another group of doofuses—"

"There's a lot of nighttime between now and morning." Helene gave him another deliberately suggestive look. Her fingers wiggled from beneath his, then crept up his thigh again. "I can think of a few ways to make those hours feel *very* nice for both of us. Can't you?"

"—which means I won't be here for long." He never was. Reid liked to make that fact clear up front, just to avoid misunderstandings and hurt feelings. "So as tempting as this is"—he let his grin broaden—"and it definitely *is* tempting—"

Helene laughed, shaking out her long blond hair. "I'm not asking you to go steady, Sullivan! I just thought we could have some fun together. But if you're too tough for a little TLC—"

"I don't like to be fussed over." That much was true.

"—then you're the one who's missing out. Not me."

Her seductive smile made him waver. They were both adults. What would be the harm in spending some time together?

"Well, I wouldn't go that far. *You* might be missing out too." Seriously considering her invitation—now that Helene had made it clear she wasn't expecting anything significant or long term between them—Reid let his gaze linger on her mouth. "I've been told *I* have some fairly talented hands myself."

"Mmmm. Is that true?" Helene purred. "Tell me more."

"Yeah," Shane cracked from the campfire. He rounded its stone-edged circle. "Tell us *all* about it, Magic Fingers."

Looking disappointed, Helene watched the camp's owner approach. She leaned back on her heels, then got to her feet, offering Reid a final, tantalizing glimpse of cleavage.

Oblivious to Helene's discontent, Shane sat heavily on the same peeled log that Reid occupied. His dark hair stood on end. His bristly jawline looked tight. He clenched a whiskey bottle in one hand. Irritably, he took a swig, then frowned.

"Don't mind me, you two." Shane gestured with the bottle. "Go ahead with planning your illicit little get-together. God knows, *somebody* ought to be getting laid around here."

"It's not going to be you, with that attitude." Helene appeared to size up the situation. She sighed in apparent—and momentary—defeat, then turned to Reid. "I'll be in my tent"—she pointed a few meters away—"if you find yourself with some energy to spare after you tuck in your girls for the night. They're adorable, by the way. So are you. Especially with them."

She winked, then glanced at Shane. "Have you thought about borrowing a baby? Even a hard case like you might get lucky if you were toting around a baby. Or maybe a puppy. A cute, tiny—"

He peered up at her. "Don't you have bandages to roll?"

"If that's a double entendre, you're *way* out of practice, boss. No wonder you're having trouble." Grinning, Helene trailed her fingers across Reid's knee, then sashayed away with a wave. "Night, boys. Try not to get too carried away with the whiskey."

Regretfully, Reid watched her leave. He hadn't wanted to mislead Helene into believing they might have a future together. They didn't. Couldn't. He'd never been able to stay put. With few exceptions, women had never been able to deal with that.

But a night of togetherness had sounded damn good. He could hardly remember what it felt like to sleep while holding close to a woman—a woman whose every feminine curve felt as familiar as his own fingerprints.

He missed it.

On the other hand, he also missed NFL football, *un*stale Oreos, and showers that reliably spit out odorless, colorless water. But Reid was getting by without those things. He could get by without nightly spooning, for fuck's sake.

What was the matter with him?

Beside him, Shane snorted. "It's too bad the Four Stooges didn't want to sleep with you." He pointed his whiskey bottle toward the row of camp visitor tents, where Binky, Booster, Asshat, and Topher had been assigned to sleep. "Maybe they would have tried harder on their pretrip fitness test if they'd thought there would be a meaningful reward at the end." He waggled his considerable eyebrows. "If you know what I mean."

"Nuns in Brisbane know what you mean. And you make a lousy pimp, by the way. Remind me to look for new management before I hit the road again." Reid grabbed the bottle. He took a swig, then winced while the liquor burned its way to his gut. Exhaling mightily, he examined the slender bottle and its contents. "This is half gone. How long have you been at this, anyway?"

"Not long enough." Shane shrugged. He retrieved the bottle with the same zeal a child used to snatch a free balloon at the doctor's office. "The fearsome foursome are leaving in the morning. I had to refund their nonrefundable deposits."

Reid frowned. "I'll cover your expenses."

"No need." Shane hugged the whiskey to his chest. He stared into the campfire. "It's not your fault. You were right to boot them. Bunch of idiots, if you ask me." He looked at Reid. "I wasn't sure about your pretrip fitness test, but you sold me."

Reid nodded, still eyeing the whiskey bottle. How long had Shane been drinking this heavily? He lifted his gaze to his friend.

No point busting his chops about it, he decided. Shane was a big boy. He could handle himself. Besides, Reid didn't like anyone poking into his private life—or offering him unwelcome "help." Being on the receiving end of too much mollycoddling made him feel weak. He doubted Shane was any different.

"It works," Reid said. "It works a hell of a lot better than believing what people tell me, that's for sure. They claim they've read the pretrip materials, then they go batshit at the sight of a harmless wombat. They swear they can meet the minimal fitness requirements, then they punk out, red faced and gasping, the first time they have to climb a hill. They promise they can handle a fifty-pound pack, then they beg me to shoulder it."

They promise to pay on time, then hop a plane to Yemin in

the middle of the night instead. It had taken Reid a solid month to pull in enough work to make up for that particular unexpected shortfall. He hadn't liked the feeling of putting his income—and his daughters' well-being—at risk, even temporarily. He had some emergency cash stashed away, of course, but that incident had taught him that "some" didn't necessarily equal "enough."

Back in the day, Reid hadn't worried about security. Now he did. For Alexis and Nicole, if not for himself. Also, to a lesser degree, for Amanda. The girl might have a freakish affection for frogs' legs dipped in Dijon mustard and dukka, but he owed her.

He wasn't the kind of guy who let loyalty fall away.

"In short," Shane said, "your theory is that most people are lying motherfu—"

"To a dangerous degree," Reid confirmed, cutting off the profanity before it could drift toward his daughters' tent. "That's why I don't ever want to be responsible for anyone but myself. End of story. There's no payoff in it for anybody."

Shane mulled that over. He took another slug of whiskey, then poked at the fire with a stick. "I've got news for you, pal. You're responsible for Alexis and Nicole."

Reid nodded. His daughters were different. He didn't feel responsible for them, exactly. Responsibility was burdensome. It was unwelcome. It was forced and compulsory. Responsibility trapped a man—especially a man who valued his freedom. What he felt for Nicole and Alexis was bigger than mere responsibility. Reid would kill or die to defend them, no questions asked.

But that protectiveness was a part of him. It wasn't the same as being on the hook for a stranger. It wasn't the same as allowing some numbnuts CEO on an adventure-travel high to ambush him with the sudden news of his deadly bee-sting allergy and then beg Reid to watch over him. It wasn't the same as carrying someone else's hopes and dreams on your shoulders and never being able to put down that Sisyphean burden, no matter what.

It wasn't the same as breaking an innocent woman's heart.

"Is that why you turned down the lovely Helene at first?" Shane swirled his whiskey, watching it gleam. "Because you don't want to be responsible for anyone else, even for one night?"

One night could become two, Reid knew. Two could lead to expectations. Expectations could be shattered. Hearts could be broken, people disappointed, children separated from mothers. . . .

Where was Gabby right now, anyway? Did she miss Alexis and Nicole the same way they missed her? Did she miss *him?*

Reid wasn't nostalgic for his marriage. He'd moved on. But no matter how hard he tried, he couldn't replace the girls' mom. He might be a whiz at whipping up campfire paella while reading Dr. Seuss aloud to his daughters, but he didn't know about braiding pigtails or being a confidante. He didn't know about getting periods or liking boys. He didn't know about a lot of things. Some nights that realization left him in a cold sweat.

But not tonight. He'd be damned if he'd give in to those maudlin thoughts. Instead, Reid grinned at his friend.

"Why the big interest in my love life all of a sudden?" he asked. "Exactly how long were you lurking over there in the shadows, Quasimodo? Do I need a restraining order?"

Shane laughed. He batted his eyelashes. "You're dreamy, Reid. Please don't leave me behind, you big, strong stud!"

Shaking his head, Reid laughed too. "If I had a dime for every time I've heard that line—"

"You'd be rich enough to buy half a gumball."

"Or the whole damn bucket of gumballs, you mean."

"Gumballs don't come in buckets, moron."

"Says the guy who's been out here with Helene for six months and still hasn't made a move. Who's the moron now?"

"I tried." Morosely, Shane took another drink. He gazed into the starry Outback night. "She said she doesn't 'do' hard-luck cases." He knocked back more whiskey. "Whatever."

Again, warning bells went off in Reid's head. If even happy-go-lucky Helene detected problems with the way Shane was handling himself these days . . . maybe something really was wrong.

But then Reid gave himself a mental shake. He and Shane had known one another for almost fifteen years now. They'd battled the elements, the landscape, and sometimes each other. They'd always come out strong in the end. His friend could cope with whatever was going on. And although Reid didn't currently have a curvy, familiar woman to cuddle up to at night, he *did* have more than his share of close friends around the world, he remembered belatedly. That had to be worth something.

Even if, right now, it didn't feel that way.

After all . . . most of his friends were very, *very* far away.

Automatically, Reid gazed toward his daughters' tent. Looking at Nicole and Alexis always made him feel grounded. In a million small ways, they reminded him that his existence mattered. That what he did and who he was counted for something.

Unfortunately, tonight someone was blocking Reid's comforting view of Alexis and Nicole. That someone was Topher.

"Take me. By myself," Topher said. "I'll pay you double."

Reid shook his head. It was as though the man had a built-in piss-off-everyone meter, and he wasn't happy unless it was constantly maxed out. "No. I'm not taking you out."

"All right. I respect your ability to haggle." Nervously, Topher hitched up his pants. "Triple. I'll pay you triple."

"There's not enough money in the world," Reid said.

"Quadruple!" Topher bargained, obviously not getting the point. He swore. "Look, dude. This team-building event is on my shoulders. It's my responsibility. If I screw this up, management will have my ass in a winch, but quick."

"Ouch." Shane winced. "Corporate life must really suck."

Reid agreed. There was a reason he'd never handcuffed himself to a desk. He couldn't conceive of spending all day indoors, toiling under fluorescent lights, being totally motionless except for his typing fingers and his flapping jaw. He wasn't a talker. He was a doer. He liked to do his doing outside, where he could feel the air on his skin—where he could draw in a deep breath. Anything else made him feel suffocated.

"Please!" Topher begged. "I need to make it look as though things went well out here. At least take a few snaps with me next to a koala or something." He held up his iPhone. "Look. I've got my camera right here. It'll only take a sec."

Reid and Shane stared blandly up at him. "For a photo like that," Shane said, "what you want is a trip to the zoo."

"I won't pretend I took you out when I didn't," Reid added. He was a lot of things, but he wasn't a liar.

"Look, asshole." Threateningly, Topher stepped forward. He balled his fists, still clutching his iPhone. "You're making this harder than it has to be. Just cooperate, and I'll—"

Reid stood, meeting him face-to-face. "The answer's no."

Topher swore again, his face reddening. "Come *on!* This is not a big deal! One or two photos, maybe a signed statement—"

"You're wasting your time," Amanda interrupted.

"He won't say he took you out if he didn't," Alexis added.

"Yeah," Nicole put in. "My dad is not a fibber!"

At the sound of his daughters' voices, Reid wheeled around. He spotted them standing with their nanny/tutor just outside their shared tent, watching the standoff between him and Topher. He should have known the trio would be drawn to the commotion.

Amanda popped another Marmite-covered cracker into

her mouth. She crunched it. "We're right. Deal with it. Want a cracker?"

"Er, yes! Thank you." Inexplicably, some of the fight seemed to go out of Topher. He tromped to Amanda's side. "I'm sorry, Sullivan. I guess the answer's no. I get it now."

Startled by his speedy acquiescence, Reid shot Topher a disbelieving look. Then he decided there was no point belaboring the issue. He wasn't a man who went looking for trouble.

Even if it did seem to find him pretty often.

Tearing his gaze from the surreal sight of Amanda sharing Marmite-smeared snacks with Topher, Reid crossed his arms. He gave his daughters his sternest look. "What are you girls doing out here? Shouldn't you be doing your homework?"

Nicole bit her lip—her longtime tell that she was about to spin up a supersize whopper. "Yes, Dad. And it's so smart of you to notice that! But the thing is—"

Alexis held up his satellite phone. "The thing is, Great Grammy Sullivan called. It's an emergency. She wants us to come home on the double."

Chapter Four

December 16th
Eric's Beachside Love Hut
San Diego, California

Mustering the last reserves of her self-possession, Karina stood in her ex-husband's kitchen, trying hard to resist the urge to hug him. It wasn't easy. With his "rock-star" eyeliner, flip-flop-clad feet, and skintight ultradistressed jeans, Eric appeared to be experiencing the mother of all midlife crises. For the first time ever, Karina felt sorry for him.

Maybe that was progress. At least she wasn't feeling sorry for herself. Or the kids. On the other hand, Eric really was pitiable. She didn't know how she hadn't noticed that earlier.

Or how she hadn't noticed that the overriding love she'd always felt for her ex-husband had morphed into something else altogether. Something subtle but appreciable. Something like . . . fondness. Mingled, of course, with the tiniest lingering urge to clap a wrench on his button fly and twist it. Hard.

She was only human, after all.

"Look, I didn't have to come here," she said, "but I did."

"Shh!" Eric interrupted. "Listen. Do you hear that?"

From the other end of the condo, the sounds of a video

game hurtled toward them. Electronic crowd noise boomed.
Loud music roared. Eric nodded, then flashed her twin devil's
horns–style "rock on" hand signals, followed by a patented
Billy Idol sneer.

"Hear what?" Karina cupped her ear. "All I'm picking up
is the sound of your lost maturity making a run for it."

"That's *Rock Band,*" Eric whined. "*Rock Band!*"

"So?"

"So the kids are going to screw up my score if I don't get
in there, pronto!" In a parody of guitar-hero machismo, Eric
treated her to a few air guitar licks. When Karina (apparently)
appeared unimpressed, he leaned sideways instead, neck
veins bulging above his skinny flannel shirt. "Kids, don't
mess up Daddy's game!" he shouted. "Daddy worked hard on
that level!"

With visible reluctance, Eric's gaze returned to her.

"I *did* come here," Karina continued patiently, wondering
when (and why) he'd paid good money for a studded black
leather wristband, "so I could tell you—in person—that
there's been a change to our holiday plans. I thought it was
only fair that you knew. We're leaving first thing tomorrow,
which means—"

"'*Our* holiday plans'? Aww, Karina. Karina. Karina,
baby." Clucking with pity, Eric shook his head. "There's no
'us' to have plans anymore, remember? We're divorced now,
so—" Eric broke off, head canted to the side like a wolf-
hound's as he listened anew to the guitar playing and drum-
ming coming from the other room. "Not that song, kids!" A
strangled exclamation came from him. He swore. "I just got
past that level too."

"Don't worry. I'm sure it will be fine."

He eyed her with displeasure. "Are you *comforting* me?"

Whoops. She had been. "Relax. It's nothing personal. It's
like a reflex for me." Realizing that meant she'd inadvertently
comforted him *twice* now, Karina inhaled deeply. She had to

focus. "The point is, I thought you should know the kids and I are going away for Christmas this year. To Michigan. To a cute lakeside resort town called Kismet. It looks *so* amazing, Eric, with snowdrifts and holiday lights and Christmas caroling—"

"Fine." Eric gave her a dismissive wave. "I know how much you've always liked Christmastime."

Right. Which explained why he'd absconded with *all* their Christmas decorations for himself? Karina frowned.

"Besides, Chelsea and I are hitting the Bahamas with her 'rents this year anyway," Eric continued, "so—"

"Her whats?"

"Her 'rents. Her *parents?* Get it? It's slang. Man, are you out of touch or what?" He shook his head, making his newly gel-spiked hair catch the sunlight. "So we'll be gone until past New Year's Day anyway." He examined his new forearm . . . tattoo? Where in the world had *that* come from? "God, Karina. It's no wonder we didn't make it." Sorrowfully, Eric raised his gaze to her face. "I'm young at heart, and you're . . ." Her ex-husband scrutinized her again, taking in her khaki Capri pants and logoed Marsden Elementary School Badgers T-shirt. "Well, you're . . . not."

Stung, Karina looked away. As though punctuating Eric's statement, Chelsea bopped into the room, all brightness and lightness and bikini-clad boobs. Next to her, Karina felt like a teenage boy. A gangly, out-of-touch, awkward teenage boy.

A teenage boy who was a big fan of the Marsden Fighting Badgers, obviously, but a teenage boy nonetheless.

Maybe that was why she kept right on talking. Unwisely.

"Well, be sure to pack your Viagra," she said cheerfully, pretending she hadn't noticed Chelsea entering. "You wouldn't want to be caught unprepared"—*in a beautiful tropical paradise*—"miles away from a pharmacy." *When you want to get busy with your stupidly limber, sexy girlfriend.* "That would be a real mood killer, wouldn't it?" *When you're in the Bahamas. Argh!*

"Oh, Eric doesn't need Viagra anymore!" Chelsea hugged his elbow to her ample bosom. "I guess he's cured!" She giggled. "Or maybe it's because I got him that special O-ring for his—"

Karina held up both hands. "Stop right there. *Please.*"

"But you should be so proud of him!" Chelsea cast a spellbound look at Eric. "Now he can go all night. Just as long as I put on his special O-ring first, of course. But that's kind of fun all by itself, since it means grabbing hold of his—"

"Seriously. I'm familiar with *all* the landmarks." Haunted by an image of her ex-husband's familiar . . . geography . . . adorned with anything that Chelsea found "special," Karina suppressed a shudder. "You don't have to explain. I get it, believe me."

"Are you sure?" Chelsea wrinkled her brows with evident care and concern. "Because your, um, generation can be sort of repressed. And from everything that Eric's said, it sounds as though you're pretty naïve in the sex department, K. I could—"

"Please don't call me that." A nickname like "K" made them sound like friends. Which they weren't.

"—help out with some advice. After all, you're a swinging single now!" Chelsea enthused. "You should be getting your groove on regularly. You're in your sexual prime, you know."

"Really? Did they teach you that in veterinary school?"

Chelsea appeared wounded. "Um, no? Not yet." She cast a confused glance at Eric. "But maybe next semester, I guess? Mostly we're studying feline distemper right now, but . . ." She trailed off. "There's always hope I'll get there! I like cats!"

Karina felt awful. Sure, Chelsea had made her sound like a wizened old crone (thirty-six wasn't that old!), but that didn't mean Karina had to resort to snarkiness. Making fun of Chelsea was like kicking a puppy. A bodacious, dim-witted puppy. The poor girl just didn't have the wherewithal to defend herself—or even (obviously) to recognize when she was being ridiculed.

Karina would probably go straight to hell for this.

Grudgingly, she patted Chelsea's arm. "I'm sorry, Chelsea."

"Oh, come on! Call me 'C'! Like on *Gossip Girl*! Please?" Chelsea begged. "Then I'll know for sure that we're friends!"

Karina inhaled. "I didn't mean to hurt your feelings . . . , C."

Was there a twelve-step program for chronic people pleasers? If so, Karina definitely needed to enroll. Yesterday.

Giddily, Chelsea clapped her hands. "Yay! I'm C! You're K!"

Helplessly smiling now too, Karina glanced at Eric. She expected her ex-husband to be enraptured by his girlfriend's bouncing breasts—or maybe to be clapping his hands in outright approval of them. Instead, he stood gazing pensively at Karina.

For an instant, they *connected,* just the way they had when they'd been married. Karina would have sworn she saw sad comprehension in his eyes—probably the full knowledge of how idiotically he was behaving by abandoning his family and shacking up with someone who said "Yay!" without any perceptible irony. But then Eric shrugged and grinned as if to say, "Hey, she came toting a *cock ring,* K!" and all bets were off.

"So anyway, back to our holiday plans—mine and the kids'," Karina was careful to specify. "We should talk about when and where to meet up after Christmas, so we can set up a switcheroo." She smiled at her own use of the term they'd adopted to describe their parental visitation drop-off routine with Josh, Michael, and Olivia. She was being *so* adult about this. So calm! Kudos to her. Seriously. "The kids and I are going to be gone to Kismet for a couple of weeks, so we might have to adjust your next visit with them just a tiny bit. Depending on what time your flight comes in from—"

"Wait." Eric held up his nontattooed arm, flashing her his studded leather wristband again. He frowned. "Let me get this straight. You're taking *my* kids away from me? On *Christmas?*"

"Well . . . yes. I guess so. Technically," Karina told him. "You won't be seeing them on Christmas day. But I'll make sure to call at least once a day, and Olivia can text you, too, so—"

"So *those* are your so-called Christmas plans?"

She wished he'd let her finish a sentence for once.

"That's what I came over here to talk about, yes." Karina nodded. Maybe the pensive look he'd given her a second ago hadn't been about regret, she realized belatedly. Maybe it had been about pure, no-holds-barred contrariness. Maybe her earlier statement about her altered holiday plans had finally penetrated Eric's thick skull, and he was genuinely upset about the change. It was hard to say. This was the "new" Eric, after all. The Eric who listened to hip-hop, drank hemp milk, and wore penis ornaments. Puzzled by his sudden vehemence, Karina chose her next words carefully. "But you know as well as I do that the kids are supposed to be with me during the holidays anyway. And you and Chelsea *are* going to be out of the country with her parents, remember? So it's not as though you—"

"As though I have any choice in the matter?" Eric interrupted. "That's right. I don't." His frown deepened. "The fact is, you're depriving me of my right to see my children."

Since when was he so pedantic about his visitation rights? He certainly hadn't been this nitpicky last month when he'd asked to skip a weekend visit. And that time his only excuse had been that he'd wanted to "catch some tasty waves" with Chelsea.

Caught beneath her ex-husband's baleful glare, Karina

stiffened her spine. There was no way she was backing down on this. No. Way. This was her chance to give the kids the Christmas they'd always dreamed of—the Christmas they deserved.

Nobody—not even Eric—was getting in the way of that.

"Eric, be reasonable." Even as the words left her mouth, Karina thought better of them. *Eric* plus *reasonable* did not compute. "Or at least listen: There's a good reason for all this." *Aside from your children's need for a happy Christmas this year.* "The B&B we're going to is an all-inclusive vacation spot specializing in Christmas getaways." *Is that the ultimate, or what?* "Stephanie was supposed to evaluate the place as her next assignment for Edgware. But Blake is really, really sick right now." *My poor little nephew.* "He has a flu bug or food poisoning or something. So Stephanie can't do the evaluation, and it's too late to line up someone else from Edgware at the last minute. Most of the other consultants are on personal leave for the holidays. Cancelling is out of the question, so Steph asked me to fill in. In secret. All I have to do is upload the evaluation forms every day—and not alert any of the other guests or the management to my real purpose at the B&B, of course."

"Ooh! Like a spy!" Chelsea cooed. "Or one of those secret shoppers! Except for a B&B, I mean. That's so cool, K!"

"Thanks, C." Ugh. She hated herself for going along with that silly nickname stuff. But it just slipped out. And at least *someone* was happy for her, Karina thought rebelliously. "The bonus is, the kids and I get a free vacation out of the deal."

"Merry Christmas to you!" Chelsea chirped.

"I know. It's sort of perfect." *Since I could never afford it otherwise. Thanks a lot, divorce.* "The kids were superexcited when I told them about it. It'll be their first time on an airplane. Their first time traveling to another state."

"Their first time abandoning their dad on Christmas."

"Their first time seeing snow! And icicles!" Chelsea shot Eric a quelling look. "I'm so happy for you guys, K."

"That's really nice of you, C."

Eric rolled his eyes. Karina ignored him. It was too bad if her ex couldn't handle her and Chelsea getting along. And while she was genuinely concerned about her little sick nephew, she was also determined to help out her sister. If by doing so she could give Olivia, Michael, and Josh a picture-perfect holiday—the kind of holiday she could never pull off on her own—well, that was a slam dunk. Eric ought to be able to understand that.

"Justin is already in Hong Kong on business," Karina explained further, "so he can't stay with Blake himself. And the job is supposed to start tomorrow, so Stephanie really needs my help. She's totally at her wit's end—"

"She must be if she's trusting you to handle things," Eric said snidely. "Everyone knows you're a soft touch when someone needs a favor, but you're not exactly competent, *K*."

Shocked by Eric's bluntness, Karina gaped at him. Since their split, he'd been distant, dismissive, and occasionally delusional. But he'd never been *mean*. Not like this. Somehow, his derision now hurt her more than everything else.

"Yes, I am. I'm competent." Sometimes she procrastinated a bit. But everyone did that. "What are you talking about?"

"Yeah!" Chelsea elbowed Eric. "That's not nice!"

"I'm *talking* about your tendency to take on too much." Eric stretched out the word *talking,* making it sound especially obnoxious. "I'm *talking* about the way you can never say no to anyone. I'm *talking* about the fact that no matter how bad you might feel about having failed with our marriage—"

"*I* failed?" Incensed, Karina stepped up. "*I* didn't fail!"

"—you can't make up for your shortcomings by bribing the kids this way." Eric crossed his arms. "Taking a fancy Christmas vacation? Using your sister's job as an excuse? It's pathetic."

Dumbfounded, Karina stared at him. She couldn't speak. But she also couldn't help wondering . . . was Eric a tiny bit right?

Lately, she *had* been feeling as though she were letting down Michael, Josh, and Olivia. It wasn't easy being the one who said no to requests for new sneakers and expensive video games. She simply couldn't afford everything they wanted. But that didn't make seeing their disappointed faces any easier to bear.

"Stephanie never liked me, and you know it," Eric said. "The two of you probably cooked up this whole scheme together just to make me look bad. I'll bet there isn't any Edgware evaluation happening at all."

"Of course there is." Karina couldn't believe he was being so churlish. "It's worth a lot of money to everyone involved too! Edgware is the biggest hospitality company in the world. They run thousands of hotels and resort properties in multiple international networks. If they decide The Christmas House concept is worth franchising, it's going to mean—"

"Oh, spare me," her ex interrupted. For the billionth time. "I don't need to hear the hard sell—the *fake* hard sell. What I don't get is how you expect anyone to believe *you're* capable of evaluating a property anyway. That really takes the cake."

Ouch. That hurt. Wounded, Karina glanced away.

Then she regrouped. Damn it, Eric wasn't going to stop her.

"I've been listening to Stephanie talk about her job for all these years. That's got to count for something, right?" She raised her head, fired up with a newfound urge to totally nail the B&B evaluation—and maybe prove Eric wrong about her in the process. "And I've already got Stephanie's preevaluation research and her notes, so that will help too. Once I'm equipped with the official evaluation guidelines, it'll be a simple matter of ticking off items on a checklist. I'm sure I'll—"

"You'll crash and burn. *If* this thing is really real. Which I doubt. Admit it—you want to show me up at Christmastime. That's what this is all about—your insecurities."

Wow. This felt unnervingly like being married to him.

Why, exactly, had she missed any of this?

In that moment, as far as Karina was concerned, all men everywhere could just leave her alone. For good. There was no reason she couldn't handle everything on her own . . . with no heartache, dirty tighty-whities, or "collectible" NBA basketball jerseys to clutter up her life. And no regrets, either.

No regrets. Now *there* was a motto she could get behind.

Chelsea shook her head. "Oh, cut it out, Eric. You're going too far, even for you." She offered Karina an apologetic look. "You know Karina loves the kids too much to bribe them! And you can't blame her for helping out her sister! She's a giving person! What difference does it make if Karina and the kids are going away for the holidays? We won't even be here."

"The details don't matter," Eric argued. Petulantly. Possibly with a special O-ring adorning his— "The point is—"

"The point is," Chelsea persisted, "that your ex-wife is getting on with her life, and you're not handling it very well. You ought to be more grown up about all this."

Silence fell. This time, it was Eric's turn to gawk.

To be fair, Karina did too. That was really . . . *insightful.*

Also, she liked the idea of herself getting on with her life. It was past time she did that. *Way* past time.

"You've got to remember, babe," Chelsea continued serenely, "that a truly strong man allows others' strength to shine."

Huh? Karina blinked. Eric wrinkled his forehead.

"I read that on my Gingerbread Latte cup at Starbucks yesterday. I thought it fit." Chelsea beamed. Offhandedly, she examined her bikini top, then adjusted its triangle cups as sultrily as one of the Pussycat Dolls might have done. "So. Are we all good? Eric, are you going to be nicer to Karina?"

Contritely, he nodded. "Yes, Chelsea. I am."

Wow. Whatever mojo Chelsea had, Karina needed some. Eric had *never* been this compliant when he'd been married to her.

"And Karina, are you going to have a fun vacation?"

A fun vacation? Karina hesitated. She hadn't quite thought of the upcoming trip in that way. She'd been busy checking flights online, making whirlwind packing lists, and conferring with Stephanie about the Edgware evaluation details.

But the truth was, this opportunity was heaven sent.

The B&B in Kismet had genuine snowdrifts. Actual Christmassy ambiance. Pine trees galore. And the B&B owners *specialized* in making their guests' holiday dreams come true—it said so right on their brochures and Web site. Visiting The Christmas House would be like stepping into one of those feel-good holiday TV movies. It didn't get much more fun than that.

She nodded. "I think the kids are going to love it."

"But what about *you*, K? You have to think about yourself too," Chelsea insisted. "It's like my mom always said—"

"Take off that miniskirt and those hooker heels?"

This, from Eric. Chelsea and Karina both glared at him.

He gave an awkward chuckle. "I guess my image of your teenage years is inaccurate?"

"You're about a million times too sleazy, I'm sure," Karina said. Although, privately, she agreed about the miniskirt.

"—she always said," Chelsea went on with good-natured doggedness, "that a vacation is when a family goes away for a good time, and their mother makes sure everyone gets it. My mom used to start every vacation exhausted from planning and come home afterward to a mountain of laundry. Don't let that happen to you, Karina. Make sure *you* have a good time too."

"She wouldn't know how." Eric fiddled with his wristband. "Karina is about as much fun as a bucket of to-do lists."

"Maybe with *you* she was," Chelsea said. "But the two of you obviously weren't a good fit. With another guy . . . who knows? Maybe Karina will have herself a wild and crazy holiday affair."

Yeah. Who knew? Maybe she would, Karina thought defiantly.

It was weird to feel so encouraged by "the other woman" in her ex-husband's life. But all of a sudden, she actually felt tempted to cut loose. To live a little. To get on with her life in a *big* way.

Eric had been right about one thing, she decided ruefully. Being around Chelsea really *was* liberating.

"Yeah!" she said, stifling a fist pump. "Who knows?"

Eric's scowl deepened—satisfyingly so. It was about time *he* was the one who'd been caught off guard. Especially by her.

He'd be caught off guard most of all, Karina promised herself, when she aced that very *real* Edgware evaluation. Eric could hardly argue that she'd made up the whole thing if Edgware officially announced they were franchising the B&B's concept and taking its worry-free Christmas-vacation idea nationwide.

"I say go for it!" Chelsea urged. "And keep me posted too." She gave Karina a girl-to-girl wink, grinning like a true confidante. "I want all the dirty details, K. You be sure to call me the *instant* something happens, okay?"

"If there's anything racy to report, you'll be the first to know," Karina told her. "I swear on my Badgers T-shirt."

She held up two fingers, Boy Scout style, but the truth was, it was an easy promise to make. There was no way in the world official good girl and devoted mother Karina Barrett was about to indulge in a supersteamy holiday fling. For one thing, she'd be working. She owed Stephanie her very best efforts.

Besides, there wasn't enough spiked eggnog in the world

to loosen up Karina that much. While a short-term Christmas romance might be . . . invigorating, she could definitely do without the aftereffects of starting up a new relationship. Even if it would be, by necessity, limited to the holidays. Possibly with a hunky, hayseed-chewing Midwesterner . . . who liked honey.

Like a dream, Honey-Buying Man's head superimposed itself on an image of a shirtless, Santa hat–wearing, muscle-bound stud. Hmmm. She liked that, actually. She liked that a lot.

Whoa. She *had* to get hold of her hormones. STAT.

"So I'd better get going. Lots to do before our flight."

Forcing a smile, Karina slung her purse over her shoulder, then prepared to gather up the kids for the drive home. Just before she headed to the video game zone, though, she realized she'd forgotten something. Something she should have come here specifically to do, but had been afraid to try until now.

She stepped up to Eric, then squared her shoulders. Wearing her sweetest expression, she asked, "By the way, can I have *my* half of our Christmas decorations, please? I noticed they were missing from the attic. You must have grabbed all of them by mistake when you moved out."

Chelsea frowned. "Eric! You didn't."

He hung his head. "Sorry, Karina," he mumbled. "I'll get them right now." He schlepped away, flip-flops flapping.

"Load the boxes into her car for her too!" Chelsea called.

He waved his assent without turning, then kept going.

Karina watched Eric hop to it. "Wow. I'm impressed."

"It's nothing." Chelsea shrugged. "Just simple directness. Men respond pretty well to a straightforward approach."

"Well . . . that bikini of yours probably helps too."

"Probably," Chelsea admitted with a grin. "A little."

She and Karina shared a satisfied, sisterly (and entirely unlikely) moment of camaraderie. Right then, Karina decided there was a lot to be said for Chelsea's methods. Even if they had led (indirectly) to the dissolution of her marriage.

Chelsea might be a little bubbleheaded, but she was also supremely self-confident—and she got results when she wanted them, too. Even from Eric. That was commendable.

"You should get one." Chelsea gestured at Karina's suburban mom outfit. "A bikini, I mean. You could totally pull it off."

Karina blinked. "Me? No way. I'm a tankini girl, all the way." Only someone as flawless as Chelsea could be so blasé about baring it (almost) all in anything less. Karina had borne three children—and her body had all the usual jiggly spots to show for it. "Besides, where I'm going, I'll have to dress for warmth. It's freezing in Michigan in December, remember?"

"Oh yeah." Chelsea grew thoughtful. Karina could almost see the gears turning in her tiny, blond-haired head. "You probably don't have much in the way of cold-weather gear, either."

"Nope. What Southern Californian does?"

"True. And even if you had it, your stuff would probably be less 'snow bunny' and more 'abominable snowman.' Am I right?"

Karina considered being offended by that comment, then decided to let it go. Her single item of truly warm clothing was a quilted parka. And it *was* pretty abominable. She'd bought it at an end-of-season sale for a trip to Lake Tahoe with Eric. In the end, they'd cancelled. They hadn't been able to find a reliable baby-sitter, and Karina hadn't wanted to risk using a last-minute substitute. With her, her kids always came first.

On later reflection, that attitude probably hadn't done her struggling marriage any favors. But how was a woman supposed to juggle everything? She was doing her best. She really was.

"Hey, don't look so gloomy!" Chelsea piped up. "We'll

get this figured out." She grabbed Karina's arm. "Come with me!"

Karina balked. "What for?"

"For getting you ready for your Christmas vacation in Kismet, of course!" Chelsea rolled her eyes. "Hello? How are you supposed to snag a hottie if you're dressed like a yeti?"

Karina winced. "'Yeti' is a little harsh."

"You're right." Chelsea gave an offhanded wave. "We haven't covered yetis in veterinary school yet. So I'm no expert, that's for sure. I don't even know if they have girl yetis or not."

Awesome. Not only did Karina resemble a gnarly mountain creature, but she apparently resembled a gnarly, *mannish* mountain creature. Had she forgotten to shave her legs again?

After a quick hairy-legs check, Karina shrugged. Her calves were (relatively) stubble free for now. But that didn't mean she intended to blow off Chelsea's offer. Against all good judgment, Karina followed Chelsea to the other end of the condo.

Not because she actually needed Chelsea's help. Or even because she was (admittedly) curious about what kinds of cold-weather clothing ideas Chelsea might offer. (Fur-lined bikinis? Fair Isle knit hot pants? A low-cut, thigh-high Polarfleece romper?) But mostly because Karina figured there was no harm in indulging her new friend.

Chelsea honestly seemed to want to help. Karina was a person who understood that sentiment intimately. She liked to help people too. It would have been unkind to refuse.

Besides, it wouldn't hurt if a smidgeon of Chelsea's bodaciousness accidentally rubbed off on her. Just in case something unexpected happened. Just in case, say, a gorgeous Honey-Buying Man stand-in happened to be staying at The Christmas House. And Karina decided to indulge herself. And *he* went for it. And together they made a few jingle bells ring.

Right. And then they lived happily ever after. Ho ho ho.

If she believed any of that, she *definitely* needed a vacation, Karina decided, then dutifully followed Chelsea to her walk-in closet and prepared to be polite about viewing skintight sweaters, zebra-print leggings, and knit caps with special lip gloss storage compartments—all the accoutrements of a midwinter seduction Karina was *so* not going to need this Christmastime.

Chapter Five

December 17th
Gerald R. Ford International Airport
Grand Rapids, Michigan, USA

Fisting his carry-on bag in one hand and Nicole's stuffed dingo in the other, Reid stood impatiently in the airport's arrivals zone. After three connections (on two continents) and more than twenty-eight hours in the air, he was tired, wired, and worried—all at the same time. He still had a few more miles to travel, too. From where he stood, it would take at least an hour to commandeer a rental car and make the drive to Kismet.

Methodically, an airport official thumbed through Reid's passport, examining its multiply stamped pages. The document was proof of Reid's globe-trotting life. He liked that. Right now, though, he didn't like the delay it seemed to be causing.

Ever since Alexis had told him about that emergency phone call from his grandmother, Reid had been pushing to get home—or at least as close to "home" as his former stomping grounds in the Midwest (or anyplace stateside) would ever feel to him.

He'd grown up in Kismet, the son of parents who both worked—like many locals—in the town's hospitality industry: his father as a hotel accountant, and his mother as a pastry chef. People like them—sometimes several generations of people like them—helped make Kismet an ideal vacation spot.

What the town might have lacked in size and sophistication, it made up for in outright charm—not to mention friendliness. Located between a riverfront and a lake, Kismet boasted an old-fashioned, picturesque downtown, multiple clapboard-sided cottages, and miles of trees. In the summertime, the place overflowed with sunburned, ice cream–eating tourists.

As soon as Reid had been old enough to understand the concept of *vacationing*—of traveling someplace you didn't live and exploring it just for fun—he'd decided he wanted to be a tourist too. Full-time. To him, Kismet had felt close-knit but confining, like the family reunions the Sullivans had held at the Kismet Elks Club. Stuck inside its four walls for a day, a kid could hardly chase his squealing cousins without getting shushed by his buzzkill aunts and uncles. Reid had wanted out. He'd gotten out. And then he'd explored the hell out of things.

But now, with Grammy Sullivan's mysterious catastrophe calling him home, Reid wanted back in. *Right now.*

Hoping through force of will to make the airport official move faster, Reid glowered at the man. It almost worked.

The official glanced up. He stabbed one ink-stained finger at Reid's passport. "Paraguay, huh? You like it there?"

"Yes, I did. I taught a parasailing class."

"See any llamas?"

"You're thinking of Peru. There are a lot of llamas there." Reid didn't want to go into details about his time on a llama ranch. Especially the manure story. Everyone loved the manure story. "Alpacas too. They're big in the textile industry."

"Hmmm. You're probably right. It's probably Peru I'm thinking of. Just had a Peruvian exporter come through here last week. Nice guy. Liked Twinkies." More poring. More delaying.

Reid inhaled deeply. Around him, the airport buzzed with movement. The other passengers moved through their designated lines quickly, then trotted off to retrieve their luggage.

Reid didn't have checked luggage. He and the girls had mastered the art of traveling with nothing but allowable carry-on baggage years ago. As long as he had Alexis and Nicole by his side, he had everything he needed.

Whatever else they wanted, Reid could borrow, barter, buy, or MacGyver into being. But he couldn't force his way through this line any faster. Beside him, Nicole sighed.

"Hang in there." He hugged her. "We won't be much longer."

"Okay." His daughter leaned her head on his arm. Her skinny arm wrapped around his waist. "I'm just worried about Great Grammy's emergency, that's all. Did you ever get through to her?"

Reid shook his head. "Every time I called, a different person answered the phone—sometimes staff at The Christmas House, sometimes one of my relatives, sometimes a neighbor." They'd all been suspiciously vague about the nature of the crisis—probably to spare him worry. "The whole place must be swamped with people. That's how Kismet is—everyone helps one another. Your great-grandparents are probably up to their ears in homemade casseroles by now. By the time we get there, there won't be anything to do except pick up a fork and start eating."

He grinned. His daughters didn't appear reassured.

"Ugh, don't talk about eating!" Alexis slumped, jutting one hip like a long-limbed, world-weary supermodel. She swept her hair from her eyes. "I'm starving right now. I just hope they have some decent food in this stupid airport. I'm *dying* for a snack."

"We'll get you something soon." Reid hugged her too. She looked tired—probably from her attempts to rewire the headphone jacks on their red-eye from Australia. "I've still got some of Amanda's Marmite and crackers in my pack—"

The airport official looked up sharply. "Did you declare those items, sir? Were they a gift? Are they open or wrapped?"

Wearily, Reid answered his questions. And several more.

In another line a few meters away, Amanda breezed through. She hoisted her carry-on items, blew air kisses to the girls, then proceeded to the terminal to wait for them. Whenever possible, Reid liked to give their nanny/tutor a little privacy—and some off-duty free time. That's why she'd spent their overnight flight and its multiple connecting legs seated several rows away with her headphones on, watching sequential in-flight movies and scarfing down junk food from her pack.

"Wow." Appearing awestruck, Nicole stood on tiptoes to peer at the airport official. "You must have the coolest job ever!"

The official blinked. And smiled. "Thanks, little girl."

"I mean, meeting all these people who are coming in from all over the place. Talking to them. It must be fun."

He paused. "You know, not many people notice that."

"*And* it's obvious you're extra good at it," Nicole nattered on, smiling at him. "The people in those lines"—she gestured sideways—"are just rubber-stamping the travelers through. But *you're* being careful to check everything. I think that's special. It's like the Dalai Lama said to me one time—"

The official boggled. "You've met the Dalai Lama?"

Offhandedly, Nicole nodded. "He was nice. I told him I liked his robes. They were a very pretty color."

Startled, the airport official glanced at Reid, who nodded in confirmation. He and his daughters had met His Holiness briefly at a reception a few years ago. Nicole had been only five or six, but she'd charmed the Dalai Lama immediately.

Sort of the way she was charming the official right now.

"'A spoon cannot taste of the food it carries,'" Nicole quoted solemnly. "'Likewise, a foolish man cannot understand—'"

"Nicole!" Alexis clutched her stomach. "No food talk!"

"'—a wise man's wisdom, even if he associates with a sage.'" Satisfied, Nicole gave the rapt airport official a keen look. "You're a sage, I'll bet. That's probably why those other airport people don't 'get' your superior screening methods."

Vigorously, the man nodded. "They don't! They really don't!" He beamed at Nicole, then blinked. Hard.

Reid peered at the airport official. Was he actually tearing up? He was. Nicole had officially moved the man to tears. Now if he would only move them forward, damn it.

His grandmother's emergency couldn't wait.

After a therapeutic exhale, the airport official sniffled loudly. He put aside Reid's passport to examine Alexis's and Nicole's documents. He nodded. After an interminable-feeling wait of forty-five seconds, he waved them all through.

"Welcome to the Wolverine State! You three have a wonderful stay."

"We will!" Nicole and Alexis chimed. "Bye!"

The man waved at the girls. Then he gave Reid a man-to-man nod. "That's a very special little girl you have there."

Reid smiled. "Don't I know it." Not every ten-year-old could cajole her way into the USA. "Thanks. Have a good day."

With the niceties dispensed with, Reid bolted into the terminal, trusting Alexis, Nicole, and Amanda to keep up as he headed straight for the rental car counter.

Within minutes, he was there. His undoubtedly grim expression helped clear his path through the crowded terminal.

Despite the hazy assurances of his grandparents' neighbors and friends, he fully expected to find disaster in Kismet. He'd already steeled himself for it. All that remained now was to deal with it, by whatever means possible. Reid was ready.

He turned. Nicole had already taken a seat on the airport's dingy carpeted floor, sharing a leftover pack of airplane pretzels with Amanda. Their backpacks lay slumped at their feet. The two of them slouched against the wall, completely at ease, even in their bustling surroundings. Looking at them as he waited in (yet another) line, Reid felt proud of his younger daughter.

There was nothing like travel to teach a person to be self-sufficient and comfortable in diverse surroundings. If he left Nicole there very long, Reid knew, she'd probably start napping.

Although Alexis was the one with a real knack for sleeping under the most inhospitable circumstances. She'd once napped her way through an arduous Jeep ride across the plains of Siberia. Their driver, Sergei, had joked that Alexis had the constitution of a Kamchatka brown bear—wanting "only to hibernate, eat, and hibernate some more!" If it hadn't been for—

Abruptly yanked from his reminiscences, Reid realized why things didn't seem quite right. Alexis was nowhere in sight.

With the dull hum of the airplane's engine filling her ears, Karina squinted at the laptop she'd propped on her tray table. It was pretty easy to read the screen, even with the glare from the window hitting it. That was because the passenger directly in front of her had reclined his seat at the first opportunity, putting Karina's tray table about a quarter inch from her lap. At this point, that thin plastic wedge was performing triple duty as a laptop holder, beverage tray, *and* inadvertent Pilates-style isometric exercise device.

She'd considered asking the man to put his seat upright again. But then the snoring had kicked in, and Karina had decided it wouldn't hurt her to tone her abs a little. Doing just that, she held her breath and sucked in her belly, the better to operate the laptop's minuscule touch pad. That was better. She could feel herself getting a six-pack already!

Besides, the man in front of her must be exhausted, she told herself. She should let him sleep. That's what she would have wanted her fellow passengers to do for her, if she'd been able to snooze during the cross-country flight.

As it was, Karina had divided her time between all three of her children, making sure they each had pillows, snacks, entertainment, and as few squabbles as possible. Even with all that effort, she could still feel the flight attendant's censorious gaze sneaking in her direction, as if it were only a matter of time before the Problem Children in Row Seventeen started raising a ruckus.

That was a look Karina was all too familiar with: wary, hypercritical, and (potentially) beleaguered—as though she were somehow being unreasonable by traveling with people who couldn't vote or pay taxes . . . or order eight-dollar minibottles of merlot (gratuity not included). She felt the effects of that look strongly, especially now that she was solely responsible for Olivia's, Michael's, and Josh's behavior most of the time.

She'd done a good job handling things, though. At least she thought she had. Mostly. Hoping to confirm that fact, Karina glanced up from Stephanie's official, top-secret Edgware checklists on her laptop, examining her children instead.

Michael slumped beside her in the window seat, his stubby legs barely bent at the knee in his adult-size seat. Just as he'd done during the first two hours of their flight, he stared at the clouds with rapt attention, captivated by that bird's-eye view of the world. From the moment they'd boarded, Michael had peppered her with questions. How did the plane stay up in the air? Why couldn't he play with his Game Boy? How far was it to Michigan? How could it be two different times in two different places when they were the same people going from here to there?

Karina had to admit, he'd almost stumped her with that last question. It was a mind bender. But that was typical of her youngest son. Michael had always been intensely curious. Except about her and Eric's divorce, it occurred to Karina. He'd asked her only one question about that: *Is Daddy coming back home?*

No, she'd been forced to answer. *Daddy's going to live at his condo now. But you'll see him all the time! He loves you lots!*

Michael's solemn-eyed acceptance of her answer still haunted Karina sometimes. Especially late at night, when she couldn't sleep. Which was much of the time, actually.

She hoped she'd handled things correctly with her divorce. If she hadn't, she devoutly prayed a little bit of Christmas magic would help smooth over the rough spots for her children.

To Karina's right, Olivia perched attentively in the aisle seat, watching the other passengers and the flight attendants. She seemed to have appointed herself the protector of their traveling group. She'd even gone so far as to soberly suggest "one of those kid leashes" for Michael, to make sure he didn't get lost in the busy airport. Olivia had also earnestly informed Karina that she had to be on red alert ("Kids get abducted from public restrooms *all* the time! I saw it on TV!"). She'd further informed Josh that he ought to be careful in crowds during their trip and maybe "get a backpack with a lock and chain," to make sure he didn't "get pickpocketed or some-thing like that."

Looking at Olivia's watchful, pugnacious little face right

now, Karina couldn't help wondering . . . when had her daughter become such a worrier? And how was Karina supposed to deal with it?

Only Josh seemed to have emerged relatively unscathed from the difficulties of the past year. It had been tough on him to see Eric move out, Karina was sure. But Josh remained mostly upbeat, interested in the usual kid stuff like video games and basketball and cartoons. Even during his first cross-country flight—which definitely counted as a nerve-racking experience for some people—Josh seemed to be coping remarkably well.

In his seat across the aisle from her, he balanced his knees on the back of the seat in front of him, keeping himself occupied by playing with a Rubik's Cube. His hair fell across his face, mostly shielding his profile. Still, Karina could glimpse his sweet, full cheeks, his childish upturned nose, and his attitude of concentration as he worked on the puzzle. Knowing Josh, he would solve it quickly. Then he would boast to Olivia about how she couldn't do the same. He would probably even—

He did not own a Rubik's Cube, it occurred to her.

Karina nudged him. "Hey, buddy. Where'd you get that?"

"It's mine." His fingers flew. "I brought it with me."

"You brought it on the plane?"

"Yep." More twisting and turning. "Pretty sick, right?"

"Sure." It was possible Josh had sneaked an extra item into his luggage. Although Karina had weighed every piece, to make sure they wouldn't exceed the limits. Still, a Rubik's Cube didn't weigh much. "Did your dad give that to you? Or Chelsea?"

Josh shrugged. "I just got it, that's all."

"Where?"

"Moooom."

"Okay, okay. Sorry. Good luck solving that thing."

"I don't need luck. I've got two sides done already." He twisted. "I'm a freakin' genius with this thing."

Karina smiled at Josh. "Don't say 'freakin'," she said, then went back to work on her laptop.

Lots to do, lots to do, lots to do. Her sister was counting on her, and so—by extension—was her nephew.

Plus, she still wanted to leave Eric gobsmacked by her efficiency and amazing butt-kicking evaluation of the B&B.

All at once, though, the official Edgware documents that Stephanie had entrusted her with—along with strict, detailed instructions for using and uploading those documents—didn't have the same appeal they had a few minutes ago.

Biting her lip, Karina glanced around the plane. Nobody here would care if she waited until she arrived at the B&B before she examined all the evaluation paperwork. In fact, that would probably be a better strategy. Then she could approach the evaluation process fresh, without being influenced by the things she was supposed to be observing for potential franchising.

If she was smart, it occurred to Karina, she would at least *arrive* at The Christmas House with no preconceptions or checklists in mind. That was only fair . . . right?

Holding her breath, she shut down the evaluation program. Almost without conscious thought, she swept her finger across the touch pad, going through the familiar taps and motions to open her e-mail software. Within seconds, the program unfurled on the screen. Her burgeoning in-box appeared. Accusingly.

Wow. She'd forgotten there were so many messages, mostly from the students she counseled at the community college. Even during the winter break, they needed her! Releasing her pent-up breath at last, Karina highlighted the first item.

She opened it. She scanned it.

Yes. She knew how to handle this.

Feeling sure of herself—possibly for the first time since stepping out of her shoes at the airport security checkpoint that morning—Karina opened an e-mail reply template. She considered the issue at hand, then started typing. She wouldn't be able to send any messages until their plane landed, of course—she certainly couldn't afford the exorbitant rates the airline charged for in-flight Wi-Fi—but that didn't mean she couldn't get a jump on helping some of her students.

Faster and faster, her fingers flew. This was actually better than her usual routine, she realized. With no Internet connection available, she wasn't tempted to read her favorite blogs or drop by Zappos to look for cute shoes. She could probably answer *all* of these student e-mails before her flight landed. That would put her so far ahead, it would be downright easy to concentrate on doing the B&B evaluation for Stephanie.

That's all she was doing, Karina told herself—just getting a head start. Clearing the decks. It was a good thing.

Then, partway through a complex reply involving transfer credits, degree requirements, and the book *What Color Is Your Parachute?* Karina heard an accusing voice ring out.

"Hey, kid!" cried the business traveler in seat 17-E. "You stole my Rubik's Cube. Give it back, you little thief!"

Just as Karina glanced up, preparing to rebut that ridiculous accusation, Josh sprang up. His face aflame with guilty knowledge, he bolted toward the back of the plane, the Rubik's Cube still clenched in his fist.

The door to the airplane toilet slammed. It locked. Uh-oh.

Olivia leaned forward, her hands balled into fists. "My brother is not a thief! You take that back!"

The businessman, apparently startled to be reprimanded by a ten-year-old girl, only stared at her. At first. Then he went right on blustering. "If he acts like a thief and runs like a thief, I'd say he's a damn thief! And I want my Rubik's Cube back!"

Laboriously, he unfastened his seat belt. He tossed aside his suit jacket, as though preparing to confront Josh.

Urgently, Karina waved her arm. "Sir, I'm sorry! I'm sure we can sort out this little misunderstanding." She lifted her laptop in her arms, then struggled to put her tray table back in its locked and upright position. It refused to budge. *Thanks, Sir Snores a Lot.* "If you'll just give me a minute—"

"Mom?" Michael turned to her. "I was wondering . . ."

"Hang on a second, sweetie." Karina pushed ineffectually at the seatback in front of her. "Are you sure that was your Rubik's Cube?" she asked the man. "Because my son said—"

"Your son is a delinquent and a liar."

"You take that back!" Olivia yelled. Threateningly.

"Honey, calm down. I've got this." Karina soothed her daughter, then felt Michael tug on her sleeve. "Sweetie, I'll be right with you," she promised him. "Just a minute—"

"You should consider therapy for that kid." The businessman waved his arm at the bathroom. "Or medication. Or maybe both."

Disbelievingly, Karina glowered at the man. "I'm a professional academic advisor. I think I'd know if my own son—"

"Isn't that always the way?" the man interrupted snidely. "The cooper's son is the one who goes without shoes."

"You mean 'the cobbler's son,'" Michael said. "The cooper is the man who makes barrels. We learned that at Old Tucson. My dad took us there, this one time last summer."

Hearing Michael's wee, precocious voice seemed to calm the man. For an instant, at least. Karina took advantage of that instant to try freeing herself again. She nudged the seat in front of her. Its occupant snuffled, then shifted.

No dice. She poked harder.

"Hey! Do you mind?" the man in front of her complained.

Karina hugged her laptop, completely exasperated. She was concerned about Josh, worried that Olivia might go into protective overdrive and physically assault the accusative businessman with her *Twilight* action figure, and distracted by Michael's ongoing yanking at her sleeve to get her attention.

Naturally, that's when the flight attendant decided to stop by, a decidedly triumphant gleam in her eye in spite of her professionally calm demeanor. "Is there a problem here?"

"Yes!" The businessman pointed at Karina. "This woman's hooligan son stole something of mine, and now he's hiding in the bathroom. I want someone to get him out of there and—"

Karina didn't hear the rest. It was probably just as well.

Michael chose that moment to quit waiting for her full attention . . . and go for anyone who would listen to his question.

"Does *anybody* know"—he asked with his arms dramatically in the air—"how Santa is supposed to find me this Christmas? In *Michigan?* Where I don't even *live* most of the time? And I don't even know if there are chimneys in those BB places? *Anybody?*"

Karina stuffed her laptop in its padded carrying case.

"I know the answer to that, Michael." She smiled into his worried little face. "And as soon as I inform your brother that an airplane bathroom *doesn't* make someone invisible, I'll give you the whole lowdown, I promise. Okay?"

Solemnly, Michael nodded. "Okay."

"Don't worry, Mom. I know the answer to that question too." Olivia appeared. Like magic, she'd somehow induced the snoring space hog in the next row to pull up his seat. She gestured for her mother to escape in the allotted free space. In a very grown-up voice, Olivia said, "I'll handle this one for you."

Surprised, Karina glanced up. Then she nodded. It was really sweet when the Barretts pulled together as a family. That was the upside to her divorce. She and the kids had definitely grown closer over the past year. Also, Josh's situation really needed to be dealt with. Any second now, the other passengers would start taking sides. Things would get ugly. On an airplane, nobody liked kids. Not anywhere near them, anyway.

"Thanks, Olivia. I'll be right back."

Karina headed to the airplane bathroom, still worried about her son but feeling slightly better. Especially once she heard Olivia's voice kick in, gentle and nurturing.

"You see, Michael," Olivia said sweetly, "Santa will be able to find you because of the RFID tag embedded in your toe."

"The *what?*" Michael squawked. "In my *what?*"

"The RFID tag. In your toe. It's what spies use for tracking down their enemies . . . and making them pay."

At her daughter's dramatically bloodthirsty tone, Karina could only shake her head. She kept going, a rueful smile on her face. Olivia's methods weren't perfect. But nobody's were. And her heart was in the right place.

That was more than Karina could (potentially) say for Josh, her lovable kleptomaniac, as she located the airplane bathroom and knocked on the locked door.

Chapter Six

December 17th
(arriving in) Kismet, Michigan
(still en route to) The Christmas House

   In the end, it took forty-three minutes to reach Kismet.

   Clutching the steering wheel of his rented four-wheel-drive Subaru Forester, Reid navigated down Main Street. His shoulders thrummed with tension. His temples ached with worry. His jaw clenched as though it might never relax. Still, he kept driving.

   It wasn't like his grandparents to call for help. But the truth was, Betty and Robert Sullivan were both in their mid-seventies now. It was possible this was the first time they truly *needed* help. Reid couldn't reach them fast enough.

   The town's traditional wrought iron street lamps flashed by. So did quaint businesses, real-estate offices, cafés, and souvenir shops. All of them stood festooned in holiday finery, from blinking lights to hand-painted window decorations to plastic wreaths of mistletoe. Festive banners stretched across the thoroughfare, announcing the upcoming and much-bally-hooed Kismet Christmas Parade and Holiday Lights Show.

   Snowdrifts piled up at the edges of the street, competing

for wintery ambiance with the icicles glittering from the shops' eaves. The whole place sparkled. It smelled like snow-fall and gingerbread. It buzzed with shoppers hurrying from store to store and reverberated with the sounds of the Christmas carols the city officials had piped in over hidden municipal speakers.

"Hmmm. This place is crazy about Christmas." Beside him in the Subaru's passenger seat, Alexis gazed out at the streets as they whizzed past. In her lap sat a cardboard box. She reached inside it and withdrew a miniature cinnamon roll. "Would you like a Minibon, Dad? They're really tasty."

"I want one!" Nicole yelled from the backseat.

"Pass those back here," Amanda suggested, hungry as usual.

"No." Reid clenched his jaw. "I don't."

"No, *thank you,* you mean." Primly, Nicole accepted the Cinnabon box as Alexis passed it back. "Use your manners, Dad."

In the rearview mirror, Amanda grinned.

Reid frowned anew. He turned the corner onto Lakeshore Drive. "My manners went missing the same time Alexis did."

"I can't believe you're still talking about that!" Alexis shot him an incredulous look. "I told you, I was *starving.* I saw the Cinnabon store and went in. I knew I could catch up with you at the car rental place afterward. Airports *do* have lots of signs, Dad. A moron could find their way around. Blind-folded."

Not the least bit mollified, Reid kept driving. He didn't want to confess how rattled he'd been by losing track of Alexis. Ordinarily, that wouldn't have happened. He chalked it up to the stress of being called home on such a mystifying basis.

"It just took a while," his daughter went on, "because I didn't have anything with me except Australian dollars."

"*I* could have convinced them to take those," Nicole said.

Chewing a mouthful of Minibon, Amanda avidly agreed.

Stern faced, Reid glanced into the rearview again, ready to referee the inevitable argument that Nicole's statement would cause. Alexis hated the thought that her sister could be better than she was. At anything. Oddly enough, though, the girls merely shared a vaguely conspiratorial look, then glanced away.

Hmmm. That was weird. What were they up to, anyway?

An instant later, the Christmas House B&B came into view, and Reid forgot all about whatever subterfuge his daughters were planning. The B&B's familiar holly-wreathed, hand-painted sign made his heart beat even faster. He eyed the place's wide, snowy grounds, then the porch-bedecked house, looking for signs of trouble. Nothing appeared overtly threatening. There weren't even very many vehicles parked in the small lot adjacent to the three-story, white-painted house and nearby outbuildings.

Was the B&B *closed?* He couldn't remember The Christmas House ever being closed. Its annual holiday activities were a mainstay of his childhood memories. That meant his grandparents had been operating the place for at least thirty years.

Thirty years . . . and all of them potentially at risk now.

Shoving the Subaru into park, Reid whipped off his seat belt. He opened the driver's side door. With one booted foot propped on the snowy driveway, he twisted around in his seat, ready to prepare Nicole and Alexis for . . . what, exactly?

Reid didn't know. He doubted it would be good.

His daughters' cinnamon-and-sugar-smeared faces met his. So did their wide eyes and nervous gazes. The combination reminded Reid of when they'd been toddlers, getting into things and making messes. Time went by so quickly. Things changed. *People* changed. Circumstances were fragile and always evolving.

Not necessarily for the better, either.

Suddenly choked with emotion, Reid tightened his grasp on the door. Frigid air poured inside, chilling him to the bone. All of a sudden, he didn't want to know why his grand-parents had called him home. He wanted to stay there, wrapped up in blissful ignorance and the sweet smell of cinnamon rolls, forever.

"You go ahead." Amanda waved him onward, her gaze filled with empathy. "We'll get cleaned up and meet you inside."

Unable to speak, Reid nodded. Then he stiffened his spine, got out of the Subaru, and went to meet the mysterious crisis that, for the first time in years, had finally called him home.

In the airplane aisle behind Karina, another passenger stepped into line. That made five people who wanted to use the restroom. Five people whose icy stares stabbed into her shoulder blades, as sharp as the icicles on The Christmas House's eaves in the B&B's scenic brochures. Casting a nervous glance back at her fellow passengers, Karina apologized again.

She knocked on the door. "Josh, please come out."

"*Moooom!* I'm using the bathroom!" Her son's muffled voice sounded stressed. "Can I have some privacy, please?"

"Look, I promise you're not in trouble. Just come out."

"No."

"We can talk about this. Come on, Josh."

A pause. "You're going to be mad."

"I'm not going to be mad. I only want to help you."

Silence. Faint clicking. More clicking. Hmmm . . .

"Are you *still* working on that Rubik's Cube?"

A guilty pause. Then . . . "Maybe."

One of the passengers in line behind Karina groaned. Another gave her a poke in the arm. "Hey, can you hurry him up?"

"Well." Karina gave a nervous titter. Maybe some humor would help? "He *did* say he was a genius at that thing, so—"

An expletive cut her off. Someone in line grumbled.

Karina raised both arms in her most contrite pose, addressing all the people who wanted to use the bathroom. If only the flight attendant weren't being so unreasonable about letting them use the first-class restroom, this wouldn't have been a problem for anyone. The first-class facilities were, of course, totally free.

"Maybe Santa will bring you a Rubik's Cube for Christmas," she told Josh through the door. "If you put one on your wish list, he'll know you want one. You could do that, right?"

The door opened a sliver. Josh appeared, still holding the puzzle toy. His lips wobbled in an uncertain smile as he held up the Rubik's Cube to show her its same-colored sides. "Did it."

His brown-eyed gaze, so similar to Eric's, beseeched her to approve. Karina felt her heart give an impossible tug.

"Congratulations, hotshot." She hauled Josh into her arms and hugged him. "I guess you really *are* a genius at that thing."

Her little boy hugged her, too, his arms tight around her middle. "That man wasn't even using it." Josh spoke in a low voice, his head pressed against her shoulder. "He was *snoring!*"

Karina thought about the rude passenger in front of her. "Yeah. There's a lot of that going around on airplanes."

"I didn't steal it," Josh went on. "I only borrowed it! I just wanted to finish it before I gave it back, that's all."

Karina wanted to believe him. But something about his statement niggled at her. Last month, Josh had "borrowed" his friend's new iPod nano—until the boy's mother had called to request its return. Last week, Josh had "borrowed" the hamster that served as his class's mascot—cage and all—and had fibbed to Karina that his teacher had asked him to take the creature home for safekeeping. Only a few days ago, her sweet little boy had "borrowed" a few extra cookies from the after-school snacks cache in the cupboard, oblivious to the impossibility of ever "returning" a half dozen already eaten cookies.

Affectionately, Karina ruffled Josh's hair. She set him apart from her in the cramped airplane space, the better to deliver him a serious maternal look. "I think you need a refresher course on what 'borrowing' means, young man."

"*You* need a 'refresher course' on not raising a juvenile delinquent!" someone shouted from the line. "Move already!"

"Yeah, lady! You and your kid get out of the way!"

"Ma'am?" The flight attendant motioned to Karina. "We're going to be making our descent toward Grand Rapids in a few minutes, so if you would please take your seat?" She addressed everyone else. "That means the captain will be turning on the FASTEN SEAT BELTS sign. Everyone will need to be in their seats, with their tray tables in the locked and upright position."

The people in the bathroom line shuffled mutinously.

Six baleful gazes shifted toward Karina and Josh, each filled with murderous intent and—most likely—a forcibly subdued urge to use the airplane bathroom. Protectively shielding Josh with her arm, Karina ignored those barbed glares. She guided the two of them back to row seventeen, feeling as though the two of them might be spitballed at any second.

She motioned for Josh to return the Rubik's Cube to its rightful owner. The businessman glared at him, but accepted it.

Just to be on the safe side—in case there were any grudges left lingering—Karina took Josh's former seat next to the man. She let Josh slip into Olivia's previous place on the aisle. Beside him in the middle seat, Olivia was still explaining the Santa situation—very matter-of-factly—to a wide-eyed Michael.

". . . it's simple," she was telling her brother. "The reindeer have GPS units installed in their antlers. That's how they navigate. That's why Rudolph is the best of all. He's the prototype." She drew in a breath. "The *robo* prototype!"

"Rudolph the Red-Nosed Reindeer is a *robot?*" Michael sounded horrified—and fascinated. He examined Olivia's face as she nodded in affirmation. He scrunched up his nose. "No *wonder* his nose glows! No ordinary reindeer could do that!"

"That's right," Olivia said. "And wait till you hear what Santa's elves are *really* making in his toy shop. . . ."

Settling in her new seat, Karina leaned back her head. *Whew.* Made it. She closed her eyes. Just for an instant.

Christmas vacation, take me away! Now more than ever, she needed a relaxing getaway. And so, it seemed, did her children.

They were all about to get one, too. If The Christmas House B&B could do half the things it promised—make gift shopping fun and easy, offer ready-made treats and holiday meals, supply seasonal activities, ensure merry times and family togetherness—it deserved to be franchised by Edgware. It really did.

Personally, she could hardly wait to find out how it fared.

"That's right. You heard me," Robert Sullivan said. "We want to unload this place. It's time. It's *past* time."

Reid gawked at his grandfather. He'd knocked on the door, rushed inside the B&B, hugged everyone, then demanded to know what the dire emergency was. Instead, his grandfather had come out with . . . Well, Reid still couldn't believe it.

Completely confused, he shook his head. Maybe if he went

along with them, this would all make sense eventually. To that end, Reid repeated, "You want to *sell* The Christmas House?"

"Yes," Betty Sullivan confirmed. Appearing wholly well and vibrantly fit in her jeans, boots, and turtleneck sweater, she moved about the B&B's cozy front room, supplying her eager great-granddaughters and their nanny/tutor with iced sugar cookies. "We've been trying to sell for five years now."

"Every time we have a sale lined up . . . *Bam!*" Reid's grandfather slammed his fist in his hand, making an exasperated sound. "The holiday season rolls around, we get all nostalgic, and we end up cancelling the deal. But not this year!"

He slid his gaze to the pile of luggage that had been neatly arranged at the landing. The arched stairway beyond it led to the house's second and third floors, where the B&B's guests stayed—and where Reid's grandparents had always lived.

Reid counted. There had to be at least twelve suitcases there, plus a few garment bags and a packed duffel. Clearly, traveling light wasn't necessarily embedded in the Sullivan family genes.

"We've been trying to retire for years now." His grandmother set down the tray of cookies on an ottoman near the fireplace. She took a seat opposite Reid, appearing entirely indifferent to the gaily decorated Douglas fir that stretched to ceiling height beside her, sparkling and flashing. "But this time, we went all the way with our plans." She took Reid's hand between both of hers, her grasp as warm as her smile. "This time, we put a big down payment on a new house in Arizona."

Taken aback, Reid asked, "You're serious then?"

"Quarter of a million dollars' worth of serious!"

At his grandfather's good-natured outburst, Reid couldn't help smiling. For as long as he could remember, Robert Sullivan had always been generous with love, treats, and surreptitious ten-dollar bills for his grandchildren. But he'd also always been careful with money, to the point of doing most of the repairs on the B&B himself. He'd painted and caulked, plumbed and tiled . . . he'd even helped construct one of the outbuildings.

In a very real sense, The Christmas House was a labor of love, handmade by Robert Sullivan (with a lot of help from Betty). The B&B was practically a part of the Sullivan family. It was their legacy. It was the place where all the other Sullivans—most of whom lacked Reid's wanderlust and still lived in Kismet—gathered for the holidays every year. That was why Reid found himself still shaking his head dubiously.

On the other hand, if his grandfather was willing to pony up a cool quarter million to make sure his Arizona retirement was secure . . . Well, *that* was serious. Really serious.

Never mind the emergency just then, Reid decided. He could see that both his grandparents appeared happy. That was enough for now. For *right now.* Later, he'd get to the bottom of that cryptic phone call, he promised himself. In the meantime . . .

Retirement? *Selling?* It couldn't be true.

Reid knew his grandparents had been talking about retirement for years. But as each holiday season had come and gone—with Robert and Betty still ensconced at The Christmas House—he'd taken their avowed eagerness to retire less and less seriously. So had the rest of the family. It had almost become a family legend. *Right. Then Grandpa's going to retire. Ha!*

Now it seemed the joke was on them. His grandparents gave every impression of sincerity this time, right down to the packed luggage at the foot of the stairs. Not to mention the new *Arizona* logoed golf visor his grandfather was wearing. Hmmm . . .

"I can't imagine this place without you," Reid said.

"Well, you're going to have to imagine it!" Robert informed him. He smiled at his great-granddaughters, who perched on the sofa on either side of him, happily crunching iced cookies. "Because it's happening. By this time tomorrow, your grandmother and I will be hitting the golf course, working on our tans—"

"Figuratively speaking, of course," Betty assured him. "We always wear sunscreen and protective clothing, and we make sure to stay out of the sun between eleven and three every day. You can't be too careful when it comes to sun exposure, you know."

"—and enjoying the high life. I might even set up my model trains again. Our new place at Carina del Mundo—"

"'Home of the world'?" Alexis translated. "Must be *big*."

"—has plenty of room. Room this overstuffed house never had!" Robert gestured at the B&B's front room. It was fully decorated with lights, embellished holiday pillows, bowls of ornaments and clove-studded orange pomanders, fat flickering candles, and even topiaries made of holly and mistletoe. "And we won't have any damn visitors for *at least* the first year!"

"Robert!" Betty protested.

"Sorry. 'Darn' visitors. For *at least* a year!"

Puzzled, Reid examined them. "I thought you liked company. I thought that's why you enjoyed running the B&B so much."

"Company, yes," his grandmother said. "But there are limits. We're getting on in years, you know. We want to relax."

His grandfather nodded at that. Vigorously.

"*And* we want some time to ourselves." His grandfather gave Betty a grinning, lascivious wink. "If you know what I mean."

Reid nodded. It was a peculiarly American mind-set to believe that people stopped being interested in sex when they got older. In other parts of the world, people understood that a fulfilling life included plenty of whoopee. No matter your age.

"That's why we want to retire. *Now*. Before it's too late."

Reid could hardly fault them for wanting to enjoy their golden years. He definitely wanted them to be happy. Still . . .

What about the emergency? What about that phone call?

Reid shot a glance at Alexis. She bit her lip, appearing to be thinking the same thing he was. *What about what's wrong?*

"All right. I hear you," Reid said. "I understand that it can't be easy to run this place, year in and year out."

His grandparents traded an enigmatic look.

"Oh, it's not *that* bad," his grandfather said. He chuckled. "Most of the time, The Christmas House practically runs itself."

"It really does," his grandmother assured him—pointlessly, since Reid was already busy preparing himself for the worst.

"All right. Fine." He got to his feet. He paced across the room, absently noting the presence of at least three dancing Santa figurines and one fireplace mantel full of already hung stockings. They even had names embroidered on their cuffs: *Karina. Josh. Olivia. Michael. Suzanne. Rocky. Neil.* "But when Alexis told me about that satellite call, I got the impression there was more to this story than a simple urge to retire. You could have told me about that over the phone, any one of the dozens of times I called. Or did no one give you my messages?"

His grandmother gazed at him dotingly. "Look at him, pacing around like that, Bob. Reid still can't sit still, even at his age. It's just like when he was little. Isn't that cute?"

"You always were a rowdy one," Robert confirmed fondly.

Wheeling around, Reid confronted them. "Just tell me: Which one of you is sick? Exactly what's wrong? And how can I help?"

At his anguished tone, Nicole gawked. Amanda paused with a cookie halfway to her mouth, compelled by the unexpected drama to quit eating. His grandparents . . . laughed. *Laughed!*

"No one is ill," his grandfather said. "We're quite well."

"I do water aerobics at the Y three times a week!"

Reid didn't believe them. "Then what's the emergency?"

Alexis and Nicole exchanged a furtive look.

So did his grandparents. Did *everyone* have a secret around here?

Reid felt too overwrought to contemplate the notion much further. "Enough about The Christmas House," he said roughly. "Enough about Arizona! I want to know the *real* reason you called me. And don't talk to me about going ten under par or taking up saguaro gardening, because I won't buy it."

"Saguaro gardening," his grandmother mused. "Good idea!"

"We already told you," his grandfather insisted. "We called you here because we want to sell The Christmas House—and we want your help with it. It'll be easy. We already have—"

Newly alert, Reid stopped. "My help? You want *my* help?"

"—a deal lined up with a global hospitality company. They're called Edgware. You might have heard of them?"

"They're big. Your cousin hooked us up with them."

"It's almost a done deal," Robert rushed on, all business now. "All that's left is for the B&B to undergo a mandatory anonymous evaluation, just to prove that we're all shipshape—"

"Which, of course, we are!"

"—and the deal will go through. It's worth big money."

"*Really* big money," his grandmother emphasized hastily. She gave a firm nod. "Believe me, hospitality companies aren't exactly lining up to invest in small inns like ours, especially these days, and especially around here. It's only because our all-inclusive holiday vacation concept is so unique—"

"We were featured on *Good Morning, Kismet*!"

"—that The Christmas House is under consideration at all. This is an opportunity we can't afford to pass up."

They both stopped for breath, seeming to have run out of chatty arguments for selling the B&B. Uncertainly, his grandparents glanced at each other. Then, hopefully, at Reid.

A certain tension filled the air. It felt a lot like the anxiety Reid sensed whenever one of his adventure travel clients had been less than truthful with him. Maybe about preparedness. Maybe about fitness. Maybe about his or her goals for undertaking a wilderness trek. Either way, it wasn't good.

At the fireplace mantel, Reid paused too. He thought about what he knew so far. Then, with sudden insight, he turned.

"You staked your new retirement house on this deal."

His grandparents swapped uncomfortable looks.

"You *literally* can't afford to pass this up," he added, "because you've already spent the money you'll get from the sale. *If* it goes through." He turned. "I'm right, aren't I?"

Silence descended. Amanda reached for another cookie.

Snowflakes drifted past the windowpane, making Reid shiver. It was warm inside, especially by the cheery crackling fire, but his reaction had nothing to do with the wintery weather—and everything to do with the abrupt letdown of the adrenaline rush that had brought him here. He'd been so fraught with worry. So determined to take charge. And now . . . Now he was merely baffled.

Why would his grandparents gamble with their future this way? Staking the B&B was crazy—especially if there were hoops to jump through before the sale could be finalized. A "mandatory anonymous evaluation" sounded like a pretty big hoop to him.

If the Edgware franchising deal fell through, Betty and Robert would be out of luck—and unable to pay for their new retirement home in Arizona, too. Given the current real estate market, they'd be unlikely to sell the B&B to anyone else.

"You have to understand." His grandmother wrung her hands, her wedding rings sparkling. "You're our very last hope, Reid."

"Hope for what?" He frowned, still confused.

"For helping us sell The Christmas House!" his grandfather said. "We need you to handle things—to make sure the sale goes through as planned. *That's* why we called you."

"But I don't know anything about real estate."

"You don't have to!" his grandmother hurried to assure him. "All you have to do is make sure things run smoothly while the secret Edgware evaluator is here. It will be a piece of cake."

"Then *you* should do it. You're the ones with experience running a B&B," Reid pointed out—reasonably, he thought.

"If we try to do it, we're likely to get all sentimental. Again," his grandfather said. "And we'll end up cancelling the deal. Again. This time, as you said, we can't do that."

Because our retirement depends on it. They didn't have to say the words aloud. The truth was evident. "Then don't cancel."

"It's not as simple as that." Patiently, his grandmother folded her hands in her lap. "The evaluation has to happen at Christmastime, because that's when the B&B is at its best. But that's *also* when your grandfather and I feel the most attached to this place. We've made a lot of happy memories here, Reid, especially holiday memories. If we try to do this ourselves, I just know what will happen: One minute, I'll be demonstrating how to make paper cutout snowflakes to our guests . . . and the next I'll be bawling into the eggnog and begging Bob to stop the sale."

"She does cry into the eggnog," Robert said. "Salty eggnog is not the tastiest eggnog, let me tell you."

Exasperated, Reid shook his head. "I don't have time. I need to line up other jobs." He couldn't take a chance with Alexis's and Nicole's security. "I have clients waiting to hear from me in Argentina and Iceland. That means I'll be either herding cattle with gauchos or skiing the chutes in Isafjordur."

His grandparents looked at him uncomprehendingly.

"The answer is no," Reid clarified. "I have work to do."

His daughters—and Amanda—scowled at him, cookies in hand.

"Real estate is hardly my forte," he felt compelled to add. "Unless it's untamed, untried, and located in some far-flung corner of the globe, and even then—" Getting off track, he regrouped. He squared his shoulders, then faced them all. "I'm an adventurer, not a salesman. You need a salesman."

"What we need," his grandfather said, "is a Scrooge."

"And *you're* him," his grandmother added. "*You* won't get sentimental about all the holiday traditions here at the B&B. You're practically immune to Christmas! That makes you *perfect.*"

Perfect, because he wouldn't get nostalgic about the B&B.

Perfect, because, to his grandparents, a sincere wish to sell The Christmas House and retire really *was* a crisis.

Perfect, most of all, because he was a Scrooge at heart.

Still unconvinced, Reid kept pacing. It was true that his world travels had left him one step removed from the traditions everyone else treasured. He really *was* unlikely to cave in to a sudden bout of nostalgia and call off the sale. His grandparents were right about that much. But his admitted lack of Christmas cheer didn't mean he wanted to hang around Kismet—of all places—trying to please holiday vacationers and hoping to impress a clipboard-wielding hospitality company evaluator.

Frankly, the whole idea sounded nightmarish to him.

"You won't have to do everything yourself," Robert said.

"That's right!" Betty beamed at him. "I almost forgot that part. All your relatives—and our neighbors—will be here to help you, Reid. Everyone's already agreed to drop in and volunteer on an as-needed basis. That will make things easy-peasy!"

"If anyone can make sure this sale goes through," his grandfather pushed, "it's you, Reid. We need you."

That almost did it. As much as Reid loved to travel the

world, he loved his family more. Loyalty was his middle name.

Teetering on the verge of agreement, he exhaled. With his head tipped to the ceiling, he examined the B&B's lovingly restored crown molding. It was edged with evergreens and starry LED white lights, lending the whole room a Christmassy air.

A Christmassy air *he* felt utterly indifferent to.

Maybe he really was a Scrooge.

"Hey, Dad?" In the silence, Nicole piped up. "What's that pine tree doing inside, with all that stuff on it?"

She couldn't be serious.

"Pine tree?" Reid stepped closer to the gaily decorated fir, with its strings of popcorn and cranberries, old-fashioned bubble lights, and glass ornaments. "You mean this one?"

Soberly, she nodded. "Yeah. I mean, it's pretty and all, but . . . What's it for? What does it do? How'd it get there?"

Everyone in the front room stared at her. Then at Reid.

Their disapproving gazes made him feel . . . itchy. He didn't like it. He rubbed the back of his neck, then gave an uncomfortable chuckle. "Honey, come on. You know what that is."

His small daughter only gazed at him. Trustingly. Blankly.

"It's a Christmas tree!" Reid blurted. "Remember those?"

Surely Nicole had seen a Christmas tree before. Admittedly, the three of them had spent much of their time in subtropical, isolated, and partially unexplored places. Their lives were made up of indigenous peoples, wildlife, and topographical maps—not carols, Santa Claus, and greeting cards. But Reid knew he hadn't deprived his daughters of *all* knowledge of Christmas. Had he?

Hoping he hadn't, Reid gazed tautly at Nicole. Her face appeared brighter than ever in the glow of the holiday lights.

"Nope." Nicole shook her head. "I don't remember those."

That settled it. It was one thing if *he* was a Scrooge. He

was a grown man, comfortably invulnerable to gooey emotion and the need to look at shiny things, burst into stupid songs, and eat candy canes once a year. But his ten-year-old daughter?

She should experience Christmas firsthand. The sooner the better. He'd obviously neglected his duty in the holiday arena.

"All right," Reid said. "I'll do it."

His grandparents exchanged relieved looks. "Great!"

"But only this once," Reid warned with as much severity as he could muster. His position was probably weakened by the gush of emotion he felt at the sight of his grandparents' grateful expressions. "If you get all sentimental this time and call off the deal, I'm out. There won't be a second chance next year."

"We won't need a second chance next year," his grandfather assured him. "The sale's going through *this* year!"

"Absolutely!" His grandmother rose. She gave him an appreciative hug. "Thank you, Reid. You don't know what this means to us. You truly don't." She trotted over to the pile of waiting luggage, then put her palms together with a businesslike air. "The keys and a few notes are waiting in your room, along with a detailed schedule for each day. It's not complicated. The staff knows exactly what to do. They're expecting you. Your cousin should be here soon to brief you on procedures, and the first guests ought to be arriving shortly after that."

Reid nodded, suddenly feeling a little jet-lagged.

"The toilet in the third room on the left on the second floor needs a little jiggle to the handle to make it quit running," his grandfather informed him. "Also, the sleigh is parked in the barn. Whatever you do, *don't*—"

"The *sleigh?*"

"For the sleigh rides." His grandfather got to his feet also. He traipsed to the pile of luggage too, adjusting his golf visor as he went. "Through the snow. With the jingle bells."

"It's all on the schedule, dear," his grandmother said.

"All right." Reid frowned. "But won't you be—"

"Here?" his grandmother interrupted gaily. She laughed. "Heavens, no! We learned our lesson last year. We're leaving."

"For Arizona. Today. Our flight takes off in two hours."

Stunned, Reid stared. "You already booked a flight? But I was halfway around the world. *Literally* halfway around the world. What if I hadn't arrived in time? What if one of my flights had been delayed? What if I hadn't come home at all?"

They both laughed. His grandfather gave him an affectionate clap to the shoulder. "Of course you came. You're . . . *you.*"

His grandparents' joyful smiles looked warm and certain. *You're . . . you.* That's right, Reid thought. He was.

And he'd traveled more than fifteen thousand kilometers to arrive at this moment. He might as well get on with it.

Heartened by their unmistakable confidence in him, Reid blinked to shake off his jet lag. He could handle this— running one tiny B&B during one uneventful holiday season with one single nitpicky evaluator to impress. He'd earn the B&B an A-plus rating for sure. After all . . . what could possibly go wrong?

In a flurry of activity, his grandparents prepared to leave. Reid carried their luggage to their waiting vehicle— a minivan driven by their ever-helpful neighbor. Hugs were given all around. Chatter ensued. Within minutes, it seemed, Reid found himself on the B&B's front porch, standing with Nicole, Alexis, and Amanda as they waved good-bye to his grandparents.

The minivan pulled around the corner, then was gone.

For some reason, its parting *honk* sounded a little mocking.

"Well, I guess that does it." Stretching out his arms, Reid enveloped both his daughters in a sideways hug. The crisp December air stung his lungs as he inhaled, preparing himself for the unknown tasks ahead. He nodded. He could do this. No problem. "Who's ready for a little Christmas cheer?"

"We are!" his daughters yelled. "Woo-hoo!"

Their nanny/tutor yawned. "I'm going to take a nap."

The three of them disappeared inside, leaving Reid alone.

Standing on the front porch, he wrapped his gloved hand around one of the ribbon-wrapped porch pillars. Experimentally, he rang one of the shiny decorative jingle bells affixed to the ribbon. He waited for Christmas cheer to wash over him.

Nada. With a shrug, Reid gazed across the snowy grounds, past the several additional decorated outdoor trees, past the multiple wooden cutout Christmas decorations, past the lights, past the snowdrifts and plastic candy canes, all the way to . . .

An airport shuttle pulled up. It disgorged about a dozen chattering, gawking tourists. All of them headed for the B&B.

Reid glanced around, waiting for the staff to materialize. Nobody appeared. The porch remained empty, except for him. Huh. That was strange. His grandparents had assured him the staff was ready and waiting to snap into action at a moment's notice.

Oblivious to the lack of trained B&B personnel, the (apparent) guests tromped closer, squashing the snow under booted feet. They pointed at the decorations. They oohed and aahed. A couple of them waved at him with mittened hands.

"Howdy-ho!" one called out. "Merry Christmas!"

Reid wasn't sure exactly what that meant anymore. Or what these people expected from The Christmas House. But he'd be damned if he'd let down his grandparents—or his own daughters.

He stepped forward, then thrust his arm in the air in a confident, jovial wave. "Merry Christmas! Come on in!"

Everyone headed in his direction. "Holly Jolly Christmas" suddenly blared from inside the house, and Reid was on his way.

Chapter Seven

Date: December 17th
Edgware Project Name: The Christmas House
Initial Impression: ~~festive~~ HUBBA-HUBBA!
Interaction Goal: ~~evaluate ambiance~~ CHAT UP SEXY GUY!

Doing her best to kick off her Edgware evaluation on the right foot, Karina stood in the foyer, furiously taking mental notes about The Christmas House. She and the kids had arrived there moments earlier, having missed the first available airport shuttle. They'd caught the second one, though, and had spent the ride marveling at the amazing *winteriness* of their surroundings.

Snow. For a California girl, it was mind-boggling.

"Mom?" Olivia tugged her sleeve. "Can we go in there?"

Karina glanced in the direction her daughter indicated. The B&B's front room stood crowded with other guests, all of whom appeared to be enjoying an afternoon cider-and-gingerbread reception. Neat. Karina smiled. "Sure. I'll be right there."

It would be easy to keep an eye on them from here, she reasoned. Also, if Michael, Olivia, and Josh stayed busy with the reception, she wouldn't have to explain what she was doing scrutinizing the B&B before they'd officially checked in.

She hadn't shared her covert mission with them. It would be smarter, Karina had decided, to keep it a secret—at least for now. Even under the best of circumstances, the Barretts weren't exactly renowned for their inconspicuousness. She couldn't risk having one of her children blurt out the fact that Karina was here to assess The Christmas House. Doing so would endanger Stephanie's job *and* the accuracy of the Edgware evaluation alike.

At her nod, Olivia, Josh, and Michael hurried into the fray with their usual mix of boisterousness and cookie-locating ability. Left on her own, Karina craned her gaze upward. The crown moldings were festooned with freshly cut evergreen garland and glowing Christmas lights. Nice.

Holiday ambiance: check. Drawing in a professional-evaluator-style breath, she furrowed her brow, then examined the remaining details in the B&B's festively decorated entryway.

A pinecone-and-evergreen wreath adorned the front door. More garland wrapped around the traditional oak banister, the foyer mirror, and the archway that led to the other room, where her children already fisted cups of spiced cider. A pine tree stood in the nook beside the staircase, fully decked out with lights and ornaments and embellished with wrapped gifts.

Holiday carols wafted from unseen speakers. The spicy scents of cinnamon, bayberry, and cloves drifted past Karina's nose. At the mullioned window nearby, red velvet curtains begged to be touched, appearing both lavish and soft at the same time.

So far, The Christmas House had all the bases covered. It looked like Christmas. It smelled like Christmas. It sounded like Christmas. It even *felt* like Christmas: magical and warm.

She liked it immediately.

"Hey, what are you doing in here all by yourself?" A man approached, tall and broad shouldered. He sported dark shoulder-length hair, a sociable demeanor, and several days' worth of macho beard stubble. Another guest, she guessed. A gregarious one. "You ought to be in the party with everyone else," he said in an invitingly husky voice. "Come on. I'll escort you in."

He raised his shoulder to indicate the reception going on in the other room. Karina wondered why he didn't simply wave his hand. A closer look told her why: Both his hands were full.

They were big, capable-looking hands, she noticed. Very arresting. One of them held a cup of spiced cider. The other held . . . No. It couldn't be. But it was. It *was*.

Feeling a ridiculous flutter in her midsection, Karina jerked her gaze from the man's hands, to his face, then back.

Back . . . to the squeeze bottle of honey in his hand.

Christmastime Honey-Buying Man stand-in. He was here! Just the way she'd imagined he might be.

Riveted by the notion that her secret fantasy man had actually materialized before her eyes, Karina inhaled to steady her nerves. Then she took a closer look. She owed it to herself to be thorough about evaluating *everything* here at The Christmas House . . . including her own potential holiday fling-ee.

It was practically fated. He *did* have the honey, after all.

"Thanks. That's nice of you." She noted his merry-looking blue eyes, his rugged jawline, his way of commanding attention as though *he* were the centerpiece of the day, instead of a bowl of holiday cider. "But won't your wife mind if you . . . ?"

Delicately, she let her question linger unfinished. She expected him to jump in with an answer. Eric had rarely let her finish a statement, much less a question. Instead, the man in front of her merely stood waiting with raised eyebrows.

Patiently. Interestedly. And (let's face it) sexily.

Karina nearly fell in love with him on the spot. How many men truly *listened* when a woman spoke? A handful? Maybe. *If* she were being generous. *And* counting talk-show hosts, who were *paid* to listen—mostly to famous, beautiful women. That meant this man's ability to pay attention—especially to a nonfamous, nongorgeous person like her—was practically a national treasure.

". . . join the party with another woman?" she finished.

There. She applauded herself for putting all the words together in the right order. But she could hardly stand there just ogling him, could she? No. No matter how much he (frankly) deserved it. There was something decidedly spectacular about the way he wore his khaki pants and stretchy thermal shirt, layered with another skintight tee. She could scarcely pull her gaze away from the shadows his muscles made against the fabric.

"No wife," he said. "I'm divorced."

Yay! This was fate, for sure. "Girlfriend?" she asked.

Her ultracasual tone didn't appear to fool him—at least if his dazzling smile was anything to go by. Through some kind of holiday magic, Karina felt that smile all the way to her toes.

"I'm on my own. Except for my daughters." He nudged his chin, this time indicating a pair of long-legged, energetic–looking preteen girls in the next room. Both wore knit caps and multilayered clothes. One appeared to be trying to reprogram the dancing Santa figurine; the other was demonstrating a dance move to Olivia, swiveling to the tune of a hip-hop Christmas carol. "They're pretty immune to the sight of their dad talking to pretty women, though, so we ought to be okay to join the party."

He thought she was pretty. Feeling a warm flush bloom in her cheeks, Karina grinned. He grinned back at her, making that flush spread rapidly . . . all the way to her giddy mid-section.

Flirtatiously, she waved her hand in front of her face. "Wow, is it hot in here, or is that just you?"

He laughed outright at that. *Yes!* She was back, ladies and gentlemen! Karina Barrett might be out of practice, but she wasn't down for the count. Encouraged, she leaned toward him.

Those few inches brought her within reach of his warmth, his presence, his indescribably delicious smell. Buffeted by a wave of wholehearted lustiness, Karina swayed. She smiled. Then, pretending to need him to steady her so she could get a leaning-sideways view of their children, she touched his shoulder.

It felt warm and solid beneath her hand. It felt *good*.

Really, really good. Great, even. Shocked by the impact that simple touch had on her, Karina trembled.

Wowsa. Apparently, sexual chemistry was real. And potent. Even (maybe especially!) between Christmastime strangers.

"It looks as though your daughters have met my daughter." She made herself remove her hand, successfully resisting an urge to pet him with it. "They seem to have hit it off, don't they?" At his nod, she smiled again. "My two sons are in there someplace too—probably next to the gingerbread cookies."

"Mmm. And your husband?" Mr. Dreamy raised his eyebrows.

"Pfft. In the Bahamas with his Pop Tart girlfriend."

"You seem surprisingly fine with that."

"Right now? I *totally* am." Karina showed him her naked ring finger. Briefly, she contemplated showing him even more. Instead, she got a grip on herself long enough to face him. "I'm divorced too. That's why we're here, actually. I needed a little help with the whole holly-jolly Christmas routine this year."

"Well, then, I guess you've come to the right place."

"Have I?" She could get lost in his eyes. They were so blue. So direct. So intense and insightful. "I'm glad."

"Me too."

His voice rasped all the way inside her, making her shiver—even in her multiple layers of cold-weather gear. Still bundled up in her sweater, shirt, T-shirt, camisole, jeans, extra sweater, scarf, hat, parka, hood, mittens, superwarm socks, and fuzzy lined boots, Karina just went on smiling.

Chelsea had been right. She *did* deserve a little fun.

This man could be a *lot* of fun, it occurred to her. He seemed genial, proficient, insanely fit, and intelligent enough not to make a fuss about theirs being nothing but a short-term holiday affair. He was conveniently unattached too.

It was hardly well mannered to start spinning sexy, illicit plans from the moment they'd met. On the other hand, he *did* have the honey. That was a positive sign. Time was wasting!

"So . . ." He lifted his gaze to her face. "What are you hoping to get out of The Christmas House experience?"

To get lucky. To get laid. To find myself sweating and trembling in your big, strong arms, begging for more more more.

Whoa. Her hormones were going into overdrive! Obviously, they considered this encounter to be nothing but a preview of the inevitable X-rated feature. Even as Karina stood there, attempting to summon up a reasonable answer to his reasonable question, she felt positively . . . overheated. Ripe. *Ready.*

Well, maybe this time she didn't have to get a grip on herself. Maybe—just maybe—this time, she could indulge.

She deserved it, didn't she? After her difficult year?

It wasn't as though she wanted to *marry* Honey-Buying Man stand-in. She just wanted to, possibly, lick him a little.

"Oh, you know." Karina raised her gaze audaciously to his, trying to clear her mind of the erotic visions clouding it. *I'm hoping for multiple orgasms. I'm hoping for you.* "I'm feeling pretty open about that." Airily, she asked, "How about you?"

* * *

How about me . . . what? Reid wondered, momentarily dazed by the unexpectedly carnal look the woman in the foyer had thrown him. He *knew,* somehow, that she'd been thinking about sex. *Sex sex sex.* With a clarity and vividness that shouldn't have jibed with Christmas carols and hot spiced apple cider, but did.

She's a guest. Be professional! he commanded himself.

It wasn't easy. Somehow he managed. Barely. Maybe . . .

"I'm just hoping to get through the next two weeks," Reid said with utter truthfulness. "I'm not usually big on Christmas. This is all Greek to me." He waved, indicating the decorations and the rollicking reception going on just beyond the foyer.

The gesture reminded him of the items in his hands. He really ought to deliver that spiced cider and honey to the two guests who'd requested them. The B&B staff had arrived—belatedly but efficiently—but Reid had remained hard at work. By now, his beverage-and-sweetener-seeking guests probably thought he'd fallen into a snowbank someplace—which seemed like a pretty good idea, just at the moment. Maybe it would cool him off.

"Well, I can help you out with that." The woman beamed, her smile lighting her whole face—or at least as much of it as he could glimpse in the tiny space not covered by her scarf, hat, and parka hood. "I guarantee I can make you see the wonderfulness of Christmas. I *love* the holidays. And I *love* helping out too!"

She also *loved* looking at him, Reid noticed, which thrilled him in a way he'd thought himself immune to by now. At Shane's campsite, Helene had scarcely been able to get a rise out of him. What was going on now, that he felt so drawn to this woman?

Trying to figure it out, he examined her. Legs. Check.

Arms. Check. Head, face . . . all appeared pretty ordinary. Also, mostly shrouded in wool and quilted performance fabrics. For all he knew, his late-arriving guest had the figure of a moose. But her eyes were kind and her voice was sweet, and her aura of perky divorcée determination drew him like a bee to honey.

In his younger, rowdier, more degenerate postdivorce days, Reid had gone through a major phase of bedding the most carefree, most innocent women . . . then trying to extricate himself from their expectations afterward. Those experiences had led directly to his policy of making an "I'm not sticking around" disclaimer before starting up a new relationship. It had been years since Reid had felt tempted to deviate from that rule.

He felt tempted now. Tempted to swerve sideways, throw out the rulebook, and just . . . *indulge.* Something about the woman in front of him made him want *more* from life. Much more.

More than any sensible woman should probably give him.

"I just got in from Australia," he blurted. "The girls and I, I mean. I won't be sticking around here in Kismet."

The woman looked surprised.

That made two of them. What the hell was he doing issuing his Standard Disclaimer? Reid wondered. He'd only approached this bundled-up woman in the first place in his official capacity as temporary innkeeper. He'd wanted to make sure she was having fun—just in case she was the secret Edgware evaluator (not likely, given her overall air of suburban naïveté). He hadn't intended to get lured in by her eyes, intrigued by her smiles, or captivated by the feel of her hand on him.

His shoulder still tingled where she'd touched him.

No. *No,* goddamn it! He had enough to handle right now. The last thing he needed was to get himself tangled up with a new woman. Especially a cute one. Especially a perky one. Especially one—he reminded himself—who would undoubtedly want "A Commitment."

Well. He'd probably already put the kibosh on that idea with his Standard Disclaimer. It tended to scare off most women.

Reid prepared himself to be disappointed.

She shrugged. "Me neither. This trip is totally off the record books for me. What happens in Kismet stays in Kismet!"

That was new. He'd never been answered that way before.

If they were *both* determined *not* to play for keeps, maybe that meant *all* the rules were blown. Maybe that meant he *could* get tangled up with her. Maybe he could unwrap that long, fuzzy scarf she had on, peel off her bulky parka, find out what she looked like under all those layers of Polarfleece and wool.

"After all, we've got two weeks ahead of us, right?" Her dimpled smile charmed him. "I'd say that's more than enough time to get to know one another better. So . . . I'm Karina Barrett."

Cheerfully, she stuck out her mittened hand.

Reid stared at it, fighting the unmistakable feeling that any contact between them might have momentous consequences. Which made no sense at all. Maybe he was still jet-lagged. Or maybe a part of him truly *liked* Karina Barrett. Nonsensically. Unfoundedly. Without reservations or even a glimpse of cleavage to sweeten the deal. Reid hesitated. Then . . . *Screw it.*

As far as he could tell, Karina wasn't even his type. And he wasn't in the market for a holiday romance anyway. It was perfectly safe to shake her hand and get to know her better.

He put down the cider and the honey. Karina's gaze lingered on both . . . or maybe, inexplicably, only on the honey. Hmmm . . .

He grasped her hand. "I'm Reid Sullivan." Mitten-to-hand

contact wasn't as satisfying as he might have hoped. Maybe that's why he went further. Unwisely, unprofessionally further. "Why don't you take off your coat and stay a while, Karina?"

Scrabbling eagerly at the zipper on her parka, Karina decided that a girl couldn't ask for a better invitation.

Well, maybe she could, she reasoned breathlessly as her mittened fingers jabbed at the metal fastening. *Why don't you let me stroke you all over?* would have rated highly. Under slightly different circumstances, so would, *Why don't you take a nap while I do the dishes, diaper the baby, and make you hot cocoa?* But as far as unexpected invitations went, Reid's was a winner. Feeling hotter than ever, she flipped back her parka hood, then hastily whipped off her coat.

Politely, Reid took it. His gaze skimmed flatteringly over her figure as Karina debated what to remove next: hat or scarf?

Taking off her knit ski cap would leave her with major hat head. *Scarf.* Definitely. She'd been a little rushed when she'd gotten outfitted with it—along with all the rest of her cold-weather gear—in the airport ladies' room before venturing outside and hopping on the airport shuttle with the kids. But she'd been determined not to turn up in the snowy Midwest looking like an unprepared blond bimbo from the sunshine state.

She'd gone overboard. Her scarf was wound *way* too tightly.

Ineffectually, she plucked at it, feeling frustrated.

It figured. A hot man invited her to undress for him (okay, *partially* undress for him), and she was all thumbs. Argh!

"Here." Reid stepped nearer. "Let me help you with that."

He had to be kidding. He was gorgeous, friendly, muscular, patient, squeaky clean, interested in listening to her, nice smelling, funny, *and* helpful? This just got better and better. Karina couldn't wait to tell Chelsea about this encounter.

I want all the dirty details, K. You be sure to call me the instant something happens, okay? Well . . . It was happening!

Even if Chelsea—probably—didn't consider *listening* to be a requisite hot-male quality, Karina did. Chelsea, in her youth, probably preferred her dates to be capable of moshing. Or maybe hacking into Facebook. Or even pulling a wicked Ollie on their skateboards. Karina knew better. Listening rocked.

Filled with anticipation—and obedient stillness—Karina stood with her chin jutting out. Reid took a workmanlike, wide-legged stance in front of her. He peered at her scarf, then gave it an experimental tug. As expected, it held fast. With easy agility, his fingers worked at the gnarled length of her scarf.

"It's a little tangled," he acknowledged as he plucked and twisted. "But don't worry—I have a lot of experience with this."

Karina considered rubbing herself on him. Just on a simple getting-to-know-you basis. She blinked, then cleared her throat. "You have a lot of experience with undressing women?"

His gaze met hers, now only a few inches away. This close, she could see that his beard stubble was real—none of that razor-trimmed, boy-band stuff sported by guys who wore Axe Body Spray and watched the show *XTreme Sports!* on TV. His mouth quirked.

"With unknotting tangled scarves," he clarified.

Making progress now, he casually brushed his knuckles along the underside of her chin. In response, a tingle swept along her jaw to her ear, leaving Karina with a sweet-sour sensation akin to biting down on the gummy worms Josh and Michael liked.

She fought an urge to knot her scarf permanently.

"I *do* have daughters, remember?" Reid's brow knit, then cleared as he pulled her scarf free. He dropped it. "Voilà."

Mission accomplished. He stepped away. She felt the loss of his nearness keenly. Preposterously keenly. On the other hand, Reid Sullivan *was* her potential holiday-affair mate, Karina reasoned. As fated by the honey. She *ought* to like him. A lot.

So far, she did. *Thank you, Stephanie, for this job!*

"Thanks for the help." Gesturing at her cast-off coat on a nearby chair and her scarf (*bless you, tangled scarf!*), Karina shrugged. "I'm new at this whole cold-weather thing. At home in San Diego—where I'm from—I mostly wear bikinis all the time."

Okay. It was a tiny exaggeration. A glib fib. But where was the harm? One teensy white lie that made her sound sexy and carefree wouldn't hurt anybody. And it might improve her chances with Reid Sullivan, superstud and B&B guest extra-ordinaire.

"Really? The B&B has a hot tub." He hooked his thumb toward the rear of the place. "If you want, we could—"

"Oh no! No, that's all right!" Karina laughed as she yanked at her cardigan, trying to remove it, too. It seemed glued to her shirt underneath it via the awesome power of static cling. Her skin crackled. "A hot tub isn't very Christmassy, is it?"

"I don't know." Reid seemed genuinely mystified by the question. He was *so* cute with his knitted brow and full-lipped frown. "Maybe if we wore those red and white Santa hats?"

And nothing else, Karina's imagination suggested. The idea had merit. She gave a serious nod. "All right then. It's a date. I'll bring the Santa hats, and you bring—"

Automatically, she stopped, semicertain he'd interrupt her. He didn't. At the realization, she swooned a little harder.

"—yourself, okay? I'm a simple girl with simple needs."

At that, Reid laughed. "No woman is simple. But I have to say . . . I'm looking forward to figuring out your com-plications."

"Oh? You think I'll be that easy to decipher, huh?"

"No. That's the whole point." His gaze roved over her, seeming to see beyond her unwieldy ensemble of flannel shirt, T-shirt, camisole, sweater, mittens, jeans, thick socks, and knee-high boots. Yep. Bundled up like a nun. Sexy. "I think you'll be challenging." His gaze lifted to her face. "I like challenging."

"In that case, I'll be sure to speak in code from here on in. And maybe wear a mask part of the time, too." Karina grinned. "I wouldn't want to disappoint you by being easy."

I'm so easy! her libido offered, panting. *Super easy!*

At her unintentional double entendre, Karina wanted to wince. But Reid didn't seem to notice. Actually, he seemed to be envisioning that naughty, seminaked hot tub scenario.

Or maybe that was just her. She bet he looked great wet.

"I doubt you could disappoint anyone," he said. "You seem so . . . generous. So giving, somehow. I can't explain it."

"Well, I *did* just hand you my coat and let you strip off my scarf. As first impressions go, that's pretty munificent."

Another smile. "It's more than that. You seem . . . special."

That's because I'm undercover. But she couldn't share that.

"You do too," Karina said. She meant it, too, she realized then. Reid *was* special—because of the listening and the helping. "And I'm not just saying that because of the honey, either."

He frowned, puzzled. Whoops. Had she said that aloud?

They both glanced at the abandoned squeeze bottle, then at each other. Then Reid smiled as though guessing her secret—one of them, at least. A long moment stretched between them—a moment that, inexplicably, felt compatible. Relaxed. *Right.*

Loath to disturb it, Karina held her breath. She hadn't done much dating since her divorce. This was all new to her. Maybe this attraction between them was merely ho-hum flirtation?

It felt like more . . . until Reid blinked and refocused.

"So . . . shall we go in?" he asked.

He angled his head, indicating the reception. It was really kicking into gear now. Karina's fellow guests were gathered in laughing, lively groups, sharing cider and stories with each other. It looked like fun. But so did Reid. Here. With her.

On the verge of agreeing—however reluctantly—Karina spied her sons, both kneeling on the floor beside one of the Christmas trees. As she watched, Michael picked up a wrapped box and shook it, then held it to his ear. Josh examined an airplane-shaped ornament, then nimbly plucked it from a low-hanging branch.

Uh-oh. Her unrepentant "borrower" was at it again.

Beside the crackling fireplace, Olivia frowned at one of the red felt stockings with embroidered cuffs. She appeared bothered by it, but Karina couldn't figure out why.

"Is something wrong?" Reid's voice penetrated Karina's consciousness, making its way past her maternal red alert. "You seem distracted, for some reason. If you don't like parties—"

"No, that's not it. I'm sorry." Why wasn't he keeping an eagle eye on his daughters? she wondered abruptly. Surely they weren't so angelic that they didn't require any supervision? "It's just that it looks as though my kids are about to give The Christmas House the full-on Barrett treatment."

"The Barrett treatment?"

"Also known as making sure nothing remains unscathed, undamaged, or otherwise unspoiled," Karina explained, newly vigilant as she watched Olivia, Michael, and Josh. "They're sort of . . . demolition experts, I'm afraid."

Reid shrugged. "They're kids. They can't be that bad."

"You haven't met them." With an apologetic smile, Karina excused herself. "I'd better run interference. It was nice to meet you, Reid. I hope we run into each other again sometime."

His smile mesmerized her. "I feel sure we will."

Yes, please! Karina thought in a dither. Why had Josh, Michael, and Olivia chosen *now* to misbehave? *Now*, when things had been going so well for her and Reid? It was as though their kid radar had detected that Mommy was enjoying some adult-style fun, and they'd acted unconsciously to derail her plans.

They'd possessed the same disruptive abilities when they'd been babies, kicking into uncanny crying jags the instant their mother had attempted to take a nap, catch up on paperwork, or log some much-needed husband-and-wife time with Eric.

"Remember." Reid's eyes sparkled. "You promised to show me a little Christmas magic. I intend to hold you to that."

Was that a double entendre too? Or just an invitation?

Either way, Karina was officially psyched. She grinned.

"You've got no idea what you're in for," she said.

Then she left Reid behind and bolted into the reception, intent on corralling her children before they unwrapped all the prop gifts, filched all the ornaments, and (possibly) performed a *CSI*-style DNA test on the traditional holiday stockings that hung all in a row on the mantelpiece.

Chapter Eight

... From the desk of Betty Sullivan
DECEMBER 17TH
LOCATION: THE CHRISTMAS HOUSE
SCHEDULED EVENT: "SNOWED-IN" RECEPTION—
3:00 P.M. TO 5:00 P.M. (DAILY)

Carrying a fresh platter of iced gingerbread cookies, Reid paused. He glanced at the schedule written—for his guests' convenience—on the B&B's chalkboard, which stood on a tinsel-bedecked easel in a corner of the front room. He adjusted the platter, frowned at his watch, then looked around him.

The cider-and-gingerbread "Snowed-In" reception should have ended three hours ago. Instead, the get-together was still in full swing. Apparently, now that all his guests had arrived, they were intent on whooping it up. The time had positively flown by.

Well, happy guests meant things were going well. And that meant Reid had been right. Overseeing The Christmas House this season *would* be an easy task—even for a Scrooge like him. To confirm that, all he had to do was look around.

The spiced cider flowed freely. The gingerbread made the rounds quickly. At times, his guests' laughter actually overrode the Christmas carols on the sound system. People were dancing to the music, talking in groups, and even plucking off decorations from the Christmas trees to wear.

As he watched, one of his single guests, a fiftysomething woman named Suzanne, wrapped a hank of gold garland around her neck. Fluffing it up like a feather boa, she danced her way to Rocky and Neil, a couple visiting from Vermont, and urged them to join in. They did. Before long, the whole room was boogying.

Downstairs, in the B&B's basement Fun Zone, more music blared—but these Christmas carols were less Bing Crosby, more 50 Cent. There was probably more dancing going on too, but Reid knew that dancing was competing with The Christmas House's big-screen TV and video game system, the air hockey and pool tables, the shelves full of board games and books, the toys for kids of all ages, and the holiday-themed snacks that were always kept stocked downstairs. All of Reid's underage guests were in the Fun Zone, currently being supervised by a conscientious and cheerful Amanda. She'd agreed to temporarily expand her role as Alexis and Nicole's nanny/tutor for the sake of helping out.

Feeling grateful to her, Reid set down the gingerbread cookies on the sideboard. A couple of guests mamboed past him. A few more started up a conga line. Several people linked arms, waved their cups of spiced cider, and sang woozily in tune to the music.

No. Not woozily. Suddenly stricken by his guests' shambling dance moves, extrabright grins, and expansive gestures, Reid realized the truth: His guests weren't woozy. They were *drunk!*

That wasn't supposed to happen. The Christmas House was a family-friendly destination. Unlike most B&B's, they'd purposely remodeled so they could offer suites that slept four or six. They'd provided activities for children (hence the downstairs Fun Zone). They'd deliberately offered nonalcoholic spiced cider and gingerbread cookies *instead* of wine and crudités, so the daily afternoon receptions wouldn't devolve into happy hour.

But somehow, some way, his guests had gotten blitzed anyway.

This wouldn't look good to the Edgware evaluator, Reid realized. Until half an hour ago, there'd been children present at the reception. What if they'd accidentally gotten tipsy?

He had to investigate. He had to make sure this didn't happen again tomorrow. There were a dozen receptions still remaining on his schedule. He had to nip this in the bud.

Decisively, Reid approached the buffet table. He chatted with some friendly guests, then poured himself a cup of spiced cider. It smelled . . . boozy. He sipped. It tasted . . . potent. It was definitely spiked with something alcoholic. Something . . . tasty.

He licked his lips, then quaffed the rest.

Fisting his cup, Reid frowned at the cider bowl. There was only a little left—maybe an eighth of the punch bowl. The only responsible, speedy, surefire way to dispose of it was clear.

Just as Reid finished his sixth cup of cider—after first holding the crystal punch bowl and shaking it to release every delicious drop—a hank of silver garland landed on his head.

He plucked it off, then wrapped it around his neck. With a flourish, he flung one end back, in the style of the Red Baron's jaunty aviation scarf. He struck a pose. His guests applauded.

Suzanne gave him a good-natured wolf whistle.

That cheerfully licentious sound reminded him of Karina. Where had she gotten off to, anyway? Reid had liked her. He'd *really* liked her. And that wasn't the spiked cider talking, either.

Recalling the promise Karina had made to show him the wonders of Christmas, Reid veered sideways. He felt unexpectedly *fine,* he realized. Maybe it was the cider that made him feel so loose and carefree. Although he typically drank harder stuff: whiskey, mescal, absinthe. Spiked apple juice was nothing! He could handle that, for sure. Of course, he was still jet-lagged, Reid remembered. That would make him feel the effects of the alcohol sooner than usual. Maybe a little more strongly too.

Straightening amid the gaiety of the raucous reception, Reid examined his guests. None of them had hair the color of sunshine, a smile that made him feel weak, or a surfeit of cold-weather clothes better suited to an arctic expedition than to a visit to Kismet. None of them were Karina. He had to find her.

It was his own fault for losing track of her, he knew. He could have followed her into the reception and met her children. He could have arranged to meet her later. He could have— Reid knew damn well—persuaded her to stay in the foyer with him.

But he hadn't. Instead, mustering the resolve of ten conscientious men, he'd quit envisioning him and Karina in a hot tub (wearing nothing but Santa hats) and had refocused on his duties at The Christmas House. He'd put his mind on the proper host-to-guest politeness track and asked if she wanted to join the reception . . . just when they'd been on the verge of something more. Just when that indescribable *moment* had happened between them, full of possibility and yearning and wanting and lust.

Yes, lust. It was bald but true. At least on his part.

But had he indulged himself? No.

So . . . shall we go in?

Stupider words had rarely been spoken. Reid remembered the disappointed downturn of Karina's mouth. He'd wanted to kiss away that frown of hers. He felt certain he could still accomplish the job. In addition, he wanted to know exactly what lay beneath all those layers of Polarfleece and wool

Karina had been wearing. He could imagine. And had. Vividly. Now he needed to discover the truth for himself.

Now that he'd solved the spiked punch problem, that is.

Congratulating himself on his innate inn-keeping talents—which he'd never realized he had—Reid headed upstairs.

Maybe Karina was getting settled in her room, he decided. He'd glimpsed her at the front desk, formally checking in, shortly after she'd gone to handle whatever alleged misdeeds her children were involved in. Which reminded him—he didn't understand why Karina was wound so tightly about ordinary childlike behavior. But . . . whatever. He didn't want to give her a parental report card. He wanted to give her a kiss. And more.

"Hey there, cuz!" someone said from behind him.

Reid turned. His cousin, Vanessa, stood with what looked like a wriggly brown-, black-, and white-spotted lump in her arms.

"I'm glad I found you." Vanessa hurried to him. Up close, it became evident that the thing in her arms was a dog. A dachshund. "I need your help with Digby, here. Usually he's fine with being around the guests, but today he's freaking out. Look!"

She turned and sort of . . . *thrust* the creature at him, dog breath and all. Its floppy ears, pointed muzzle, and big brown eyes met Reid's puzzled gaze. So did something else.

"Is that dog wearing a sweater?" he asked.

"Of course he is. It's cold out." Vanessa tightened her hold, worriedly nuzzling Digby as the dog squirmed and whined. "Besides, that's his signature look. Digby is the official mascot of The Christmas House! He always wears his souvenir sweater, especially to the "Snowed-In" receptions. We sell tons of these getups each year to our guests who want mementos for their pet companions."

She rearranged Digby to show a knitted-in version of The Christmas House's holly-wreathed, hand-painted logo, as seen on the sign in front of the B&B. It was smart, Reid had to admit.

"Nice cross-marketing effort," he admitted. "But I was just on my way to do something"—he gestured upstairs, where (he hoped) he'd find Karina again—"so if this can wait a while—"

"You're going upstairs? Excellent. You can take Digby with you." Nodding, Vanessa offloaded the dachshund into Reid's arms. He had no choice but to accept the warm, wiggly, snuffling dog. Digby felt surprisingly sturdy—capable, potentially, of knocking down a few of his tipsy guests, bowling ball–meets–bowling pin style, if he got loose and agitated at the reception. "He'll do better away from all the hubbub," Vanessa explained. "Just until he calms down. You'll see all his stuff. He usually sleeps in the attic room—the small one at the very top of the stairs."

"That's my room." Reid had moved into it because of its size. It had felt cozy and, with its pitched roof, a little bit familiar. Like a tent. "You mean I'm bunking with the dog?"

"Looks that way." Vanessa grinned. "Thanks, cuz. And hey—I'm glad you're back, even if it's only for a little while."

She came closer and hugged him, silver garland and all. Still holding Digby in one arm, Reid hugged her back. At the contact, he felt . . . something. It reminded him—suspiciously—of homesickness. But he knew that couldn't be it.

As his grandparents had so adeptly pointed out, Reid wasn't the least bit sentimental. Even if he *had* grown up in Kismet with Vanessa as his tomboyish sidekick, nearly his same age and always ready for adventure. And even if he *hadn't* seen his cousin for the past, oh, too many years.

I missed you, he wanted to say. *I wish we didn't live so far apart.* When he released her, what emerged was, "I think somebody spiked the cider at the reception."

"Really?" Vanessa pulled away, frowning. "That's weird.

And potentially problematic, too. Especially with the secret Edgware inspector lurking around." She bit her lip, appearing troubled. Then she waved her hand. "It was probably just an accident, though. A teenage prank. A onetime thing. I wouldn't worry about it. We've got other things to think about right now."

Like Karina. Reid sighed. Then he snapped out of it.

"Other things to think about? Like what?"

Vanessa gave him a curious look. "Like the annual Christmas hokey pokey dance." She gestured toward the front room. "It's what's up next, and I said I'd lead it. The guests *love* it."

Reid shuddered. "No better time for me to take care of old Digby, here, then. Just put him in the bedroom?"

Vanessa nodded. "Give him a treat and a few minutes to settle, and he'll be out like a light. Trust me."

"Will do." Wrangling a firmer grip on his doggy burden, Reid headed upstairs. "Okay, Digby!" he sang out. "Let's gooo!"

He could have sworn he heard Vanessa laugh.

"That cider was *definitely* spiked," she said. "This is going to be the most awesome Christmas hokey pokey ever!"

Tiptoeing down the attic hallway, Karina could have sworn she heard singing. Not Christmas carol singing, which had been going on in rowdy fashion downstairs for quite a while now—since before she'd safely seen Josh, Michael, and Olivia downstairs to the kids' Fun Zone, then joined the reception herself—but lullaby singing. Curious, she edged toward the sound.

Through a partially opened door, she glimpsed Reid Sullivan. He stood beside a floor cushion. On the cushion lay a snoozing dachshund. The dog—wearing a holiday sweater—seemed to be snoring.

Had Reid been singing a lullaby to a dog? Adorable!

Even more curious now, Karina hesitated near the doorway. Should she say something? She didn't want to wake up the dog.

Standing in plain sight, Reid bent. He scrutinized the dachshund. Then he stood, wearing a relieved expression. Karina recognized that expression—mothers of babies everywhere did.

The baby—*er, dachshund*—was finally asleep.

On the verge of announcing her presence, she saw Reid reach for his waffle-knit thermal shirt. It appeared to be his only concession to the cold December weather. She paused. Waited.

Almost as though he were rewarding her patience, Reid pulled off his shirt. He bunched it up and tossed it on the comfortable-looking bed, his biceps and shoulders flexing.

He was still wearing a T-shirt underneath. But he looked mighty fine with one less layer obscuring his muscles.

Karina couldn't help reacting. It just happened. *"Mmmm."*

Alertly, Reid glanced up. He spied her in the doorway.

Pertly, she held up the sprig of mistletoe she'd been carrying. She'd found it in her room and—after several cups of hot spiced cider and two fortifying gingerbread cookies—had been inspired to employ it in her new quest to teach Reid about the wonders of Christmas. She hadn't expected to use it so soon.

"Mistletoe." She wiggled it. "Traditionally, people kiss under this stuff to ensure good luck in the coming year."

Reid's gaze darkened. "Interesting. Tell me more."

"Ancient Celts considered mistletoe an aphrodisiac."

"You don't say?"

She nodded. "It's supposed to be magically capable of warding off evil spirits. Oh, and putting out fires, too."

Not that it was doing much to put out the fire Karina was currently experiencing. *In her pants*. Ha!

Ugh. That was terrible. What had gotten into her?

"Hmmm. I didn't know that." Reid came closer. "What else?"

Her mind went blank. Her mouth went dry. "Um, I don't know. I didn't expect to run into you so soon." Karina swallowed hard. "I was about to go looking for you downstairs."

"Looks like you found me." Reid gave her a deliberately provocative look. It felt *so* irresistible. "Now what?"

His mouth was surprisingly close to hers now, Karina noticed offhandedly. His hands touched her hands; his hips swayed, almost making contact with her hips. Their bodies met, exchanged warmth, then met again.

How had they gotten this close, anyway?

And did she really care about how? No. They *were* this close, Karina realized as she stood in the open doorway with him. She felt powerless to resist the pull between them. She also felt light-headed with neediness—hungry with an insatiable appetite that no amount of cookies or cider could assuage. "Now I hold up the mistletoe"—she did so with a shaky hand—"and we kiss for good luck. Christmas style."

Contemplatively, Reid glanced up at the mistletoe.

He nodded. An instant later, his mouth met hers. Softly.

Way too softly. Urgently, Karina grabbed his head with her free hand, startled to feel the silkiness of his hair between her fingers, then pulled him to her. Reid felt hard and good and strange and new and right against her, and she wanted more. She wanted it all. Right now. "More," she breathed. "I want it all."

Reid delivered. Starting with their next kiss, he opened his mouth wider. He moaned, then hauled her nearer. The sprig of mistletoe wobbled. It fell away as Karina gasped, caught beneath the onslaught of Reid's lips and teeth and tongue. Mmmm. *Yes.*

Breathlessly, she leaned back. "You're good at this."

"I'm a quick study." He kissed her again. "C'mere."

She did. They flattened together against the open door, mouths moving, hands roving, breath mingling with murmured words and a needfulness that didn't require conversation to be satisfied. Karina's skin prickled. Her heartbeat soared. Her mind raced, drunk with possibility.

"I can't believe I'm doing this!" Wantonly, she arched her back to allow Reid better access to the next layer of her clothes. She helped him take off her sweater. Eagerly, she kicked off her boots. "I'm not usually like this at all."

"Maybe all these clothes have you overheated." Reid knit his brow as he studied her myriad layers. Expertly, through a tacit agreement they both shared, he removed her hat next. "You're wearing way too much. It's not that cold here."

"Actually, it's *much* hotter than I expected." Mindless of her staticky hat head, Karina gave a grinning nod. Her hair could stand up and dance a cha-cha for all she cared. Right now, she needed more of this. More of Reid. She urged him closer, then tugged at his T-shirt. "Take this off," she commanded.

"It probably smells like dog. That's why I was—"

"Just do it." They could discuss his animal welfare policies later. Karina licked her lips. "I want to see you."

At that, his gaze flared with interest. A moment later, his T-shirt landed on the bed behind him. Reid gave her a heady look, then nudged the door. It closed with a subtle *snick.*

This is really happening, Karina realized. The "wild and crazy" holiday affair Chelsea had predicted had arrived right on schedule. *Oh boy!*

Hazily, she kissed Reid again. His bare skin felt hot to the touch, his broad shoulders nearly singeing her fingertips. Very naturally, she ground her pelvis against his, wholly unable to help herself. Her reward was a preview of coming attractions. In his pants. *Ha!* She cracked herself up, Karina thought woozily.

Had she, possibly, drunk something other than spiced cider?

Who cared? Reid wanted her. She wanted him.

Right now, Karina wouldn't have had it any other way.

Smacking her hands on his chest, she backed Reid up to the bed. Then she tipped him onto it. She studied him. Lasciviously.

"You know what?" she asked in a dreamy voice. "I think I'm starting to feel the wonder of Christmas already."

"I think that's my line," Reid told her, grinning. "You're supposed to be teaching *me* about Christmas, remember?"

"Oh yeah?" Karina asked. "Well, get ready to learn, then."

The two of them smiled at each other, entirely in sync.

Then Karina jumped on the bed and lost herself in the moment, knowing that forever after she would associate the mingled fragrances of mistletoe, bayberry, and dog biscuits with the single most sexually gratifying night of her life.

She hoped.

Almost half an hour later, she knew.

Fa la la. Fa la la. *Fa la LAAAA!*

Wiggling her bare toes with utter satisfaction, Karina shot a smug smile at Reid. He panted beside her, lying sideways on the bed, half tangled in the snowman-print flannel sheets. At the wonderful, amazing, hot-hot-hot sight of him, she sighed.

"So . . . how do you like Christmas now?" she asked.

"I'm not sure." He rolled over and kissed her, then ran his hands along the length of her naked torso. "I think I need another lesson to find out. I might need *several* more lessons."

"Do you really think you're up for it?"

Saucily, Reid raised his eyebrows. He aimed his gaze lower. Much lower. All the way down to his . . . mischief maker.

"Oh, I'm up for it," he confirmed. Then he pulled her into his arms again, gave her a smile, and proceeded to prove it.

Naughty or nice is way overrated, Karina decided as she felt Reid's body cover hers, igniting a new burst of giddiness and heat in her midsection. *Naughty wins, all the way. . . .*

Chapter Nine

... From the desk of Betty Sullivan
DECEMBER 18TH
LOCATION: THE CHRISTMAS HOUSE
SCHEDULED EVENT: "VERY MERRY" BREAKFAST—
7:00 A.M. TO 9:00 A.M. (DAILY)

Squinting at his grandmother's elegant cursive handwriting, Reid frowned. He couldn't imagine what made breakfast "merry."

Jingle bells on the napkins? Christmas cutlery? Pancakes griddled in the shape of reindeer and snowmen and angels?

Reid didn't know. But a "very merry breakfast" was on The Christmas House agenda first thing today, so he'd have to find a way to be in charge of it—for the sake of his guests *and* acing the Edgware evaluation. With any luck, the kitchen staff were already downstairs hard at work on some mouth-watering merriment.

Well, that meant he'd better get a move on too. Reaching for a pair of boots to go with his flannel shirt and jeans, Reid glimpsed something silvery, shiny, and fluffy—a cast-off piece of Christmas garland. He'd been wearing it last night, he remembered, just before he'd encountered Karina.

Karina. At least once, she'd worn that garland too. Playfully. Seductively. Accompanied by nothing but burnished bare skin and a smile. Momentarily abandoning his plans to get dressed, Reid picked up the garland. He held it to his cheek.

His heart rate kicked up a notch. Helplessly, he smiled.

Damn, but he liked Karina. He liked her enthusiasm, her gentle demeanor . . . even her habit of wearing way too many warm clothes. Getting through all those layers last night had been a little like embarking on a geological expedition—a sexy one, with a superhot reward at the end. Remembering everything he and Karina had shared, Reid smiled more broadly. He didn't feel particularly well versed in Christmas lore (yet), but he looked forward to enjoying some future "lessons" at Karina's hands.

And all right . . . so she was officially a guest at the B&B. Maybe hooking up with her hadn't been his most brilliant move to date. But he *had* issued his Standard Disclaimer first, so she wouldn't get hurt. And minding The Christmas House wasn't a real job for him, so enjoying a little private time with Karina wasn't a real problem, either, Reid reasoned. It wasn't as though he intended to set her up with free accommodations, a deluxe suite, or a lifetime supply of logo-embellished doggie sweaters. Reid felt pretty sure they both understood the temporary (and hot!) nature of their liaison.

He also felt pretty sure that he'd left Karina with a favorable first-night impression. *Yes, yes, yes!*

Remembering her breathy cries, he almost wished Karina *was* the secret Edgware evaluator. Because theirs had definitely been an A-plus-worthy encounter—at least until her three children had wandered upstairs at bedtime, looking for their mother.

He'd never seen a woman get dressed that quickly.

It had been all Reid could do to grab her, give her a fast good-bye kiss, then watch with a grin as Karina had slipped surreptitiously from his room to hers, just in the nick of time.

That was going to be a fine arrangement, he decided as he dropped the silver garland on the bureau for safekeeping, then dragged on his boots. He opened his door for Digby, then stepped aside to let the dachshund scamper into the hallway.

Following the dog—after a stealthy, satisfactory check on his still-slumbering daughters in their adjoining room—Reid stopped at the door of the room opposite his. Inside, Karina was probably still asleep, he decided. He imagined her dressed in a silk and lace nightie, with her curly blond hair tousled across a pillow, and felt a fresh wave of longing.

"You know, I would have let her spend the whole night in my room," Reid confided to Digby in a low voice. He crouched to scratch between the dog's ears, still contemplating Karina's closed door. "Hell, I would have let all four of them sleep in my room." He sighed. "Does that make me a sucker, or what?"

Yep! It does! Digby's tongue-lolling canine expression seemed to say. *Join the club, human. Sit, stay, roll over!*

The dog was right. Brought up short by the alarming thought that he'd been fully leash trained and brought to heel after a meager couple of hours in Karina's arms, Reid frowned.

How had she gotten a room so near him anyway? He didn't think any of the guests had been assigned attic rooms. Usually, those rooms were reserved for family members—and the occasional live-in B&B worker who'd fallen on temporary hard times and needed a place to stay. In Kismet, Robert and Betty Sullivan were notorious soft touches. Their doors were always open.

When they retired and moved to Arizona permanently, the entire town would be saddened, Reid realized. His grandparents would definitely be missed in Kismet—and at the B&B.

Whoever eventually wound up running the place as an Edgware franchise couldn't possibly offer the same warmhearted touches his grandparents had. When it came to some things, efficiency and profitability couldn't trump caring and genuine interest.

Speaking of which . . . It was possible that his (admittedly) cursory glance at the B&B's guest registry software had left him with the wrong impression about Karina's room assignment, Reid decided. Or someone had rearranged things. Or Karina had made a special request.

It wasn't inconceivable that she might have pulled some strings to be near him—to "accidentally" run into him last night. In Reid's experience, women had hatched more convoluted schemes to get to know him. Compared with some of those antics, Karina's room reshuffling was pretty tame.

It was flattering to think that she'd gone to such lengths for their Christmas "lesson." And the truth was, they'd both enjoyed the results. No harm, no foul, Reid decided. Even after a long trip, some serious jet lag, and a few too many cups of spiked cider, he'd still possessed the mojo to hook Karina hard.

Who knew what he could accomplish well rested and sober?

With a new swagger to his steps, Reid pounded his way downstairs, eager to find out. Digby followed him. First he had a schedule to keep, though, starting with that "very merry breakfast." Focusing on that, he made his way through the darkened B&B to the back of the house. At this hour—shortly after 5:30 A.M.—the place felt deserted but no less Christmassy. The lights might be dimmed and the candles snuffed, but the whole B&B still exuded the requisite holiday ambiance. The hallway smelled like cinnamon and spice . . . and coffee. Led by the promise of an aromatic pick-me-up, Reid entered the brightly lit, bustling kitchen.

There, two cooks were already on duty. The countertops stood piled with cutting boards and metal work bowls, chef's knives and whisks, loaves of bread and wire baskets of eggs. At the professional range, one cook in a long white apron flipped a skillet full of vegetables; another tended a pan of bacon.

It looked as though everything was coming along capably. Helping himself to a cup of coffee, Reid stood amid the activity and delicious smells, deciding what to tackle first. Digby sauntered to the doggie door and let himself outside. The door's flexible covering closed with a *whap,* admitting a gust of frosty air. It barely made a dent in the kitchen's steamy atmosphere. Tea kettles whistled on the stove, unleashing spires of vapor; more water boiled for poached eggs.

At Reid's elbow, baker's racks full of muffins stood cooling, emitting the fragrances of ginger and apples, pumpkin and chocolate chips, oats and hazelnuts. A bowl of freshly baked granola waited on the countertop beside an array of sliced fruit. As far as Reid could tell, when it came to breakfast, "very merry" meant "ridiculously over the top." There was enough food here to satisfy an army, much less a few guests, some assorted family members, the neighbors, and the usual staff.

Alexis and Nicole would love it. So would Amanda—especially if there were a few regional specialties included, like Michigan cherries, maple syrup, and apples. His daughters' nanny/tutor had never visited the Midwest before, but she seemed to have an affinity for the place already . . . particularly the food.

Reid hoped the Edgware evaluator liked an oversize breakfast too. He couldn't forget what he was really here to do: impress him (or her, he still wasn't sure) with an unforgettable Christmassy experience. Part of earning that A-plus rating he wanted—the rating Reid had all but promised his grandparents he'd get—was feeding the Edgware evaluator a series of scrumptious meals.

The B&Bs in the Kismet area were known for their cuisine, whether down-home or gourmet, decadent or healthy, or somewhere in between. The Christmas House had always occupied a place of pride in the community, hiring all the best available cooks and bakers to create its *spécialités de la maison.* As far as Reid could tell, when it came to being evaluated, the B&B's gastronomic artistry was one of its never-fail aces in the hole. Over the years, it had earned multiple awards to prove it.

"Okay! I've got the sideboard set up with holiday-patterned plates, napkins, and cutlery," a woman said in a cheery tone. She entered the kitchen via the entry opposite Reid, which led to the sun-splashed room where the guests dined. "I've got the glasses and the stands for the chafing dishes all lined up too. So whenever you're ready to start taking out food, we're set."

She was perky. She was capable. She was . . . Karina?

Baffled by the sight of her in the B&B's kitchen, Reid stared. This image didn't jibe with his earlier, more seductive vision of Karina snuggled in her flannel sheets wearing next to nothing.

Then, he'd almost been able to feel the silk and lace beneath his hands. Now, this Karina—the real Karina—stood expectantly across the kitchen with an organized demeanor and twenty pounds of cold-weather clothing covering the body he now knew damn well ought to be flaunted, admired, and loved.

In that order. Repeatedly. Over and over and over again.

Rapidly, Reid counted. He estimated that Karina was wearing two different sweaters, a fleece top, one T-shirt, thermal underwear, tights, knit socks, hip-hugging corduroy pants, and a long, fringed fleece scarf—a different scarf than she'd been wearing yesterday. And not a single hank of silver garland, either. At the sight of all that wool and Polarfleece and buttoned-up knitwear, Reid felt his heart inexplicably . . . soften.

Damn, she was cute. He wanted to tell her so. But first . . .

"Good job." Smiling, he gestured toward the dining room, where Karina had evidently been . . . working? Hmmm. "You know, if you'd told someone you couldn't pay for your room, I'm sure other arrangements could have been made—arrangements that didn't include forced kitchen labor. Like a different credit card?"

Noticing him at last, Karina smiled. Her eyes brightened. Her cheeks turned pinker. She opened both arms as though on the verge of running across the room to give him a hug.

Knowing her, Reid thought with pleasure, that might even be likely. Karina Barrett, he'd learned last night, really was generous to a fault. She was also much kinder than any person needed to be—especially in a world filled with Binkys, Boosters, Tophers, and Asshats.

Reid had never known himself to anticipate a kindly *hug* with so much ferocity. But there it was. He wanted her, layers and all.

Unfortunately, he had to wait. Because in the next instant, the two cooks he'd noticed earlier snapped to attention. They shot panicked looks at each other, then turned.

"Sorry, Chef!" one cried. "Good morning, Chef!"

"Sorry, Chef!" The other saluted with a spatula. "We didn't see you there, Chef! What can we do for you, Chef?"

At the cooks' harried—and militaristic—greeting, Reid raised an eyebrow. He was familiar with the conventions of kitchen staff—which explained all the Chef-iness—but that didn't explain why both cooks seemed to think *he* was in charge here.

"Please, go back to what you were doing." Reid waved his arm, indicating the stove. "I'm not in charge of the kitchen."

"Ah, but that's where you're wrong, cuz." Vanessa breezed in, toting a potted poinsettia in the crook of each elbow. She set down the holiday plants, then took off her quilted coat and her hat. Smiling, she gave him a good-morning hug. It was nice. But it did nothing to assuage his desire for the hug he'd expected from Karina. "In the absence of our *former* head chef, you *are* in charge—of the B&B *and* the kitchen."

"What happened to the head chef?" Reid asked.

"*You're* in charge of the B&B?" Karina asked.

Their questions overlapped. Reid stared at Karina. Karina stared at him. His cousin, Vanessa—apparently sensing a fraught undercurrent in the room—left them gawking as she poured herself a cup of coffee. She sipped it with gusto, then exhaled.

She must have missed out on the spiked cider last night, Reid realized. She was (possibly) the only one. Judging by the watery, bloodshot gazes the two cooks had given him, the liquored-up cider had been popular with the guests and the staff alike.

"Our *former* head chef was stolen away by those rat bastards at Lagniappe at the Lakeshore," Vanessa told Reid, naming The Christmas House's chief competitor in Kismet. "Apparently, while we were all here enjoying spiced cider and gingerbread, the Lagniappe at the Lakeshore owners were out wooing our chef with promises of imported matsutake and a brand-new snowmobile."

"*You're* in charge of the B&B?" Karina asked again.

Reid didn't understand why she appeared so gobsmacked by the idea. After all, he'd greeted her in his official capacity yesterday. He'd inquired about her hopes for her stay at the B&B, just as his grandmother had suggested he do with each guest. Granted, he hadn't made a point of his management role at The Christmas House, but he'd thought it would be obvious.

Also, he'd been a little . . . distracted by her.

"Yes. This year, Reid's running the whole show!" Vanessa answered for him. She grabbed an abandoned chef's toque from the countertop and plopped it, unhelpfully, on his head. "There. Now you can really enjoy the whole 'Chef! Yes, Chef!' experience." Grinning, Vanessa leaned confidingly toward Karina. "Secretly, I think he likes being kowtowed too. He always was pretty bossy, even as a kid."

"*You're* in charge of the B&B," Karina said again.

This time, it wasn't a question. It was an affirmation of the facts. Facts that shouldn't have made a bit of difference between them but appeared—somehow—to be affecting everything. And not necessarily for the better, either.

Trapped unwillingly in his role as The Christmas House Scrooge, Reid nodded. "Yes, I'm in charge of the B&B."

Almost imperceptibly, Karina drooped. Like a vivid flower being smothered by sixteen layers of sweaters and thermal underwear, she lost a little of her original perkiness. Her gaze met his, swerved away, then dimmed as she closed her eyes.

When she opened them again, she straightened her spine too.

"All right then." Karina looked around, as though in search of a sense of purpose. "Well, I guess all this talking has put me a little behind with the juice!" She chuckled, then picked up a pair of slender glass carafes, one full of freshly squeezed orange juice and one full of cranberry. She headed for the dining room. "I'll just put these on ice! Back in a minute!"

Watching her go, Reid couldn't help feeling mystified. When Karina had first seen him this morning, she'd appeared as ready as he had to tear off their clothes and kick off round two of the getting-to-know-you mambo, preferably in bed.

Now, she couldn't get away from him fast enough.

Why had Karina cooled toward him? Reid wondered. Sure, some women might have been disappointed to learn about his temporary inn-keeping job. It wasn't exactly a hard-core, thrill-a-minute job (unlike his usual globe-trotting gig).

But Karina hadn't struck him as the adrenaline junkie type—even by proxy. Last night, they'd enjoyed their share of between-the-sheets pillow talk—some of which had covered his work, and hers as an academic advisor—but she hadn't seemed particularly invested in Reid's exciting, travel-intensive job.

In fact, she'd mostly been interested in his big, hard—

"Beast!" The minute Karina left the room, his cousin smacked his shoulder. "You did it again, didn't you? Not even twenty-four hours in town, and already you're breaking hearts."

"Huh? I didn't break anybody's heart."

"What's the matter with you, Reid?" With a disapproving clucking sound, Vanessa crossed her arms. She shook her head in apparent disbelief. "Can't you keep it in your pants for one day, at least? You can't afford to be distracted right now. Grammy and Grandpa are counting on you."

"I know they are." Wistfully, Reid stared in the direction Karina had gone. He glimpsed her puttering around the dining room, artfully rearranging pots of snowy white amaryllis to make room for the juice station. "Don't worry. It'll be fine."

Exactly whom was he reassuring? Vanessa? Or himself?

If it was his cousin, he failed. Big-time.

Vanessa scoffed. "You didn't even try to deny it! You *did* sleep with her." Another head shake. "Poor Karina."

"'Poor Karina'?" Feeling affronted, Reid redirected his gaze to his cousin. "What's that supposed to mean?"

"Well, now she's going to be hooked on you, isn't she? Just like they all are," Vanessa pointed out. "And you didn't exactly rush over to her with hugs and kisses this morning, did you?"

He'd wanted to. He'd wanted to hug Karina. And kiss her. And more. Much more. But that was none of Vanessa's business. Besides, Reid had barely recognized Karina before the cooks had—evidently—derailed his mojo. He still didn't understand it.

"Women *need* those thoughtful gestures, you know. Karina probably thinks you pawed her like a Christmas cracker and then threw her away," Vanessa accused. "How could you?"

"For the last time, I *didn't*." Reid thought about it a little harder. "Well, technically I *did,* but it's not what you think. It was very, *very* mutual and kind of . . . sweet."

Sweet? What the hell? Astounded by his own words, Reid clamped his mouth shut. That didn't stop Vanessa's knowing look.

"What's she doing down here in the kitchen anyway?" For distraction's sake, Reid pointed at Karina. At the gesture, his chef's toque wobbled. He ripped it off his head, then tossed it aside. "Last time I checked," he informed his cousin, "it wasn't B&B policy to extract slave labor from our guests."

"It still isn't." Vanessa slurped more coffee. Evidently willing to leave aside the matter of his heartbreaking ways for now, she shrugged. "Karina volunteered to help, that's all. She was up early, like me. I ran into her—outside on the porch, of all places—and when she heard about the problem with the *former* head chef, she offered to lend a hand. She's really nice. Very helpful. And yes, very *sweet.*" His cousin's frown deepened. "I noticed that about her right away, which is all the more reason you shouldn't be messing with her heart, Reid!"

So much for leaving aside matters of heartbreak.

"I didn't mess with her heart!" he protested. "If anything, *she* messed with *my*—" At his cousin's abruptly interested— and all too familiar—look, Reid broke off. He swore. For an instant, he'd forgotten about Vanessa's inveterate matchmaker tendencies. "Look, just leave this alone, all right? I have enough to think about without you doing your lonely hearts routine on me."

"'Lonely hearts routine'?" Owlishly, Vanessa gazed across the kitchen. She knelt to pet a newly returned Digby, who flopped on the rug to gnaw at his snow-encrusted paws. "I'm sure I don't know what you mean," she protested. Implausibly. "Besides, the important issue here is—"

"Is the fact that Lagniappe at the Lakeshore *stole* our prime asset!" Ordinarily, Reid didn't like to interrupt. But he had to get Vanessa back on track. As she'd so wisely pointed out, their grandparents were depending on him. On them all. For the B&B to earn the stellar Edgware rating it deserved, they needed their head chef in the kitchen. "You knew the head chef—"

"The *former* head chef," Vanessa muttered darkly.

"—so you probably know more about the ins and outs of this problem than I do. We need him to run the kitchen, right? So what will it take to bring him back?"

"A sense of loyalty." Vanessa sniffed, her head in the air. All the Sullivans valued fidelity. "Which he doesn't have."

"What about higher pay? A better snowmobile?"

"A bribe? It just might work. Turnabout *is* fair play."

Reid didn't like the vengeful gleam in his cousin's eyes. He shook his head. "Not a bribe. A fair wage." He glanced around the kitchen. On closer examination, it appeared less bustling and more driven by sheer panic. Which made sense, given that they were shorthanded by one very necessary employee. "Although the head chef must have been paid pretty well, so why—"

"Because Lagniappe at the Lakeshore wants to put us under, that's why!" Vanessa said. "You haven't been here for a while. You don't know how cutthroat things have gotten. Since the economy took a nosedive, we've all been fighting for smaller and smaller pieces of the tourism pie—especially in wintertime, like now."

Reid nodded again, easily believing her. As a lakeside destination, Kismet traditionally earned most of its tourism income during the summertime, when even Michiganders flocked there to enjoy the town's idyllic ambiance. Wintertime was a tougher sell. That was part of the reason his grandparents had devised The Christmas House concept in the first place.

It had begun—simply enough—with Betty's genuine enthusiasm for the holidays, which she'd been happy to share with the B&B's guests. Unexpectedly, her wholehearted take on tradition had sparked a chord with their wintertime visitors. Word had spread.

From there, it had been only natural to expand the idea to encompass other holidays, from Independence Day to Valentine's Day. Then a travel writer had visited a few Decembers ago and had subsequently written a rave review—accidentally calling the B&B The Christmas House instead of its original moniker of The Holiday House. Despite a correction, the new designation had stuck.

To capitalize on the resulting publicity, the Sullivans had rechristened the B&B as The Christmas House, and the rest was history. These days, aside from a few (understandably) confused newcomers, everyone understood it was a year-round destination, with special emphasis on holiday getaways. Next, the local TV station had featured the B&B on *Good Morning, Kismet!,* someone from Edgware had watched the segment, and now . . .

Now Reid was screwed unless he came up with a new chef.

Torn between his duty to his family's beloved B&B and the need to find out what was going on with Karina, he glanced to the dining room. It looked as though Karina had rearranged those pots of amaryllis at least twelve ways. She examined them, dithered, then rearranged some more. She glanced in his direction.

Their gazes locked. Reid felt his heart give a hopeful leap. Maybe he'd misunderstood. Maybe things were fine.

He couldn't have broken her heart already . . . could he?

Right on cue, Karina jerked away her gaze. With apparent huffiness, she picked up an ice bucket, then left the room.

With a sigh of disappointment, Reid grabbed his rental car keys, then did his best to get down to work too. His family was counting on him. They had to come first. But so far, things didn't look good. This already felt like the least "very merry" breakfast on record . . . and it hadn't even started yet.

Chapter Ten

Date: December 18th
Edgware Project Name: The Christmas House
Amenities Offered: ~~full breakfast buffet~~ MORNING-AFTER
AWKWARDNESS (HANGOVER OPTIONAL)
Pluses/Minuses: ~~absentee employees~~ TOTAL CHANGE OF
PLANS!

Feeling like an idiot, Karina gouged the metal scoop in the ice machine's bin one more time. She shoveled ice into her bucket mechanically, her mind filled with one terrible thought.

She'd slept with the man whose B&B she'd come to secretly evaluate! What kind of person did that make her?

Certainly not an ethical one. Or a sensible one. Or even—regretfully—a carefree one. Not anymore. Because she could hardly continue her ho-ho-ho holiday affair with Reid while she was anonymously evaluating his business . . . could she?

No, Karina told herself firmly, scooping another load of ice. She couldn't. It wouldn't be right. Now that she knew who Reid really was—and what he was really responsible for—she couldn't ignore the facts. She couldn't let herself go, indulge in some holiday fun, or even break out that honey she hadn't been able to try yet. She was hamstrung, tied to her moral principles and her stupid, inconvenient sense of fair play.

She'd have to leave Reid alone. It was the only way. The few hours they'd spent together would have to be their last.

Stung by the thought, Karina missed the bucket with her next scoopful. Ice pinged to the floor of the anteroom adjacent to the kitchen, scattering like lumps of see-through coal in a naughty child's Christmas stocking. Reacting too slowly, Karina grabbed for one, juggled her bucket, lost hold of the scoop, then dropped the whole caboodle. More ice spun out of control.

Swearing, she dropped to her knees to retrieve all of it.

She'd really *liked* Reid, too. He'd been . . . sweet. Also, hot, sexy, considerate, fun, skillful, and ambidextrous.

At first, she'd thought she'd been so into him because it had been months since her last sexual encounter. But it hadn't taken more than a few kisses—and a few especially passionate moves on her part—to realize that something more momentous was happening between them. Something special. Karina had never felt so drawn to a man in her life— not even Eric.

Could she really give up all that incredible connectedness for the sake of a favor? Even a favor she'd promised her sister?

Maybe Stephanie would understand, Karina mused as she scrabbled for more dirty fallen ice and shoved it in the drain beneath the ice machine. Maybe Stephanie would realize that good men were few and far between—her own luck with Justin aside—and let Karina off the hook for the evaluation. Maybe she would . . .

. . . sacrifice her job for Karina's love life?

No. Karina couldn't ask her to do that. Family came first. Loyalty and responsibility came second. And hot monkey love?

Well, in her case, hot monkey love came in dead last.

With her mind made up, Karina nodded to herself. Whatever it took to resist Reid, she'd have to do it. She couldn't
tell him the real reason for her decision, of course. But she
owed it to herself, to Stephanie, and to The Christmas House
to put her covert mission there ahead of her own libido. It
was only right.

"Hey." With a hesitant air, Vanessa Sullivan wandered into
the anteroom. Dressed in alternative-chic clothing, with her
dark, shaggy hair shaped almost like a Mohawk, she made an
arresting picture. A picture of freedom. Freedom, Karina
thought semiresentfully, to wear an eyebrow ring, eat brown-
ies for breakfast, *or* indulge in holiday nookie if she wanted
to. Some people had all the luck. "Are you doing okay in
here?"

"I'm fine. Thanks." Offering her a smile, Karina retrieved
her abandoned bucket. She stood and brushed off her knees.
"Sorry it's taking so long to set up the juice station. I had a
little accident with the ice machine, but it's all good now."

"Okay. Great." Vanessa studied her. She gestured uneasily
toward the nearby kitchen. "I'm sorry about . . . whatever
happened back there between you and Reid. Do you want to
talk about it?"

Yes! I'd love to! Grateful for the offer, Karina sagged
against the ice machine, fighting an urge to discuss the fact
that Reid was running the B&B until she fully understood
it—and all its implications.

Talking was how she wrapped her head around her feelings, her thoughts, and her plans. Granted, she'd already sent
a few deliriously happy text messages to Chelsea. She'd also
received some questionable (and hilariously bawdy) advice
in return. But right now, she didn't need another Go, K! Way 2
hit that, hott stuf! message via SMS. What she needed was a
compassionate and wise listener.

Unfortunately, as much as Karina liked Vanessa, Vanessa

simply couldn't be the helpful sounding board she needed. Because just like Reid, Vanessa was part of the B&B's management team. That made her off limits as a real confidante.

It also explained why Karina had run into her that morning, outside on the front porch. Vanessa had been arriving to report the traitorous head chef situation and help with breakfast. Karina had been taking stealthy photos of the B&B's "*actual (not representational or previously published) exterior*" for her Edgware report. It had been all she could do to formulate an excuse for her high-tech borrowed camera and furtive notebook scribblings. She thought Vanessa had believed her hastily dreamed-up cover story about wanting mementos for her family scrapbook. With the hangover she'd been fighting since before dawn, it was hard to tell.

Reminded of the sorry state she'd awakened to find herself in, Karina touched her forehead. Yep. Her raging headache was still in full force, hammering on her skull. Her eyes still felt runny and bleary; her tongue felt fuzzy. She doubted all those aftereffects could be remnants of her impulsive fling with Reid. She'd only ever felt this way a few times before, usually after a wild Halloween, Christmas, or New Year's Eve party.

All the evidence pointed to one thing: The innocent-looking spiced cider last night had been spiked with something much more potent than cinnamon and nutmeg—even though children had been present for much of the reception. That should probably go into her report, Karina realized. It would be a black mark for sure.

"Thanks, but I should finish this first." Regretfully, she gestured to the ice bucket. "That juice isn't getting any colder, and I promised to get the buffet set up. I appreciate the offer to talk, though. That's really nice of you."

"It's not nice. It's my guilty conscience talking."

Guilty conscience? What in the world could Vanessa have to feel guilty about? Fisting the scoop, Karina went after more ice. But she couldn't resist flicking Vanessa a curious glance.

Even without verbal encouragement, Vanessa kept right on talking. "It's all my fault, what happened between you and Reid," she confessed, flinging her hand in the air. "I'm really sorry, Karina. When I saw you at the reception yesterday, I thought you and Reid might hit it off. He's nice, you're nice, you're both divorced. You know. So when I checked you in—"

"That's right!" Karina remembered, belatedly recognizing her. "You *were* manning the front desk last night!"

"I swapped out your typical second-floor reservation for a special attic room. A room right across the hall from Reid's. With the hope you two would run into each other, and maybe something would click. I *know* I shouldn't have done it. Believe me! But I really love Reid, and he *so* deserves to be happy after the rotten way his ex-wife treated him, and it wouldn't kill him to settle down to a regular grown-up lifestyle, either, especially for the sake of my two nieces, and I just thought . . . Well, the bottom line is, I thought I could make a good matchup between you two." At that, a proud gleam came into Vanessa's gaze, despite her apologetic demeanor. "That's kind of my thing—making hookups between people," she admitted. "I've been doing it since middle school. I have a whole bunch of successful relationships to my credit. You wouldn't believe how many weddings I get invited to. It's ridiculous!"

Almost breathless after her long-winded explanation, Vanessa waited, with blatant hopefulness, for Karina's reaction.

"Reid's ex-wife was mean to him? What happened?"

Darn it. She shouldn't have asked that question.

She was supposed to be forgetting about Reid, not digging up details about his past. What was she thinking?

That she felt sorry for him, that's what.

Nobody deserved to have his heart broken. Especially

Reid. Reid was interesting and talented and kind and generous. . . .

And off limits! She couldn't forget that.

"No. Never mind." Shaking her head, Karina finished scooping up ice. She shut the ice machine's sliding door. As though the bucket could cool her avid interest, unstoppable libido, and poor hopeful heart, she clutched it against her chest. "Don't tell me. It's none of my business. Really."

Vanessa gave her a shrewd look. "Then you *do* like him!"

"Well . . . Who wouldn't? He's handsome, smart, and nice."

Vanessa beamed. Obviously, she and her cousin were close.

"But I'm not in the market for a relationship right now," Karina protested. *A holiday fling? Yes. A relationship? No.* Lamely, she added, "I just don't think it's a good idea."

"Why not? Are you involved with someone else?"

"Unless my TV boyfriend, Nathan Fillion, counts . . . No."

A grin. "Then what's the problem? Is it your kids?"

"So far? No." Seriously considering the question for the first time, Karina shifted the ice bucket from her chest to her hip. "In fact, if Olivia, Josh, and Michael got along with a man I was dating, that would mean big points in his favor."

"Excellent. Reid gets along *great* with kids!"

Uh-oh. Yet another way Reid was irresistible. Terrific.

Fortunately, he hadn't officially met *her* kids yet, Karina reminded herself. Thanks to the way she'd scampered off to disrupt Josh's petty theft–athon, Michael's gift-guessing extravaganza, and Olivia's suspicious analysis of those Christmas stockings, Reid probably believed her children were budding juvenile delinquents. He probably dreaded meeting them.

Now, thanks to her vow to nix things between them, he wouldn't have to. Umm . . . yay? Dispiritedly, Karina sighed.

"It's no use, Vanessa. This year, I have all I can handle just dealing with Christmas." *And my undercover Edgware evaluation of your family business.* "It's the first

holiday since my divorce. I really need it to be special for
my children."

Astutely, Vanessa nodded. "Right. What about for you?"

Why did everyone keep asking her that? "If they're happy,
I'm happy," Karina said firmly. "Which means I'd better deliver this juice and make sure they get some breakfast. Thanks
for the talk, though. It's been nice making a friend here in
Kismet."

Leaving Vanessa behind—before she could crack and confess her inescapable longing for Reid—Karina hustled off to
the dining room, ready to make sure she thought more about
Christmas carols and tinsel than she did about Christmas affairs and nookie. No matter what it took . . . and it was going
to take a lot—especially after having experienced Reid.

By the time her second full day as a stand-in Edgware evaluator dawned at The Christmas House, Karina figured she
was doing pretty well. So far, although she'd met all the other
guests, a couple more Sullivans, and some helpful local residents, no one had guessed her secret mission. She'd managed
to compile a pretty respectable assortment of notes about the
B&B's day-to-day operations, its amenities, its schedule of
events, and (to a guiltily lesser degree) its staff, too.

She hadn't yet uploaded those reports, of course. She
hadn't had time. Or an opportunity. Besides, her admittedly
sketchy ability to resist procrastination—even at the best of
times—was no match for the ongoing stress of trying to make
sure Michael, Josh, and Olivia had a perfect Christmas (while
simultaneously trying to keep them out of trouble).

That hadn't been easy. Michael persisted in questioning
everything—including Karina's ever-present note and picture taking, which made performing her evaluation duties
trickier than she'd anticipated. Josh continued "borrowing"
assorted items, from the safety scissors used to craft paper

snowflakes during the B&B's daily kids' Fun Zone sessions to the peppermint candy canes that had been stockpiled for Christmas tree–decorating class. Olivia insisted on informing Karina of every potentially dangerous item in their midst, from the "identity theft!" threat posed by the personally inscribed (but otherwise innocent) holiday stockings on the mantel to the terrors of multicolored chaser lights (with "deadly lead dust!" on their wires).

"I promise I won't lick any wiring this Christmas," Karina told her daughter as they trooped across the B&B's snow-covered grounds with the rest of the guests. They were on their way to this season's inaugural horse-drawn sleigh ride, and Karina had bundled up in an assortment of items on loan from Chelsea's closet. Her jeans barely fit over her thermal underwear and thick socks. She felt extremely bulky. "And I'll wash my hands very thoroughly if I handle anything. Cross my heart."

She made the ritual cross-my-heart gesture, then smiled.

Her daughter wasn't appeased. "You'd better." Huffing in the snow, Olivia tromped onward, her small face creased in a frown. "I refuse to lose another parent if I don't have to."

That brought Karina up short. She signaled for Josh and Michael to stop, then crouched with her hands on Olivia's arms. She gave her daughter a serious look. "You didn't lose your dad. He loves you very much! We both do. *Double* cross my heart."

She made the cross-my-heart gesture again.

Olivia refused to look at her. As the other guests kept moving in jolly groups toward the B&B's outlying barn, Olivia stood with her booted feet planted. "Maybe. But for how long?" she demanded. "Things could change at any second, you know. Things have a way of changing just when you don't expect it."

Like a divorce that happens and breaks up your family.

She didn't have to say the words aloud. The sentiment

behind her expression was clear . . . and it broke Karina's heart.

"Our love for you won't change," she assured Olivia. "Our love for you—and your brothers—will always stay the same, no matter what. Just because your dad and I are apart now—"

"Hey!" Michael blurted. "It's Reid! Hi, Reid!"

"Hey!" Happily waving, Josh joined in. "Hi, Reid!"

Both her sons swiveled with eager grins on their faces.

"Can we go hang out with Reid?" Josh asked, hopping on one foot. "He promised to let us steer the horse-drawn sleigh!"

"He's the *coolest!*" Michael added. "He has a tattoo!"

Karina was familiar with Reid's tattoo. She was pretty sure she'd licked it at least once. Fortunately, the practice hadn't been toxic . . . only titillating. She wished she could try it again. But she'd sworn off Reid. For good. Even if he *was* gazing at her with a supersexy expression just then. And waving, too.

It felt almost as though they belonged together—as though she and the kids had come out here to be with him. Ridiculous.

"Can we, Mom?" Michael yanked her sleeve. "Huh? Can we?"

"Michael, I'm having a very important conversation with Olivia right now. So please give me a minute, then we'll—"

Abruptly, Karina noticed that Olivia was staring in Reid's direction, too. She was probably wondering who he was and why her brothers were so excited to see him. Which made two of them.

All right. Fine. Karina gave in. "You two know Reid?"

Beside her, Olivia gave a gusty, world-weary sigh. "Mom. Please. *Everyone* knows Reid. He's, like, everyone's friend."

"Awesome." More alarmed now than ever, Karina nodded. She couldn't think of a single reason to deny her sons' request to hang out with Reid—at least not one that wouldn't arouse undue suspicion. "Sure, go ahead. Olivia and I will catch up with you in a sec."

"Speak for yourself, Mom!" Olivia disagreed. "I feel fine now. I'm going to go say 'hi!' to Reid." She ran ahead, waving, with her winter boots kicking up plumes of snow. "Hi, Reid!"

Josh and Michael bolted toward The Christmas House's innkeeper too, their coat hoods flopping behind them. Wearing mittens, hats, scarves, and boots, they converged like playful puppies on a happy-looking Reid. Snatches of their excited chatter drifted on the icy-feeling wind, referencing some of the activities they'd (apparently) enjoyed at the B&B while Karina had been busy sneaking around to evaluate the place.

Watching her children clamor for Reid's attention, Karina felt her heart expand . . . then sink. It was good that her kids liked Reid. It was also terrible that her kids liked Reid.

If Olivia, Josh, and Michael got along with a man I was dating, that would mean big points in his favor.

When she'd made that statement to Vanessa yesterday, she'd been telling the truth. Dating someone who didn't connect with her children was unthinkable. But it didn't seem as though that would be a problem with Reid, Karina noticed. Even a person who *wasn't* wearing a hat, hood, and scarf over her face could see that Reid had (somehow) totally bonded with Michael, Josh, and Olivia. Not that she could blame them. He was pretty amazing.

So were her children, of course.

"Hey, Mom!" Eagerly, Olivia gestured to her. "Look at the horses! Reid says I can feed these carrots to them!"

She waggled a bunch of carrots, holding them by their feathery green tops. Swerving her gaze from those carrots, Karina examined the pair of Clydesdales that had been harnessed to the sleigh. The massive horses were wearing jingle bells. The bells emitted a burst of cheery sound whenever they moved.

At the moment, the horses were moving as much as they could—given the constraints of the harnesses—as they anticipated Olivia's carrot treat. One of them nickered. It edged closer to Olivia, opened its mouth, then showed her its big yellow teeth.

"Be careful!" Startled, Karina waved. Visions of her daughter's mittened hand being mistaken for a weird new vegetable swirled in her mind. "Watch out for those teeth!"

She hurried over, vigilant and wary. But Reid, who stood a short distance away, only smiled. He seemed oblivious to the potential dangers of allowing a ten-year-old girl to put her mittened hand close to a horse's snapping teeth. Even as the horsey treat drama continued to unfold, he remained nonchalant.

Karina stopped in front of him. "What's the matter with you?" she asked, hands on her hips. Agitatedly, she gestured at Olivia. "She could be hurt! Are those horses even tame?"

Reid's carefree gaze transferred to her. "Hey, you're talking to me again." His smile broadened. "That's great."

So was the effect his nearness was having on her libido. Even though they were standing in the cold December weather, surrounded by several other guests, Karina suddenly felt a lot warmer. She also felt as though stripping off Reid's puffy vest and sweater and getting him naked might be fun. *Lots* of fun.

"You didn't answer my question. Is that horse safe?"

"You know," Reid mused, "I could swear you've been avoiding me the past couple of days. Did I do something to upset you?".

"Is that horse safe?" Karina repeated. Doggedly.

His statement about her avoiding him wasn't something she could honestly address. It was better not to discuss it.

If Eric had been there, the concept of Karina passing up

a conversation would have blown his mind. So would her newfound sense of purpose and determination. She was a new woman now, Karina reminded herself. She was a new woman who would not be drawn into discussing her short-lived holiday affair to remember. No way.

"Is that horse safe?" she asked again, standing her ground. "Or will I have to get Olivia a new thumb for Christmas?"

"No. She'll be fine." Grinning as though he found her motherly concern hilarious, Reid nudged his chin in the direction of the Clydesdales. "My own daughters are over there."

"Right. But you're the world's most lackadaisical parent."

He seemed unfazed. "Because I don't hover over my girls the way you do with your kids?" Another shrug. "I'm okay with that."

"Well . . . still." Irked but running out of steam, Karina glanced away. A few of the other guests had noticed their discussion, but they didn't seem especially interested. She'd get no help from the more cautious-minded parents who might be "hovering" nearby. "I just think you should have asked my permission first. I'd like to be consulted about potentially dangerous activities—especially when they involve my children."

"Okay." Reid nodded. "As soon as I run across something that fits that description, I'll let you know."

How could he be so blasé about this? Feeding carrots to horses the size of Hummers *was* dangerous—and potentially problematic for The Christmas House, too. Especially with regard to their Edgware evaluation. If she was going to be a truly responsible and thorough evaluator, Karina told herself, she ought to note all hazardous activities in her report.

Possibly with a recommendation to shut them down.

The risky activities, of course—*not* The Christmas House.

But maybe she was getting a little drunk with power, it occurred to Karina. Because just then, she almost relished the idea of drawing a black mark on the B&B's evaluation report. That wasn't like her at all. Besides, it wasn't Reid's fault that he was off limits to her (and therefore making her cranky with his very presence). He couldn't help that . . . just like Karina couldn't help cringing a little as she watched Olivia reach up to pet one of the horse's necks. Next to that huge creature, her daughter appeared very small and fragile.

She also appeared, as she looked over her shoulder at Karina, absolutely delighted. A broad smile wreathed her features, lending them a lightness Karina hadn't seen for a long time. That smile was just what she'd hoped to see on this trip.

Reid had managed to produce it after three minutes.

Shaking her head, Karina hugged herself. Maybe she *was* a little too protective sometimes. Maybe Reid had a point.

"Olivia really seems to love horses," he said.

Smarty-pants. "What little girl doesn't?" Karina asked, not yet ready to concede that point. Giving in to Reid's laissez-faire approach to parenting still felt too risky to her.

Reid's gaze stayed on her. "Do you want a turn, too?"

"With the horses?" Karina scoffed. "Ha! No, thanks."

But a part of her *did* want a turn, she realized with embarrassing clarity. Apparently, there was a horse-loving preteen buried somewhere inside her. And she wanted out.

Forcibly shoving her down, Karina stuffed her hands in her pockets. She toed the snow with her boot. "I'm fine right here."

"That's not what I asked you." Reid's gaze told her he thought she was *fine,* all right. It also told her he was confused about why she'd been avoiding him. He grabbed her hand, then lay a carrot in her mittened palm. "Here. Go ahead."

"I can't. Really. I'm the mom. I—" Torn, she scrutinized the carrot. It was pretty long. Her fingers would probably be safe from those horsey chompers. "I should set a good example." She glanced up at Reid's angular, stubbled jaw, dark brows, and penetrating eyes. He was so *dreamy!* But she couldn't think about that now. She raised her chin. "I should do the right thing."

"All the time? That's not even possible."

"Sure, it is. If I try hard enough." Her sister was depending on her to do exactly that, Karina reminded herself.

"Go ahead." Reid nudged her. "Go crazy. Be reckless."

He didn't know what he was urging her toward. Obviously, his statement could be construed in more than one way—including a way that would lead them both to another hot-hot-hot liaison in his big, comfy sleigh bed back at the B&B. Because the more Reid encouraged her to cut loose, the more tempted Karina felt to throw caution to the wind, burn her Edgware evaluation notes, and throw herself headlong into . . . well, *him.*

Given that—and the thrillingly sensual memories that nudged at her just then—approaching an SUV-sized horse suddenly felt like the lesser of two evils. Karina fisted her carrot.

"Fine. I will!" she said, then marched over, ready to go for it.

Chapter Eleven

... From the desk of Betty Sullivan
DECEMBER 19TH
LOCATION: THE CHRISTMAS HOUSE
SCHEDULED EVENT: "JINGLE BELLS" SLEIGH RIDE—
10:00 A.M. TO 2:00 P.M. (DAILY)

Leaning against the gaily painted side of the B&B's old-fashioned sleigh, Reid chuckled. He couldn't take his gaze off Karina. Standing next to Holly and Ivy—The Christmas House's longtime lead horses—she appeared terrified, eager, and rebellious at the same time.

As he watched, she clenched her carrot in a viselike grip. Tentatively, she waggled it toward Holly.

The old mare whinnied, then bared her buckteeth.

Karina flinched. She took a step backward. Her three kids offered up encouragement. So did Alexis and Nicole. With their usual adventurousness, Reid's daughters gently pushed Karina. She nearly did a face plant into Holly's shaggy, horsey flank.

She righted herself, visibly screwed up her courage, then examined her carrot. Carefully holding it, she raised it again.

Holly snatched it away. She crunched it down, sending

orange carrot bits and equine spittle flying. The Clydesdale wasn't a graceful eater, but she was an eager one. Ivy nosed over, looking for a treat of her own. Olivia brightened, then gave her mother a selection from her cache of carrots. Everyone watched as Karina fed Ivy. The horse greedily chomped away.

"Yay! I did it! Twice!" Karina flung her arms in the air.

Looking delighted, she danced a little jig, kicking up snow. All the girls cheered for her. A few of the other B&B guests applauded. Michael and Josh merely grinned, macho style.

Reid grinned too. Karina was adorable. He didn't know why she'd been avoiding him, but he had his suspicions— chief among them that he'd hurt her feelings, the way Vanessa had claimed.

If that was true, Reid owed it to Karina to make it up to her—by being her friend. Her *platonic* friend, if that's what she wanted. With the necessary exception of Gabby, he'd never attempted to remain friends with an ex—especially not a one-night-stand ex. But this time, it felt necessary. Reid wanted to do what was right for Karina. He wanted to make amends. He wanted—

Her. He wanted *her*. He wanted to indulge in a crazy amount of headboard-banging, screaming-to-the-rafters sex with *her*.

But he wasn't going to. This time, Reid planned to be smart about things. He planned to take sex out of the equation altogether. That way, he could still spend time with Karina *without* being distracted from his work at the B&B and his promise to his grandparents. It was a win-win. A slam dunk.

If he wasn't sleeping with Karina, Reid reasoned, it would be impossible for her to sidetrack him from his job at The Christmas House. After all, how diverting could a *platonic* female friend be? Especially a platonic suburban divorcée friend with three kids and a mortgage? Karina was so settled and content, she might as well have *Homebody* tattooed on her forehead.

They were total opposites. Despite the effect Karina had on him, she wasn't exactly his dream girl. Despite the sexy times they'd shared in his bed (and on his room's settee and in his room's triple-showerhead-equipped shower), Reid figured it would be easy to move Karina to the friend zone.

Absolutely. The strategy was genius. He felt justifiably pleased with himself for having come up with it, late last night, while pondering Karina's newfound aloofness over a cup of wassail punch. *Never back a Sullivan into a corner,* he thought to himself now. *Because we're masters at maneuvering.*

Speaking of maneuvering . . . Still leaning against the sleigh while his guests chatted, Reid studied Karina's derrière as she moved. *Nice.* Bootylicious. But oddly bulky too. He'd swear she was wearing three pairs of underwear. How was that even possible? Maybe if he stripped off one pair with his teeth—

Nope, he reminded himself staunchly. Underwear removal was probably not a platonic-friend activity. Except in the case of a freak underwear emergency—an example of which didn't come readily to mind . . . no matter how hard Reid tried to think of one.

"Preride run-through's finished." Nate Kelly, one of the obliging Kismet locals who'd volunteered to pitch in at Reid's grandparents' behest, joined Reid at the sleigh. Folding his massive arms, Nate gave Karina a convivial nod. "So who's the new girl? Looks like she's got you totally wrapped up, Sullivan."

"Takes one to know one. I hear you're bound and tied to another teacher—Angela Wright, right? And her daughter, Kayla?"

"That's right." Nate, a former NFL lineman—and current industrial arts/home economics teacher at Kismet High

School—gave another nod. He didn't appear the least bit bugged that Reid had basically, in a man-to-man, regular-Joe fashion, called him whipped. "Yes, Angela and I are together now. Couldn't be happier either! That's why I can tell what's up with you."

"Nothing's up with me. You're crazy."

"She doesn't look familiar," Nate observed. "Is she from around here? What's her name?" He paused, waiting for answers from Reid. None came. Jovially, Nate kept talking. "Your daughters sure seem to like her. Look at them all together over there."

Reid did. Nate was right, he was surprised to notice: His daughters *did* seem to like Karina. Even now, Alexis and Nicole laughed at something Karina said. Karina smiled at them, then tucked back a hank of Alexis's long, hastily brushed hair. Ordinarily, his older daughter would have bristled to be "fussed over" that way.

But when it came to Karina, Alexis merely brightened . . . then edged closer and kept on chatting.

Nicole did, too. As Reid watched, his younger daughter pointed at Karina's scarf—a pink spangled thing that looked as though it belonged at the Barbie Dream House. (Reid knew more about the Barbie world at large than was probably recommended for an adult his age—or anyone else.) In response to Nicole's interest, Karina removed her scarf, flipped it over Nicole's shoulders, then performed an elaborate knot-tying maneuver.

The end result explained why Karina had needed *him* to intervene with her tangled scarf the other day . . . but it appeared to thrill his daughter. As though she were on a Paris runway, Nicole marched with kooky high-legged steps alongside the paddock fence, stopped to strike a pose, then giggled and came back.

Reid had never seen his daughters act so . . . girlishly.

What was going on here? Sure, he got along famously with

Josh, Michael, and Olivia; that was true. But Reid's instant rapport with the Barrett kids wasn't the same as this. It wasn't the same as Karina causing his two multilingual, globe-trotting, sari-owning, stubbornly individualistic preteenagers to suddenly morph into the modern-day equivalent of California Valley Girls.

"Name?" Nate pushed. "Rank? Serial number? Anything?"

Reid blinked. What were they . . . ? Oh yeah. Karina's name.

"Sorry, Nate. She's Karina Barrett. Just another guest. From California. San Diego. And her three kids." Reid watched her. "Yep," he confirmed pointlessly. "Just another guest."

Nate grinned, then shook his head. "If *she's* just another guest to you, then I'm the Sugar Plum Fairy."

"Really? *The Nutcracker?* You like that stuff?"

"Hey." A mock threatening frown. "Don't diss higher culture, dude, just because you feel vulnerable right now."

"Speak for yourself. I don't get vulnerable." To prove it, Reid smiled. "Hey—don't you have a sleigh ride to orchestrate?"

Nate gave an affirmative sound. "Which reminds me—if the Edgware deal goes through, will the new franchisee still keep the horses on-site? I promised Angela I would check on that."

Surprised, Reid glanced at him. "You know about Edgware?"

Nate shrugged. "Most of the town does. We're pretty bummed about it actually. I'd hate to see another business sell out."

"Lagniappe at the Lakeshore wouldn't mind."

"Maybe. Business has been pretty bad lately. I guess they probably need all the advantages they can get over there."

"You sound as though you feel sorry for them."

"I do." Semiapologetically, Nate spread his arms. "I'm a lifetime Kismet resident. I plan to stay here, no matter what. My loyalties are probably a little different from yours."

Since you're leaving after the holidays, Nate's expression said. *You big Scrooge.* It was an accurate—if unspoken—appraisal. If he did everything right, Reid figured, he and the girls could be back on the road by New Year's Day, with Amanda in tow.

"Probably." Reid couldn't argue the truth. The longer he was in town, the more he realized it: *Everyone* in Kismet felt unswervingly loyal to the place. That allegiance seemed to apply to The Christmas House too. All the townspeople who'd dropped by to volunteer or visit had told him they wished the Sullivans could keep running the B&B—especially during Christmastime.

No wonder his grandparents had summoned Reid from the other side of the world. He was, quite literally, the only un-sentimental person Robert and Betty Sullivan knew. He was the only person who could—and *wanted to*—make sure the Edgware sale succeeded.

Speaking of which . . . If the secret evaluator had come out for the inaugural sleigh ride, he (or she) was probably getting tired of waiting. Reid clapped his hands, then spoke up to summon everyone. "Okay, we're just about to get started!"

From the corner of his eye, he glimpsed Karina. She turned to face the sleigh, wearing a childlike expression of wonder—and downright eagerness, too. Earlier, she'd stifled her inner horse-crazy girlishness. He didn't want her to similarly stifle her inner holiday-loving hedonist . . . which Reid knew damn well she'd do, given half a chance.

"Nate and I will take out the first group in a few minutes. Then we'll proceed in order from there, so that everyone gets a sleigh ride," he told his guests. "In the meantime, we have hot cocoa and apple cider donuts to keep everyone warm, along with some lessons in making snow angels and building snow forts."

"Yay! Snowball fights!" some of the kids shouted.

Smiling, Reid signaled to The Christmas House staff,

who'd brought along the goodies and other supplies. At his
nod, they lined up everyone behind a red-and-white candy-
striped velvet rope, turned on some holiday tunes, and kicked
off the activities. His guests cheered. Amanda, along with the
B&B worker who usually dealt with the kids' Fun Zone activities, rounded up the children.

With that dealt with, Reid approached Karina. "Let's go.
You and the kids are in the first group."

"Us?" She tapped her well-bundled chest. "But we can't be
first. We're . . . Well, you've already made an exception to let
Olivia—and me—feed the horses." Prettily, Karina blushed.
"Which was very nice of you. But you should take someone
else first. There's no reason we should get special treatment."

She seemed alarmed by the very idea. He didn't know why.

"There's every reason you should get special treatment,"
Reid told her, smiling. "But the reason that matters right now
is that I don't want to make my introductory sleigh ride with
anyone else. I want to take you first. You and the kids."

Reid gestured at them. All five had already clambered into
the sleigh. Now they chatted amiably with Nate. Michael
waved his arms. Nicole laughed. Josh pantomimed feeding a
horse—and being a horse. Olivia held her nose, making some
sort of joke. Even Alexis, seated tantalizingly close to the
sleigh's radio and GPS unit, ignored those gadgets in favor of
twirling her hair and borrowing Olivia's lip gloss.

"See?" Reid pointed out. "Ordinarily, my daughter Alexis
would be hacking into the radio and reprogramming the GPS
unit to take us to the Upper Peninsula for homemade fudge.
But even she's mellowed out."

And embarked on a makeover program. Taken aback by his
daughter's primping, Reid did a double take. He didn't think
he'd ever seen Alexis *or* Nicole actually primp for something.

"I'm glad. She's a sweet girl. So is Nicole," Karina said sin-
cerely. She wrung her mittened hands together. "But I don't
want to be treated differently than any other guest. Okay?"

It seemed important to her. Reid couldn't imagine why.

"You already have been treated differently," he pointed out with a grin. "Or did you think I greeted all my guests with a—"

"Stop right there!" Blushing again, Karina cut him off before he could describe any of the tantalizing, mind-bending, entirely X-rated things they'd done together. "I'll admit, your 'greeting' did make me feel pretty special. But when it comes to the sleigh ride, I want everyone to get a fair turn."

"They will. I promise. But for this first ride, I want to go out with someone who won't be looking for every flaw in the experience. Someone who will be nice about my first attempts at maneuvering a decrepit old Santamobile. Someone like you."

Karina swallowed hard. "Someone like . . . me?"

Was she really going to make him lay it out for her? Reid nodded. "Someone nice and noncritical. Okay? How about it?"

She bit her lip, then blinked. "Okay. Time's wasting! Let's get on that sleigh ride!" With every appearance of enthusiasm, she straightened her spine and marched to the sleigh.

Reid didn't know how she made that simple maneuver look so delectable. But she did. Just watching her *walk* made him feel hot. So far, he sucked at platonic friendship. But he was going to do better. Just as soon as Karina removed her derrière from view, so he wouldn't feel so irresistibly drawn to look at her.

There. Karina took her place on the sleigh's front bench, right beside Nate. Reid felt about a million times better— until he caught another glimpse of Karina's face and realized something even more alarming: He was looking forward to showing her the sights on the B&B's holiday sleigh ride route even *more* than he was looking forward to admiring her backside.

If that wasn't scary, he didn't know what was.

Given the choice between getting frisky with Karina and

continuing to have these unaccountably . . . *gooey* feelings toward his new platonic friend, Reid knew what he would choose. It wasn't exactly the stuff of high-minded poetry and literature, either. It was down and dirty. It was raw. It was primal and naked and necessary. It was (kind of) against the rules of Reid's new foolproof plan to responsibly run the B&B, too.

Seated in the driver's seat, Nate cleared his throat. He hefted the harness traces, then gave Reid a pointed look. "Shall we get going, boss? Or are you staying here?"

And miss a chance to experience Karina's first sleigh ride? Screw that. Ignoring all the warning bells in his head, Reid strode to the sleigh. He got in. "I'm going. Ho ho ho!"

Chapter Twelve

Date: December 19th
Edgware Project Name: The Christmas House
Guest/Staff Interface Opportunity: ~~horse-drawn sleigh ride~~
SNOWBANK MAKE-OUT SESSION . . . WHOOPS!
Interaction Goal: ~~quantify guest enjoyment and evaluate~~
~~viability of franchising services~~ DON'T LET THIS HAPPEN AGAIN!

Snuggled on the sleigh's bench seat with the crisp wintery air in her face, the horses' jingle bells jangling, and the sleigh whooshing past some of the most scenic forest she'd ever experienced, Karina sighed. She *loved* this. The sleigh ride was idyllic, her children were behaving impeccably (and seemed to have become fast friends with Reid's daughters too), and she felt more hopeful about her first postdivorce Christmas than she probably had a right to.

If this was the kind of experience she could share with Olivia, Michael, and Josh, she was doing okay.

The only problem was Reid. He'd insisted on sitting right next to her, and he was downright impossible to ignore. He looked good. He smelled good. Even worse, he was being *nice*.

Ever since finding out he was the B&B's manager, she'd

been trying so hard to behave coolly toward him. Why wouldn't he get the message? Instead of following her lead and silently enjoying the scenery, Reid talked to her, pointed out all his favorite landmarks . . . and made her feel closer to him than ever before. Instead of accepting her extra layers of clothing as a reason to feel less attracted to her, he smiled and tossed her admiring looks. Instead of growing conveniently uglier and less appealing the longer she knew him, he appeared distractingly dishier and even more irresistible.

Why, oh why, did Reid have to be so *charming?*

Desperate for diversion, Karina dug in her coat pocket. She withdrew the high-tech camera Stephanie had lent her, then started snapping pictures. The beautiful horses. The bucolic scenery. The white-barked birch trees standing in the snow. The hills. The snow-flocked evergreens. The volunteer help, Nate Kelly, ably maneuvering the sleigh over hill and dale as the metal runners made a sprightly *whoosh-whoosh* sound on the snow.

Idly, Karina wondered if Nate was licensed for this job. If he wasn't, that would be a black mark against the B&B too.

"So, are you sure Mr. Kelly is up for this work?" she asked Reid, striving for a sense of *non*-secret-assessment-evaluator airiness. She nodded toward Nate. "Driving the sleigh, I mean. You must need a special license for that, right?"

Typically, Reid appeared unbothered. "Probably."

"But does he have one?" Karina pressed.

A shrug. "According to Vanessa, he's been helping out at The Christmas House for years. He seems pretty good at it."

Watching Nate drive the sleigh, Karina had to agree.

"Seriously. You can relax," Reid advised her. "I wouldn't bring anyone out here if I didn't think it was safe."

He thought she was being her usual overcautious self, Karina realized. Well, that was better than having him think she was an undercover Edgware evaluator. Wishing she could just tell Reid the truth—*without* compromising her mission and Stephanie's job—Karina decided to quit interrogating him for now.

Instead, she took a few more digital snaps of the children. Miraculously, all five of them were experiencing the sleigh ride with no iPod headphones or handheld PSPs in sight. Clearly, the Christmas House had worked some sort of holiday magic on them. Their faces looked bright and pink-cheeked in the afternoon sunshine.

"You don't have to take your own pictures, you know." Reid pointed to her borrowed camera. "That's one of the services we provide here. Our staff takes expert video and still photos of our guests—strictly with their consent—so everyone can enjoy their vacation without experiencing the whole thing through a camera lens." He indicated the trio of miniature, state-of-the-art, remotely operated digital cameras mounted to the sleigh. "It's part of The Christmas House's all-inclusive package."

"I know. Sort of like a supersize version of the postride pictures they offer you at Disneyland, right?" Karina laughed, hoping she sounded carefree—and *not* like a corporate superspy sent to find fault with Reid's family business. Even if she (technically) was. "But I like taking my own photos." *For my secret Edgware report.* "For my . . . scrapbook. As keepsakes."

"Right. I should have known you'd be the sentimental type."

"Guilty." Cheerfully, Karina nudged him. "You're not?"

Reid looked away. "Never had a reason to be."

"Surely your daughters gave you a reason?"

He gazed back at them, crowded in the rear bench seats, with a world of love plain in his face. "They gave me a reason to live. A reason to become a better man. But a reason to get all schmaltzy?" He pulled a goofy face. "Nope. Not yet."

Somehow, Reid's denial made Karina feel sorry for him. She couldn't imagine what it would be like not to treasure every moment and milestone of her children's lives—not to feel moved by each one. "Huh. I practically live through my children."

He transferred his gaze to her. "That's a mistake."

"It can't be." The very idea flew in opposition to everything Karina stood for. Being there. Helping. Giving her all, especially to her children. "I know it might seem that way to someone like you. You travel around the world with your kids—your life is one big nonstop party. But my life is a lot more grounded than that."

Reid's gaze narrowed. "It's my job, not a party. And traveling around the world is a good thing. It's broadening."

"I guess you're probably right. For you, at least." Karina shrugged. "All I know is . . . even if I *could* travel the world, I wouldn't. Not at my kids' expense. I mean, there's school, and friends, and—"

"Are you suggesting I'm hurting my daughters somehow?"

The intensity in his eyes spooked her. So did the way he interrupted her—an unusual occurrence for Reid. Maybe this wasn't the first time he'd heard this particular criticism.

"No! Not at all!" Karina assured him. "Everyone can see you're a wonderful father." *She'd* certainly noticed how protective, gentle, and affectionate Reid was with his daughters. But that didn't mean she was blind to the truth. "It's just that . . . Well, not everyone wants to put themselves first, the way you do. Not everyone *can* do that. You're fortunate Nicole and Alexis are up for the adventure."

"They *love* the adventure." He appeared convinced of it. Unerringly, thoroughly convinced. "They're proud of traveling all over the world. I'm proud of them for doing it."

"And I'm proud of all the work I put into being a mom. Maybe motherhood won't always be front and center for me, but right now it is. That's not a 'mistake,' for me or anyone else."

Reid mulled that over. "You can love your children—and

you can be a good parent—without sacrificing everything for them."

"That's easy for you to say. You're a man! Men have it easy."

"We do?"

She nodded. "Think about it: When you take over child care duties, even for a couple of hours, you're 'helping' or 'doing a favor' for their mother. The whole world pats you on the back for something that should have been your responsibility in the first place."

Reid's gaze remained fixed, compassionately, on hers. "And when a man takes over for more than a few hours? For all day, every day, three hundred and sixty-five days a year? What then?"

"Uh . . ." He had a point. Darn it. "Well, I guess then you're a hero. Like you."

But Reid only shook his head, even as the snowcapped scenery continued to fly by and the jingle bells went on ringing. "I'm no hero. I'm just a guy who's trying to do the best he can, day by day. Just like you're a woman who's trying to do the best she can, morning and night. Neither of us has to be perfect to be good parents. We just have to be there, mixing it up and taking a few punches whenever necessary."

Karina grinned at that. "Interesting view. Parenthood as full-contact sport?"

"Sometimes it feels that way." As though reminded of some *other* full-contact "sport," Reid glanced at her latest multiply layered ensemble. She'd swear he had X-ray vision. *Sexy* X-ray vision. "I call 'em like I see 'em."

Unwisely thrilled by his suddenly suggestive attention, Karina squirmed on her seat. "And what do you see right now?"

A woman I want more of, she expected to hear, anticipating their usual flirty banter (and grudgingly preparing herself to resist it). Or, *a woman who's driving me crazy with her three-pairs-of-thermal-undies-augmented, extra-luscious booty.*

Instead, what emerged from Reid was . . .

"I see that your seat belt isn't fastened." His gaze zoomed to her lap. He frowned. "The sleigh doesn't have airbags for safety—at least not yet—but it is supposed to have seat belts."

He craned in his seat to make sure the children were all securely buckled up. They were. He returned his attention to Karina. She twisted on her seat, looking for her seat belt.

"Found it." She held up its frayed edges. "It's broken."

"That's weird. It looks as though it's been cut in half." Wearing a concerned look, Reid fished around in the seat. He withdrew a lone buckle that had been wedged, uselessly, beneath her hip. "This clasp has been snapped clean off too. See?"

Karina did. This wasn't a good sign for the B&B. Someone at The Christmas House obviously wasn't doing his or her job. She hoped it wasn't an endemic problem. Trying to view the incident as a simple oversight—and not an indicator of yet another black mark against the B&B—she flung aside the seat belt remnants.

"Well, I can't use this, then. I'll be fine, though." She poked Nate's huge shoulder to get his attention. "Hey, Nate! Take it easy on the way back, okay? My seat belt is broken."

Nate saluted. "Gotcha. I'll be extra careful."

Fortunately, they weren't traveling very fast. All the better to enjoy the views, the Christmassy ambiance, and the snowfall that began drifting down, just like in one of those holiday-themed TV movies.

Thrilled by the snow's picture-perfect fluffiness, Karina relaxed. So did Reid . . . mostly. He shot an occasional accusing glance at her nonfunctioning seat belt, though. And when they reached the top of the next hill, he seemed to come to a decision.

He signaled Nate. "Hey, Nate. Pull up here for a minute, okay? I'm going to switch places with Karina."

"Oh, you don't have to do that," she protested. "I'm fine!"

"I won't have you in danger," Reid said. "We're switching."

The sleigh pulled to a stop, leaving the horses prancing in the snow. All around them, a peaceful field stretched for what seemed like miles. The crisp wintery air filled Karina's lungs. Her nose tingled with cold. She felt warm and protected, though—protected because Reid was chivalrously looking out for her and warm because she could glimpse, *waaaay* down the hill, the faraway B&B, with its barn and outbuildings and multiple Christmas trees.

It looked just like an old-fashioned holiday card—like one of those lithographic prints from Currier and Ives, with gilded edges and an elegant script greeting inside. Except it was real.

Karina sighed.

Reid stood. He gestured for her to do the same. Karina did.

At the same instant, the Clydesdales stamped and blew. One of them reared in its traces. Startled, Nate yanked the reins.

It was no use. The equine team, apparently spotting their home base at the paddock and barn, were ready to go home.

They bolted into motion, heading downhill. One minute, Karina was balancing precariously in the sleigh, trying to trade places with Reid . . . and the next, she was falling. She reached for something to steady herself, caught hold of Reid's hand, and felt him yank her. Hard. They both teetered sideways.

An instant later, the sleigh swerved violently. Karina lost her footing on its icy floorboards. Her mitten slipped off, leaving Reid grasping it—and Karina grasping nothing at all.

"Mom!" Olivia yelled. "Mom! Sit down!"

"Grab Reid!" Josh added. "Grab his hand!"

Karina couldn't. The next thing she knew, she was toppling crazily over the side of the sleigh. She landed on a big pile of snow, inches from the whooshing runners.

The sleigh flew past. Jingle bells rang merrily in her ears. Then . . . all was silent.

* * *

The minute Reid felt Holly and Ivy jerk the sleigh off course, he knew exactly what was happening. His grandfather had tried to warn him about this. He hadn't had a chance to finish.

Whatever you do, don't— Robert had started to say, when they'd been having their last-minute discussion about the B&B. Now Reid could easily guess the rest: *Don't let the horses see the barn before you're ready to let them haul ass toward home.*

The Clydesdales' eagerness had brooked no argument. When a pair of beasts weighing sixteen-hundred-pounds decided it was time for a hay-and-oats happy hour . . . well, it was time for a hay-and-oats happy hour. Period.

At first, Reid had thought he could hold Karina. Then her mitten had come off, and he hadn't been able to.

Damn that unusable seat belt of hers! He'd swear it had been tampered with. Clearly, someone wanted to shut down The Christmas House—or at least make them fail their evaluation.

Reid didn't know who. Plenty of townspeople seemed to be likely suspects, though, given their reluctance to see The Christmas House become an Edgware franchise.

Or maybe Lagniappe at the Lakeshore was behind this latest act of sabotage. Obviously, they'd already poached the B&B's head chef. Reid suspected they might have spiked the cider at the reception too. But exactly how far would they go to get a leg up in the competition for Kismet's tourism dollars?

Reid wasn't sure. He didn't have time to ponder the issue, either. Because even as those questions crowded into his mind, all hell broke loose. Karina toppled out of the sleigh. All the children shrieked. Nate struggled to control the horses. Reid assessed the situation, then took the only conceivable action.

Like a cliff diver in Brontallo, he jumped off the sleigh.

He hit the ground hard, seeing stars. With a final roar from Nate, the sleigh coursed merrily—but unstoppably—downhill.

The jingle bells clanged out of earshot. All was silent.

Shaking his head, Reid pushed up from the snow. He took a look around, got his bearings, then spotted Karina. She lay like a fleece-covered lump near a snowdrift just ahead of him.

It felt as though it took forever to run to her. Reid did, then fell to his knees beside her. With a practiced glance, he took in her posture, breathing, and vital signs. He framed her face with his gloved hands, carefully examining her features.

"Karina! Say something!" he cried. "Are you all right?"

"I'm fine." She cracked open one eye. "Are *you* all right?"

"Me? Who cares about me?" Immeasurably relieved to see her looking back at him, Reid exhaled. Sure, Karina was looking at him with only one eye—pirate style—but she seemed to have full comprehension of her surroundings.

At the realization, he wanted to laugh, cry, swear . . . or maybe dance the way Karina had done after she'd fed those carrots to Holly and Ivy (those traitors). Instead, he stroked her cheek. "It's you I'm worried about," he said. "You took quite a tumble from the sleigh."

"Nah. We weren't going that fast." She opened her other eye. Languidly, she flung her arms to her sides in the snow. Snowflakes drifted down to sparkle in her hair and on her hat. "At least not until *you* managed to leap out headfirst! By then, the horses were really running hard. Are you crazy?"

He didn't know what she meant. "I had to get to you."

"That's nuts." Karina gave him a beautiful smile. "It's also why I stayed here and played dead until you reached me. I could hardly let all that effort go unrewarded, could I?"

"You *played dead?*" Reid could hardly comprehend it. Trying to, he boggled at her. "Why in the hell would you do that?"

"So you could rescue me, silly." Her smile turned cock-eyed. Maybe she was concussed. "If I'd gotten up and jogged over to meet you, it would have been anticlimactic at best. Right?"

She was *definitely* concussed. "So you flopped in the snow and took a nap?"

"Sort of." Beaming now, Karina pushed up to a sitting position. As though proving her hardiness, she jumped nimbly to her feet. She gave a dramatic bow, then performed twelve jumping jacks. "See? I'm fine. Stop looking so worried, all right?"

"Oh man." Finally understanding she was okay—*and rubbing his face in it!*—Reid advanced on her. "You are *so* getting it."

Unconcernedly, she pursed her lips. "Getting what?"

"This." He grabbed her. Kissed her. Felt her warmth, her curviness, her pliant body as she surrendered against him. One kiss became two. Two became three. Three became . . . "Ahhhh!"

Reid fell backward, pushed by Karina. She followed him down to the snowbank, then grabbed a big handful of snow.

Gleefully, she rubbed it in his face. "Gotcha!"

Well. *That* couldn't be allowed to stand. No matter how damn cute Karina sounded while ambushing him. Sputtering, Reid groped blindly for a snow clump of his own. He found one.

This time, it was Karina's turn to howl with surprise.

They rolled apart from one another. Wetly, Karina blinked. Snow stuck to her hat, her hood, and her scarf. It clung to her eyelashes, then began melting. She rubbed her hands together.

Then she tackled him again, a fistful of snow leading the way. Reid grunted as woman and coldness both hit him at once.

"This is awesome! I always wanted to have a snow fight! And now I have. Officially." Triumphantly, she straddled him. "And I won, too. Woo-hoo!" Her grateful gaze slipped to his.

"Thanks for playing along. I know it's kind of lame for a grown woman to have a snow fight."

"It's not lame." *Especially this part, where you're on top of me.* Reid groaned, wishing there were about twelve fewer layers separating them. "It's fun. You're allowed to have fun."

Karina bit her lip. "Do you think the kids are okay?"

"They're probably having a snow fight of their own by now."

Propping her hands on his chest for leverage, she peered downhill. She squinted. "You're right. I think I see them." Her gaze returned to his. "I should get back to the barn. They're probably worried about me. I *did* just fall out of a moving sleigh, you know. It was practically a near-death experience!"

Reid examined her. Pleasurably. And at length. "You seem pretty perky for someone who just defeated the grim reaper."

"I'm tougher than I look. Also, I'm well padded today. I'm pretty sure my thermal underwear acted as a shock absorber."

Pretending to evaluate that theory, he squeezed her cushioned ass. He nodded. "Good thing you bundled up then. Thank God for your wimpy California girl constitution."

Laughing, Karina swatted away his hands. "Hey. Don't bad-mouth the Golden State. You just might like it there."

For a heartbeat, Reid actually considered the possibility. He imagined himself inside Karina's undoubtedly cozy house in San Diego, with her right next to him—and all their assorted kids close by—listening to the roar of the surf outside.

He liked the beach. It would be a good place to get married. *If* a person wanted to get married, of course.

"I've been to California. I doubt I'll go back for a while."

"Oh." Karina's face fell. "Well, that's your loss, I guess. And here I was, right on the verge of inviting you for a visit."

Reid froze. "You wanted me to come to California?"

Actually . . . yes, her wistful expression said, silently and irrefutably. *I wanted you to come to California.*

For a long moment, they gazed at one another. Reid's mind filled with a few more enticing images. Karina in a bikini.

His daughters laughing, arms full of textbooks, as they got on a school bus. Karina's kids cracking jokes, playing video games, and learning Reid's secrets of spelunking and campfire cooking.

Him, settling in. Him, hanging up his traveling shoes.

The idea felt surprisingly appealing.

"Nah. Kidding!" Karina rolled off him. "Boy, are *you* ever gullible!" Not meeting his eyes, she sat near the snowbank. She yanked up the thick socks she had on beneath her snow boots and tucked-in jeans, giving all her attention to that mundane task.

"*I'm* gullible?" Did he actually feel *wounded* by that remark? Impossible. "If that's what you call leaping off a moving sleigh, all Superman style," Reid said, "then I guess gullible means something other than I thought it did."

"You're right." Still holding herself apart from him, Karina plucked off her one remaining mitten. She examined it, then pocketed it. "That *was* a grand gesture." Finally, she looked at him. "Thanks for rescuing me . . . you big show-off."

Her expression was unreadable. Reid felt confused.

Was she grateful to him or not? Did she want him or not? Did they have a chance of being friends . . . or not?

Also, what the hell was wrong with his usual mojo, that he was even contemplating these stupid questions in the first place? It wasn't like him to feel uncertain. Usually, Reid felt supremely confident with women. All women. All women everywhere.

But Karina . . . Karina was another story altogether.

If they were going to be friends—platonic friends—he'd better quit imagining her naked, Reid told himself abruptly. Because if she'd actually been wearing as little as his libidinous mind insisted on showing him, she'd have been frostbitten for sure.

"That's me. A big grandstander, all the way." Better to be thought of as bigheaded, Reid decided, than to let Karina know the truth: He'd been scared out of his mind for her. And filled with remorse that *his* sleigh might have seriously hurt her. He vowed to get to the bottom of the snafus at The Christmas House. But first . . . He yanked off his gloves and offered them to her. "Take these," he said gruffly. "You don't want to get cold."

She scooted a few inches nearer. "Thanks."

They sat together, almost shoulder to shoulder in the snow, while Karina pulled on his gloves. On her, they appeared comically oversized—which only reminded Reid exactly how delicate, how vulnerable, how *necessary* to him she was. Her accident had shaken him up. Remembering it now made him feel twice as determined to make sure things went well at the B&B.

That meant he had to make doubly sure he didn't get distracted again. He had to make sure he focused, damn it!

But there was something about Karina's nearness. It stirred up all his emotions. It tempted him. It *lured* him. As though by moving closer she'd triggered some sort of unstoppable chemical reaction, Reid couldn't stop thinking about kissing her again.

Maybe he'd try being platonic another day.

He turned to her. She turned to him. Their faces hovered only a few inches apart, their breath turning into frosty plumes in the wintery air. Driven by an overpowering need to feel her again, to know her more deeply, Reid lifted his hand to her jaw.

Her skin felt warm and smooth beneath his bare palm, and since Karina remained still, he decided that maybe this was an okay platonic-friend activity. Maybe he'd been acting too rigidly all along. Experimentally, he stroked his thumb over her cheek.

At that, she widened her eyes, suddenly awakened to what was happening between them. Almost imperceptibly, Karina swayed toward him. She dropped her gaze to his mouth. She drew in a raspy, anticipatory breath—one that matched his own—and then . . .

"Do accidents happen often at The Christmas House?"

Startled by her question, Reid blinked. "What?"

"Is what happened to me today an indication of a larger problem with the B&B's safety policies," she pressed, "or is it a onetime fluke, like the spiked cider at the reception?"

Expectantly, Karina gazed at him. Her demeanor seemed oddly businesslike, her attitude brisk, and he wondered why she would interrupt a kiss for a question that clearly could have waited.

Then he realized the obvious truth. She was *Karina.* Even at the best of times, she was a worrywart. As her friend, Reid needed to put her mind at ease. Striving to do that—instead of enjoyably kissing her again, the way he wanted to—he casually dropped his hand.

Friends friends friends. Be her friend first!

He shrugged. "I hope it's a fluke. I haven't been around often enough to know for sure." He gave her the capsule version of his coming-home story and his grandparents' request that he run the B&B this Christmas season. "The trouble is, we're being evaluated for a potential franchise sale right now—"

Karina went still beside him. "Evaluated?"

Reid nodded. "Right. Anonymously. By a secret risk-assessment evaluator from a hospitality conglomerate called Edgware. They want to franchise The Christmas House concept, but they need to make sure it's a good investment first."

"Oh. That seems like, um, good news. Right?"

"Right." Another nod. "Edgware has a reputation for being really tough, though, so we can't afford to have any more screwups. The good news is, I know what happened with the horses, and I can fix the seat belt on the sleigh, too. So as long as nothing else goes wrong," Reid said, "I think we'll be okay. We've solved a few of the potential problems already."

He told her how he'd promoted one of the longtime cooks

to replace their pilfered head chef. He explained how he'd hired another cook to help out—a recent graduate who'd come highly recommended from the local culinary school.

"Given a little time, I think the new kitchen crew will work wonders," Reid said. "Whether that will happen in time to impress the Edgware evaluator remains to be seen."

"And you *want* the sale to go through?" Intently, Karina gazed at him. "I mean, if the B&B has been in your family for decades, maybe you'd rather it *didn't* get sold off and franchised. Maybe you'd rather the deal fell apart completely?"

At her blatantly hopeful expression, Reid couldn't help laughing. Clearly, Karina would have sided with the Kismet residents—and Nate—on the question of who should run the B&B.

"Nice try. But I'm not the sentimental type, remember?"

She slumped in her parka and hood, seeming disappointed.

Wanting to cheer her up, Reid gave her a companionable nudge. "If it makes you feel any better," he confided with a fresh grin, "I'm starting to feel a major moment of nostalgia for ten minutes ago, when we weren't talking about work."

She laughed. "Me too. Believe me!"

He angled his head, confused by that.

"I mean, I liked the snow fight better!" Karina explained, catching his undoubtedly perplexed expression. "That was fun."

"Yes, it was." He rested his forearms on his upraised knees and gazed at her, feeling a moment of camaraderie stretch between them. "All I can say is, it's a damn good thing *you* weren't the Edgware evaluator." He chuckled. "I'll bet he— or she—would *not* have felt like having a spontaneous snow fight just moments after being thrown from a runaway sleigh."

Karina gazed at the snowy horizon. In the distance, the town of Kismet stretched toward the frozen lake, then circled around it. Houses and businesses lined the adjacent riverbank.

"Maybe they would have," she mused, hugging herself.

"Maybe your impression of the anonymous evaluator is too harsh."

Reid laughed. "All right, Pollyanna. You're hired."

"Hired? For what?"

Her expression of naïveté made him feel a million times more cynical than usual. Had he really gotten that jaded over the years?

"I could use someone to keep up everyone's spirits while we deal with the evaluation. It's stressing out the staff." Only half joking, he nudged her again. "Want the job?"

If she did—if it had been a *real* job—he'd have even more reasons to see her, Reid realized. The more he considered the idea, the more he liked it.

"Everyone is stressed out?" Karina bit her lip. She shook her head. "That's awful! Do you think that's why the former head chef left to work for that other B&B across the lake?"

"The evaluation stress might have had something to do with it. Or it could be that Lagniappe at the Lakeshore simply made him a better offer. Period. Not everyone believes in loyalty."

Finally, Karina looked at him. "But you do?"

"It's my second guiding principle."

A smile quirked her lips. "Aha. Right after . . . ?"

"Right after number one: Don't let a lady freeze to death in the snow." Reid stood, then extended his hand to help her get up, feeling strangely at peace. It had been a long time since he'd truly confided in anyone. Talking with Karina had been nice—even if it *hadn't* ended in the sexy snowbound liaison of his dreams. "Come on. Let's get you back to a warm fire before your lips turn blue."

Karina took his hand. For a moment, her gaze met his head-on—and he'd have sworn he glimpsed pure desire in her eyes. But then she blinked, squeezed his hand, and got to her feet.

"A fire sounds nice," Karina said. "But I'm *so* wet right now. First I'm going to have to take off all these clothes."

Reflexively, Reid tightened his grasp. Karina gave him an impish, not quite innocent smile, then sashayed downhill.

Oh man. Christmas had better come soon, Reid thought. Because while he was waiting for the big day to finally arrive—and free him from his obligations to The Christmas House—his amateur attempts at platonic friendship just might kill him.

That's if unrequited lust didn't finish him off first.

Watching Karina turn and motion for him to join her, a big smile on her face and a sexy wiggle in her hips, Reid realized it was shaping up to be a race: his good intentions versus his animal nature. Before Christmas Eve, he was bound to crack.

It was inevitable. But would he give in to friendship and gooey emotion first? he wondered. Or would the need to join with Karina until they were as close, as sweaty, and as carnally satisfied as possible emerge victorious in the end?

From where Reid stood, it looked like a dead heat.

And from where Karina stood?

Well, Reid hoped like hell she couldn't tell how much she was getting to him just then. Because if she ever realized exactly how he felt about her, he wouldn't stand a chance. His globe-trotting ways would be headed straight for the permanently endangered list, and his heart would be as malleable as holiday fudge in her hands. And no right-thinking man wanted that.

Did he . . . ?

Chapter Thirteen

Date: December 20th
Edgware Project Name: The Christmas House
Guest Service Rating: A+
Guest Accommodations Rating: A+
Guest Satisfaction Rating: F— (SCORE COULD EASILY BE
IMPROVED, GIVEN ADDITIONAL ONE-ON-ONE ATTENTION FROM
ACTING B&B MANAGER)

Okay. So Karina would be the first to admit that deliberately taunting Reid with the idea of getting naked in front of
a nice, cozy fireplace wasn't exactly fair. But was it fair that
he'd tortured her yesterday with all that touching and gazing
into her eyes? Was it fair that he'd intrigued her with his
retelling of how he'd returned stateside to help out his elderly
grandparents? Was it fair that he'd stood there, all handsome
and brawny and wonderful, and called her *Pollyanna?*

Of all the heroines of literature, song, myth, and Disney
musical features (animated and otherwise), the very last one
a grown woman wanted to be likened to was Pollyanna. Seriously. Nobody trotted out a sexy Pollyanna costume at Halloween, looking to shed her ordinary persona and try out
something a little more *stupidly optimistic.*

Even more than all that, though, it wasn't fair that Reid had confided in her! Until he'd done that, Karina had been doing all right. Not perfectly, but all right. She'd managed to hold her ground and resist jumping into his arms—at least any more than she already had before their snow fight. Then, listening to Reid describe the ongoing Edgware evaluation and his efforts to cope with it—all while trying to bring together the stressed-out staff of The Christmas House—she'd positively *melted*.

What kind of man put aside his work and traveled halfway around the world (literally) to help out his family? What kind of man good-naturedly shouldered the worries of a dozen B&B staff members and dedicated himself to helping them? What kind of man truly believed in things like loyalty and trust?

The kind of man she was deliberately deceiving, that's who.

Brought up short by that reminder of her unwelcome role at The Christmas House, Karina stopped in the midst of tromping downstairs at the B&B. With her arms full of wrapped gifts, she gazed at the tableau below her. As usual, the foyer looked cheery, all decked out in traditional Christmas regalia. The front room sparkled with holiday lights, two Christmas trees, and a full contingent of her fellow guests. In their midst, Karina glimpsed Reid, looking more charming and handsome than ever, with his tough-guy build and burgeoning beard stubble.

Was it her imagination, or had his beard grown even darker?

As she watched him, trying to decide, Reid laughed with Rocky and Neil. Suzanne wandered over too, then launched into another one of her anecdotes. She was, Karina had learned, a born storyteller. Reid could be quite the raconteur too, she'd noticed, with a variety of stories based on his travels.

With a sigh, Karina gazed longingly at Reid. He didn't have to know she was here, pining over him. While he was occupied with the other guests, she could look her fill. She could imagine the two of them together having a Christmas all to themselves. She could fantasize that Reid *did* want to come to California, that they'd blend their two families into one happy bunch, that they'd find some commonality in their approaches to life and be better people because of being together, that they—

Right on cue, Reid glanced up at her. He smiled.

Karina smiled back. She just couldn't help it. A grin nudged at the corners of her mouth, spread to the rest of her face, then seemed to fill her heart with lightness. She liked Reid *so* much. Being forced apart from him was so unfair!

As though punctuating that fact, Karina's cell phone rang, kicking into a mocking ringtone rendition of "Santa Baby."

She wrenched her gaze away from Reid, who went back to his conversation. She adjusted her armload of wrapped gifts, took out her phone, then glanced at the display. *Stephanie.* Uh-oh.

"Hey, Steph! How's it going?" Deliberately making her tone cheerful, Karina swiveled on the staircase. She headed back upstairs, where it would be quieter. "How's Blake?"

"He's feeling better," her sister said. "His fever's down."

"That's great!" Relieved to hear her nephew was recovering, Karina ducked into an alcove. Like every other nook and corner of The Christmas House, it was heavily decorated, boasting an array of garland, lights, and potpourri. She sank on a chair, letting her gifts fall to her lap. At the window beside her, snow drifted past the panes. "What does the doctor say?"

"Mostly to keep an eye on him and let him rest."

"That's easier said than done with a four-year-old, right?"

"No kidding!" Stephanie laughed, sounding more like her usual self. "I'm pretty relieved, though. It was touch and go for a while there." She inhaled. "So . . . how's the evaluation going?"

"Um, all right. It's a little tricky to focus"—*with the man of my dreams in constant proximity*—"but I think I'm compiling a good assortment of notes about The Christmas House."

"I checked the Edgware database. You haven't uploaded anything yet. Are you having trouble figuring out the system?"

"No. It looks pretty straightforward—a lot like the system we use at the college to keep track of our students." *Speaking of which . . . None of my students have contacted me lately. That's strange. Don't they need me anymore?* "I've been really busy, that's all. They have a lot of holiday activities here."

"I know! I'll bet Olivia, Michael, and Josh are loving it."

"They are." *Especially the parts that involve Reid, Alexis, and Nicole.* "They've already made some new friends here, too."

Stephanie sounded glad. "I knew they would. How about you?"

"I've . . . met some people too. Everyone is very nice."

"Karina! You're not spending all your time working on your Edgware evaluation, are you? You're supposed to be having fun too! I know all those checklists and spreadsheets can seem daunting—"

There are spreadsheets? She'd been diligently filling out the appropriate Edgware checklists every day, but she hadn't noticed any spreadsheets. Uncomfortably, Karina recalled reviewing the files her sister had entrusted her with. Frankly, she *had* found them daunting. She'd better get busy. Busier!

"—but they're not that time-consuming. The trick is to chip away at them, day by day, instead of saving them up for the end of your stay." Steph laughed. "You don't want to wake up the day after Christmas and have a bunch of Edgware homework to do."

Nope. I want to wake up the day after Christmas in Reid's arms . . . with a brand-new life stretching ahead of us.

No. Wait. She couldn't want that! She wasn't in the market for a new life. Was she?

"I know, Steph," Karina said. "I promise I'll get it done."

"I know you will. Thanks again. Talk to you soon!"

After a little more chitchat, they said their good-byes. Karina disconnected her call with Steph, then noticed she had a few new text messages from Chelsea. She debated opening them.

Then she shook her head. Chelsea's messages would have to wait. Karina simply couldn't deal with her ex-husband's girlfriend right now. All of a sudden, it felt as though she had a million things to do and not enough time to do them in.

Frazzled and guilt stricken, she headed downstairs. First she'd add these gifts to the growing pile beneath the communal Christmas House tree in the foyer. Then she'd hunt down Michael, Olivia, and Josh and make sure they were having a good time. Then she'd review all the Edgware paperwork, check in with her incommunicado college students, try uploading her evaluation notes, participate in a few more holiday activities with her children, buy the few remaining gifts on her list . . .

Argh! All at once, her Christmas vacation was running dangerously low on holiday spirit, Karina realized. And despite her usual can-do attitude, she had no idea how to fix it.

". . . and that's how you make an igloo," Reid said. "One block at a time, all around the circle, until you have a good shelter from the cold." He hunkered down, exaggeratedly rubbing his arms and blowing on his hands. Then he stepped inside the igloo circle and relaxed with apparent warm bliss. "See?"

For this demonstration, Reid had employed a makeshift four-sided wooden form to make snow blocks. In the wilderness, he'd have compacted the snow by stomping it with his feet, then cut out blocks with a snow saw to form an emergency shelter. That meant this igloo wasn't 100 percent authentic. But the two Barrett boys, who'd ventured onto the B&B's snowy grounds with him today, didn't seem to care.

"Cool!" they cried in unison. Identically bundled against the cold, Josh and Michael gazed at the snow blocks Reid had compacted. "How did you learn how to do that?"

"I spent some time on an expedition in Greenland."

"Greenland?" Michael wrinkled his nose. "Where's that?"

Debating how best to explain geography to a six-year-old, Reid looked around. In the end, he located a fallen tree branch, then used it to draw a crude map in the snow. He started out with a depiction of Greenland, then expanded his sketchy drawing to encompass Australia, Africa, Japan, and Spain.

"Wow," Josh said. "You've been to *all* those places?"

"All those and more." Reid smiled. "I like traveling."

Michael frowned. "Do Alexis and Nicole like traveling too?"

For the first time, Reid debated how to answer that question. Ordinarily, he would have been certain. *Yes. My daughters love traveling!* But right now, with Karina's words from yesterday still ringing in his ears, he wasn't so sure.

Even if I could travel the world, I wouldn't. Not at my kids' expense. I mean, there's school, and friends, and . . .

"I think they do," he said honestly. "I hope they do."

"I'd miss my room," Michael told him. "And all my stuff."

"I'd miss my friends," Josh added. "And my PS3."

"But you're traveling right now, and you like it." Reid started on another snow block. He guided the boys as they copied the steps he demonstrated. "You've got a nice room here at the B&B, right? And you're making new friends while you're here."

"I guess so." Josh shrugged, then dug his knees deeper in

the snow. "It's not the same, though. Those are vacation friends. Everyone knows vacation friends aren't real friends."

"Yeah." With boyish exuberance, Michael compacted another snow block in his mittened hands. Josh stacked it on the igloo's foundation. "You don't care that much if your vacation friends are nice to you or not, because if you don't like them, you can just go do the next activity in the Fun Zone all by yourself."

"Yeah." Sagely, Josh nodded. "And even if you really, *really* like them, it doesn't matter anyway. Because you're going to be leaving in a week or two. And so are they. So why bother going crazy making friends? You might as well stay by yourself."

"Or with your brother," Michael added. He smiled at Josh.

"I'll take real friends over vacation friends any day. Vacation friends are okay, but they're temporary." Josh made a face. "Just like my dad. He's temporary now too. We only see him on the weekends. And his girlfriend, Chelsea, is *always* there."

Temporary didn't sound good—at least not when it came to fathers. Reid glanced at Michael, wondering at his reaction to that. But the youngest Barrett boy only heaved a sigh.

"I wish Alexis and Nicole were my real friends," he said.

Aww. Reid couldn't help smiling at that. "You do?"

"Yeah." Michael nodded, still packing the snow. "They're nice. And Nicole shared her cookies with me one time too."

"Don't be stupid." Josh poked him, wearing a look of brotherly disdain. "You can have cookies whether you have friends or not. There are tons of cookies all over this place!"

While Michael and Josh debated the relative availability of cookies, Reid gazed contemplatively across the snowy grounds. Not far from the B&B's main building, he spied Alexis and Nicole. They sat hunched together in The Christmas House's decorated gazebo, knee-to-knee and face-to-face.

Their pose appeared serious. Their demeanor practically screamed *isolated.*

Did his daughters share the Barrett boys' views on vacation friends not being "real"? For Nicole and Alexis, travel was their life. Did that mean Reid had deprived them of authentic friends?

Struck by the notion, he examined them more closely.

As though sensing his scrutiny, Alexis and Nicole glanced up. They saw him watching. They froze. Then Alexis elbowed her sister, Nicole clamped shut her gaping mouth, and they both jerked themselves into blatantly innocent postures. All but whistling with unconvincing cartoony nonchalance, they got up and headed back inside. His daughters, Reid was reminded, would make terrible poker players . . . and probably had, in the Outback.

Aside from being an expert guide and unrepentant whiskey lover, his friend Shane was also pretty fond of five-card stud.

"Hey, Reid." Josh looked up. "Did you ever eat whale?"

"Or shark?" Michael's eyes gleamed. "How about walrus?"

"No, yes, and yes." Pulled from his pensive state of mind by their questions, Reid redirected his attention to the diminutive igloo they were building. "How about you guys?"

"Ugh! No way!" Michael collapsed into giggles. "Yuck!"

"I'd do it." Josh squared his shoulders. "No problem."

"Hmmm. I see." With a thoughtful nod, Reid smiled at the boy. "Now *you,* Josh, would make a good poker player."

"Really?" Josh appeared delighted. "You think so?"

"You can already bluff. That's half the battle," Reid declared. The boy reminded him of himself just then. The realization made him feel . . . almost nostalgic. It might have been nice to raise boys, he thought. He'd have liked to have had a larger family. But he'd put those plans on hold when things had gone south with Gabby. "If you want, I'll teach you how to play sometime," he offered the Barrett boys. "We can use pinecones for chips. There are lots of those lying around here."

"Nah. We should bet real money!" Michael's eyes lit up again. "I'm pretty good at games. Even aggravating ones, like Chutes and Ladders. I think I could win. And I *don't* want any boring old pinecones either. Who wants to win pinecones?"

Reid laughed, shaking his head. "I think your mother might have something to say about us playing poker for real money."

"I doubt it." Josh neatened the edges of a block of snow. "You wouldn't *believe* what it takes before our mom even notices what's going on! She's been pretty distracted lately."

"Yeah." Michael nodded. "She took us to school when she was wearing her PJs."

The boy made a face, clearly aggrieved at the memory.

"Shut up, Michael!" Josh frowned at him, then shot a self-conscious look at Reid. He gave his brother a shove. "It wasn't a big deal. At least we *have* a school. Alexis and Nicole don't. We're not supposed to rub it in, remember? Olivia told us—"

"I *wasn't* rubbing it in! *I* think it's cool that Alexis and Nicole have their own teacher all to themselves. Amanda is nice. If Mrs. Wheeler would be just *my* teacher, that would be great!"

Josh glanced at Reid. "He's in love with his teacher," he explained, rolling his eyes. "It's a stage. We've all been through it. But Mrs. Wheeler is *not* exactly thrilled."

At Josh's world-weary tone, Reid stifled a grin. "Mrs. Wheeler is probably just playing it cool, that's all," he said. "First-grade teachers are famous for being especially lovable. So it's no wonder Michael's fallen for this one."

"See, Josh? *Reid* understands!" Michael crowed. His gaze, glowing and happy, settled on Reid. "Thanks, Reid."

"No problem. I'm happy to help," Reid told him. "Just

remember, when the time comes to move on from Mrs. Wheeler—"

"I'll *never* move on!" Michael vowed, eyes wide. "Never!"

"—just promise me you'll let her down easy, okay?"

Michael appeared to consider that. Then, solemnly, he gave Reid a nod. "Okay. I promise I'll be gentle with Mrs. Wheeler."

"Good man."

"But I still won't ever quit loving her!"

"I know." Reid gave Michael's knit cap an affectionate tug. He smiled at the boy. "Once you give a woman your heart, you don't ever get it back. Not all in one piece anyway."

Josh nodded. "He means because it's broken," he informed Michael in a sophisticated tone. "Women break your heart."

"Not all the time," Reid surprised himself by saying. "Sometimes, a woman makes your heart feel bigger too." *Like your mom does to me.* "Sometimes, I feel as though my heart is just pushing at my chest, growing way too big to be contained."

Josh squinted. Nodded. "That's just a hard-on, Reid. It happens to every guy some of the time. You'll get over it."

Straight-faced, Reid looked at him. "You think so?"

"Yeah. It's not a big deal. My mom told me so." Josh sighed. "She wanted to give me a book about it too, but she decided to wait until my dad was around to have a 'discussion.'"

Josh shook his head, as though the vagaries of adult interaction were beyond ridiculous. Reid smiled at him, wondering if Karina knew exactly how far afield her motherly attempts to explain love and anatomy to her son had gone.

"I have to disagree with your mom on that one," he said. "It's *always* a big deal." And not in a ribald sense either. Love—and hard-ons—were nothing to joke about. "The first time a girl makes you feel as though your heart is getting bigger, Josh . . . Well, you won't ever forget her, that's for sure."

"Like Mrs. Wheeler!" Michael piped up.

"That's right," Reid agreed, adding another snow block.

"Sure," Josh declared. "Maybe. Until you go and get divorced from her. Then I'll bet you forget all about her."

And the three kids you had with her too! his wounded expression said. Saddened by his tone, Reid frowned. He couldn't help whatever hurt feelings Josh had about his parents' divorce. But he could tell the truth now. So that's exactly what he did.

"Some people are way too special to be forgotten about," Reid said. "I'd put the two of you firmly in that category."

Michael grinned openly. Shyly, Josh ducked his head.

"Not just anyone learns how to make an igloo this quickly," Reid pointed out as proof. "You boys are geniuses at this."

This time, Josh did look up. Then he grinned too.

More importantly, though, he also withdrew from his pocket Reid's B&B keys. With an oh-so-casual movement, Josh dropped the keys on the snow, just out of sight behind their miniature igloo. At the movement, Reid raised his eyebrows.

He'd noticed when Josh had pinched his keys, of course, right before the boy had lofted that diversionary question about eating whales. Josh might have the makings of a budding poker player, as Reid had pointed out, but he was hardly a master thief. His actions had been easy to track—especially for Reid, a man who'd traveled among the world's best pickpockets.

"Hey, you found my keys." Reid plucked them from the snow.

Josh's cheeks colored scarlet. "Uh, yeah. I did."

"In your pocket," Reid clarified. "You stole them."

"No, I didn't! I borrowed them, that's all."

"You stole them. That's wrong."

"I couldn't help it." Josh gulped. "I was upset."

"Learn to help it," Reid told him. "Practice. Whenever you feel like sneaking something into your pocket, just wait. Thirty seconds, two minutes . . . whatever you can manage.

You can do it. Eventually, you won't feel like taking anything anymore."

"Oh yeah? Well, maybe I don't want to." Stubbornly, Josh stared at the igloo. He folded his arms, his parka crinkling. "Maybe that's a stupid idea, and I'm not going to do it."

Reid shrugged. "Okay. Suit yourself." He nudged Michael, jolting the boy out of what appeared to be a growing fascination with his miscreant brother. "Hey, good job on that last ice block. How about if we take a break for some hot cocoa?"

"Yeah!" Michael leaped to his feet, snow pants and all. His knees were caked with snow. "Do you have marshmallows too?"

"I think so. We can check with the cooks." Reid smiled at him. Then he turned to a sulking Josh. "You coming, Josh?"

The boy ignored him, his butt firmly planted on the snow.

"If you're going to stay out here," Reid said, "see if you can straighten up that bottom row. Our igloo looks crooked."

With relish, Josh kicked his booted foot through one of the snow blocks they'd made. It shattered upon impact.

Blandly, Reid examined the damage. Beside him, Michael goggled. He took Reid's hand. Reid squeezed it reassuringly.

"You can join us inside whenever you want, Josh," he said.

Then he guided Michael back toward The Christmas House for that cup of cocoa. Behind them, snow blocks disintegrated under Josh's kicking feet, sending powdery flurries into the air. Reid just kept going. Next to him, Michael glanced back worriedly.

"Josh looks mad," he said. "Is he going to be okay?"

"Yep." Reid tossed his keys in his gloved hand, listening to the grunting and kicking behind him. A clump of snow sailed into the air, then shattered on Reid's head. Brushing off its remnants, Reid gave a nostalgic grin. He couldn't help being reminded of his own childhood . . . all over again. "Josh is going to be fine. Just as soon as he gets whatever's bugging him out of his system."

"But . . . wait." Michael's worried gaze met his. "Don't you think we should stay here and talk to him about it? That's what my mom does. She talks. A lot. About everything. She says talking helps people."

"Talking is good," Reid agreed. "But maybe not this time."

"Not this time?" Michael seemed flabbergasted at the very idea—and a little thrilled too. "Why not?"

"Because we might need to save our energy," Reid said, still listening to Josh's destructive fury as they walked toward the B&B. "We might need to build Josh more than one igloo."

Chapter Fourteen

... From the desk of Betty Sullivan
DECEMBER 21ST
LOCATION: THE CHRISTMAS HOUSE
SCHEDULED EVENT: "OLD-FASHIONED GARLAND
MAKING: POPCORN & CRANBERRIES"—2:00 P.M. TO
4:00 P.M.

By the time Reid encountered his fourth mishap in two days' time at The Christmas House, he started feeling fed up. First, someone left on a hose outside overnight, causing the B&B's pipes to freeze and creating an impromptu ice patch in the front yard. It looked dangerous—and it was—until Reid recruited Nate and a few other locals to purposely thicken the ice and turn it into a bona fide (if pint-sized) ice-skating rink. Then it looked like fun, especially to his more adventuresome guests.

"You're lucky you caught this." Nate shook his head as he watched their winter visitors glide across the ice on borrowed skates. "Someone could have slipped and fallen out here."

"And sued the B&B for all it's worth!" Vanessa added.

"It's fine now," Reid said. "Especially with the warning signs and temporary fencing we put up." Then he went on to deal with the next disaster: a huge, black gash of graffiti plastered on one of the B&B's signature transport vans.

Standing beside Reid as he examined it, Josh woefully shook his head. "It looks like the van that takes you to prison."

Feeling concerned despite himself, Reid frowned. "How do you know what the van that takes you to prison looks like?"

"Easy." Josh affected a macho pose. "Video games."

"Huh." Warmly, Reid tugged on the boy's hood. "Figures."

"We could have it repainted," one of Reid's staff members suggested. "But the van would be out of service for a few days."

"That won't work. We've got our annual holiday lights tour tonight!" Agitatedly, Vanessa consulted their grandmother's schedule. "It's one of the biggest events of the year in Kismet, aside from the Christmas parade. How are we supposed to transport all our guests to Glenrosen"—the neighborhood most famous for its holiday lights display—"if we're short a van?"

"I dunno." Then the staff member suggested, "Travel in shifts?"

"That could work," Reid agreed. He didn't understand the appeal of staring at other people's yards full of Christmas lights anyway. Boooring. But then he glanced at Vanessa, who was worriedly scrutinizing her clipboard, and knew he had to solve this issue. For her. "I have another idea," he said. "Wait here. I'll be right back. I need to consult with an expert first."

Ten minutes later, upon Reid's instructions, Amanda was leading all their guests—children and willing adults alike—in a spontaneous decoupage session. Armed with a full contingent of craft supplies, a couple of stepladders, and a great deal of holiday cheer, Nicole and Alexis's nanny/tutor tackled the job with her usual vigor. In a surprisingly short period of time, the offensive graffiti was gone—replaced by cheerful, handily shellacked holiday gift wrap, completely covering the van.

Dubiously, Michael peered at it. "It looks like Christmas barfed all over the van." Slowly, he grinned. "I *love* it!"

"It's . . . unique," Karina said when she saw it. Alexis and Nicole, who hadn't strayed far from her side for days, nodded in agreement. They twirled their pink spangled scarves. They bobbed their heads, making their glitter-covered, felt reindeer-antler headbands wiggle. "It definitely says 'The Christmas House.'"

At their headgear, Reid did a double take. His daughters usually weren't fans of girly, froufrou accessories. But for the duration of their time stateside, Reid had decided not to bug them about it. Alexis and Nicole were getting older. Maybe they were enjoying having Karina's feminine influence in their lives. They definitely seemed to be enjoying Olivia's "sisterly" influence. The three girls had become nearly inseparable.

Besides, it wasn't long before the third problem popped up, and Reid had to deal with that. It started out innocently enough. He came downstairs one morning, feeling as though he'd slept surprisingly well for a man who'd spent several consecutive nights celibately alone in his big, empty sleigh bed, and found himself stepping on . . . something. Frowning, he lifted his booted foot and plucked off a shard of . . . something.

Squinting, Reid identified it. A piece of gift wrap.

It felt wet and sloppy, and it looked frayed at the edges, too. Realizing it was probably a remnant of the van decoupage session, he threw it in the trash, then went to get some coffee.

Partway there, he ran into Vanessa. His cousin already had her coffee. She held her cup aloft as she scrutinized the hall floor. As he watched, she balanced on one foot, then pulled a scrap of red and green gift wrap from the sole of her boot.

"There's gift wrap out here too, huh?" Reid asked.

"Yeah. It's weird. I've been finding these bits of paper all over the place today." Vanessa crossed the hallway to discard the errant gift wrap in a bin. Then she directed her gaze higher, to his darkly stubbled jawline. Her grin broadened. "You too, Sasquatch?"

Reid rubbed his face. "I'm on strike from shaving."

"Hmmm. Any particular reason?"

Reid thought of Karina—and the way she'd all but purred as she'd stroked his shadowy beard, the one night they'd been together. "It reminds me of happier days. Until they come back, I'm not shaving again. It's . . . a Zen tactic I learned in Tibet."

"Uh-huh. Since when is a nookie beard 'Zen'?"

Busted. Reid decided to play dumb. "Huh?"

"If Karina is over you already," his cousin opined regretfully, "then growing a gnarly nookie beard won't help."

"It's not gnarly." And the idea of Karina being over him didn't bear thinking about. Offended, Reid frowned at the floor. He spotted a few more scraps of gift wrap. He bent to pick them up. "And I've never heard of a nookie beard. You made that up."

"Hmmm. Maybe I did. Maybe I didn't." Giving him a contemplative look, Vanessa slurped more coffee. "Either way . . . do Alexis and Nicole know you're pining over their new best friend? They might have something to say about your hooking up with Karina, now that they're so close with her and Olivia."

"No. But who knows?" Reid said semidefensively. "They might be fans of the idea of my hooking up with Karina."

Which was ridiculous, it occurred to him. His daughters didn't even know about him and Karina. As far as he knew, they hadn't even guessed about his onetime liaison with her. But Reid sure as hell hadn't asked Alexis and Nicole if he could do the wild thing with Helene. So why was he considering what his daughters' reactions to another hookup with Karina might be?

He'd always shielded Nicole and Alexis from the romantic side of his private life. Over the past few years, Reid had turned down more invitations than he'd taken advantage of. He hadn't wanted to create conflicts with his daughters' needs or compromise the time he wanted to spend with them. Thinking about things now, though, Reid realized it might be nice if he could have a relationship with a woman openly. Lovingly. Enjoyably.

"For all you know," he told his cousin, "Nicole and Alexis might give their blessing to my being with Karina." *So there.*

His triumph was short-lived. Vanessa gasped.

"Aha! You've thought about it then!" she said. "You've thought about what Alexis and Nicole would think if you and Karina got together full-time." Vanessa's know-it-all grin broadened. Aggravatingly. "That means you're serious, cuz!"

He was? "I never said that. You're getting ahead of—"

"You're really into Karina! Oh. My. God!" Vanessa put down her coffee cup, then busted into a dance move. "Alexis and Nicole are going to have a stepsister! And stepbrothers! Cool!"

Belatedly, Reid realized he had to ignore this outburst. Vanessa was only upping the ante in an effort to make him confirm or deny her suspicions. This was a fishing expedition, pure and simple. He couldn't play along. It was better, he'd learned, *not* to encourage Vanessa's matchmaker tendencies.

His cousin thought she was a master relationship builder. In reality, she was terrible at knowing who might be happy together. She would do better as a professional *breakup* artist. But everyone who knew Vanessa loved her too much to put an end to her "hobby." When confronted with Vanessa's joyful pride in her "skills," everyone who knew her simply caved in . . . and let her go on believing in her supposed romantic expertise.

One of these days, Reid knew, someone would regret that.

"It's about time you quit gallivanting all over the place and settled down to a regular life," Vanessa said. "We've all been waiting for you to come to your senses, you know."

No. Reid hadn't known that. But he should have guessed, given the thinly veiled criticism he'd been getting from his Kismet friends, neighbors, and relatives about "being responsible" and "getting on board" with a "normal job." Even Karina had jumped in with both feet, Reid remembered, on the day of her sleigh ride accident. She'd all but come out and said his globe-trotting ways were selfish and unfair to his daughters.

He hadn't liked that much. That's why he hadn't given it any further thought. Although he *had* thought about Karina. . . .

"Does Karina know how you feel?" Vanessa prodded. "Did you tell her? What did she say?" She hugged herself. "I *knew* it! I knew the two of you would be a perfect match. Yes! Score!"

Uh-oh. On second thought, if Vanessa thought she'd put together him and Karina, they were doomed for sure.

Uneasily, Reid frowned. He needed to end this. Now.

"There's more wrapping paper under that table." He headed in that direction and picked it up. "It's forming a trail. . . ."

He tracked the remnants of tattered, twisted, occasionally sodden bits of colorful paper. Some were gilded. Some were textured. Some were stuck together with tape fragments. All led down the hallway toward the B&B's front room.

"I can tell by your stupid macho silence that you haven't said a word to Karina about how you feel." Vanessa trailed him, her voice and footsteps right behind him. "You've got to tell her that you love her! You were just like this before you and Gabby got engaged. Do you remember? You were moody and curt—"

"Shut up. Pick up the paper."

"See?" Vanessa crowed. "Moody! And curt! It's love!"

"It's not love." Abruptly, Reid brought a larger scrap of gift wrap to his nose. It smelled familiar. "It's liver treats."

His cousin laughed. "Look, I know you've been living in some pretty remote locales lately, but if that's your idea of a romantic declaration, we have a *lot* of work to do. What if Karina is vegan? Liver treats won't exactly endear you to her."

"No." Impatiently, Reid waggled the paper at Vanessa. "It's liver treats. On the gift wrap." He took a few more steps, all the way into the B&B's front room. "Somehow, for some reason, someone smeared liver treats all over this wrapping paper."

A rhythmic thumping sound alerted him to a possible outcome of that action. Reid followed it . . . all the way to Digby the dachshund. The dog lay amid dozens of ripped-apart gift packages, tail wagging madly, as he tore into another box.

"Oh. No." Vanessa exhaled. "Look at all the packages!"

"Or at least what's left of them." Peering through the wreckage of chewed-up gift wrap, Reid identified sweaters and scarves, toys and books, CDs and games and bottles of perfume. Swaddling them all were festively colored drifts of slobbered-on wrapping paper, courtesy of Digby. "No wonder I slept so well last night," Reid said. "My hyperactive roommate was—"

"Stop!" Vanessa held up her palm. "Don't shatter my illusions! Now is *not* the time to reminisce about your hot date." She added encouragingly, "Unless it was Karina?"

"—down here destroying all our guests' Christmas gifts."

Without Digby snoring, pacing, and playing with his chew toy all night, Reid realized, he'd been able to snooze freely.

Appearing baffled, Vanessa picked up a floating scrap of gift wrap. She sniffed it. Winced. "Phew. This stuff stinks!"

"Digby seems to like it." Reid patted the dog. He shooed him outside, then methodically began cleaning up gift wrap.

When his guests got wind of this destruction, they wouldn't be happy. They'd entrusted the B&B with their gifts, which had been accumulating under both Christmas trees for days now, following several B&B-sponsored shopping trips. The Christmas House had promised to keep those gifts safe. Instead, they'd inadvertently allowed them to be strewn far and wide, separated from their identifying tags, and dappled with dog drool.

How, Reid wondered, was he going to explain this?

"Did someone actually smear liver treats on wrapping paper and leave it under the tree?" Mystified, Vanessa picked up an empty box lid. She used it to corral the paper she gathered. "If so, we'd better keep that in mind for next year. No dog treats allowed. Nothing edible, period. That way, next year—"

"We won't be here next year. Edgware will be."

"Oh. Yeah." His cousin sighed. "Still . . . What a mess!"

"And nobody wrapped up liver treats." Reid extracted a piece of gold foil from beneath a chair. "This stuff is all over the packages. It's tucked into the folds, made into a paste and smeared all over the outside edges. It's sabotage. Again."

"Sabotaged by liver treats?" Vanessa sighed. "Come on."

"Do you have a better explanation?" Reid asked.

"No, but—" Vanessa broke off, shaking her head. "Our guests are going to be disappointed when they see this. And the Edgware evaluator . . . Ugh. This makes us look totally inept. We'd better get busy." His cousin dropped to her knees beside the closest Christmas tree. She scooped up more paper, then stuffed it in the rapidly filling box lid. "If we hurry, we can replace the most ripped-up gifts with empty boxes. You know—stand-in gifts. That will buy us time to replace what needs to be replaced, surreptitiously identify which gifts belong with which guests—"

"No stand-ins. And no sneaking around, either. We'll have to let everyone know what happened, right up front," Reid said. "Maybe at the 'very merry breakfast' this morning." Had he just said "very merry breakfast"? With a complete lack of irony? This place was changing him—and not for the better. "We'll have to describe the ruined items, offer to replace them at the B&B's expense, reunite everything else with its proper owners—"

"No! We can't do that." Vanessa shook her head. "These are Christmas gifts, remember? *They're* supposed to be surprises. And *we're* supposed to be providing our guests with a picture-perfect Christmas! We can't just announce what's left here and wait for people to claim it. That would totally ruin the holiday—especially for the kids. They're bound to recognize their wish list items being talked about." Again, she shook her head. "Do *you* want to explain there's no Santa Claus?"

"Well," Reid began, "if someone has to do it—"

"Argh!" His cousin dropped her hands to her hips, both fists full of crumpled gift wrap. "You really *are* clueless about Christmas, aren't you? We. Can't. Do. That. We have to be sneakier, or we'll spoil all the surprises!"

Reid frowned. "Lying to kids is never the answer."

"Whatever, Scrooge. I suppose you crushed Nicole's and Alexis's hopes about the Easter Bunny and the Tooth Fairy too?"

"What hopes?" As far as he knew, they hadn't had any.

Vanessa gave a clucking sound of disapproval. "I say we hide this whole mess, go downtown and secretly buy new things, then concoct a good cover story—one that *won't* clue in the Edgware evaluator to our latest mishap. There's still plenty of time before any of our guests wake up and discover this."

At the doorway, a flicker of movement caught Reid's eye. He glanced up, now on his hands and knees as well, and glimpsed someone standing there. Karina. She wore at least three sweaters, one scarf, jeans and boots, and a concerned frown.

"Discover what?" she asked. "What's going on?"

Reid shut his mouth, suddenly self-conscious about his "nookie beard." But Vanessa had no such compunctions about gabbing.

"Karina! Thank God!" his cousin exclaimed, looking relieved. "You'll help us, right? You *always* help. You're a real lifesaver—like when you helped organize the van decoupage."

Karina helped with that? Surprised, Reid gazed at Karina.

"And the hand-painted signs for the new ice-skating rink too." Obviously proud of her protégée, Vanessa waved her hand toward Karina. "You were instrumental in making those, right?"

Karina was involved with the ice-skating rink?

"So we should have guessed you'd show up here, right in the nick of time," Vanessa concluded happily. She gave Karina a shorthand retelling of the damage Digby had wrought—minus Reid's suppositions about sabotage. "You're like our very own magical Christmas elf, Karina. By now, you're practically a staff member of The Christmas House. Heck, you're practically a member of the family!" Meaningfully, Vanessa raised her eyebrows at Reid. "Isn't she, Reid? Isn't Karina practically a Sullivan by now?"

"Sure." He wished Vanessa would put the kibosh on her matchmaking routine—at least while Karina was here. "Almost."

Even if he'd wanted to, though, Reid couldn't deny the truth: He liked having Karina nearby. Just seeing her there made him feel better. He liked seeing her smile, her overload of sweaters, her sexy, curvy hips in those jeans of hers. . . .

Suddenly aware of the wistful way he was watching Karina, Reid made himself quit. He cleared his throat.

His cousin was staring at him. Smugly. And knowingly.

Clearly pleased by his reaction, Vanessa transferred her gaze to Karina again. "Hey! I was thinking . . . Do you want to go downtown with me later to replace some of these gifts?"

"Um, okay." Shooting Reid a cryptic look, Karina tucked something in the pocket of her outermost sweater. Her camera. "If there's a problem with the communal gift exchange, though, I'd just as soon keep my replacement gifts in my room, where they'll be safe. I hope you don't mind."

"You don't have to worry about that," Reid said, wanting to reassure her. "This was a onetime incident. Nothing like this has ever happened before. Ordinarily, everyone keeps their gifts down here in big piles beneath the trees, then unwraps them together at the party on Christmas Day. It's usually a lot of fun. At least *I* liked it, when I was a kid here at the B&B. It was like spending Christmas with a gigantic extended family."

Karina blinked. "You spent your Christmases here?"

Reid nodded. So did Vanessa. "Every last one of them! We both did. Those were the days, right, Reid? Grammy's fudge, Grandpa's big piles of popcorn and cranberries to string—"

"Grandpa's swearing whenever the cranberries rolled under the TV set and got squashed before we could get them out. He'd be unearthing petrified cranberries all the way till July." Reid sighed, recalling those long-ago family get-togethers with more fondness than he expected. "You know what? We should have a cranberry-and-popcorn-garland-making class this year."

"It's already on the schedule," Karina surprised him by saying. She took a careful step forward through the wreckage, then bent to scoop up some stray gift wrap. "I remember reading about it—'Old-Fashioned Garland Making: Popcorn and Cranberries.'"

Reid frowned. How could Karina know The Christmas House's detailed schedule of activities more thoroughly than he did?

"Wow." Vanessa laughed. "You're good, Karina! Are you sure *you're* not the top-secret Edgware evaluator? Those people are rumored to have special spying gear *and* photographic memories."

"No photographic memory here." Karina gave an unsteady grin. She wadded up more squelchy gift wrap, then tossed it into a bin. "It's just very important to me that this Christmas be perfect—for my kids' sakes. I can't help noticing the details."

Reid couldn't help noticing how jumpy she seemed. Probably, he realized, straight-arrow Karina wasn't entirely comfortable with Vanessa's covert plan to replace the guests' gifts.

Well, neither was he. As far as Reid was concerned, honesty was always the best policy. It would be better to come clean to everyone—all at once—about the damage that had been done, then deal with the consequences as they arose . . . including the consequences of the Edgware evaluator's take on the situation.

He liked knowing that he and Karina were on the same page when it came to telling the truth, though. That was important. Like loyalty, honesty mattered to him. It mattered a lot.

"It probably wasn't the best idea to leave all these gifts down here in the first place," Karina mused in a quiet voice. "I realize the big B&B Christmas party is a tradition—a tradition that involves unwrapping both these huge piles of gifts all together during the party—but sometimes tradition has to bow to practicality. Sometimes it's important to consider liability issues, allergies, insurance premiums, potential theft—"

"Whoa! You sound just like Scrooge over here!" Vanessa laughed, glancing from Karina to Reid. "Take it down a notch, Ebenezer. We've been doing things this way for years!"

"Well . . . maybe you should reconsider that." Karina cast a shuttered glance at Reid. "Maybe, if you said you were sorry and explained to all the guests that you made a mistake, the Edgware evaluator wouldn't knock off too many points for this incident."

Reid stared at her. "What do you know about the evaluator? Do you know who it is?" He'd been trying to guess for days. So far, he'd suspected (and dismissed) Suzanne, Rocky, and another guest, all in turn. But Karina was friends with everyone here. She might have learned something important. "If you've got some inside information about the Edgware evaluation—"

"Geez, Reid! Grill the poor girl, why don't you?" Protectively, his cousin moved to Karina's side. "If you don't want to admit we made a mistake, then don't. Just go along with my plan, and there won't be any apologies necessary. Chances are, the Edgware evaluator didn't even have any gifts under the Christmas trees. Why would he? He's faking!" Vanessa then amended, "Or she is." Looking frustrated, she frowned. "Whoever it is, he or she is only pretending to celebrate Christmas with us."

"That's true," Reid said. How much did he owe someone who was a professional sneak, anyway? "The evaluator's holiday probably hasn't just been wrecked by Digby's snack attack."

"Probably not." Confidently, Vanessa lifted her chin. "So if you *don't* make a big public announcement out of this, the evaluator doesn't ever have to know. We can just gather the tags, discuss the problem with the affected guests *privately,* then get on with our Christmas. Easy peasy."

"Easy peasy, huh?" Vanessa's tactics *would* lead to the same end result as his plan, Reid considered. The affected gifts would be replaced and/or reunited with their appropriate tags, then placed back under the Christmas trees. The holiday would go on, with the Edgware assessor none the wiser. And Reid could get back to spending time with Karina. That sounded pretty good to him. Torn between doing what was honest and doing whatever was necessary to get a positive evaluation for his grandparents, he hesitated. Then he shook his head. "Nope. I'm not hiding this. I'm telling everyone the truth at the 'very merry breakfast.'"

"What?" Vanessa wailed. "Those poor kids! No Santa!"

Karina didn't seem happy about his decision, either. Maybe she was worried the surprises of Olivia's, Josh's, and Michael's gifts would be spoiled, Reid decided. Or maybe the Barrett kids still believed in Santa. Karina *was* a traditionalist, after all.

"With the provision," Reid allowed, "that we speak to the adults and clear the children from the room first."

His cousin harrumphed. "That will only help partway. We'll still get marked down on our evaluation for this! That nitpicky Edgware evaluator probably isn't an eight-year-old, you know." She frowned. "Whoever the evaluator is, they'll be there in the room when you come clean about this. They'll know everything."

"That's true," Reid agreed. "But the fact is, we blew it. We didn't safeguard these gifts." He thought again about his theory—that someone had sabotaged those gifts by doctoring them with liver-treat spread, knowing Digby would likely tear into them. He didn't want to bring it up again, though. Vanessa was skeptical, and Karina didn't need to know. He'd already groused enough to her about running the B&B, when he'd unloaded about how stressed the staff was feeling. "If telling the truth means we get dinged on our evaluation . . . Well, we'll just have to make up for it by doing better in some other area."

Determinedly, Reid smiled, satisfied with that solution.

An instant later, he smelled . . . something. He sniffed.

"Hey." Vanessa sniffed too. "Is that smoke?"

"I think so." Concerned, Reid went to investigate.

It looked as though they'd have to start "doing better" in some other area later. Because apparently, problem number four was on its way . . . and it had the potential to be a real doozy.

* * *

It was not a doozy. It was only a minor mishap, Reid realized almost immediately, caused by the inattentiveness of the B&B's kitchen staff . . . with one surprising addition.

"Amanda? What are you doing down here?" Skidding to a stop in the center of the kitchen, Reid recognized his daughters' nanny/tutor first. He spotted the charred pot of smoking liquid on the stovetop second. He realized he would not have to evacuate The Christmas House or call the fire department third. Relieved but confused, he scanned the room. "Is anyone hurt?"

"No. We're fine. We're all fine!" Nervously, Amanda smiled. She cast a shaky hand toward the abandoned sauce pot. Its contents still emitted smoke into the stovetop's whirring exhaust fan. "Rodrigo was showing me how to make caramel sauce to go with the gingerbread French toast this morning—"

Impatiently, Reid glanced at the new cook—the one he'd hired from the local greasy spoon. Rodrigo shuffled his feet.

"—and we, um, got a little distracted, I guess." Amanda's cheeks blazed pink as she glanced at Rodrigo again. "The next thing we knew, the sugar was burned, the pot was completely blackened, and the caramel sauce was ruined."

Hazily registering the arrival of Karina and Vanessa, who'd followed him from the scene of the gift-wrap disaster in the front room, Reid frowned. He still didn't understand exactly what had happened here. Amanda and Rodrigo had gotten "distracted." So what? They weren't solely responsible for breakfast.

"Where were the other cooks when all this was going on?" he asked. "Shouldn't someone have noticed when the smoke started?"

On the other side of the kitchen, the remaining cooks suddenly got *very* busy with the breakfast preparations.

"Well, *you* noticed!" Amanda laughed. "So I guess that's—"

"They were in the other room, giving us some privacy." Uneasily, Rodrigo straightened. He flicked an apprehensive glance toward his fellow chefs. "I asked them to do it."

Beside him, Amanda gasped. "You did? Awww. *Rodrigo!*"

Rodrigo blushed. He smiled at Amanda. "I just wanted a few minutes alone with you," he confessed in a tender voice. "I knew I would never have the nerve to make my move if they were here."

"Well, you made your move, all right!" She squeezed his hand, appearing overjoyed at his admission. "And I'm glad! So what if the caramel burned?" She giggled. "We'll make more!"

"I'll make a million sweet things with you, *cariño,*" Rodrigo promised with love-struck earnestness. "If you'll let me, I'll fill your whole life with sweetness!"

"Awww!" Karina and Vanessa exclaimed as one. "They're so cute together!"

Reid didn't think so. "You nearly burned down my kitchen."

"But we found true love in the process," Rodrigo said in a dreamy voice. He snapped his gaze to Reid. "And we're sorry about all the smoke! Very, very sorry!"

On the verge of haranguing them both for being so careless, Reid stopped. He glanced at Karina. She was watching Amanda and Rodrigo, wearing a big smile, her eyes filled with . . . yearning?

Even as he wondered about that, he found himself caving in.

"Well, what's done is done," he said. "Just don't let it happen again." With as much sternness as he could muster, he added, "You'll have to redo that caramel sauce too."

Somehow, his warning lacked gusto. And machismo. And

authority, too. Feeling beleaguered and out of sorts, Reid confronted all the astonished gazes that met his.

"Come on! It's Christmas!" he blurted. "Lighten up. If I started firing people over accidents, we'd all be out of work."

He turned, ready to make a stomping exit from the kitchen before he could become 100 percent sappy and ruin his Scroogey reputation forever. But Amanda's voice stopped him.

"Then you're okay with this?" his daughters' nanny/tutor asked him. "You're okay with me and Rodrigo? That's *great!* I've been so worried about how to tell you, but now I won't have to be."

Reid searched her glowing face. Was he really that forbidding to talk to? "Amanda, I can't tell you who to love," he said as gently as he could. "I'm your boss, not your—"

"No! I mean, *tell* you, tell you. All of it." Hastily, Amanda sucked in a breath. She traded a warmhearted glance with Rodrigo. "I've decided to emigrate to the states and attend culinary school full-time. Here in Kismet, just like Rodrigo did. It's my calling! It really is. You know I've always been interested in food, right? I mean, I was always eating *something,* no matter where we went or how weird the food was."

Amanda was staying here? But . . . he needed her. He needed her for Nicole and Alexis. Reid frowned. "The girls and I are leaving right after Christmas. I already have jobs lined up."

Again, Amanda inhaled. Rodrigo squeezed her hand.

"This is a good thing," she said. "Alexis and Nicole like it here in America. If *you* decide to remain stateside for a while too, like everyone here at the B&B has been talking about your doing, they can go to a regular school! They won't need me to tutor them anymore. And since you're running the B&B now—"

"That's temporary," Reid reminded her. "The Christmas House is being sold. After this year, it'll be out of my hands."

"—which you really seem to enjoy doing, and are really good at because of how great you are with people, it will all work out perfectly." Amanda's pleading gaze met his. "Please understand, Mr. Sullivan. I've loved being Alexis and Nicole's nanny. And you've been awesome to work for! Honestly, you have been. It's just that . . . well, I have to follow my heart."

"You've known Rodrigo for less than a week!" Reid said. "How can you change your whole life based on one week?"

"I don't know." Amanda shrugged. "All I know is, I'm going to. When it's right, it's right. I have to do this."

Nearby, Vanessa murmured in agreement. Karina remained silent—but she appeared to be paying unusually close attention to the conversation. Probably, she was a closet romantic.

It was a good thing *he* was immune to sentimentality, Reid realized. These kinds of over-the-top decisions belonged in books and movies, not in real life. Not in *his* life. How was he going to manage without a nanny/tutor for Alexis and Nicole?

"Don't be mad about this!" Amanda begged. "Please. I'll stay in touch. It's not as though I'm abandoning you, you know."

Reid scoffed. "I don't feel abandoned."

But he did. A little.

What the hell was happening to him lately?

"It's about time you and the girls had a regular life anyway," Amanda said. "A normal, responsible, settled-down life. With schools and car pools and a home that *isn't* a collapsible tent, a shabono, a bivouac sack, a bordei, *or* a quinzhee. Without me to worry about, you can all have that!"

"What if I don't want all that?" Reid demanded. "What if I like living in a quinzhee?" He'd spent enough nights in one of those snowy shelters to know they were effective, if not exactly cozy. "It's easier to build than an igloo and just as warm."

Amanda smiled. "You'll like living in a real house more."

"No, I won't." Reid folded his arms, feeling annoyed. "What if I think that's a stupid idea, and I'm not going to do it?"

And what if that sentiment reminded him of . . . something?

It reminded him, he thought abruptly, of Josh. And his temper tantrum outside the igloo.

That igloo was only a snow pile now. It remained to be seen whether Josh would require more than one igloo to work out his feelings about his parents' divorce. Reid was ready, if he did. And Michael had already promised to help him with it, too.

"You can't fight this forever, Magellan," Vanessa told him, bouncing on her toes with every evidence of gleefulness. "Sooner or later, you're going to have to admit it: It's time to grow up, quit wandering the globe, and get down to real life."

Screw that. Reid refused to be keelhauled into a settled-down life he didn't want—a life full of sentimentality, and secrets, and lies about Santa Claus. It wasn't for him.

At least it never had been before.

Meeting their expectant gazes, Reid frowned.

"What it's time for," he said with dignity, "is getting this place back on schedule. I have a B&B to run and a candle-light snowshoe Christmas caroling expedition to plan for—"

Their amused faces only aggravated him more.

"—so if you'll all excuse me, I'm leaving."

Then he stomped outside, ready to hunt down a dozen pairs of snowshoes . . . and forget this incident had ever happened.

Chapter Fifteen

Date: December 21st
Edgware Project Name: The Christmas House
Social Responsibility Rating: A+
Environmental Initiatives Rating: A+
Guest/Staff Interaction Rating: B— (IMPROVING RAPIDLY!)

Strangely enough, it was the swearing that drew her in.

Passing by the open doorway of The Christmas House's management office, Karina heard a colorful string of curse words. She stopped, unsure if she'd really heard them. After all, the B&B's customary Christmas carols were playing on the sound system, the other guests were milling around enjoying the daily "Snowed-In" reception, and she *had* been moving in a rush.

For the past several hours, she'd been frantically running to and fro, helping Vanessa deal with the wrecked Christmas gifts, pinch-hitting for the B&B's usual floral arranger (who was out sick), scribbling notes in her Edgware log, watching a holiday-themed family movie with Michael, Josh, and Olivia, taking surreptitious photos of the B&B's holiday décor, trying to boost the morale of the stressed-out maid she'd found crying outside her room (another guest had complained that his towels didn't smell "Christmassy enough"), dodging a few more text messages from Chelsea, setting up Eric and the kids with their daily videoconference call on her laptop, and consoling Suzanne about the difficulties of buying gifts at the last minute . . . not to mention offering Reid a minor "out" when it came to the Edgware evaluation.

Karina still couldn't believe she'd done that. What kind of secret evaluator volunteered to amend her rating (essentially) on the basis of a heartfelt apology?

Not that she'd thought Reid would go for it. He'd appeared awfully tempted to take Vanessa's advice and try a cover-up of the gift-wrap disaster instead. And then, just when it had appeared that Reid felt no loyalty toward someone who would only pretend to celebrate Christmas with them at the B&B, he'd surprised Karina by announcing he was going to tell the truth.

In the end, Reid might not have a perfectly run B&B (or a replacement nanny/tutor for his daughters), but he did have integrity. Which was (potentially) more than Karina could say for herself. Because in her latest daily Edgware report, written immediately after the "very merry breakfast," she'd purposely downplayed the gift-wrap incident. Technically speaking, that meant Karina had kept her promise to Reid . . . by offering less than 100 percent disclosure on her evaluation. It was enough to make her feel crazy. And conflicted. And disloyal—both to her sister and to Reid. But the truth was, she'd done her best not to think about those issues. She'd been way too busy.

For the past few days, in fact, she'd been helping, shopping, volunteering, spending time with her children, assessing the B&B, arranging flowers, chatting, laughing, touring the Glenrosen holiday lights displays, resisting Reid, and doing her best Pollyanna routine with The Christmas House staff. (Not that she intended to call it that. Ever.) Now, lingering outside the management office doorway, with its decorative trim of evergreen garland, red velvet ribbon, and glowing lights, Karina went still for the first time in hours.

She listened. Then, just as she'd almost decided she'd imagined the whole incident, that un-Christmassy sound came again: an eloquent burst of profanity unlike any she'd ever heard.

Recognizing that voice, Karina smiled. Against her better judgment, she poked her head around the door frame. Reid sat on the office floor amid a jumble of wires and bulbs, his hands full of tangled strings of holiday lights. He swore again.

"Wow. That's impressive. Are you even speaking English?"

Reid looked up. The moment he saw her, the thunderclouds in his expression skittered away. He smiled, then shook his head.

"No, it's French." He demonstrated. "In any language, the easiest words to pick up are the swearwords. They're the ones you hear most often. I can pick a fight in twelve languages, then curse in six more when I get thrown in jail for brawling."

"Oh, come on. You've never been in jail!"

He raised his brows. "Where do you think I got my tattoo?"

Involuntarily, Karina sent her gaze toward his tattoo. She recalled licking it. A rush of heat flooded through her.

"Not jail." She raised her gaze again. "A bordello?"

His tattoo was certainly provocative enough. But maybe that was only her impression. Everything about him made her hot.

Like his laughter, which she heard plenty of now.

"It wasn't a bordello." He gave her an amused, reflective look. "You have no idea what my life is really like."

"Oh yeah?" Irresistibly tempted, Karina took a step nearer. Now she stood at the threshold of the office, fighting an urge to help Reid with those tangled light strings. Helping was in her nature. That was innocent, right? That wasn't failing to resist him for the sake of completing an unbiased and fair evaluation. It was only helping. "Why don't you tell me?"

He quirked his mouth. "By now, I'd have thought Vanessa would have filled you in on every last detail about me."

"She did. I interrogated her pretty heavily while we were shopping downtown. Kismet is charming this time of year."

The interrogation part was true. So was the part about Kismet. She could tell Reid thought she was joking, but Karina *had* peppered her new friend with questions about him. Now she knew a lot more about his upbringing, his history with his ex-wife, Gabby, his progression from restless teenager to footloose world traveler, his views on fatherhood, his likes, his dislikes, his past and his future. All afternoon, she'd told herself she was merely passing the time . . . merely using the common ground she and Vanessa shared as a conversation starter.

Now, Karina admitted the truth to herself: She'd been looking for common ground between her and Reid. She'd been looking for an excuse *not* to avoid being with him. She'd been looking—wistfully and romantically, inspired by Amanda and Rodrigo's unlikely love story—for a tiny glimmer of hope.

Entirely unknowingly, Reid gave her one. "If you're not too busy," he said, "I could use some help untangling these light strings. It's a job that needs four hands to be done properly."

"You want my help?" That was music to her ears.

A nod. "I want . . ." *You,* his heated gaze said. In blatant demonstration of that fact, Reid lowered his voice to a husky, sensual, goose bump–causing level. "Your help. Yes."

Thrilled beyond all reason, Karina shook her head. "Nope, I'm not too busy! Are you kidding? I *always* have time to help. Ask anyone!" She dropped her purse, her Edgware camera, and the box of chocolate-peppermint bark she'd bought to cheer up the maid, leaving everything on the floor outside the B&B's management office. With her booted toe, she nudged everything to the side, where Reid wouldn't see it and realize she *had* been busy already. She didn't want any reason for him to turn down her help, now that he'd actually asked for it. "I'll hold the lights," she offered in her most eager tone, "while you tell me all about what your life is 'really like.' Deal?"

"Hmmm. I don't know." Reid grinned, his shadowy beard highlighting his vivid smile and devilish nature. "Are you sure you're up for it? I've been to some pretty dark places."

Karina shrugged. "I've got enough brightness for us both. Bring it on, tough guy. And pass those lights too."

Several anecdotes later, Reid glanced from Karina's shining face to the clock on the management office wall. He blinked.

Nope. He wasn't imagining things. He'd just spent almost two hours telling Karina what his life was "really like," and she hadn't so much as yawned. She hadn't gone to get a whiskey bottle, suggestively offered him a "massage," challenged him to a fistfight, whipped out a deck of cards, or told him to grow up, be responsible, and get a thirty-year fixed-rate mortgage on a split-level two-bedroom house in the burbs.

Everyone else he could think of would have done one (or more) of those things inside the first ten minutes. Apparently, he'd been keeping company with some pretty impatient types all these years. Which was fairly obvious, it occurred to him. Almost everyone he'd ever been close to had been a thrill seeker like him. Like him, they'd all wanted more. They'd wanted it harder. Faster. Different.

Exotic, untested, and dangerous.

It didn't get much more dangerous than this closeness he felt with Karina, Reid realized. It didn't get much more real.

On the face of it, that sounded ridiculous. But there was no denying the truth. Right now, sitting companionably next to Karina, Reid felt the same clench in his belly, the same uptick in his heartbeat, the same surge of adrenaline he always did when tackling something risky. Evidently, this was what he got for throwing down that idiotic request for Karina to help him.

Remembering it now, Reid stifled a grin.

He hadn't really needed *help* untangling Christmas lights. He was a grown man! He was a man who'd scaled Kilimanjaro, ridden camels, gone deep-sea diving, and survived a month in the Arctic Circle. The plain truth was, Reid didn't need *help* with much of anything in life. He never had. But something had made him ask Karina to stay tonight . . . and right now, he was glad he had. Even if doing so had required a tiny little fib.

I want . . . your help. Yes.

He hadn't wanted her help. For him, the idea was laughable.

What he'd wanted, Reid knew, was *her*—irredeemably and constantly—the same way he had since he'd met her. He knew he should have resisted the urge to let Karina stay with him (and especially to spill so many of his secrets to her the way he just had), particularly since Karina probably agreed with Vanessa and everyone else that he should be different.

Settled. Staid. Stagnant. Unhappy.

Reid felt none of those things now. Sitting there with Karina, he felt *good*. They were surrounded by neatly bundled piles of holiday light strings, being serenaded by the distant sounds of The Christmas House's ever-present carols, and he'd just given her the CliffsNotes version of his adult life. And Reid felt . . . *happy*. He felt comfortable. He felt understood.

It was weird. It was unexpected. But he liked it.

"That was a surprise this morning, about Amanda." Karina gave him a compassionate look. She shifted atop the office rug, probably settling in for a long chat . . . but only succeeding at reminding him of sleigh beds and stolen hours and one particular California suburbanite divorcée who was astonishingly limber, when properly motivated. "I'll bet it won't be easy to let her go," she said. "What do you think Alexis and Nicole will say?"

Reid had been concerned about that very thing. He'd been trying not to think about it. He'd been succeeding too, thanks to the thorny problem of the tangled holiday lights. Now, deprived of the distracting necessity of work to do, he frowned.

"I think there are more light strings in the attic."

He leaned sideways, preparing to push to his feet. Karina stopped him with a hand on his arm, her gaze steady and warm.

"Oh no, you don't. That won't work with me."

He liked the feel of her hand on him. He considered all the myriad ways to get more of that feeling and settled on the idea of closing the office door as a kick-starter. With a side-long jab of his foot, Reid accomplished the task. "What won't work?"

"Wiggling out of the conversation that way." Karina tugged him back to a seated position atop the rug, beside her. "You're talking to a master procrastinator, right here." Apparently oblivious to the closed office door, she pointed both thumbs at herself. "Whenever I get upset, I *immediately* find something else to focus on." Even as she said it, she seemed startled by the realization. She forged onward. "It might be my students' problems, my kids' behavior, items on my to-do list. . . . Whatever it is, it means I'm *not* dealing with whatever I'm supposed to be dealing with right then. Usually, for me, that's my feelings. Maybe it's the same way for you. You don't want to talk about your worries about Alexis and Nicole, so you—"

"That's not what I'm doing." Reid glanced across the rug at Karina, feeling as though he'd done more than enough talking for one night. Her latest sweater was a fluffy, oversize cardigan, he noticed. It appeared uniquely touchable and was all the more intriguing for it. He scooted closer. "I'm not procrastinating. I have a lot to take care of. That's all."

She nodded. "That's what makes procrastination so nefarious. It's easy to convince yourself it's necessary." Then Karina shook her head, as though denying the whole idea. "But it's only a distraction—a distraction that gets you nowhere." Appearing stricken all over again, Karina frowned. "It's got to be squashed. *Squashed,* before it gets worse!"

She pantomimed smashing a bug between her palms. With WWE-worthy ferociousness, she pretended to pulverize it. Then she looked up, triumphant and a little dazed. Reid doubted Karina realized exactly how much she'd just revealed about herself.

"So," he asked, "with all your helping and volunteering and running around . . . what are *you* trying to avoid thinking about?"

Given her ferocity, it had to be something pretty major.

Surprised, Karina stared at him. She drew in a breath.

"Who says I'm procrastinating?" she asked.

"I do." He stared back at her. He bit his lip, waiting.

"Screw the tangled Christmas lights," Karina blurted. She eyed him seductively. "You want to make out?"

"I thought you'd never ask," Reid said. He took her hand, pulled her closer, and decided he liked the idea of being her partner in crime. He liked it a lot. He also decided it wouldn't hurt one damn bit for procrastination to win this round.

Not if it brought him Karina.

Breathless, overheated, and with her curly hair now as tangled as the holiday light strings initially had been, Karina got to her knees atop the rug. She smiled, then straddled Reid.

Willingly, he submitted. Even though they were both still fully clothed, this was rapidly becoming her new favorite position. From here, she could admire Reid's muscular chest, his sculpted face, his expression of pure delight as she flexed her thighs and settled more comfortably on top of him.

Ah. She liked this. She liked this a lot. She could do this all night—with a few variations included, of course. Like a pantsless version, an entirely naked version, a reverse-cowgirl version. Unfortunately, her new position also brought the desk clock into her line of sight. Karina couldn't help noticing, through her dreamy-eyed gaze, that hours had passed since she'd first entered the office. *Hours.* She could scarcely believe it.

"You realize this is only procrastination at work," she panted, still reeling at the revelation she'd had earlier. "You realize this behavior isn't doing either of us any good."

Reid groaned. "You're right. We're going to have to deal with our issues." He brought his hands to her waist. Slowly, he slid his palms higher. He cupped her breasts, making her nipples harden beneath her multiple sweaters. "Sooner or later."

"Yes. Yes!" Closing her eyes, Karina swayed. That felt *so* good. Except they were supposed to be talking, she remembered. "Yes, we will," she repeated in a slightly more controlled voice. She opened her eyes again. "Now that I've recognized my procrastination pattern, I'll have to be on guard against it."

"Right. You'll have to be vigilant." Reid caressed her again. With fluid movements, he tugged off her cardigan. With relish, he eyed the additional sweater she'd put on beneath it, then toyed with its hem. "You'll have to be sure you don't get caught up in something else. Something distracting."

"Right." She bit her lip, then gave in to an urge to kiss him. Their mouths met, stretched wide, explored in a slippery arc that made words extraneous. "Mmmm. What were we saying?"

"That you want to focus on what's happening now." Smiling,

Reid slipped his hands beneath both her remaining sweaters, her T-shirt, and her lacy camisole. Unerringly, he closed his hands on her bare breasts. How had he known she wasn't wearing a bra beneath her camisole? "Concentrate," he suggested. "Focus."

"Okay." The way he was rubbing his thumbs gently over her nipples made focusing feel surprisingly easy. Breathily, Karina exhaled. "I am. I'm focusing." An idea struck her, making her go motionless in a way that only allowed Reid greater access. "Wait. Focusing doesn't count as procrastinating, does it?"

His throaty rumble confirmed it didn't. "If it helps, you can close your eyes. Just lean forward, come a little closer to me, let your eyelids drift shut, and then—"

Ah. Karina sighed as his tongue swirled over her nipple, bringing it to an ever-tauter peak. Impatiently, Reid groaned. He tugged off her remaining sweaters. They landed beside the bundled-up holiday lights. He pushed her T-shirt and camisole higher, baring her other breast. At the feel of his mouth there, she rocked forward, mindlessly driving her pelvis against him.

She needed a little more. No, she needed *much* more.

"Mmm," she said, striving for words. Eventually, she found a few, tucked in between breathy gasps. "We wouldn't want to allow any loopholes in the focusing process," she managed, her voice husky with needfulness. "That could be dangerous."

"Yes." Reid cupped her derrière, then tilted himself upward. "That could be very dangerous." A pause. A slow, hard, demonstrative thrust. A gentle inquiry: "Are you focusing?"

"Yes." Karina gave her answer honestly. Immediately. Hoarsely. "Right now, I'm thinking about how hard you feel."

His answering groan made both of them tremble.

"I'm thinking about how much I enjoyed feeling you inside

me last time." Excited by the very memory, Karina quivered anew. Together, they'd been good. Very, very good. "I'm thinking about how much I want to feel you again, big and hard and—"

"Remembering isn't feeling." With a dark, warning look, Reid flipped her in his arms. An instant later, he loomed over her, balanced on his elbows and knees, eager and ready, just as powerful a presence as she remembered. "I want you to *feel* this," he said. "I want you to feel everything, forever."

"Forever?" Woozily, Karina fluttered her eyelids, struck by the romantic notion inherent in those words. Was Reid really as quixotic as he sounded? She couldn't tell. Even as she opened her mouth to respond, the sound of a moving zipper stopped her.

Concentrating hard, she focused. Was it hers? Or his?

Hers, she realized with an initial pang of disappointment. That tiny, raspy sound was the zipper sliding down on her jeans.

She would much rather have heard Reid's zipper coming undone, Karina knew. She imagined those tiny metal tracks gradually coming apart, slowly revealing the bulge she'd been rocking against just a few minutes earlier, treating her to an up-close and personal view of Reid's . . . *Wait.* With her heart pounding, Karina stilled. Then she arched upward, needing more.

She needed more of Reid's hands on her, she realized belatedly. Much more. Because while she'd momentarily lost focus, he'd unzipped her jeans, nudged them down a few crucial inches, and . . . *ahhh.* How did one man manage to have hands that talented?

Tossing her head against the cushy office rug, Karina became compellingly aware that she was already wet, already swollen, already impatient for more. More more more.

Was this really *her,* she wondered in amazement, writhing

on the floor in a sexy man's arms, all but begging him to take her?

It was. And the knowledge of that thrilled her. She'd never before been as bold as she'd been with Reid. *Was being,* right now, with Reid. But even without the excuse of spiked cider or months' worth of pent-up lustiness to blame, Karina knew what was happening between her and Reid was about more than physical needs. This was about taking chances, making a change . . . doing something that was wholly for herself and no one else.

Suddenly alarmed by that idea, Karina stopped moving.

"Wait. Let me touch *you,*" she whispered. "Let me—"

"Not yet. Don't spoil my fun." Reid paused, resting the heel of his hand against her. The gesture felt less like a break in the action . . . and more like a promise of what was to come. "You're supposed to be concentrating on focusing, remember?"

With those small, swirly motions he was making, drawing her closer and closer to the edge, it was pretty tough to forget.

"I know I am, but—" But something still nagged at her. With her heart pounding and her head whirling, Karina clenched her fists. Her whole body thrummed with desire. Her hips arched upward all on their own, searching for completion. And yet . . . "But I have to do more for *you* first. Otherwise, you won't—" She panted, stalled for an answer, even as Reid waited. *Won't what?* her impatient mind demanded. Only one answer supplied itself: "Stay. You won't stay! Just please, let me touch you."

Desperately, she reached for him, nearly able to grasp the cold kiss of his zipper tab beneath her fingertips. Instead, she felt the hard clamp of Reid's hand on her wrist. He stopped her, held her, then levered over her with his eyes fiercely on hers.

"Nothing on earth could make me leave you. Especially right now," he promised. He kissed her, slowly and thoroughly, and with much more tenderness than his harsh tone suggested. Gently, he pulled her against him. "No more of that. All right?"

"All right." Karina nodded. Maybe she *wasn't* yet a master of on-the-spot, impromptu liaisons. "Thank you. I'm sorry—I didn't mean to derail all the focusing. Please, go on."

Reid smiled. "So polite." He sounded amused—and affectionate too. He gazed into her eyes, then exhaled deeply. He shook his head. "It's no wonder I love you, Karina. There's no one else like you—no one in the whole wide world."

"Well, you'd know, having traveled through most of it."

"I would." A somber nod. "It's true. You're special."

"Well, there's definitely no one else who'd let you get away with using *I love you* that cavalierly, that's for sure." Karina laughed, grateful to Reid for keeping the conversation going. "I knew there'd be awkward moments when I started dating again"—*like the one thirty seconds ago, when I blurted, "You won't stay!"*—"but now, thanks to you, I'll be ready for anything when I get back home and start whooping it up."

"I mean it," Reid insisted. "You have no idea how unusual this is for me." He kissed her again. "Believe me, I did *not* want Vanessa to be right about us. But she was. She *is*. So . . . I'm afraid you won't be dating anyone else when you get home."

His self-assured smile made her heart turn over. Reid was so cute when he pretended to be jealous. So tough. So sweet.

"Oh yeah?" Teasingly, Karina rolled her eyes at him. It was fun to see this lighthearted side of him. It was fun to banter with him this way, too. "Exactly how do you plan to stop me?"

"Easy. I plan to ruin you for any other man. When I get done with you, no one else will possibly satisfy."

"Ooh!" Karina grinned. "Big words."

"That's right. Big words, from a big man."

With a grin as wide as hers now, Reid touched his profile to hers. They lay together on the rug, side by side, touching from nose to toes, in a way that felt uniquely close—uniquely *them*. Reid pillowed her head with his bicep. Karina felt surprisingly comfortable there with him, talking and joking.

"There's a problem with your plan, you know," she said.

"My 'big words, big man' plan?" A head shake. "Can't be."

"There is. Unless you're in California or I'm here, I'm going to date someone else eventually—no matter how unsatisfying they might happen to be." Karina gave a pretend regretful sound. "I won't have any choice. A woman has needs, you know."

"Mmm." Reid stroked her hair. "Needs, hmmm?"

"That's right. And it's way too freezing for me to live here in the Midwest. There aren't enough sweaters in the world."

"You're not trying hard enough." Reid gestured at her discarded cold-weather gear. "Three sweaters? Amateur."

"I'm sorry, but three is my limit." Growing restless now, Karina cradled Reid's face in her hands. His beard felt soft and spiky beneath her fingertips. "Mmm. I *do* like this, though."

"You like my beard?" He seemed surprised. And pleased.

She nodded. "I'd like to feel it . . . elsewhere."

Reid caught her intimation immediately. He smiled at her. "I knew I was right not to shave," he said. Inexplicably.

"And that would be because . . . ?"

"Because this gnarly nookie beard of mine worked," Reid told her. "It *did* bring back happier days. It brought back *you*."

Smiling and bemused, Karina shook her head. "I hate to break it to you, but your beard is probably not a good-luck charm. That doesn't make any sense at all."

"I disagree." Reid shrugged, then went on gazing at her. He trailed his fingertips over her cheek, appearing wholly absorbed in the shape of her face, the curve of her smile, the texture of her skin. "But the important thing is, I'm glad you're here."

"Now *that* makes sense. I approve."

"And since my nookie beard has worked so well, I'm going to test the theory even further," Reid said. "Until you say you love me back, this beard of mine is sticking around."

"Ha! You're in for a long wait then," Karina joked. She wiggled as Reid kissed his way down her body. "Because I'm just using you for your body, pal. Your big, strong, extrahot—"

"You're using me for my body?" In midkiss, Reid glanced up.

Something in his rough tone made her look at him twice. For a heartbeat, Karina had second thoughts about teasing him.

What if Reid meant it? What if he really *did* love her?

After all, Rodrigo loved Amanda after only one week. . . .

But before Karina could regroup, Reid pulled up her shirt and camisole again. He gave her belly a teeny, affectionate nibble, then made his way to the waistband of her panties. He hooked his fingertips inside, sending a cascade of goose bumps skating along her skin from hip bone to hip bone. All thoughts of true love and weeklong holiday affairs flew away.

"I thought we'd moved past the sex-only phase," Reid said. "But for now, using me is enough. I'm yours." In a mock stern voice, he added, "Just remember, the fate of my beard is in your hands. Until you feel like saying you love me too, it's staying—no matter how rugged and macho it makes me look."

In demonstration of those dire consequences, Reid nuzzled her. Slowly, he let his beard trace the area just above the tiny bow decorating the low waistband of her Christmas-print panties.

"Mmm. That tickles," Karina breathed. Feeling dreamy eyed again, she grabbed Reid's head. She stroked his neatly trimmed beard, then smiled at him. "I have to tell you . . . you're not exactly incentivizing me with this tactic of yours. If you keep that up, I'll never want to admit a thing! Much less—"

Much less say that I love you. It sounded so . . .

Unbelievable? Preposterous?

No. Perfect. It sounded *perfect*.

But Karina couldn't risk it. What if Reid really was joking? She'd look like a naïve fool for taking him seriously. She'd already been down that road with Eric. This time, she wanted a new road. A new future. A new *her,* with new freedom.

Besides, what were the odds she'd find true love during her very first postdivorce fling? She could hardly hope for *that*.

She had to be a realist, Karina knew. Eric might have emerged from their broken marriage with a new relationship, but she couldn't possibly be that lucky. Especially with a man like Reid—a man who was gorgeous, thoughtful, *and* good with kids, *and* great in bed.

"Much less," she repeated, switching tactics on the fly, "let you out of this room before I'm finished with you."

"Oh yeah?" Reid's smile looked downright provocative. "I like your attitude. You'd do well on an adventure travel trip."

He wants to travel with me! Secretly elated that Reid thought she would fit into his globe-trotting life—however impractical that would be—Karina smiled at him. "Hmmm," she pretended to muse. "I don't know about that. With my schedule, they'd have to be short trips—but frequent ones. I'd probably need a guide to take me there too. And good guidance is *so* hard to find. . . ."

"Oh, I'll take you there, all right." His husky tone made his tantalizing meaning plain. "I'll take you anywhere you want to go. You just hold on and try to focus a little harder this time, all right? Because I'm going to have to start over from the beginning, and I don't want you to miss anything."

"Okay. I'm ready." Karina wriggled in anticipation. Breathlessly, she nodded. "I have a feeling things are about to get good."

"They're about to get very good," Reid promised.

"Very, *very* good," Karina emphasized, caught up in a newly riveting memory of the first (and last, and only) time they'd been together. Reid touched her again, this time sweeping his fingers past that tiny ribbon on her Christmas-print panties. Filled with pleasure, Karina gasped. He really was . . . "*So* good!"

Tossing her head on the rug, she tensed in renewed eagerness. She could hardly wait for more, could scarcely breathe for needing him, could think of nothing else except—

An unusual popping sound was heard. Everything went silent.

No Christmas carols. No chattering. No guests or staff members moving around outside the management office. Nothing.

A loud thump sounded on the door. "Reid! Come quick!"

Perplexed, Karina opened her eyes—just in time to see . . . Well, nothing. She couldn't see her hand in front of her face. But she could feel Reid leaving her. She could feel him moving away, hear him murmuring something apologetic, groaning in frustration.

"Something's wrong," he said. "I'd better get out there."

Now? she wanted to wail. *You can't leave now! Things are about to get good!*

A flashlight came on, small but powerful. Reid shined its beam near her, illuminating the rug—and her disappointed face.

"I'm sorry," he said. He looked it, too. "I know the timing couldn't be worse. But the way things have been going around here lately, this could be pretty serious."

"I know. It's okay." Rapidly setting herself to rights, Karina got to her feet. Gently, she touched his arm. "You go ahead. I'll be out in a second. Maybe I can help somehow!"

"Maybe." Reid kissed her, the gesture hasty but full of promise. Briefly, he framed her face with his hands. "Later?"

"Later," Karina affirmed. She watched him move efficiently around the office, their near liaison temporarily on hold as he prepared to take charge of the B&B's latest emergency. With one final backward glance, Reid opened the door. Then he disappeared into the darkness that shrouded The Christmas House.

The power must have gone on the fritz, Karina realized. That meant the lights were out, the heat was out, the Christmas music was nonfunctioning, and the guests were stuck in a cold, dark, totally *non*festive B&B. Reid couldn't ignore any of that.

Argh. Was the entire northwestern Michigan power grid out to get her, or what? She and Reid had been close. *So* close.

"I'll *definitely* see you later," Karina agreed, even though Reid couldn't hear her anymore. Her thoughts whirled, caught up in the potential importance of Reid's *I love you*— and his so-called "threat" to keep that cute beard of his until she told him she loved him too.

What was she supposed to do about *that?* She'd never been faced with a dilemma like that before. Confused and thrilled and conflicted, Karina sighed. "But first . . . I've got work to do too."

Then, reluctantly, she headed for the door to gather her things. Whatever this incident was, it was destined for her Edgware report. And Reid could *not* be around to see her working on it. The consequences of that could be *really* disastrous. . . .

Chapter Sixteen

... From the desk of Betty Sullivan
DECEMBER 21ST
LOCATION: THE CHRISTMAS HOUSE
SCHEDULED EVENT: "COOKIE BAKING & DECORATING:
GINGERBREAD, SPRITZ, PFEFFERNÜSSE, AND MORE!"
—6:00 P.M. TO 8:00 P.M.

When Reid left the B&B's management office and aimed his flashlight beam to illuminate his path, the first thing he saw was the long hallway table. Serendipitously, it was fully outfitted with neat rows of candles—candles that had been affixed to easy-to-use holders and arrayed next to reusable lighters, destined for candlelight snowshoe Christmas caroling later tonight.

Reid grabbed a lighter, along with an armful of candles. As he headed down the hallway with them, flashlight at the ready, he heard The Christmas House's guests milling around, talking. It sounded as though they were speculating about the problem. Then he heard the staff, working hard to reassure everyone. Next he heard Vanessa, cracking a joke about Santa's "naughty Christmas elves" keeping everyone in the dark so their boss could get his work done and knock off early this year.

Someone wandered by. Neil, using his cell phone screen as a miniature flashlight. A couple of guests mimicked him. Their cell phone screens peppered the darkness with blueish squares. They provided insufficient light to safely guide anyone's path, though, and the whole B&B was starting to feel increasingly chilly, Reid realized. Clearly, the power had gone out, taking The Christmas House's atmosphere of holiday cheer along with it.

"This sucks!" someone complained. "I'm not having fun."

"Whoops!" A crunch was heard. "Sorry! I think I just stepped on someone's gift." A bunch of ornaments jangled. "And bumped into one of the Christmas trees too. Sorry, everyone!"

A collective groan went up. More people grumbled, their voices filled with growing discontent.

"This is ridiculous. How long before the power comes back on?"

"Are we going to have to find someplace else to stay tonight?"

"Doesn't this place have emergency backup power?"

"Don't worry, everyone," Vanessa called out. "We're working on the problem. We'll get the power back on ASAP, I promise."

"The lights are on across the street," Suzanne pointed out, "so it's not a citywide outage. What's wrong with this place?"

"Yeah! First you wreck our gifts," someone else said, "then you leave us in the dark. And now the cookie-baking session is going to be late, too! My kids were looking forward to that."

"Mine too! And it's getting cold in here. Brr."

"I'm going online—on my phone!—right now to complain. Your triple-A rating is totally taking a nosedive after this!"

"Sorry for the inconvenience, everyone." Reid reached the front room, then waved his key chain halogen light to get his guests' attention. "There'll still be time for gingerbread and spritz and pfeffernüsse later on, I promise. Just hang tight."

He handed out the first candle. Helpfully, he lit it, too. He examined the crowded room, then charted a path to distribute the rest of the candles to his restless guests. Lacking another strategy—or simply drawn together in the dark—they appeared to have all gathered in the front room. He guessed misery really did love company . . . and the holidays really did bring out the worst in people sometimes—even though his mission at The Christmas House was to ease holiday stresses, not add to them.

Vanessa sidled up to him, wearing a sweater and an admonitory expression. "Hey, cuz," she said in a low voice. "I'd watch those promises of yours. I called an electrician to come out, but he said it could be hours before he gets here. We might not have time for the cookie-baking and -decorating session."

"It's a tradition," Reid said firmly. "We'll do it."

"But the ovens are out!" his cousin argued. "The cookie dough is all prepared, but by the time the power comes back on, all the chefs will be finished with their shifts. They're already working really long hours for us. We can't ask them to stay even later tonight."

Another candle. "We'll figure out a way."

"I hope so." Vanessa elbowed him, her face jolly in the semidarkness. "By the way, how did things go with Karina?"

I told her I loved her. "Fine. They went f—" He stopped. "No. Wait. What makes you think I was with Karina?"

"Oh, come on. Don't play dumb with me! Why do you think I volunteered for management duty tonight? I thought you might be . . . indisposed." Vanessa waggled her brows. "Just helping out!"

"M. Y. O. B." Reid frowned, reverting to the lingo of their shared teenage years. "And I don't need any help. I never do."

At his elbow, someone tugged his sleeve. He glanced down.

Olivia stood there, her skinny arms filled with candles, another reusable lighter, and a few extra candleholders. She must have grabbed all those items, Reid realized, when she'd seen him handing out candles to the B&B's guests.

Her face looked pensive in the gloomy light, but when she saw him looking, Olivia brightened. "Hi, Reid! Can I help you?"

"Oh, sweetie. That's so nice of you!" Vanessa said. In a wiseass tone, she added, "But Reid doesn't *ever* need any—"

Help. It didn't take a genius to read her mind.

"Sure!" Reid smiled at Olivia. He shot his cousin a cease-and-desist look. "As a matter of fact, I was just thinking I could use some extra hands for this job. Come on, Olivia." He pointed with a candle. "Let's hit that corner over there."

"The one in the opposite direction of Vanessa?"

"Yep." He moved in that direction, handing out candles.

"What does she think is so funny, anyway?" Olivia cast a backward glance at Reid's cousin, who was still watching them. "She looks like she's about to crack up about something."

"Vanessa has a weird sense of humor." Reid motioned for another candle. "Hey, good job on finding those candles."

Olivia shrugged, small and diligent by his side. "I checked the fire extinguishers too. They're all fully charged."

Hmmm. That was . . . oddly cautious, for a ten-year-old. "Good to know." With a nod, Reid gave Olivia another candle to hand out. She watched as he lit it for a waiting B&B guest.

"Be *sure* to hold your candle upright," Olivia advised the guest in a concerned tone. "And don't let your candle get too close to anything flammable, like curtains or pillows or gift wrap! There's always a danger of fire getting out of control."

"It's not that big a danger. We have working fire extinguishers." Reid winked to reassure his budding worrywart helper. "Just use reasonable precautions," he reminded his confused-looking guest, "and everything will be fine."

They walked toward the next guest. "You can't know everything will be fine!" Olivia disagreed. She shook her head, looking determined. "Things happen, you know. *Bad things.*"

"That's right," Reid agreed. "Absolutely. But most of the time, the things people worry about the most never happen. That means they've spent all that time worrying for nothing."

"Nuh-uh. That's not true," Olivia told him. She issued the next guest a candle—and her standard warning notice—then looked up at him. "Worrying helps you get prepared for things."

"Really?" Reid ducked closer to the guest, issued *his* standard reassuring rebuttal to Olivia's warning notice, then kept moving alongside his helper. "Worrying is a good thing?"

Olivia nodded. "It's like a fire drill for your brain. It helps you think about what to do if stuff goes wrong."

"That's an interesting premise."

"Which, by the way, you should have at this place," she went on, knowledgably. "Fire drills, I mean. There hasn't been a single fire drill since we've been here. Except the one I made my mom and brothers do on our own." Olivia's jaw tightened. "Saving people's lives isn't a joke! There's probably a law or something that you're breaking by not having fire drills."

He peered at her stubborn, supercautious, skepticism-filled face. "Aha! So *you're* the one. You're the Edgware evaluator!" Reid shook his head in amazement. "Man. No wonder they had me fooled. Their evaluators are deep, *deep* undercover."

Olivia giggled. "*I'm* not the Edgware evaluator!"

"Are you sure?"

Another nod. "I don't even know what that is." She gave him an anxious look. "*Should* I know what that is?"

"No!" Wanting to assuage her worries—not add to them—Reid hugged Olivia to his side. Together, they handed out more candles—and more warnings/reassurances. As they worked the room, Reid glanced down at the little girl. She reminded him of Karina. Generous. Smart. Sweet. But a little too apprehensive for her own good. "You know," he told her, "I'm intrigued by that worrying theory of yours. Do you really think it's true? Do you really think worrying is like a fire drill for your brain?"

Intently, Olivia glanced up at him. By now, the guests surrounding them were almost 100 percent in possession of lighted candles. That meant he could glimpse her troubled expression clearly. And *it* worried *him*. He wanted to help her.

"Yes," she said. "I really think so. Worrying is a good idea. People just don't get that. I'm extra good at it, too."

Being "extra good" at worrying sounded awful. Casually, he asked, "Is that so?"

"Uh-huh." Olivia gave a vigorous nod, seeming reassured to be talking about this with someone. "Whatever's going on, I can usually think of about a *million* ways things could go wrong," she explained. "Then I fix all of those problems in my head."

"Wow." Reid hoped Alexis and Nicole didn't have heads stuffed full of emergency scenarios and virtual fire drills. Making a mental note to have a father-daughter talk with them after the cookie-baking session, he nodded at Olivia. "That's really something. It *does* sound like you're good at worrying."

"I like to think of it as *planning*," Olivia clarified, tossing her scarf over her shoulder. "And I have to be good at it. Because my mom is really bad at preventing disasters."

Reid bet he knew exactly which "disaster" Olivia was referring to. If she'd reacted to her parents' divorce the

same way Josh had, she probably still wasn't A-OK with
the situation.

"I'd sure like to know more about that," Reid said. "In my
job, I do a lot of work with people who are worried." *Reasonably so, since we're scaling mountains, exploring rain forests, and geotrekking in subzero temperatures.* "If I could give
them some new advice, they'd probably appreciate it."

"Well . . . Just tell them to worry more! They'll get better
at it the more they practice. It's just like playing soccer. I'm
on a team back home, you know."

"That's . . . very encouraging of you." Reid stifled a grin.
At the same time, he felt an entirely unexpected urge to give
Olivia another hug—and do whatever he could to protect her
from *everything*. "But I'm looking for some practical tips. Do
you think you could help me out with that?"

"Sure. *If* it can happen in a week. We're leaving soon."

Unhappily reminded of Karina's imminent return to the
land of sea and sunshine, Reid nodded. "Okay. Here's what I
want you to do. Every time you're worried about something,
write it down. Then write down all the fire-drill solutions you
have. Okay?"

"That's it?" Olivia shook her blond bangs from her eyes.
She eyed the Christmas tree—probably examining it for potential choking hazards. "That doesn't sound very helpful
to me."

"Trust me. I think it will be."

"You think giving people a list of all my worries will help
them somehow? I don't know. Usually you're pretty smart,
but that doesn't sound like a very good plan to me."

"You'll be giving them all your solutions, too," Reid reminded her. "Think of it as a case study: learning by example."

Dubiously, Olivia wrinkled her nose. "I guess I could do
that. There's a whole pad of paper in our room upstairs. I
could use that. Although I might run out of paper." She appeared newly uneasy. "I'd have to ask my mom for more. Or

buy some in Kismet. Or borrow some from the front desk. Or get some from Josh."

"See?" Reid said. "You're 'planning ahead' already. Wow."

Privately, he was dismayed at how easily worries crowded into poor little Olivia's brain. How did she make it through fifth grade every day without totally freaking out? Just making a decision at lunchtime—fish sticks or veggie burgers?—could launch a quandary of epic proportions. Olivia would still be debating the pros/cons of eating and deciding what to have while her friends headed out to enjoy recess.

Reid hoped his plan would help her. From where he stood, it looked like a long shot. But he specialized in tough situations.

"Hey, there are Alexis and Nicole!" Happily, Olivia waved at her new friends, appearing—all of a sudden—as though her myriad worries were forgotten. She waved them over. "Where have you guys *been?*" she squealed. "It's been *crazy* around here!"

Reid's daughters threw him a pair of cursory greetings and a wave. Then, excitedly, they huddled with Olivia. The laughing threesome appeared utterly natural together . . . and utterly indifferent to the grown-ups in the room as they compared notes on what they'd been doing when the power outage had happened. Right on cue, Michael and Josh wandered upstairs from the kids' Fun Zone. They joined the girls, Josh with a candle held in one hand and Michael with a copy of *How The Grinch Stole Christmas.*

"Well, that answers that question." Karina appeared beside Reid. She nodded toward their united children. "My kids were here with you, and your kids were wandering the halls with me! I ran into Alexis and Nicole while I was looking for Michael, Olivia, and Josh," she explained, "and convinced the girls to come along with me. I wanted to make sure everyone was okay."

"They seem . . . amazingly fine." Reid smiled at her.

"Thanks for corralling Alexis and Nicole. That was nice of you."

"Well . . . They insisted they were fine in the dark as long as their PSPs still had juice," Karina confided. "But between you and me, I think they were relieved to have an adult take charge and bring them here safely with everyone else."

"Maybe." Reid doubted it. His daughters were much too independent to behave like normal preteens. They didn't need Karina's mother hen routine any more than he did. Thinking better of saying so—and risking hurting her feelings—he jabbed his chin toward the group of chattering children. "Look. They really get along, don't they?"

"I know. They really do." Karina gazed at them, then smiled up at Reid. She squeezed his arm. "That's cute, isn't it?"

"It's adorable." Vanessa broke into their conversation with a know-it-all grin. "Just like I knew it would be. You guys are *totally* the new Brady Bunch! Minus one, of course—I guess you can't have everything." She aimed a practical glance at Reid. "The electrician is here, cuz. And things don't look good."

Left on her own in the midst of the (newly) candlelit B&B reception, Karina watched Reid leave with Vanessa to consult with the electrician. She'd used candlelight to finish making a few handwritten notes for her Edgware report. She'd made sure her children—and Reid's—were safe and happy. She'd double-checked with the staff to see if there was anything else she could do to help. There hadn't been. Now, at loose ends, she snuggled into her warm sweaters, debating what to do next.

If there'd been time—and a stand-in baby-sitter who *wasn't* probably canoodling with Rodrigo someplace dimly lit and cozy right now—Karina might have gone upstairs and started getting ready for her "date" with Reid. His promise of *later* still rang in her head, making her feel doubly impatient for their next opportunity to be together. As it was, though, she had to hang around until things were settled here. She might as well—

Her cell phone tweeted out its incoming SMS tone.

Chelsea. A glance at her cell phone screen confirmed it.

Well, there was no time like the present to see what urgent issue had caused Chelsea to text her almost hourly for the past few days. Curious, Karina opened the latest message.

K! WHERE ARE U? she read. DID I DO SOMETHING WRONG?

Guiltily, Karina edged to a corner of the B&B's front room, then thumbed out an answer. NO. JUST BUSY. SORRY. WHAT'S UP?

ERIC AND I ARE OVER came next. Then, I HATE THE BAHAMAS!

Feeling shocked, Karina stared at her cell phone. Her ex-husband and his bodacious bikini-clad girlfriend had broken up?

Karina hesitated, waiting for a well-earned bout of schadenfreude to sweep over her. After all, Eric's fling with Chelsea had caused the breakup of her marriage. It had made him behave like a punk-obsessed, video game–playing idiot. It had upset her children and caused her endless turmoil. Given the circumstances, Karina figured she deserved to feel vindicated.

Instead, she only felt sad. Soberly, she thumbed out another reply to Chelsea. SO SORRY, C. CALL ME. MAYBE I CAN HELP?

Almost instantly, her cell phone rang.

Moving toward the hallway, where it might be a little quieter, Karina prepared herself to answer. Maybe the college students she was paid to advise didn't need her help over Christmas break this year, she realized, but this one *particular* college student did, and Karina intended to do her best to help her. If that meant patching up her eyeliner-wearing ex with his supersexy, twentysomething paramour . . . well, so be it.

* * *

"See? This here's your problem." The local Kismet electrician jabbed one callused finger at the electrical panel. He nodded at Reid to make sure he was paying attention, then jabbed again. "You've got yourself a one-hundred-amp system here. That's not enough for all that fancy gadgetry and all those big light displays. What you need to do is heavy up to a two-hundred-amp setup, like your newer houses on the other side of the lake have."

The other side of the lake. Where Lagniappe at the Lakeshore was located, Reid couldn't help noticing. Grr.

"But we've been using the same Christmas lights for years," Vanessa mused. Standing beside Reid and the electrician with a flashlight in her hand, she cast the electrical panel a worried glance. She looked at Reid. "We've never had a problem before."

"Could it be sabotage?" Reid asked bluntly. "Rewiring or tampering? Could anything else have caused this problem?"

"Hard to say." The electrician scratched his head. "Can't think why anybody would want to tamper with anything."

Unfortunately, Reid could. Lagniappe at the Lakeshore would love to shut them down, by whatever means possible. But he wasn't likely to get very far with that line of reasoning with the kindhearted electrician. The man clearly couldn't conceive of Kismet's business rivals harboring any ill will toward each other.

Feeling resigned, Reid agreed to an immediate partial upgrade of the power system. He paid the electrician—out of his own pocket, for the sake of expediency.

"You know, it would save a few watts to take down some of those lights you've got all over this place," the electrician advised. He finished writing an invoice and a work order for a new sub-panel and a power surge arrester, then handed the paperwork to Reid for his signature. "They look nice, sure. But even with the upgrade I'm installing, there're only so many amps to go around. You're pushing your luck with these overloads."

"We've never had a problem before," Vanessa reiterated. "How are we supposed to make this place look like a festive winter wonderland if we don't have all our Christmas lights?"

"Dunno." The electrician shrugged. "Use your imagination, I guess. Those orange-and-clove pomanders don't draw any power, and they look pretty this time of year. My wife makes 'em. They make good gifts too. Fit right in a stocking, nice and neat."

Reid's cousin gave a frustrated sound. But Reid only paused, struck by a new idea. The electrician was right. All they needed was a little imagination. Lagniappe at the Lakeshore couldn't take away their innovation. They could dent their spirits only *if* the folks at The Christmas House allowed them to.

"Come on," he told Vanessa. "Let's leave this job to the experts. We've got some Christmas cookies to bake and decorate."

"But . . . the power isn't even back on yet!"

"Prob'ly won't be for an hour or so," the electrician specified with a dour expression. "That's *if* things go well."

"That doesn't matter." With new vigor, Reid grabbed his coat, then headed outside to one of the B&B's outbuildings. "For the strategy I'm thinking of, we don't need electricity."

The best part of the cookie-baking and -decorating session wasn't the cookies, Reid realized shortly after he hauled his cousin outside to help him set up. The best part wasn't the colored sugars, sprinkles, red and green icing, or silver dragées. Instead, the best part was the awestruck looks on the faces of the children as Reid carried in each platter of freshly baked cookies, then set them in the staging areas Vanessa had arranged. One area was for cooling cookies, one was for ready-to-decorate cookies, and one was for finished, fully decorated cookies. There were a few of each type of cookie lined up in each zone already, tempting everyone to start nibbling.

"Hey, be sure to save some icing for the cookies." Smiling, Reid swiped a dab of frosting from Michael's cheek. The boy grinned back at him. "You can't eat all of it between batches."

"Oh, that's not a problem," Michael assured him, licking his fingers. "We can just make twice as much frosting!"

"Good solution." Amused, Reid double-checked the battery-powered camping lanterns he'd found in the outbuildings. Vanessa had arranged them down the centers of the tables, where they provided plenty of light despite the still-nonfunctioning power.

"Hey, Reid!" Olivia waved at him. "Look what I did!"

He peered at the cookies in front of her. "Is that . . . ?"

"Yes! A gingerbread family!" Proudly, she smiled at it.

Reid did too. He tilted his head. "It looks like—"

"Yep. It's us!" With her fingers stained red and green, Olivia pointed out various cookies, assigning each an identity. "There's you, and me, and my mom." All three featured prominent smiling faces made of icing. "This one's Michael." It was small but adorable. "This one's Josh." It was stumpy and skewed. The next two cookies were lovingly decorated with sparkling sugar and extra sprinkles. "And these two are Alexis and Nicole!"

"Aww!" His daughters exclaimed, glancing over. "Cute!"

"Nice work, Olivia." Reid wiped his hands on his bibbed BBQ apron—which he wore atop his jeans and flannel shirt, beneath his puffy, quilted vest—then glanced around the room. The adults were still occupied with some gung ho project of Karina's in the front room. All the children were here busily decorating. There wasn't much chance he'd identify the Edgware evaluator here. But Reid couldn't help looking. He'd been doing it all week. "Keep it up. You're doing great," he told Olivia. "And have fun!"

"I will," Olivia promised. "Oh! Wait!" She tugged his sleeve, then showed him a small pad of notepaper situated at her elbow. Several pages were flipped back, as though they'd already been used. The top sheet showed a handwritten list of worries. A *long* handwritten list. "I already started my list. See?"

Reid swallowed hard. That was a pretty scary list. But he didn't want to alarm Olivia. "Good job," he said. "I can't wait to read it." *And help you deal with all those worries, too.*

Olivia beamed at him. Reid hoped he could live up to the trust she was so obviously placing in him. But before he could ponder that concern any further, Karina arrived from the other room. Her blond hair looked tousled. Her chin was smudged with frosting. But her smile was as wide—and as beautiful—as usual.

Instantly, Reid felt better—about Olivia's problems and everything else, too. Whatever went wrong, he'd figure out how to deal with it. He always did. Besides, there was no way he could feel anything less than happy around Karina.

It's no wonder I love you, Karina.

Even without her writhing half naked in his arms, even with her simply approaching him now, Reid knew it was true. And he was glad. He might not be a man who examined his feelings deeply . . . but he did recognize those feelings (eventually) when they smacked him upside the head with their intensity.

He wasn't afraid to express them, either. He might not have wanted other people to tell him how he felt—he swept the room with a grumpy gaze, eyeballing his interfering matchmaker cousin, Nate, Angela, and everyone else who'd advised him—but once Reid knew how he felt, he laid it on the table. Fearlessly.

Although he *was* afraid—a little—that Karina wouldn't

reciprocate those feelings. After all, she *had* admitted that she was only using him for his body. And she *hadn't* admitted that she cared about him, too. Although she *had* approved of his beard.

Contemplatively, Reid stroked it. It *was* his good-luck beard, damn it. He didn't care what anyone else said.

"Wow. I can't believe this worked!" Karina stood beside him, arms folded over her chest, and watched the B&B's young guests as they went to town decorating Christmas cookies. "What made you think of baking cookies on the barbecue grill?"

"Something the electrician said sparked an idea," Reid told her. He lifted the edge of his chef's apron and wiped the icing from her chin. "I figured, if it's possible to grill pizzas, it should be possible to bake other things on a barbecue grill."

"And we wouldn't need electricity to do it. Genius!"

Reid shrugged. "People bake without electricity every day, all over the world. They use tandoors or hornos, shichirins or woodstoves—all kinds of ovens. I knew that already. All I needed was a different perspective to remember it."

"Well, if you can't get a new perspective at Christmastime," Karina said cheerfully, "when can you?"

"Christmas had nothing to do with it." Reid crossed his arms. "I would have had the same idea at any time of year."

"Maybe. But would you have had the same impetus to do it?"

He didn't know what she meant. "Probably."

"Admit it." With her eyes sparkling, Karina nudged him. "You wanted the cookie-baking and -decorating session to happen. Vanessa told me how determined you were. She told me what you said." Here, Karina adopted a he-man stance, with her arms held out at her sides. She lowered her voice—presumably in mimicry of him. "It's a tradition!" she growled. "We're doing it!"

Reid smiled. "Funny. But don't get hung up on thinking I'm secretly sentimental. I'm no Christmas-crazy traditionalist."

"Sure. That's what you say *now,*" Karina agreed. "But once you get a load of what I've been planning in the other room—"

Vanessa arrived, appearing pleased. "Sorry to interrupt you two lovebirds," his cousin said. "And by the way, you two look completely adorable together. Have I mentioned that?"

"You might have," Reid said drily. "Once or twice."

Karina only smiled. Gently, she squeezed his hand.

"But I thought you'd want to know," Vanessa went on, "that the electrician is almost finished. Another fifteen minutes or so, he told me, when I went to check on his progress just now."

"That's great!" Karina brightened, smiling in the lamplight. "That means the problem is solved then, right?"

"It's solved for now," Reid agreed. "We should be set for the rest of the season. But the B&B will need more extensive upgrades later—especially if Edgware wants to split up the suites into smaller rooms and increase occupancy."

"Is that likely? That sounds expensive," said Karina.

"It could be very expensive." Reid checked his watch, realized it was almost time to retrieve the next batch of baked cookies from the grill, and decided to cut to the chase. "But it probably won't matter. Most likely, Edgware will glean all the information they can about The Christmas House's concept during their assessment, then demolish the place and build a more cost-effective B&B on the site after they've acquired it."

Karina looked appalled. So did Vanessa. "Demolish it? They're going to *demolish* it?" Vanessa shook her head. "Nobody said anything about taking a wrecking ball to this place."

"That's the risk we take with selling." Reid shrugged. "It's business. Grammy and Grandpa must have known that might happen when they made the deal with Edgware."

"I doubt it," his cousin said darkly. "They're not that cold-hearted. Some of our guests have been coming here for years, Reid! *Years!* Where are they supposed to go now?"

Why was she asking him? As though in search of an answer, Reid looked around the room. The staff members—and a few of the older children—glared at him, almost as if *he* were the one leading the wrecking crew. "If Lagniappe at the Lakeshore has its way," he said, "some of them will probably go there."

His cousin's frown deepened. So did Karina's.

"You act as if you don't even care," Vanessa said. "Don't you want The Christmas House to stay in the family?"

Of course Reid wanted that. He liked the idea of this place being here, welcoming and Christmassy, just the way it had always been. Just the way it was in his memories. Just the way it had been all week. It wasn't *unthinkable* that he'd get a jones for a family-style holiday someday. It was just unlikely.

"It's not up to me. The B&B isn't mine to keep."

"But it *is* yours to keep!" Vanessa insisted. "It's all of ours! It belongs to everyone in the family. In a way, The Christmas House belongs to everyone in the community."

Reid disagreed. But before he could say so, several of the B&B's guests crowded into the room. They appeared fully prepared to do . . . something. And it probably wasn't decorate cookies. Maybe they'd planned a protest about the power outage?

Perplexed, Reid watched as Suzanne moved to the head of the excited, jostling group. Rocky and Neil arranged themselves just behind Suzanne. Everyone else filed into position, including a few of the formerly grouchy guests to whom Reid had distributed candles earlier. Now, though, everyone appeared enthusiastic and downright merry.

What was going on? Reid wondered. He sensed a certain expectancy in the air, along with a growing eagerness. The newly arriving guests glanced at Karina. She glanced at them, appeared to realize what was about to happen, then held up her palms.

"Wait, everyone! Now isn't the best time. I'm sorry."

"Right," Reid agreed. He didn't know what was going on here, but when he glanced at his watch, he knew one thing for certain: Those cookies were probably on the verge of becoming charcoal briquettes by now. "I've got to get the next batch of spritz cookies off the grill." He hooked his thumb toward the B&B's expansive backyard, where the grills were set up. "So—"

But his guests ignored him *and* Karina. Obviously acting through some sort of prearranged signal, they raised their lighted candles. With their faces bright in the glowing light, they began to sing.

The melody began softly at first.

O holy night! The stars are brightly shining . . .

Reid recognized the song. He frowned in confusion.

"Wait. Hang on just a minute." He raised his hands to quiet the crowd. "I know you're probably all bored, with no power—"

But the impromptu carolers only cast proud, conspiratorial glances at Karina, then raised their voices a little higher.

O holy night!

Beside him, Karina blushed. She nodded, then joined in.

"—but we'll have the electricity back on very soon!"

Vanessa elbowed him. "Don't be an idiot, cuz! They're not singing because they're *bored*. They're singing because they're full of Christmas spirit—and they're trying to share it."

"Share it?" Reid looked around. Some of the children were singing now too, their sticky, frosting-covered fingers waving, their heads bobbing with the rhythm. "Share it with whom?"

"With you, you dolt!" Vanessa said. "Listen, will you?"

O holy night!

Baffled, Reid frowned. His cousin began singing too.

He looked at Karina. She stopped singing, just for a second. She squeezed his hand again, then leaned closer.

"I knew you wouldn't have time to accomplish the cookie-baking and -decorating session *and* the candlelight snowshoe Christmas caroling," she told him, "so I . . . sort of . . . helped things along while I was in the front room waiting for you. We might not have snowshoes on, but we've got the rest right!"

First, it struck Reid that she'd been *waiting* for him. That had to be a good sign. Next, it struck him that Vanessa had been right. Someone *was* trying to share their Christmas spirit with him tonight—a Christmas spirit full of generosity and goodwill and love. And that person was Karina. Because that's what Reid felt flowing from her to him in that moment: *love.*

Even as the candles flickered and the next verse of that old Christmas carol swelled around them, Reid felt love. He felt beloved.

O holy night!

He felt . . . merry. In a flash, the realization hit him.

This was what Christmas was all about. Feeling love. Sharing love. Being together. Now that he'd experienced it—for the first time in over twenty years—he didn't want to let it go.

He also didn't want to disappoint Karina. Which explained why, when Olivia handed Reid a lighted candle—along with a cautious look and a silently mouthed *"Be careful!"*—he took it.

Stepping closer, Reid began to sing. And as he added his deep, infrequently used baritone to the reverent carol in progress, he knew somehow that he'd never be the same again.

Stupid freakish sentimentality had its damn stranglehold on him at last, Reid realized as he sang along. It was going to turn him into some kind of caroling fool. Maybe it already had.

And he was glad. Glad, glad, glad. *O holy night! . . .*

Chapter Seventeen

Date: December 22nd
Edgware Project Name: The Christmas House
Evaluator Guidelines: ~~remember: you're working!~~ REVEL!
Evaluator Caveats: ~~jet lag, personal biases, and/or home-sickness may cloud judgment~~ SUFFICIENT FRUITCAKE,
EGGNOG, AND/OR TRIPLE-CAFFEINATED PEPPERMINT MOCHAS MAY
BE REQUIRED TO KEEP UP STAMINA FOR LONG "ASSESSMENT"
HOURS (AKA, ROMANTIC INTERLUDES WITH REID SULLIVAN ...
WOO-HOO!)
Evaluator Notes: THIS MAY BE THE BEST CHRISTMAS EVER!

"And *that's* why I liked him so much." Alexis drew up her
knees, then hugged them close. She'd been sitting in the
B&B's snug window seat with Karina and Nicole for the past
half hour, describing parts of her family's monthlong stay in
New Zealand. "It wasn't the accent, I swear!" she emphasized. "It was that Liam was *nice*. And cute. And *so* good
with his hands, too!"

Surprised, Karina blinked. Alexis might be a little world-
lier than was typical, but she was still an eleven-year-old girl.
It couldn't possibly be appropriate for her to be considering a
particular boy's, um, *dexterity.* Could it?

"Liam could disassemble a cell phone in thirty seconds flat!" Alexis went on, her eyes shining with remembrance. "Or an engine, or anything! He was perfect for me. Totally perfect. My dad didn't get that, though. Not like *you* did, Karina. You knew what I meant from the minute I started telling you about Liam."

Karina smiled. "Well, I *have* had crushes on boys before."

"It's not just that," Alexis insisted. "It's that you like talking about boys. About me! My dad tries. He listens. But—"

"But he's pretty clueless about things sometimes," Nicole confided in a cheerfully matter-of-fact voice. "Especially about us. I think it's because he uses up all his energy traveling around and taking his clients into the Outback and stuff."

"Uh-huh," Alexis agreed. "He gets busy, then poof! He quits paying attention. It's like with Liam. Just when things were getting good, my dad had to go and get another job in stupid Timbuktu. He should have known I wouldn't want to go there!"

"It was Uzbekistan," Nicole specified primly. "Amanda would be disappointed to hear you mess up geography like that."

"Oh yeah? Well . . ." Alexis waved her arm, her pert, pretty face turning newly truculent. "Amanda's opinion doesn't matter anymore, now that she's deserting us to go to culinary school. And to stay here with Rodrigo! So who cares about geography?"

"Oh yeah. That's right." Nicole gave a sad little sound. "I forgot. . . . Amanda's staying here."

Both girls lapsed into silence, thoughts of Liam forgotten. Sitting between them with the wintery winds blowing snow at the windowpanes, Karina felt her heart go out to Alexis and Nicole. It wouldn't be easy for them to lose their nanny/tutor.

"Amanda must feel almost like family by now," she said.

The girls nodded. "She *is* our family. My dad and Amanda—they're all we have. Most of the time, at least." Nicole gazed out the window, looking past the jolly, cling-on

Christmas decorations someone had affixed to the panes. "We don't see our mom very much. She *wants* to spend more time with us, but—"

"But she travels a lot doing biodiversity research. She finds rare species of plants and figures out how to preserve them." Alexis poked at the knee of her jeans, keeping her head down. "It's not her fault she can't be with us more often."

"Sometimes that happens." Karina nodded, commiserating with them. "Even families who all live together in one place don't always get to spend as much time together as they'd like to."

Skeptically, Nicole looked up. "Does that happen to you?"

Karina nodded. "I always wish I had more time with my kids. But I have to work and run errands and—you know— *sleep* once in a while." She broke off, punctuating her statement with a grin. "Because, despite all the rumors, I'm actually *not* superhuman."

"You seem pretty good to us," Alexis declared, glancing up from her jeans at last. "You seem *awesome,* Karina! You always have time to talk with people. You always try to help everyone. *And* you have cute scarves to share. That's pretty good too."

"Yeah. Olivia, Josh, and Michael are *so* lucky." Nicole flashed her newly painted fingernails. "My dad and Amanda never thought of doing my nails for me. I *love* this nail polish!"

"Well . . . thanks, girls. I've been having fun with you, too." It was true. Karina hoped Reid didn't have some fatherly policy she'd violated with that DIY manicure. She doubted it. When it came to parenting, Reid seemed pretty freewheeling. "But I always want to do better, *especially* with Olivia, Josh, and Michael. Like with this Christmas. It's our first one with just the four of us, and I want it to be the best one ever!"

Both the Sullivan girls appeared mystified.

"I don't think you can do anything to make Christmas

better," Alexis told her. "It's not like an engine part you can tweak or a component you can swap out of something. Christmas is something that just happens. It just . . . is what it is."

Nicole nodded. "I don't think you should worry about it too much. Alexis and I might not have had much experience with Christmas until now, but it seems like *everyone* loves it. Automatically! Everyone here at The Christmas House does, that's for sure. So Olivia and Michael and Josh probably will too."

"*I'm* starting to love Christmas," Alexis admitted.

"Me too!" Nicole said, her eyes wide. "I didn't know if I would. But wrapping up gifts and singing Christmas carols and eating cookies sure beats playing 'Spot the Kangaroo.'"

"Even my dad is getting into it," Alexis added. "*That's* something we never expected. Did you hear him singing?"

"I sure did." At the memory of Reid adding his deep, rough voice to the B&B's rendition of "O Holy Night!" Karina smiled anew. When it came to Christmas, Reid had been a pretty hard-core holdout. But somehow, her impromptu caroling session had gotten to him . . . and things had blossomed from there. Ever since that night, Reid had begun participating in the B&B's holiday activities with extra vigor. "Your dad was great."

He was pretty adorable, too. There was nothing quite like seeing a burly, bearded, six-foot-tall world traveler hunkering down with the kids to set up toy train tracks around the Christmas trees, laughing with the adults over the Pin the Tail on Rudolph game they'd established in the front room, or lingering on the front porch to point out Kismet's multicolored holiday lights as they glowed across the ice-locked lake.

"This morning, I caught my dad putting on Digby's doggie sweater—*and* telling the dog how 'Christmassy' he looked." Nicole flickered her fingertips again, still admiring her manicure. "If that's not some kind of miracle, I don't know what is."

"*Love* is a miracle." Alexis waggled her eyebrows at

Karina. "And I bet Karina agrees with me, don't you? Especially now?"

Catching a glimmer of movement outside the window, Karina gave a distracted nod. Then she squinted. A taxi glided to a stop along the icy, snowbank-bordered street outside the B&B.

"I think my dad agrees with that too," Nicole added in an equally meaning-laden tone. "Love is *totally* a miracle."

"Mmm-hmmm." As the taxi's doors opened and its passengers emerged, Karina twisted in the window seat to get a better view. The B&B was full. That meant the new arrivals couldn't be guests of The Christmas House. So who could be out there?

". . . even though *lots* of women like him," Nicole was nattering on, not noticing Karina's distractedness. The little girl lapsed into silence, giving Karina an expectant look.

Belatedly, Karina realized she'd lost track of the conversation. At the same time, it occurred to her that *Chelsea* might be out there. Chelsea, who'd been so upset about the situation with Eric that she'd threatened to leave the Bahamas early. Karina had been able to convince her that bailing on a luxury vacation with her own parents wasn't exactly going to "show Eric a thing or two." But you never knew with "C."

Envisioning herself sharing a room with her ex-husband's girlfriend at the crowded B&B, Karina shook her head. Maybe it wouldn't be that bad, she told herself. She could glean more savvy dating tips—in person this time—like the one Chelsea had texted her a few days ago. MAKE HIM WAIT, K! MAKE HIM BEGGG!

Beg, *her?* Preposterous. On the other hand . . . Karina imagined Reid pleading for a seductive favor and realized the idea had a certain arresting appeal. Maybe Chelsea had something there. . . .

"So do you love him or not?" Alexis demanded, leaning

sideways in the window seat to catch Karina's attention. "We have a right to know, you know. We're kind of involved."

The girls lapsed into a frustrated silence, clearly waiting for an answer from her—even as Karina realized it wasn't Chelsea who'd shown up at The Christmas House. The first passenger to get out of the taxi *was* a woman, though. The next was a little boy. The third was a man. As Karina watched, he waved off the driver's offer to give change for his fare. Then all three turned to face the B&B. At the sight of them, Karina gasped.

"Well?" Nicole demanded. "Do you? Do you, Karina?"

It was her sister, Stephanie. And Blake. And Justin.

"Of course! Of course, I do!" Karina blurted. Whatever the girls were alluding to would have to wait. She grabbed her coat, then hastily dragged it on. A hat and scarf came next. "I'm sorry, girls. We'll have to finish this later. Right now, I've got to go!"

With the image of her sister's family filling her mind, Karina headed for the front porch. She was excited to see Steph, Justin, and Blake, of course. But she had to intercept them. She had to make sure they didn't blow her cover. She had to make sure everything was okay, everyone was happy, and things were good—with her family and with the Edgware evaluation.

As Karina left the window seat, Alexis's voice trailed after her. "Well, you heard her," the little girl said, her tone distinct. "I guess that means our next step is clear."

"I guess it does," Nicole agreed. "We'll have to—"

But Karina didn't hear the rest. She opened the B&B's front door and stepped onto the snowy porch, calling out a greeting to Stephanie, Justin, and her adorable, beloved nephew.

Standing at the B&B's snow-covered corral fence, Karina wrapped her scarf more tightly around her neck. At the edge of the corral, little Blake held out a carrot to Holly (or maybe Ivy). The Clydesdale bit into it, sending horsey spittle flying.

Blake laughed, delighted. Justin's eyes went wide. Making a face, he whipped out a bottle of hand sanitizer. He squirted some in his son's palm. Beside Karina, Stephanie turned her face to the sky, idly trying to catch a snowflake on her tongue.

"I'm happy to see that Blake is feeling better." Karina strived to sound as though her heart *weren't* still galloping in her chest like a hyperactive hamster on a wheel. It wasn't easy. Stephanie had given her a shock by arriving in Kismet. "He seems fully recovered. And he seems to like feeding the horses, too."

"Yes, he does like the horses." Her sister nodded. "Is that why you hustled us out here to the corral? We didn't even have a chance to see the inside of The Christmas House! I'm dying of curiosity. So what if they're at one hundred percent occupancy right now? It's not as if we plan to stay here tonight, so—"

"So *that's* why we can't go inside!" Karina interrupted, her sister's frequent-traveler/evaluator lingo ringing in her ears. "The Sullivans might find it suspicious if you started quoting statistics about their B&B's occupancy rates, insurance premiums, and staff turnover rates for the past decade."

Also, they might find it suspicious to discover that the spy in their midst was someone they trusted and welcomeed like a family member.

"Oh. You think so?" Stephanie caught a snowflake at last. She gave an elaborate gulp, then grinned at Karina. "Come on. I'm a professional. I'm not going to do something stupid."

Something stupid . . . like not file the Edgware reports.

Her sister didn't have to say it. The observation hung between them all the same, implicit but no less troublesome.

It seemed pretty obvious to Karina that Stephanie had arrived to make sure the evaluation she'd entrusted her with—

the evaluation Karina felt less and less enthusiasm for as she grew closer to the Sullivans (and to Reid)—was getting done.

She edged closer, keeping her face turned toward the B&B's barn instead of Stephanie, feeling like a character from a cheesy spy movie. "I *have* filed most of the reports," Karina revealed, moving her lips as little as possible. "You don't have to worry about that. And the checklists are almost done too."

"Oh, I'm not worried." Stephanie gave her a curious look. In a surprised, animated tone, she asked, "Is *that* why you think I came here? Because you think I don't trust you to file the Edgware reports in time?" She sighed. "Oh, Karina . . ."

"Shhh! Keep your voice down." Anxiously, Karina glanced around the picturesque grounds. She peered behind the sleigh. "Someone might overhear you and realize what's going on."

"Yes. Hmmm. 'What's going on.'" With a puzzlingly enigmatic frown, Stephanie leaned on the corral fence. She didn't strive for the least bit of surreptitiousness. "Yes, *I'd* like to know 'what's going on.' In fact, *that's* why I'm here."

"What's why you're here?" Karina frowned. "If this is because nobody thinks I can get anything done because of my *very minor* procrastination tendencies," she said, remembering the caustic way Eric had pointed out her shortcomings when she'd told him about the Edgware job, "you should know that I recently had a breakthrough about that. I think I know how to lick it."

Focus, came Reid's sexy voice. *Are you focusing now?*

Filled with inappropriately seductive memories, Karina fidgeted. She felt her cheeks heat, even as the rest of her grew increasingly chilly. Standing outside, she knew she would never become accustomed to the wintery weather here in the Midwest.

"Please. Your procrastination issues are not why I'm here." Appearing amused, Steph gave a dismissive wave of her gloved hand. "Besides, your need to help everyone all the time is a far bigger issue than procrastination ever thought of being. You just can't say no." She paused. "Thankfully, not even to me."

"Gee, thanks for the pop psych analysis." Feeling slighted, Karina shook her head. "I'm glad you're benefiting from my weak spots. Any other flaws of mine you want to point out while you're here? You *did* take a plane all this way. . . ."

Her sister appeared to realize she'd overstepped. "I'm sorry. I didn't mean to come off so critically. *I* think you're wonderful." Stephanie held out her arms. "Hug it out?"

Karina relented. They shared a sisterly hug—a big, awkward, bundled-up, sisterly hug. As they made contact, their padded and weatherproofed coats nearly caused sparks to fly. Their wooly scarves and hats crackled with static electricity. They both laughed, holding out their arms like two Michelin men.

"Yikes! We are *such* California girls!" Stephanie said.

Karina agreed, still smiling. And all at once, she felt much better. She wasn't used to fending for herself yet. With Steph here, she realized, maybe she wouldn't have to anymore.

"Thanks for coming," Karina said, genuinely meaning it. She gazed at her sister, feeling grateful for her presence. "It wouldn't have occurred to me to ask for help with the evaluation, not in a million years. But now that you're here—"

"Oh, I can't help with the evaluation." Stephanie held up her gloved hands, shaking her head. "I wouldn't know where to start. I'm not the one who's spent the past week here. It wouldn't be fair. I can advise you or help with paperwork, but—"

"But you can't take over?" Karina's heart sank.

"No. It doesn't work that way. If an evaluator can't finish an assessment, the whole thing is scrapped. The company doesn't like doing that, though. Obviously, it costs them money."

"That makes sense." Karina had only glanced at the full set

of Edgware company guidelines. Most of them hadn't applied
to her, she'd decided. Overall, the company's rules had
seemed lengthy, comprehensive, and painstakingly intricate.
They'd appeared to provide for every possible eventuality—
corporate bureaucracy in triplicate. "But if you didn't come
here to check up on me, and you didn't come here to take over
the evaluation, then why did you and Justin and Blake come
to Kismet?"

Stephanie grinned. "Isn't it obvious?"

"No." Karina thought about it. "Although Josh, Olivia, and
Michael will be thrilled to see you. The only part they didn't
like about having Christmas here at The Christmas House this
year was *not* getting to see their aunt and uncle and cousin."

"Aww. That's sweet!" Steph gazed toward the B&B, as
though hoping to spot her niece and nephews there among the
sparkling holiday lights, swags of evergreen garlands, and
tall, decorated Christmas trees that were visible from the win-
dows. "We're looking forward to seeing them too."

"Right. I'll get them in a sec. And . . . ?"

"And . . . ?" Stephanie gave an overly innocent arch of her
eyebrow, obviously playing dumb.

"And why else did you come here?" Karina pressed.

"Oh. Right." Amused all over again, Stephanie nodded.
She gazed across the fence as her husband offered another
carrot to one of the Clydesdales. Her very-healthy-seeming
son looked on, clapping his mittened hands with glee. Nate
Kelly stood to the side, just out of earshot, supervising snack
time. "I came here because you've been so distracted over the
phone. Because you've been filing reports late, even though,
most of the time, you're relentlessly punctual. I'm here because you've been calling less and less as the week's gone on.
And I'm here because"—here her sister paused, clearly relishing the next item in her baffling list—"one of your texts to
'C' went astray."

Uh-oh. "You got one of the texts I sent to Chelsea?"

"That's right."

Double uh-oh. "And you're, um, wondering . . . ?"

"I'm wondering"—her sister's smile broadened mischievously—"how things went when you wore Chelsea's leopard-print camisole the next time you had some 'private time' with 'Mr. Wonderful.'"

Hearing the nickname she'd bestowed on Reid—purely to protect his anonymity, of course—Karina felt her face flush. On the occasion in question, things had gone well. Very well.

At least until the power outage had occurred.

"In my own defense," she said, "he really *is* wonderful."

"He must be, if he's distracted *you* from doing a favor you promised. Usually, you're super-reliable, Karina. So what—"

"I'm so sorry, Steph!" Karina interrupted before Stephanie could go on. She didn't want to disappoint her sister any further. She had to explain. Except she couldn't. "I didn't mean for any of this to happen. It just . . . did. I couldn't help it."

"That's funny. You sound like your rat bastard ex-husband did when he confessed his affair with Chelsea."

She did, kind of, Karina realized. Maybe she'd been too hard on Eric, it occurred to her. Maybe he and Chelsea really *had* found true love together—at least temporarily. Despite Karina's efforts on the phone, Chelsea still seemed convinced she and Eric wouldn't reconcile. Sidestepping that issue for now, Karina kept talking. "I swear, I'm not letting it affect my evaluation. I made a promise to you, and I'm keeping it!"

"Honey, that's very generous of you, as always." Her younger sister moved closer, her face filled with compassion. "But *you* come first with me, before any job. You must know that. If you need to bow out, I'll understand. I promise I didn't come here to browbeat you into completing the evaluation."

"You didn't? But you said I was usually 'super-reliable.' And you sounded so annoyed! You know I hate when someone's mad—"

"Karina, stop it!" Stephanie shook her head, a new sense of empathy in her expression. "I'm sorry. I was being sarcastic, that's all. I promise I'm not mad. You're *still* super-reliable, as always. Of course!" She gave Karina a speculative look. "And *I'm* still insanely curious about Mr. Wonderful. So spill!"

Karina shut her mouth, reluctant to talk about Reid.

But her sister didn't follow her lead. "He *must* be pretty special, to make you this jumpy. And after you quit calling me as much, and mis-sent that text, I guess I was just hoping . . ."

Karina was almost afraid to ask. "Hoping what?"

"Well, I was hoping you'd finally get what you're wishing for this Christmas," Steph said. "I wanted to be there when it happened. Something told me it might be this year."

"What I'm wishing for?" Jokingly, Karina made a face. "Have you been looking at my wish list?" She sighed theatrically. "I know it's *unlikely* I'll score a new car and a pair of pants that magically make my butt look smaller, but there's always hope."

"No, silly!" Stephanie hugged her. She leaned back, giving Karina a serious look. "I know the contents of your *real* wish list better than that." She paused, then sucked in a preparatory breath. "I want you to have the family of your dreams."

That wasn't what she'd expected to hear. Struck by the depth of her sister's insightfulness, Karina couldn't help staring in surprise.

I want that too, she thought. *I do.*

Most of the time, she tried not to dwell on things she couldn't have. But more than anything, Karina knew, she wanted a happy family—a close-knit, united, loving family. She liked to be settled down. She liked to care for people. She liked closeness and security and feeling needed. All those things came from having a family—especially a family at Christmastime.

She and the kids were a complete family, of course. They

were. But if they could somehow find even *more* love to share . . .

"You deserve everything you've been wishing for and more!" Stephanie went on. She gazed at Karina intently, as though she could somehow compel her hopes into being. "You do! You deserve real happiness, Karina. More than anyone else I know. If that means starting over with Mr. Wonderful, then do it!" Steph gave her a mock ferocious fist waggle. "You know, provided he passes my rigorous sister test and proves he'll be amazing to you."

Helplessly, Karina shook her head. She didn't know how her sister had intuited so much from several phone conversations, some e-mails and texts, and one (in-progress) heart-to-heart, but she didn't doubt her sister's insight. She and Stephanie had always been close. This was just another example of that.

"I can't, Steph," Karina protested. "I've only known him a week! He *is* wonderful, but I've got to be sensible for once."

"Really?" Her sister tilted her head. "Why?"

"Why? Because I—" Karina broke off, gesturing in a way she hoped would send a few scintillating thoughts to her brain. Nada. She exhaled, her breath frosty in the wintery air. "I don't know. Because I'm a mom. Because I'm responsible for my children aside from myself. Because I've made mistakes."

"So? Who hasn't?"

"You don't understand. Didn't you hear me? It's only been a week! I can't possibly know Re—know *him*—well enough to risk it."

"You dated Eric for a year and a half," Stephanie reminded her. "You were engaged to him for another two years. That's three and a half years. And look how *that* turned out!"

Well, that was true. Karina had been with Eric a long time before they'd gotten married. Their marriage had still ended badly. A long-term acquaintance was no guarantee of happiness or marital success. Conversely, a short-term relationship probably wasn't doomed to fail. But Karina wasn't ready to admit it.

Silently, she gazed across the B&B's grounds toward the lake. She glimpsed people ice-skating. People ice fishing. People going about their lives *without* being paralyzed by doubt.

She wasn't one of them. She needed certainty and schedules. She needed promises and to-do lists. She needed accomplishments—big and small—to bolster her as she went about her days.

But she also needed Reid.

Tentatively, Karina looked at her sister. "I didn't come here to find Mr. Wonderful. It wasn't supposed to happen this way. I was going to date a while, maybe sign up for one of those online services, get to know someone *slowly,* at my own pace—"

"It's Christmas!" Steph urged in a jolly tone, kicking up some snow. "Why don't you take a chance on a miracle, for once?"

A miracle . . . Something about that reminded Karina of her conversation with Alexis and Nicole. They'd appeared unusually intent about the subject at hand, but she wasn't sure why.

"You know what?" She faced her sister. "Do you mind if we cut this short? I just realized there's something I have to do."

"Something to do with Mr. Wonderful? Who is he, anyway? Another guest? A neighbor?" Waggling her brows, Stephanie nodded at Nate. "They seem to make 'em pretty hunky around here."

"I'll tell you later." Breathlessly, Karina hugged her sister. Now that she'd made her decision, she had no time to waste. She wheeled around, then stopped. Then she turned again. Excitedly, she asked, "If I bring the kids out to see you, do you think you and Justin can baby-sit a while? I don't know how long this will take, so I can't make any promises, but—"

"Of course! Don't worry about a thing." Stephanie winked. "Justin and I accidentally booked two rooms at a hotel downtown—dangers of easy online booking and two over-achievers with laptops." She grinned. "We have adjoining suites, so there's plenty of room for everyone. Josh and Michael and Olivia can even stay overnight, if you want."

"Thanks. I might." Biting her lip, Karina hesitated. Standing in the snow, feeling warmed from the inside out, she gave her sister one final look. "This isn't crazy, right? Good things happen at Christmas, don't they?"

"More than any other time of year," Steph assured her. With a fond smile, she shooed Karina away. "So go make a miracle!"

For a divorced single mom, it didn't get much more miraculous than a reliable overnight baby-sitter and an urging to follow her heart. Grateful to have both, Karina nodded.

"Wish me luck," she said, then headed for The Christmas House to find her children and set her new plan in motion.

After all, Karina realized as she hurried through the snow, the B&B was officially the place where holiday dreams came true! Their brochures and Web site promised it. With decades of satisfied guests behind the inn, it couldn't possibly lead her astray . . . could it?

No way, she decided, and just kept going.

Chapter Eighteen

... From the desk of Betty Sullivan
DECEMBER 22ND
LOCATION: THE CHRISTMAS HOUSE
SCHEDULED EVENT: "DAILY DOUBLE FEATURE" —
1:00 P.M. TO 5:00 P.M.

Standing in The Christmas House's semidarkened private theater room, Reid supervised the showing of the afternoon's holiday movies. His grandparents had combined a downstairs utility room and an unneeded formal dining room to create this popular area of the B&B, complete with six ascending rows of cushy stadium-style seating, a high-def and surround-sound-enabled viewing system, and all the holiday ambiance that made the rest of The Christmas House so irresistible.

Even to him. As crazy as it sounded, Reid found that he suddenly had a real fondness for mistletoe and poinsettias, flashy ornaments and dancing Santas, Christmas carols and garland and all the rest of the seasonal accoutrements. He was even enjoying the movie that played on-screen right now—a family-focused tale about Ebenezer Scrooge, the ghosts of Christmas past, present, and future, and the miracle of second chances.

Someone sneaked inside the room, briefly sending in a glimmer of afternoon light. Reid glanced in that direction.

At the sight of Karina standing there, obviously searching for someone, he believed in the miracle of second chances all over again. Because he'd all but given up on finding someone to love, Reid realized in that moment. He'd told himself he could be happy just traveling and working and taking care of Alexis and Nicole. But while all those things were fulfilling, they weren't the same as being with someone who really understood him. They weren't the same as savoring the connectedness of a night spent pleasurably in bed with a woman he cared about. They weren't the same as loving a woman and (maybe) being loved back.

They weren't the same as Karina.

Ghostly movie images flashed over her as she stood there. She spotted him at last, then edged past the rearmost row and came eagerly toward him. Dressed in her colossal coat, hat, scarf, boots, jeans, and innumerable sweaters, Karina waved. Her smile broadened. She moved faster, her arrival making Reid remember how much he looked forward to Christmas morning this year, and all the lasting surprises he hoped it would contain.

Not gifts. Not candy canes. *Karina*. That's all.

"Is everything all right?" Reid asked when she reached him. "You look—" He broke off, studying her with new bafflement. "Different, somehow. Did something happen?"

"You could say that." With barely suppressed merriment, Karina took his hand. She squeezed it as she glanced at the rows of movie-watching guests. "Can you leave for a few minutes?"

"For you? I can leave for the day. All day, every day."

Decisively, Reid gestured at the B&B staff member who'd accompanied him to the theater room. He exchanged a few signals with her. They both nodded. Just like that, things were settled.

"I'm yours," he told Karina. "Where to now?"

"Your room," she said without missing a beat. "There's something important we need to take care of."

Reid could think of several important things he wanted to take care of with Karina. Smiling, he led the way. Together they raced down the hallway. They flew past the B&B's front desk.

"Hold my calls!" Reid yelled to Vanessa as they passed his wide-eyed cousin. "Hold down the fort! Hold everything!"

Vanessa laughed. So did Karina, breathlessly, as Reid tugged her up the stairs. Halfway to the second floor, he stopped. He kissed her. He framed her face in his hands, pushed them both against the banister, and kissed her again. *Ah*.

"I think that movie got to you," Karina said. "You're like Scrooge *after* the ghosts visit, and it's Christmas morning."

"It feels like Christmas morning. And it's about to get even better," Reid promised. "So what are you waiting for?"

He smacked her delectable backside, just to get her moving. Karina squealed, then headed upstairs. Reid might not have been able to discern what was different about her, but he liked it.

He liked it even more when they reached his room. Karina wasted no time getting close to him. The moment the door closed, she whipped off her coat, hat, and scarf, left everything on the floor where it landed, then threw her arms around him. A second later, she was kissing him, already working at the buttons of his flannel shirt.

"Hey! Hey . . ." Thrilled to find himself there with her, Reid covered her hands with his own. He interlaced their fingers, then squeezed. "Now that we have some free time, we might as well take things slowly. We've waited a long time for this."

"But it's only been a few days since we were together."

"I know." He kissed her again. When he raised his head, all

he could see was Karina's face, her warm smile, her slightly dazzled expression. "It's felt like a *very* long time, too."

Smiling even more broadly at that, Karina nodded.

Yesterday, after the power outage (and despite their promises of *later*), they hadn't managed to find a minute to be alone together. The cookie-baking and -decorating session had run long. So had the snowshoe-free Christmas caroling. Afterward, Michael had gotten a tummy ache from scarfing down a few too many gingerbread men. Then Nicole had confronted Reid about her new manicure, giddily flashing her pink-painted fingertips and all but daring him to lay down a few stern fatherly laws.

He hadn't, of course. Not about something so inconsequential. But just as Karina had needed to stay by Michael's side, Reid had needed to deal with his daughter. Fortunately, he and Karina had both understood the delay.

Now, though, there was nothing holding them back. There was nothing to keep Reid from pulling Karina into his arms, running his hands down her back, and cradling her derrière in his palms, just the way he liked to do. There was nothing to keep Karina from tugging aside his shirt collar, kissing his neck, and inciting a whole new wave of wanting. Damn, that felt good.

With his heart hammering, Reid arched his neck. He wanted more of this. He wanted more of *her.* Almost panting, he lowered his mouth to hers again. This time, their kiss felt sweet, full of yearning and promise and all the hopes he wanted to share.

"I think *you're* a little different today, too," Karina said. She nuzzled his neck as she resumed unbuttoning his shirt. "You seem . . . I dunno, *freer,* somehow. More open."

Reid shrugged. "This is what happens when a tough guy like me caves in to Christmas." He grinned. "Give me a few jingle bells and a nutcracker figurine, and it's all over. I'm gone."

"I'm gone, too," Karina said. She spread her palms over his chest, then gazed up at him with every impression of giddiness. Then, surprisingly, seriousness. "Reid, I'm crazy about . . ."

You, he waited breathlessly to hear. *I'm crazy about you.*

". . . this." Another giddy caress. "I really love . . ."

You, barreled into his head. *I really love you.*

". . . being with you!" Karina finished.

It looked as though his beard was staying, Reid realized. While those sentiments were close, they weren't what he wanted. They weren't *I love you.* They weren't going to break his razor out of retirement, the way he'd promised Karina they would.

Almost as though she'd realized as much, Karina ducked her head. She sighed. For an instant, she appeared troubled.

But then she gazed back at him, her eyes full of certainty and generosity and desire, and Reid quit caring—for the moment, at least—about the flagging powers of his nookie beard and what it might mean if his good-luck charm was failing him.

Right now, he had Karina. That's all that mattered.

"I have an idea," Karina said, delivering him a saucy smile. "I'm obviously feeling a little tongue-tied right now. Instead of talking, why don't I just *show* you what I mean?"

"That might work," Reid agreed with a playful nod. "Some cultures are very skilled at nonverbal communication. You can share all kinds of things with your eyes, your hands—"

"Your mouth." Karina dropped her gaze to his lips. With a confident gesture, she raised herself on tiptoes and kissed him.

Reid approved. "Now you're getting it."

"No, I think *you're* getting it," Karina said. Then she proceeded to show him, in all sorts of detailed and pleasurable ways, exactly how things were going to go down between them.

* * *

It was all different this time.

That's what Karina realized, late in the afternoon, as she luxuriated in Reid's nearness . . . and lounged in his bed, feeling fully sated and pleasurably cocooned from the rest of the world.

Now when she touched Reid, it wasn't simply to revel in his rock-hard abs and honed physique. It was to share her delight in their togetherness. When she kissed him, it wasn't simply to savor the slow glide of his mouth across hers. It was to communicate that she wanted to be with him, now and always. When she opened her arms and legs and welcomed him inside her, urging him closer and closer, it wasn't simply to enjoy the intimate union of their bodies coming together. It was to experience as much unity with him as possible—and to make that unity last.

Despite a couple of frustrating attempts earlier, she hadn't been able to say the words she'd come here to say—but that didn't mean she didn't feel the emotions behind them. As Karina lay beside Reid amid his snowman-print holiday bedding, face-to-face with the pale wintery sunshine splashing over them, she *definitely* felt plenty of emotions. Revelation. Happiness. Gratitude. Surprise. But most of all, she felt love.

Love.

With all that she'd been through in her failed marriage, that wasn't easy to admit. Not even to herself. *Love* meant risk. Could she really take a chance, Karina mused, that her holiday affair could become something more? Could she really trust herself to feel these feelings . . . and not get burned?

She wasn't sure. And until she was sure . . .

Well, until she was sure, she couldn't tell Reid that she loved him. No matter how crestfallen he'd looked when she'd offered a substitute: *I really love . . . being with you!*

When she'd first tried saying it, Reid had seemed ready to

bolt for his razor and eradicate his beard for good. But then Karina had stumbled over the words. Reid had quit figuratively leaping for a quick "she loves me!" victory lap with his razor. And Karina had found herself there, lamely throwing out double entendres instead of telling him what he needed to hear.

I love you, Reid. I love you.

It was the truth, yes. Karina couldn't deny that. She *did* love Reid, with all her heart. But she couldn't risk revealing it. Not yet.

A part of her still feared it was *her* fault Eric had left her. A part of her still had so many unanswered questions: Could she have done more? Could she have made Eric happier? Could she have cared for him, nurtured him, *helped* him more? And if she could have . . . would it have made a difference?

Not knowing the answers to those questions (and many more besides), Karina snuggled closer to Reid. She didn't want to think about her ex-husband, his sexy young (potentially ex-) girlfriend, or her latent shortcomings as a person and a wife. She wanted to tell Reid that she cared for him. That she *loved* him.

She wanted to tell Reid that she believed they belonged together. Lying there in his arms, snug and safe, she believed they could be happy together. She even believed, surrendering to a goofy grin at the thought alone, that their children could blend together in one happy mash-up of serendipitous togetherness and laughter and seven-under-one-roof boisterousness.

Reid wouldn't care, it occurred to Karina, if Josh pick pocketed his wallet, if Olivia wrapped him in protective padding and yards of caution tape, or if Michael peppered him with brain-teasing questions from now until forever. Reid was just that easygoing. He was just that loving. And for her part, Karina knew, she wouldn't mind if Alexis hacked into her laptop, if Nicole sweet-talked her into relaxing every rule she had, or if Reid's daughters kept her up late every night with giggling and girl talk. She enjoyed their company just that much.

So tell him how you feel! Karina's heart urged. *Do it!*

But even as she inhaled a steadying breath, preparing herself to do exactly that, Karina felt Reid shift at her side. He raised his hand, then trailed his fingertips lovingly over her cheek. He smiled with evident joyfulness, almost as though the mere sight and feel of her brought him incredible bliss.

She was so lucky, Karina thought then, to have found him. Because the sight and feel and nearness of Reid made her happy, too. She'd known it outside at the B&B's corral with Steph, and she knew it now. Her holiday affair had just turned a corner. All that remained now was sealing the deal.

I love you! she thought.

No, too simple.

Guess what? Time to shave your beard!

No, too obscure. Reid might mistake her declaration of love for a grooming critique.

Merry Christmas! I'm giving you my heart!

No, too cheesy.

I love you! she sampled again.

Yes, maybe. Simple, sure. But simple things were also classic. Like Converse sneakers, shiny silver holiday tinsel, and "I'll Be Home for Christmas." It was good.

It could work. And yet, somehow, something still stopped her. It didn't feel quite like fear this time. It felt, as Reid went on gazing adoringly into her eyes, a little bit like . . .

Deception. That was the problem! She was deceiving Reid by not telling him she was the secret Edgware evaluator, Karina realized. And until she came clean about that, she could hardly profess her undying love for him. Undoubtedly, Reid would sense she was hiding something. It would be a wedge between them. He might even stop stroking her in such a loving, seductive way, making her heart rate pick up speed and her breath hitch and—

No. She had to do this. She had to tell him the truth. Her sister wouldn't blame her for it, Karina told herself. Stephanie had practically come out and ordered her to put her personal life over the B&B's assessment. She would understand.

Inhaling deeply, Karina looked at Reid. She was ready. She was ready to tell Reid she was the undercover Edgware evaluator.

At the same instant, he lifted his gaze to hers. "I'm starving!" Reid announced. Jovially, he rubbed his flat belly. "You want to sneak downstairs and find something to eat?"

It was a moment of decision—a moment Karina chickened out of. "Sure! I think Rodrigo has been teaching Amanda how to make fruitcake—good fruitcake, with lots of nuts and whiskey."

"Mmm. Sounds tasty." Reid kissed her. He rolled over, grabbed his jeans, then tossed a few clothes on the bed for her.

When Karina didn't instantly grab them, Reid raised an eyebrow. "You might cause a furor if you go downstairs naked." He shrugged, grinning. "But I'm up for it if you are."

"No! I'm coming." Hastily, Karina snatched up the first layer of her borrowed cold-weather gear, then slid out of bed. She missed its warmth almost immediately. Within seconds, she was suitably dressed. "You can't keep me away from a good fruitcake. We might need it to keep up our strength for later."

"We'll *definitely* need to keep up our strength for later."

Pulling her close—this time beside the bed—Reid brought his mouth to hers. He smiled, then tickled beneath her chin with his fingers. At her laughter, he smiled. Then he gave her a long, serious look. "I'm glad you came to get me this afternoon. I've been wanting this—wanting you—even more than I realized."

His sincerity brought a lump to her throat. Feeling utterly

uncourageous, Karina swallowed hard. "I'm glad too," she said.

For now, she decided, this would have to be enough. This closeness, this sharing, this being united with Reid. It would *have* to be enough. At least until she found a little bravery.

And as for all the rest? The secrets, the evaluation, the fact that they lived on separate continents most of the time?

Well . . . they'd deal with those problems when they had to. Or maybe, if she was lucky, a Christmas miracle really would occur, Karina told herself as she linked hands with Reid and headed downstairs with him. Maybe she and Reid would awaken on Christmas morning to find the family of their dreams already waiting for them. Maybe they would magically keep that newfound family together . . . on Christmas day and all year long.

And maybe those butt-shrinking jeans really *did* exist, Karina told herself with a cynical shake of her head.

This was a B&B, not a miracle factory. No matter how much she hoped otherwise, the only one performing any miracles around here would be her, when she finally found the courage to come clean to Reid and admit her true mission at The Christmas House.

Someday. Someday soon. Maybe right after the fruit-cake . . .

The day before Christmas Eve, Reid stood in the snow outside the B&B, fully equipped in a coat, boots, and hat. Beside him, Olivia stood outfitted in much the same fashion—except her boots were pink and featured Hello Kitty, her hat boasted a pompom on top, and her coat was a lot smaller.

Patiently, the little girl held a fistful of heavy-duty plastic twist ties in her mittened hand, waiting for his instructions. Reid motioned to her, as he'd done several times already. Olivia handed over a twist tie, then watched as he used it to expertly affix a part of The Christmas House's nearly life-size handcrafted crèche to its supporting post.

Olivia wrinkled her nose. "Why wasn't this up already?"

"The nativity scene?" Reid stepped back, surveying his work. He steadied the figure of Joseph, then glanced sideways to catch Olivia's nod. "We try not to leave it exposed to the elements too long. It's too delicate to handle much weather."

"It looks pretty sturdy to me."

"Appearances can be deceiving." Reid motioned for another twist tie, then studied the placement of the manger. "This crèche is more fragile than it looks. It's pretty special, too. A local artisan made this for my grandparents almost thirty years ago. It was one of the first decorations we used here."

"It's an heirloom, then?"

"Exactly. It's an heirloom."

"So you probably don't want it to catch fire," Olivia observed. "Or rot. Or get moldy. Or be chewed on by gophers."

Reid raised his eyebrow. "Gophers?"

"They're *very* damaging to property. Maybe even people."

"Do you have some kind of supergophers in California?"

The little girl bit her lip. "I don't think so."

"Then we're probably safe from gophers gone berserk." Reminded of something by Olivia's litany of possible hazards, Reid motioned for another twist tie. "How's your list coming?"

"Great! It's *super* long now!" Eagerly, Olivia scrabbled to take off her mittens. She reached inside her coat pocket. "You won't hardly believe it. Do you want to see it?"

"Well . . . I've got my hands full here." Matter-of-factly, Reid gestured to the crèche. "Maybe you could read it to me?"

Olivia did. While a light snow drifted down on them and Reid continued to set up the nativity scene, little Olivia recited her list of worries and potential (sometimes comically far-fetched) solutions. It turned out that her fears ranged from failing grades, to falling anvils, to . . . well, attack gophers.

When she'd finished, Olivia glanced excitedly up at him.

Reid felt frozen in place. Partly because of his inherent empathy for all the unnecessary trepidation Olivia had been experiencing. Partly because it was damn cold in Michigan in December. He didn't know how he'd ever survived the Arctic.

Just at that moment, he didn't want to go back to the frozen north anytime soon, either. Maybe adventure travel was losing a little of its luster for him. Temporarily.

"Well?" Olivia prompted. "What do you think? Do you think this list will help the people you work with who are afraid?"

At her hopeful expression, Reid felt his heart soften. He set the nativity scene's manger in place, then remained in a hunkered-down position where he'd be on eye level with Olivia.

"Maybe," he said. "Let's break it down."

"Break it down?" Olivia glanced at the B&B's front porch, where Karina and Stephanie stood talking. "What's that mean?"

"Well, there's a lot of information on your list. You did an excellent job with it!" Reid told her. "What we need to do now is verify what's there. Scientifically."

Olivia rolled her eyes. "Now you sound like Michael!"

"I don't mind that. Michael's pretty smart." Reid had never met a brighter or more inquisitive first-grader. "And so are you, to have put together such a comprehensive list."

Olivia preened beneath his praise, her cheeks pinkening.

"So the next step is: How many of the things you were worried about actually happened?" Reid affixed the manger more securely, then glanced at Olivia. "How many of your solutions did you use? Did you ever use more than one solution? Two?"

Uncomfortably, Olivia stood on one foot, then the other. She adjusted the figure of Mary. She gazed at her mother and aunt again, clearly reluctant to answer his questions.

"A rough percentage estimate would be fine," Reid assured her in his most relaxed tone. He wanted to avoid spooking her. He wanted to help her. "Or if you don't like math—"

"Hey! Girls can be *great* at math! Don't stereotype me!"

"—you can just give me a letter grade. How useful do *you* think this strategy would be for my clients? A? B? Or C?" Reid gazed at her in all seriousness. "And I wasn't stereotyping you. I'm sorry. I know girls can be great at math. Alexis sure is."

"I like Alexis," Olivia nattered. "Nicole too. She's nice."

Reid didn't take the bait. "Is misdirection on your list?"

"I don't know. I don't even know what misdirection means." Keenly, Olivia eyed him. "My mom would know. She's smart too. Except about my dad. I mean, she *still* thinks he would have stayed with us if only she'd been a little nicer to him."

All at once, something Karina had said to Reid flooded into his mind. *But I have to do more for you first,* Karina had told him desperately. *Otherwise, you won't stay. You won't stay!*

Now, that statement finally made sense. Karina believed her ex-husband wouldn't have absconded to the Bahamas with his "Pop-Tart" girlfriend if only she'd been "nicer" to him somehow.

"I can't imagine your mom being anything less than nice."

"Nobody can. Not even my dad." At the very idea, Olivia shook her head. As though sensing she'd struck on a winning diversionary tactic, she blathered on. "My dad told me and Josh and Michael that he just fell in love with Chelsea, and that was that. He said it had nothing to do with my mom *or* with us."

Well, at least the man had *some* sense, Reid thought. He may have been foolish enough to let Karina go, but he'd also been responsible enough to reassure his children about his divorce.

That was something. But it wasn't enough. Otherwise,

Olivia wouldn't have come here toting a worry list as long as her arm.

Refocusing, Reid motioned for another twist tie. Olivia obliged. He set the handcrafted figure of a crook-toting shepherd in place next. Beside him, Olivia went on fidgeting.

"All right! *Fine!*" she blurted. "It was zero, okay? *Zero!*"

Finally, Reid's patience was rewarded. "What was zero?"

"The number of times anything on my list actually happened," Olivia admitted. Grumbling, she toed the snow. "Zero is also the number of times I had to use one of my solutions."

"Oh. I see." Mulling that over, Reid steadied an angel.

"I didn't want you to know about that part. I wanted you to think I had a really good list—a list that would help the people you work with! I didn't think you'd ask me if I *tried* any of the solutions on it." Olivia glared at her multiple pages of notepaper. "I was proud of this list. But now I see it's just a stupid bunch of useless worries. That's no good to anybody!"

"I wouldn't go that far," Reid said gently. "It's been useful to me, to help me understand"—*you*—"a few things."

"But none of that stuff ever happened," Olivia groused, her shoulders slumped. "It was just like you said—a waste of time."

"Was it really wasted, if you learned something?"

"It *was* wasted, if you can't use my dumb list!"

Compassionately, Reid gazed at her. "I think I'll get by. I don't mind changing tactics. It's part of my work. When you're faced with a blizzard or a hurricane shows up, sometimes you have to change course. There's no point arguing with reality."

"But what about the people you work with?"

"Hmmm." Reid glanced up at the steel-gray sky, pondering that question. "I guess it's possible my clients need to learn the same thing you did: that worrying doesn't help much."

With a dour frown, Olivia said, "I don't think they'll

want to learn that. I know *I* didn't. What am I supposed to do now?"

"Now that you don't need mental fire drills every day?"

Her gaze looked tentative. She nodded. "Uh-huh."

"I dunno." Reid shrugged. "You could think about Christmas instead. Or horses or math problems or pink glittery scarves."

"Or the next *Twilight* movie!" Suddenly, Olivia seemed fully cheered. She grinned at him, her eyes sparkling. "Without worrying, I'll have *tons* of room in my head for other things. Like Jacob." She sighed. "He's dreamy. I have all the *Twilight* action figures, you know. They're classic collectibles."

Aha. "So *that's* why Alexis and Nicole have abandoned Barbie and Ken in favor of Bella and Edward," Reid said.

"Probably." Olivia nodded, seeming reassured—and completely worry free—for the first time since he'd known her. "Bella and Edward are good investments. All properly licensed and authorized *Twilight* merch is a good investment, in my opinion."

Reid grinned. "'Merch,' huh? You sound like an expert."

"Well . . . maybe I am! I *will* need something to take the place of my expert worrying—I mean, *planning*—right?"

"Right."

"But if you get any merch, don't open the boxes."

"That's what Nicole told me," Reid said. "She said it affects the collectible resale value." He shook his head. "I have the feeling being stateside is changing my daughters in more ways than one."

They hadn't quit dropping hints about staying in the states (maybe) forever, either.

"Well, I wouldn't worry about it too much," Olivia said with a cocky grin. "I hear worrying doesn't get you anywhere. And sometimes surprises are nice, anyway." Impulsively, she moved closer and hugged him. "I feel better about things now. Thanks, Reid."

Startled but pleased, Reid hugged her back. "No problem, kiddo." He smiled at her. "Hey, if I wind up staying here in the states, can I hire you to be my personal tween pop culture consultant and licensed memorabilia advisor?"

"Sure!" Olivia laughed. "But you'll have to move to San Diego for that. I think you'd like it okay, though. It's nice."

All at once, the idea had a definite appeal. Reid nodded. "I do like the beach. And you never know what might happen. Christmas *is* a time for miracles, you know."

"Hey." Olivia gave him a chary look. "I recognize that line. You stole it from The Christmas House brochure!"

"Guilty. I only borrow from the best source material." Still grinning, Reid heard his cell phone ring. He took it out, then glanced at the display. *Robert Sullivan.* Uh-oh. What could his grandparents be calling about? "Sorry, Olivia. I've got to answer this."

She nodded, leaving him to accept the call.

On the other end of the line, his grandfather cut right to the chase, barely taking time for a hello. "Reid, I have bad news. The Christmas House sale is off. Edgware just cancelled."

Chapter Nineteen

Date: December 23rd
Edgware Project Name: The Christmas House
Guest/Staff Interface Opportunity: ~~team-driven Christmas karaoke contest~~ POINTLESS, NOW THAT THE EVALUATION IS CANCELLED
Interaction Goal: ~~assess feasibility of duplicating services across international Edgware properties~~ HELP REID !

Watching Reid and Olivia working on The Christmas House's nativity scene across the B&B's wide expanse of property, Karina crossed her arms over her bundled-up chest. She sighed.

"I don't know what they're talking about over there," she told Stephanie, "but Reid obviously has a knack for relating to Olivia. Maybe it comes from raising two daughters?"

"Could be. From what you've told me, Reid has had to do his parenting on his own for all these years. Sometimes in actual wilderness areas! With no family or anyone except Amanda to support him." Appearing suddenly distracted, Stephanie withdrew her vibrating cell phone. She glanced at its screen. "Sorry. It's a message from work. I'd better find out what's going on."

"Go ahead." Karina waved her sister to the other side of the porch, where the B&B's porch swing had been wrapped and decorated with candy cane stripes. "I'll wait for you here."

"Okay."

Stephanie headed in that direction, passing Josh on the way. Karina smiled at her son, surprised to see him outside away from the B&B's Fun Zone—and doubly surprised to recognize the item he held bundled—along with something else she couldn't fully see—against his chest.

"My purse!" Astonished, Karina accepted it from her son. "I lost track of this"—*on the night I almost did the wild thing with Reid on the management office rug*—"on the night of the power outage. Thanks, Josh! Where did you find this?"

He shrugged, appearing peculiarly self-conscious. "On the floor in the hallway. It was just sitting there, so I—"

Uh-oh. Karina had seen that expression before. She knew what it meant. "So you 'borrowed' it?"

Josh nodded. "Yeah. But only for a couple of days! And I didn't take anything out of it, either, I swear! I thought about it," he admitted. "I knew there'd probably be money in there, and I wanted some cash to spend at the Kismet Christmas parade tomorrow." He slumped, staring down at the remaining item in his arms instead of meeting her gaze. "But I tried Reid's idea of waiting first, *before* I took out anything, and it worked!"

Dumbfounded, Karina frowned at her son. She didn't understand. "Reid told you to steal my purse?"

"No." Josh grinned as though the idea were preposterous. "And I didn't know it was *your* purse, either. Not until later. But Reid told me the next time I felt like sneaking something I shouldn't—I should just wait. Like, thirty seconds or two minutes or whatever. Reid said that eventually I wouldn't feel like taking anything anymore. He said I just needed practice."

"Practice at *not* 'borrowing' things?"

"Not stealing things. Right. Because stealing is wrong."

Karina had been trying to drive home that point for months now. How had Reid managed it in the course of a week?

"I'm glad you made the right decision, Josh. I'm happy to have my purse back, too. I was worried about losing it."

"Well, now you can quit worrying. And you can have this!"

Proudly, Josh offered her the other item he'd been holding in his arms. Karina took it, recognizing the box of chocolate-peppermint bark she'd bought as a Christmas gift for the maid.

"I didn't eat *any* of that candy, either!" Josh bragged. "Even though it looked really good." Her eight-year-old son gave a resigned shrug. "I guess that means I'm fully rehabil-itated."

Vowing to take a closer look at the ratings on those video games her son liked playing, Karina hugged him. Then she cast a curious glance at her sister. Stephanie remained hunched over her cell phone, tapping a reply to her message from Edgware.

"So . . . Let me get this straight," Karina said to Josh. "Reid taught you all this stuff? About stealing? And waiting? And practicing until you didn't want to take anything anymore?"

"Yep. It worked, too. Reid is, like, a genius!"

"Yes, he is." Temporarily at a loss for words, Karina strived to say something wise. "I guess you should thank him."

And so should I. Josh's "borrowing" had been a worrisome issue—an issue Karina was grateful to have (seemingly) solved.

"I already did thank him!" Josh assured her. "I wrecked his homemade igloo." His grin widened in rascally fashion. "Twice."

"Oh. Um . . ." Karina hesitated, still not understanding how all this had occurred. Or exactly what it signified. Men were . . . different, sometimes. She watched as Reid spied Josh on the porch. The two exchanged masculine waves, one gigantic and the other much smaller. Obviously, Reid was okay with his twice-savaged igloo. "In that case, I'm happy for you, Josh."

"Me too, Mom." Suddenly, he seemed very wise. "Me too."

"I'm very proud of you, too."

"Thanks." Josh licked his lips. He folded his hands behind his back, then grinned. "So . . . Can I have some of that candy?"

Karina laughed. "Go ahead. You've earned it." She gave back the box of chocolate-peppermint bark. "I have a replacement."

"Yum!" Snatching the box, Josh raced back inside. "Hey, Michael!" he yelled. "I *did* get the candy back! You want some?"

As the B&B's wreath-adorned front door slammed and Josh's gleeful voice faded, Karina turned to her sister again—just in time to see Stephanie pocket her phone, her expression dire.

"Steph? What's wrong? Was it bad news?"

"You could say that." Gloomily, Stephanie approached her. "This job is over with. The Christmas House sale is off."

"What?" Shocked, Karina stared at her. "It's off?"

A nod. "Edgware is pulling out. They've cancelled the evaluation. I'm supposed to catch the next plane and get ready for a job in Edinburgh. Blake is fully recovered now, so I'm going to do it. I already texted Justin and notified my boss."

"What do you mean, they're cancelling?" Karina asked. When Reid found out, he'd be devastated. "How can they do that?"

"Easily. Edgware holds all the cards here. They've got the leverage." Stephanie cast a sympathetic glance at Reid. "I hope the Sullivans weren't counting on this sale. The company is notoriously hardheaded. I doubt they'll change their minds."

"Is it me? Is it something I did wrong? Something I

didn't do?" Suddenly filled with worry, Karina stared at her sister. How could she appear so calm about this? "I did my best. I did!"

She hated to think *she'd* somehow cost Reid's family the B&B sale they wanted. If her evaluation was somehow faulty . . .

"No, you didn't do anything wrong." Steph gave her an empathetic head shake. "My boss didn't give specifics, but I got the impression this place just didn't measure up. Once an evaluation site fails to meet the required hospitality metrics, that's it. No deal. Edgware is pretty picky. And you *did* mention the B&B has had a rash of unfortunate incidents lately."

Stephanie's shrug suggested that those incidents explained it all—that the various mishaps and mix-ups they'd encountered over the past week had simply proved too damning for Edgware to take a chance on The Christmas House concept. Maybe Stephanie was right, Karina realized. She was the expert, after all.

"So you're going to leave? Just like that?" she asked. "But we've only had a couple of days together! Blake has been having so much fun with Michael and Josh and Olivia." Her nephew had even befriended Alexis and Nicole. "I was hoping we'd all be able to spend Christmas together, here at the B&B."

"I was too. I'm sorry, Karina. I don't dare turn down the Edinburgh job," Stephanie said. "I'm gunning for a promotion—one that will let me manage assessments instead of traveling nonstop—and this is the next step in proving myself to my boss." She gave Karina a downhearted look. "You understand, right?"

"Of course I do. If there's anything I can do to help—"

"I'll let you know." Her sister grinned. "Count on it. I asked for your help at least once already, didn't I?" She gestured at the B&B. However unsatisfactory it had been to Edgware, it was still a charming place. "I won't hesitate to do it again."

She hugged her tightly. "Thanks for all the work you did. I promise, it *isn't* your fault the deal fell through."

Karina had her doubts about that. She traded a few more planning details with Stephanie, then waved off her sister so she could return to her hotel and start packing. But even as Karina did all those things, she remained preoccupied—not with her potential failure as an Edgware evaluator, but with Reid.

All during her conversation with Steph, he'd been finishing the setup on the B&B's crèche. He'd been chatting and laughing with Olivia. He'd been *happy,* just as he'd been during the past few days with Karina. Did he know about The Christmas House's failed sale?

If he didn't by now, she guessed, he would soon.

When Reid got the bad news, Karina wanted to be there. She wanted to help him. At the least, she could lend an empathetic ear and offer Reid a chance to vent his frustration and fears.

If he had any fears. Looking at him now, she doubted it.

"Okay!" Olivia called distantly, snagging Karina's attention. As she looked on, her daughter hugged Reid, then waved good-bye and ran across the yard. "See you later, Reid!"

Reid held up his palm in an answering good-bye, smiling.

Touched by their camaraderie, Karina kept watching. Her daughter and her . . . boyfriend? . . . lover? . . . *cariño?* . . . were so cute together. Seeing them together really warmed her heart.

The moment Olivia vanished from sight, Reid's smile dimmed. He turned away—probably to retrieve his toolbox and spare plastic twist ties from the snow.

Instead, he punched a tree.

Okay. More accurately, Reid smacked his palm on the trunk of the B&B's big sugar maple in obvious frustration. But whatever the specifics involved, the whole tree appeared to vibrate in response. The naked branches swayed. Reid growled.

Uh-oh. He'd *definitely* gotten the bad news already. He'd apparently been hiding his feelings until now, for Olivia's sake.

Awash in sympathy, Karina slung her purse over her heavily bundled shoulder, then tromped across the snow toward him.

Who knew sugar maples were so fucking hard?

Glaring at the tree, Reid smacked its trunk again. He felt filled with frustration, consumed by an overwhelming sense of helplessness. His grandparents had asked him to do them one favor. One tiny, mildly inconvenient, freaking Christmastime favor. And he hadn't been able to do it. He'd been brought to his knees by the challenges of running a damn B&B—a B&B whose cheesy holiday schedule he hadn't been able to pull off.

Not once. Not on time. Not the way he'd wanted to.

The moment things had begun going well, another unbelievable mishap had occurred. The spiked cider at the reception. The traitorous head chef, stolen away by Lagniappe at the Lakeshore. The sleigh ride, during which Karina had nearly been concussed. The frozen pipes. The ice patch–turned ice-skating rink. The graffiti-covered van. The gift-wrap disaster, caused by Digby's intrinsic doggie craving for liver treats. The smoky scare during Amanda and Rodrigo's inattentive caramel sauce making. The power outage, which Reid still thought was the result of sabotage. The near riot he'd faced when Vanessa had learned that if the B&B sale went through, the place would likely be demolished, taking all its happy memories with it.

Well, that was no longer an issue, Reid thought. Then he gave a growl of displeasure and walloped the maple tree again.

"Hey! Hey, stop that. You're going to hurt yourself."

Karina. At the sound of her voice, Reid felt all the fight go out of him. Surrendering, he dug his gloved fingers into the tree bark. He lowered his forehead to its chilly surface. Even as its coldness restored some of his equanimity, he still felt . . . *so much.* But he was stuck here. All he could do was *feel* the frustration and disappointment and impotence inside him.

This time, Reid couldn't get away. And he hated it.

All at once, he wanted the distraction of river rapids to tackle, of mountain peaks to climb, of sky-diving tours to lead. But here in Kismet, his usual distractions didn't exist. He hated that too. Reid wanted to get away from the B&B and everyone in it—except he couldn't. His guests were counting on him. He still had a lot of goddamn Christmas magic to deliver.

With a few murmured words of empathy, Karina came nearer. Awkwardly, she wrapped her arms around him. She peered into his stony face, obviously concerned that he'd been pummeling a tree.

"Are you all right?" Gently, she reached for his wrist. She tugged off his glove, then winced at the sight of his hand. "Your palms are bleeding. I think one of them is already swelling up. Whatever the tree did, it's time you forgave it."

Against all odds, her joke culled a grin from him. Feeling that tiny smile burble up from somewhere inside him, Reid could scarcely believe it. Soon enough, though, despair crashed through again, turning his mood as black as fireplace soot.

Karina went on cradling his hand. She pulled it close to her heart, then gazed up at him with her usual compassion. "Let's get you inside, where we can clean up these scrapes."

"It's nothing. I'll be fine." Reid withdrew his hand. The abrupt movement made the icy air sting his wounds. It didn't endear him to Karina, either. She stared at him in bafflement.

"Well, I want to make sure. Just let me help you."

Help was the last thing Reid needed. It was the last thing he *wanted* to need. He'd already failed to give his grandparents the means to their dream retirement in Arizona. He didn't intend to line up for a bunch of mollycoddling as an encore. Empathy and helpfulness wouldn't make Edgware reconsider. Nothing would. It was time he faced that—with or without a sugar maple rematch—and got on with things. Resolutely, Reid shook his head.

"You know me better than that," he told Karina with a wan smile, believing it to be true. "You know I don't need help."

"You mean you don't *want* help," she said in a remarkably chipper tone. "Wanting and needing aren't the same thing, you know. Looking at you now, I'd say you definitely need some help." She had the temerity to grin, just like the Pollyanna he'd likened her to. "And I'm the perfect person to give it."

"I just need to be left alone for a while." Setting his jaw, Reid took back his glove from Karina. He gathered his crèche-building equipment, picked up his toolbox, then gave Karina a warning look. He'd thought she understood him. Especially after all the time they'd spent together and all the closeness they'd shared. But just in case . . . "This doesn't have anything to do with you. I'll be fine. After an hour or two, I'll be back."

"But you won't be fine! You might feel even worse in an hour or two!" Urgently, Karina grabbed his arm, trying to keep him with her. Trying to help him. "I really have the impression that something . . . important has happened. Tell me? Please?"

He stared at her hand on his arm, feeling—as impossible as it seemed—even worse. It was bad enough that the Edgware sale hadn't gone through. It was even worse that he'd had to hear the bad news directly from his disconsolate grandfather, over the phone, with (he'd swear) his grammy crying on the extension.

Now Karina wanted to go all mother hen on him, even though he'd told her to back off? It was as though she wanted to revel in his misfortune—to dissect all his mistakes, gloat over his failure, and kick him when he was down. Obviously, Karina didn't understand him at all. Maybe she never had. With his usual patience worn thin, Reid shook off Karina's hand.

"If you want to help, leave me alone."

Then he hefted his toolbox and headed for the B&B.

Watching as Reid walked away, Karina could scarcely endure the helplessness she felt. It wasn't possible that Reid didn't need her. There had to be *something* she could do to help.

I have to do more for you first. Otherwise, you won't stay. You won't stay! Panicked at the thought, Karina ran after Reid. She grabbed his arm again. Luckily, he stopped. His gaze swept her face, appearing every bit as wintery as the weather.

Suddenly chilled, she shrugged deeper into her coat.

"I'm not taking no for an answer!" she said, feeling doubly determined to help him. Maybe because her involvement with Edgware had contributed to Reid's troubles. Maybe because she couldn't stand seeing anyone upset. Maybe—and this was the one Karina believed—because she loved him. "Right now, you need me, Reid. I'm sticking by you. I'm helping you, no matter what!"

Her impassioned promise only made him appear stonier.

"I don't need help." Fisting his toolbox, Reid enunciated every word. "Face it, Karina. As much as you're dying to 'help' everyone, in the end you're just a glorified school guidance counselor. And I'm no student." Bitterly, he waved her away. "So save the Little Miss Helpful routine. I don't need it."

I don't need you, Karina heard, and felt twice as wounded.

What did she have to give, if not her help? Her love?

The two were practically the same thing. She knew that.

"I'm a college academic advisor!" she specified archly. "And *I* don't need *this*." With dogged persistence, she planted her booted feet in the snow. "Yet I'm still here—for you."

"Don't you get it? I don't want you to be here. Not now."

He sounded exactly the way Eric had, it occurred to Karina, on the day he'd asked her for a divorce. Then, her ex-husband had refused to work out the problems between them. He'd simply left her to be with Chelsea. Then, Karina had buckled. She'd believed her shortcomings had caused everything, so she hadn't fought back. Not for herself, and not for her children.

But this time, with Reid, things were going to be different. They *had* to be different. Because Karina *had* to help him. She had to prove to him—to herself—that she could succeed. She had to prove that if difficulties arose in a relationship, she could solve them. Maybe then she'd have the courage to risk being with Reid, heart and soul. Maybe then she'd believe she could love someone and not wind up abandoned in the end.

Maybe then their Christmas fling could be something more.

For all those reasons—for her heart and soul—Karina stood her ground. No matter how hurt she felt—and she felt *very* hurt by Reid's snarky digs at her career expertise—she wasn't backing down. "But now is when you *do* need me!" she insisted. "I know about Edgware, Reid, and I know you probably feel responsible—"

His gaze sharpened. "What do you know about Edgware?"

"Well, just that the, um, B&B sale fell through." Too late, Karina realized that, in her haste to reassure Reid, she'd backed herself into a corner. The bad news had just come from Edgware. Only the people directly involved—like the Sullivans, Stephanie, and (unfortunately) Karina—could have known about it. With no other choice—and with Reid on the verge of walking away—she decided to go for broke. There was no point hiding the truth now. She hauled in a deep breath. "But you're not responsible for what happened! I know, because *I* was the secret Edgware evaluator. I was the one filing reports. So that means—"

Reid's horrified expression finally registered. He looked as though she'd kicked him. Desperately, Karina kept talking.

"—that means *I'm* the perfect person to help you now!" she insisted, pleading with him to understand. "I know all the rules. I know how things are supposed to work at the company—"

"'The company'?" He shook his head. "You work for Edgware?"

He was taking the news pretty well, Karina realized. He seemed very calm. Almost eerily so, in fact. Newly worried, she nodded. "Yes. But only on a stand-in basis! I was doing a favor for my sister. She's the one who was supposed to come here."

"And tell Edgware our concept isn't worth franchising?"

"No! I mean, yes, Stephanie was assigned to do the B&B evaluation. But she hadn't made up her mind about The Christmas House yet. Her report probably would have been great! You know, other than mentioning those few incidents, of course. Those would have to have been included, for accuracy's sake." She was rambling now, getting off track. Hastily, Karina regrouped. "But my nephew got sick at the last minute, and Stephanie couldn't come. So I came here in her place." She broke off, tardily realizing that disclosing all this could still get Stephanie into trouble with Edgware. "And I did my best to do a fair evaluation," she finished lamely. "At least until today."

"Right. Until today, when you let the hammer fall on this place," Reid said, misunderstanding her. "It was *your* evaluation that cost us the sale. It was *your* evaluation that crushed my grandparents' hopes and dreams." He shook his head, not meeting her gaze as he fisted his glove, staring across the

278 *Lisa Plumley*

snowy yard. "I should have known. I should have seen it! You were always so interested in everything that went on here."

"I was! I am! I love it here at The Christmas House!"

"You were always behind the scenes, rolling up your sleeves and pitching in without even needing to be asked. I thought you did all that because you liked us." *Liked me,* his tightly held jaw said. "Because you wanted to be a part of things. Because you recognized the magic in The Christmas House—the same magic I grew up with—and wanted to belong to it. I thought you wanted to belong to the same fucking magic you made me feel, all over again. Why else would you make me feel that?"

Suddenly, his gaze did swerve to hers—with new vehemence. Karina quailed beneath his anger. "I'm sorry, Reid! I—"

"I'm sorry too. Because there wasn't any truth to any of it, was there? You didn't care about this place. You didn't care about helping or belonging. You didn't care about *me.* You were just a spy, sneaking around, hoping to derail the sale."

"No. I was never hoping to derail anything!" Karina promised. She wanted to apologize again. She wanted to explain herself further. But what mattered now was helping Reid feel better. So, with effort, she focused on finding him a solution. "Maybe I could rewrite some of the reports," she offered in a newly positive tone. "Maybe I could upload the checklists I haven't turned in yet. Maybe I could write additional explanatory notes!" She moved closer to Reid, belatedly realizing that, as long as he was here, there was still hope. Clinging to that hope, she said, "You know, I *did* try to help you. I downplayed the gift-wrap incident in my daily report. And I de-emphasized the power outage too. That could have happened to anyone! So really, I wasn't a spy. I was a . . . helper."

"You," Reid said simply, "were a liar."

"But . . ." Feebly, Karina gestured, pointing out the aid she'd already tried to give him. "But can't you see? My reports could have been even worse! If I'd included every little thing that happened, my reports would have been even more damning."

Reid appeared unimpressed. "So you lied to your boss, too. You lied to everyone. Is that supposed to make me feel better?"

"Well, I can see where it would make you feel less special," Karina joked. Her attempt at wit fell predictably flat. Still desperate to find a resolution, she reverted to practicality again. "All I'm saying is, even though the B&B has some problems, none of them are insurmountable. Maybe next year, or two years from now, Edgware will reconsider."

"My grandparents needed this sale now." Reid swallowed hard. "They already spent the money they would have received. Foolishly, I know. But they counted on Edgware. They *trusted* them." His gaze was fierce and unrelenting. "They trusted a faceless corporation the same way I trusted its spy. Not that I would expect *you* to understand trust."

"Me? Why not?" Karina blinked, hurt that he kept calling her a spy—that he kept digging at her. "I understand trust!" She gave a helpless, shaky laugh. "I'm still me, after all."

"Right. You're still you." Reid's expression was unforgiving. "And who is that, exactly? Who are you, Karina? Because I sure as hell don't know anymore . . . if I ever did."

"Yes, you do! You know me." Struck by his harsh tone, Karina took a step back. "After all we've been to each other—"

"We've been nothing to each other," Reid said coldly. *"Nothing."* The fact that he'd purposely interrupted her—again—to deliver that cutting statement said volumes about his desolate mood. "What we had was a meaningless holiday affair. Now it's over and done with, just the way it should be."

"Over? We're not over." Drawing in another deep breath, Karina reminded herself that people said cruel things when they were upset. Her training and experience proved it. "You're just saying that because of the evaluation. But you know *me*. You do!" She gave another shaky laugh. She timidly smiled. "You're just upset right now. I understand. Later, we'll—"

"There won't be any 'later.'"

"Of course there will be." Karina tried to chuckle, but her throat felt as dry as dust. Mustering cheerfulness was impossible. "I care about you. You care about me. It's not even Christmas Eve yet," she pointed out in a last-ditch attempt to make him listen to reason, "so *technically* our holiday affair can't be over with. It's simply not time to call it quits."

"You're right. It's past time." Reid examined his bloodied palms, then his bruised hand. When he lifted his gaze to hers, it really was as though he'd never known her. It was as though he'd never talked with her, laughed with her . . . kissed her and declared his love for her amid his snowman-print flannel sheets in The Christmas House's attic room. "It's going to be hard enough to finish out Christmas this year. For my guests' sake—to keep as much holiday cheer going as we can, given all that's happened—I'd appreciate it if you'd leave the B&B."

Karina felt her jaw drop. "Leave? Now?"

Reid glowered at the sugar maple tree. "Now."

"But I—" *I was looking forward to sharing Christmas with you. With our children. With Vanessa and everyone else.* "I don't want to leave. What will I tell everyone?"

A shrug. "You could make up a lie. You're good at that."

"I'm not good at that! I'm not!" Karina felt tears well in her eyes. Angrily, she dashed them away. "Reid, I never lied about how I felt about you! I never lied about that."

Invulnerable to her pleading, Reid gazed at her. Beneath the "nookie beard" she'd teased him about only days ago, his face appeared even harder—even more unmoved—than before. "Maybe not," he said, "since you never told me how you felt."

Oh yeah. She hadn't. *Until you say you love me back,* he'd told her with a smile, *this beard of mine is sticking around.*

He'd never shave that beard now, Karina realized. Except maybe as a gesture of hopelessness—as proof that he'd given up on her for good. Because even if she told Reid the truth— even if she told him she *did* love him back, right then and there—she doubted he would believe her.

The irony was, if she hadn't pushed so hard to help him a few minutes ago, she might not have overstepped that line. She might not have accidentally blurted out her knowledge of the Edgware cancellation. She might not have started the ball rolling toward this awful, inevitable-feeling conclusion.

Now, not only had she failed to help Reid, but she'd also managed to make things irrevocably worse between them.

He didn't want her love. He didn't want her help.

He didn't want her explanations. He didn't want *her.*

"But I *did* feel it!" Karina cried, remembering the joyfulness she'd experienced in Reid's arms. "I did! I was just afraid to tell you, for—for so many reasons." *Many of them to do with life-altering moments like this one.* The thought gave her the courage to rally one final argument. "If what we had was so 'meaningless,'" she demanded, "then why are you still here?"

For an instant, she thought she'd gotten through to him. Reid blinked. He gazed at her. His expression eased into the one she recognized so well—the one that looked as though everything he wanted could be found in her eyes . . . in her heart.

But then Reid shook his head, and her hopes were dashed.

"I have no idea. Be out of the B&B by nightfall."

He turned away, his shoulders wide and bleak against the snowy, sparkly, almost Christmastime world that Kismet was such a part of. Then he paused, seemed to reconsider, and delivered a fluent helping of multilingual swearing.

"I'll make sure you have a room someplace in Kismet," Reid said in a grudging, suspiciously hoarse voice. "I wouldn't want Olivia, Josh, and Michael winding up on the street."

He does care. A little. Not much. But more than zero.

Feeling her heart expand, Karina held her breath. *Don't bother,* she wanted to say, all proud and strong. *I'll find someplace to stay myself.* But she didn't have many options.

With her mind awhirl and her pride scattered, she nodded.

"Maybe Lagniappe at the Lakeshore," Reid mused, giving her one last over-the-shoulder glance. "You'd fit right in there."

Karina frowned. "But you said the people at Lagniappe at the Lakeshore are a bunch of cheating liars who'd as soon sabotage The Christmas House as they'd sing 'Silent Night.'"

A heartbeat passed. "Exactly," Reid said.

And then he was gone.

Chapter Twenty

... From the desk of Betty Sullivan
DECEMBER 24TH
LOCATION: KISMET (AKA "THE MERRIEST TOWN IN MICHIGAN")
SCHEDULED EVENT: ANNUAL "KISMET CHRISTMAS PARADE AND HOLIDAY LIGHTS SHOW" — ~~10:00 A.M. TO MIDNIGHT~~
WHO CARES ANYMORE?

With a steadiness and certainty born of long experience, Reid laid out all his supplies. He arranged a towel, a bar of shaving soap, a sleek-handled brush, and his favorite razor on the vanity, which stood tucked under the eaves in the bathroom of his attic room at the B&B. Soon, he was ready to get started. No excuses. Karina didn't love him. That was that.

So his "good-luck" beard was history, starting . . . now.

Except one of the maids had arranged holiday garland around the mirror, he noticed sourly. That had to go first. There was no way he could concentrate on getting rid of his erstwhile "nookie beard" while all that Christmassy stuff was hanging around, distracting him with its stupid jolliness. This was a delicate job. It demanded the utmost focus and deliberation.

He didn't want to wind up spending Christmas all bandaged up like The Invisible Man in that old movie, did he? Hell, no. He'd scare his own children and everyone else's, besides.

Except Karina's kids. As much as he wanted to, he wouldn't get to see Josh, Michael, or Olivia. But that didn't mean—

Swearing, Reid tore down the garland. With relish, he stuffed the jolly-looking evergreens in the trash can. In triumph, he put his hands on his hips and glared at the trash.

The garland poked out again, springing back to life like the sappy, unforgivable hopefulness that had plagued Reid ever since he'd turned his back on Karina in the yard yesterday.

It had taken everything he had not to turn around again. Not to promise her a room at a hotel downtown *and* a permanent place in his heart . . . in his life. But just when he'd felt on the verge of caving in completely, he'd glimpsed his grandfather's battered Flexible Flyer sled, with its steel runners and iconic red and tan body, propped there on the front porch, and he'd remembered. He'd remembered all those Christmases growing up at The Christmas House—all those Christmases his grandparents had given him, and his parents, and Vanessa, and all the rest of his cousins. He'd remembered . . . and he'd kept walking, damn it.

Because Reid owed his loyalties to the people who were counting on him. He owed everything to the people who loved him—especially to the people who weren't afraid to say so. He didn't owe anything to a woman who'd lied to him from the moment they'd met—a woman who hadn't quit lying, all the way to the end.

I did feel it! I did! I was just afraid to tell you. . . .

Karina's words still echoed in his head. They tempted him to abandon everything he knew. They tempted him to put what he wanted before what he'd promised. They tempted him to lay down his loyalties and (literally) sleep with the enemy.

But Reid couldn't do that. Not now.

He couldn't do that any more than he could keep this pathetically optimistic "nookie beard" on his face any longer. The plain truth was, he'd given up hope yesterday. Now his beard made a mockery of everything he'd once succumbed to, including Christmas cheer . . . and the unending hope that Karina would love him back.

Determinedly, Reid met his own gaze in the mirror.

Damn. He looked like hell.

Swearing, he turned his head for a better look. A fresh angle didn't help. The events of the past twenty-four hours had taken their toll on him. Out of the corner of his eye, Reid glimpsed the garland, slowly unwinding itself from the trash can and trying to spill onto the floor. Undoubtedly, the damn stuff would wend its way back up the mirror if given the least bit of leeway. With new prejudice, Reid crammed it down. With his foot.

Okay. Shaving. Trying not to stare at the dark hollows under his eyes, Reid turned on the water. He splashed his face. The maneuver wasn't strictly necessary. He'd gotten out of the shower only moments ago. But it felt like a fitting prelude.

Wholly of its own accord, his gaze fell to the towel he'd arranged. A row of printed Santas gaped up at him, their idiotic grins making a joke of his misery. He couldn't tackle the job of shaving his beard in this environment. It was way too ebullient. Frowning, Reid stomped across the floor in his thermal T-shirt and flannel PJs. He slam-dunked the Santa towel in the trash.

But that didn't feel right, either. Bothered but still determined, Reid picked up the soap anyway. With efficient movements, he worked up a lather, then brushed it on his face. Half his face. Because as he did so, he happened to glimpse the reflection of his sleigh bed—and its holiday-print bedding—in the bathroom mirror.

Grinning snowmen? They smirked up at him, reminding

him of better days, better times . . . better versions of himself, before he'd been drop-kicked back to reality by Karina's confession.

A part of him wished she'd kept her freaking honesty to herself. She'd already lied to him. She'd gotten away with it, too. Why not let him believe what he wanted? That maybe she did care about him, that maybe Christmas really could be a time for miracles, that maybe he could be a hero for his family?

Scoffing at the thought, Reid dropped his shaving brush.

Four minutes later, he was on the move, an impressive bundle of holiday bedding, towels, garland, candles, wreaths, and other assorted tchotchkes in his arms. If The Christmas House had had an incinerator, then that fiery hell would have been his preferred destination for all this red and green junk. As it was, Reid decided to settle for the upstairs closet that served as a housekeeping station for this part of the B&B.

Halfway there, he ran into Vanessa. His cousin glanced at his suspiciously merry bundle, lifted her gaze to his face, then frowned in commiseration. "Still missing Karina, huh?"

What did she know? Nothing. Yesterday, Vanessa had had the gall to suggest he'd made a mistake in asking Karina to leave.

Angrily, Reid shouldered past her. Or at least he tried to.

Easily blocking him, Vanessa plucked out one of the Santa towels. She wiped off his half beardful of shaving soap, then shook her head. "Admit it, cuz. You're no good without her. We could all see it. Karina brought out something special in you."

"Yeah. Disillusionment." Reid sighed, then noticed his cousin's hat and coat. "Are you up here for a reason?"

"Yes. To make sure you're still going to the annual Kismet Christmas parade. It starts in an hour."

Reid shook his head. "I'm not going. I've got several calls in to Edgware. I think I could still change their minds."

"Aww, Reid. I know you don't want to quit, and that's admirable. But don't you think there's a break-even point here? Even Grammy and Grandpa said—" Vanessa broke off, her gaze falling to the other items in his arms. She tugged out one of them, then wagged it at him accusingly. "Is this Digby's holiday sweater? Did you *steal* the sweater off our dachshund's back?"

"It was more of a wrestling match, really." Reid pointed. "You can still see the tooth marks."

"Digby's, I hope."

He nodded. "I liberated that dog. Digby hated Christmas."

"You mean *you* hated Christmas. And the moment you started liking it again—the moment you started *feeling* it again—"

"Now you're just talking crazy." Reid grabbed the doggie sweater, added it back to his pile, then dumped the whole caboodle in the housekeeping closet. "I didn't feel a thing."

At least not anything I can't forget. Eventually.

Sighing in apparent censure—or maybe sadness—his cousin shook her head. "You are not the same man I used to know."

Reid only shrugged. "That's probably true."

Since Karina, he felt turned inside out and upside down. First, those changes had made him feel brand new. Now they only made him feel gullible and wrecked and curiously hollow.

"But it doesn't have to be true!" Vanessa actually grabbed his arms and shook him. Or tried to. He was a lot bigger than she was. Exasperated, she poked his shoulder. "Don't you get it? If you would just *forgive* Karina for keeping her secret, everything would be fine! She did what she had to do—for her sister's sake. *You,* of all people, should understand that." Another poke. "Karina is loyal! She's sweet and helpful and kind. She's special, Reid. The rest of us have forgiven her. All the guests, all the staff, the neighbors, Nate and Angela, Amanda and Rodrigo, Grammy and Grandpa. Everyone. Even *your own children* have forgiven Karina. You should too."

At the thought of Nicole and Alexis, Reid felt his resolve strengthen. He couldn't afford to weaken. Not when giving in meant leaving his daughters vulnerable to loving a family of Barretts who could never be trusted to love them back.

Judging by the way Alexis and Nicole had bonded with Karina and her children, they'd probably come dangerously close to making the same mistake he had—to loving the wrong person.

But Reid still had time to fix that. That was his specialty, wasn't it? Taking the big risks before anyone else? Heading straight into danger, figuring out the potential hazards, and protecting other people from them?

He hadn't managed to protect his grandparents. They'd chosen him to run The Christmas House this holiday season specifically because of his lack of sentimentality. Reid had repaid them by falling headlong into . . . stupid sentimentality.

He didn't know if he could forgive himself for that. But he still thought he could repair the damage—if his busybody cousin would get off his case and leave him alone for once. And if someone at Edgware would return his calls (their voice mail messages all claimed the executives were out until New Year's Day). And if he could explain himself to his grandparents.

I fell in love, he imagined himself saying. *I fell in love at Christmastime, with a wonderful woman—and her three children.*

Betty and Robert Sullivan would never buy it. Their Scrooge-like grandson smitten with a homebody suburban divorcée from California? Their globe-trotting, multilingual, eel-eating great-granddaughters morphing into members of the Brady Bunch?

His grandparents would laugh themselves silly at the idea.

"I knew coming home for Christmas would be a mistake." Reid frowned at Vanessa, at a loss to explain how bereft he felt. He never should have allowed himself to enjoy the holidays again—to allow sentimentality to creep in and ruin him. "I have a beard to shave," he announced, then headed back to his room.

This time, Reid resolved, he'd get the job done.

With a heartfelt sigh, Karina set the last wrapped gift on her Kismet hotel room's wide bureau. She took a step back, then examined the small pile of gifts and, next to it, the tabletop Christmas tree the hotel management had provided. It was the kind of tree that emerged intact from its cardboard box, needing only to be bent into shape, with LED lights embedded in its artificial branches and miniature ornaments stapled on. There was even a diminutive star glued to the tree's plastic tip.

"There!" Karina announced with forced cheerfulness. "Now we're all set for Christmas tomorrow. We'll sleep in—"

Her children all looked at her cockeyed. "No one *ever* sleeps in on Christmas morning," Michael said. "Sheesh, Mom."

"—unwrap our gifts," she continued, undaunted, "have a nice celebratory breakfast at the restaurant downstairs—"

"It's closed on Christmas Day," Olivia pointed out.

"—*or* a festive hotel room picnic with muffins and juice that I'll buy after the Kismet Christmas parade today—"

"I don't care about the parade anymore," Josh said.

"—and then, if the airline cooperates, we'll all go home!"

Finally finishing her announcement, Karina beamed at them. It wasn't easy. Heartbreak permeated every part of her, leaving her feeling weary, sad, and hopeless. All she wanted to do was climb into bed with a TV remote and a distracting *non*holiday movie—and maybe a giant chocolate Santa (or three) to make herself feel better—and forget the past week had ever happened.

But she couldn't do that. Olivia, Michael, and Josh were counting on her. She still wanted to give them a perfect holiday. Her personal heartache couldn't interfere with that.

"What if the airline *doesn't* cooperate?" Josh asked.

Before Karina could reply, Olivia did. "We'll think of something else," she assured her brother. "Don't worry."

Surprised, Karina gawked at her daughter. All of a sudden, she realized, Olivia had quit forecasting doom at every turn. She'd quit trying to protect them all from potential dangers. In fact, Karina thought, Olivia had become downright easygoing.

"Most of the things people worry about don't ever happen," Olivia went on, knowledgeably. "Reid told me that. It's true."

Reid. Again. Would his influence never end? While Karina was grateful that Reid had helped Josh overcome his sticky-fingered tendencies—and had, apparently, also helped Olivia see the world in a less worrisome light—Karina didn't want to think about Reid. She didn't want to remember what might have been.

She didn't want to love him, either. But she still did.

"Reid told me that being smart is the best," Michael piped up, "because it never goes away. It only gets bigger, the more questions you ask. So Mom, why didn't we just go home already?"

"Because the airlines were all booked. Lots of people want to travel during the holidays. If an earlier flight opens up, we'll take it," Karina said. "Otherwise, our original plan sticks: Christmas in Kismet, and leaving a few days later."

"Hey!" came a thin-sounding voice from the open laptop on the hotel room bed. "Isn't anybody going to talk to *me?*"

Eric. Karina had set up a videoconference call for the kids. Evidently, they'd gotten distracted by her announcement.

"I'm all done talking, Dad!" Michael pushed away from the laptop. He waved, then blew a kiss. "Bye! Love you!"

The two of them exchanged good-byes via screencast. Karina checked with Olivia and Josh, making sure they'd had their turns too. They had. Resigned, she trooped to the laptop, ready to confront the image of her ex-husband . . . complete with palm trees, beach sand, and sultry blue Bahamian skies in the background.

All those things were there, with the unexpected addition of a red and white felt Santa hat on Eric's head. It clashed with his eyeliner and the multiple chains around his neck, but at least he was trying. Affectionately, Karina smiled at him.

"Cute hat, Eric. That's nice of you."

Appearing embarrassed, he snatched it off. He fussed with his hair, deftly arranging those product-laden strands. Without the merry frame of the Santa hat, he didn't look so good.

Concerned, Karina frowned. "Hey, are you okay?"

Her ex-husband scowled. Too late, Karina remembered how much Eric hated it when she comforted him or offered advice.

In fact, she realized, Eric hated help of all kinds. Just like Reid did. Was that an issue with all men, she wondered, or only the ones she—Ms. Helpful—had the misfortune to fall for?

"No!" Eric blurted. "I'm not okay. Chelsea and I are still on the outs, Kari. She's changed somehow. And I don't like it."

Surprised by his use of his old nickname for her, Karina picked up the laptop. She sat on the bed, then arranged the laptop on her knees. Warmly—and welcoming the distraction of a problem to solve—she peered into its built-in camera with all the compassion she could. "Changed how? Can you describe it?"

Eric nodded. He started talking, his volubility doubtless enhanced by the pair of tropical umbrella-wielding drinks he appeared to have enjoyed already—at least if the tabletop display of empty glasses beside him was to be believed.

Within moments, Karina was in her element. She nodded and asked questions, listened and probed for more, empathized and brainstormed as her ex-husband described his relationship problems. It seemed that Chelsea had begun asserting herself, starting the day they'd met up with her parents in the Bahamas.

"And it only got worse from there!" Eric complained. "The next thing I knew, Chelsea had an opinion on everything! Where we went. What we did. What *I* wore!" Mournfully, he shook his head. "It's like she became someone else, Kari." He lifted his accusing glare to the camera. "It's like she became *you*."

"Well, that's flattering, Eric." Karina smiled, liking the idea that her friendship had had a positive influence. "But more likely, Chelsea just remembered who she was *before* she met you. Sometimes, when people are around their parents, they revert to their younger selves temporarily. Most people experience that phenomenon to some degree around the holidays. In large and small ways, they inadvertently find themselves stepping into old familial roles. That's part of the reason conflicts tend to be repeated at Christmastime. Everyone is reenacting their—"

"Right. I get it." Impatiently, Eric held up his hand. His studded-leather wristband glinted in the beachy sunshine. "I wasn't looking for a psychology lecture, Einstein."

Pleased, Karina hid a smile. She *was* pretty smart when it came to advising people. Even if her students had (mysteriously) stopped contacting her for help between semesters.

"I wasn't looking for any of *this,* either!" Eric went on. "Chelsea is exciting and all. I mean, come on!" Wide-eyed, he gave a lascivious gesture. "Have you seen her? She's—"

"Gorgeous, I know." Karina gave him a wind-it-up signal. "—but the best thing about Chelsea was that she didn't bug me, you know?" Eric said. "She let *me* be *me*. No matter how dumb that might have been sometimes, she never hassled me. She was impressed by everything about me. I liked that about her."

Drily, Karina said, "I can see where you would."

"But now," Eric said, "all that is gone! I don't like it."

"That's understandable. So what do you want to do next?"

"Easy." Brightly, her ex-husband sat upright. He fixed his own laptop camera with a gimlet gaze. "I want you to tell me how to get the old Chelsea back—the one who thought I was the bomb."

Karina shook her head. "I don't think I can do that. If Chelsea was downplaying her own confidence and assertiveness to get along with you better"—which, based on the conversations Karina had had with Chelsea lately, seemed probable—"it's actually a *good* sign that she feels free enough to be herself."

"Bah!" Eric waved off that notion. Tipsily, he pouted. "Can't be. Chelsea's new 'self' makes *me* feel teeny tiny."

And that was the crux of the problem, wasn't it? Karina realized abruptly. She watched as her ex-husband blearily accepted another umbrella-garnished beverage. Eric wanted to feel powerful. And *that* was what Karina hadn't given him.

Her marriage hadn't ended because she hadn't been nice enough. Or because she hadn't helped Eric enough. Or because she hadn't been able to fix their relationship problems. It had ended because she'd married a man who wanted a Barbie doll for a partner—not a real, live, confident woman with a mind of her own and a very normal tendency to nurture the people she loved.

Nearly knocked over by the revelation, Karina blinked.

"I'm sorry, Eric," she said. "But if you can't handle Chelsea's self-confidence, the problem is with you, not her."

Her ex-husband thought about that. He tried to sip his drink—and was forced to chase his straw around the glass instead, lips puckered like a blowfish. He'd never looked more . . . needy. But wasn't everyone needy? On some level?

Right now, Karina needed love. Her children needed an exemplary Christmas. Stephanie needed a job that allowed her to spend the holidays at home. Eric—and maybe even Reid, it occurred to her—needed to feel powerful. Capable. Invulnerable.

"Well, I guess that settles that, then," Eric announced.

Snapped back to attention, Karina gazed at him. "Settles what? We've only just started talking about this, Eric. You're going to have to—"

"That settles that between us!" Bobbing around on his beach chair, Eric set down his drink. Then he righted his laptop, straightening her view of him. "It's official, babe!" he said magnanimously, beaming at her from the videoconferencing software. "This thing with Chelsea was just a stupid mistake. I'm over it! We can be a family again, Kari! You, me, the kids—"

Startled, Karina snapped shut her laptop.

Eric's voice cut off. Heart pounding madly, Karina glanced around, wondering if her children had overheard their father's careless promise. *We can be a family again! You, me, the kids—*

All Karina had ever wanted was for Olivia, Josh, and Michael to be happy. Likely, they'd never stopped hoping she and Eric would reunite. Would it really be so bad if they did?

She knew Eric. She cared for him. Now she knew exactly what had caused their marital problems, too. He'd made a mistake. One mistake. But mistakes could be forgiven, right?

Cautiously, Karina contemplated her children. Olivia flopped on their hotel room's second bed, watching cartoons with the sound turned down. Josh sat cross-legged on a nearby chair, playing PSP. Michael hunched near the Christmas gifts, lightly running his fingertips over each one, undoubtedly calculating their individual dimensions and estimating the probability that one of them contained a Transformers toy meant for him.

How much did their happiness mean to her?

Everything.

Holding her breath, Karina opened her laptop. Knowing exactly how momentous this decision was, she smiled at Eric.

"All right," she said. "Let's talk about this."

Despite his resolve, Reid didn't get very far. Sure, he'd cleared the bathroom—and his attic B&B room—of deleterious Christmas paraphernalia. And yes, he'd worked up a good head of lather and slathered it on (again), fully prepared to demolish his so-called good-luck beard for good and *prove* (goddamn it) that he was finished hoping Karina would love him. But then . . .

"Dad!" Nicole hurried into his room, her stuffed dingo clutched in one arm. She stopped in his bathroom doorway, then gasped. "Oh no! What are you doing with your beard?"

"I'm going to shave off this beast, once and for all."

"But . . . Aunt Vanessa says that's your 'nookie beard.'"

"Aunt Vanessa is a little bit crazy sometimes."

"Really?" Nicole's eyes widened. "Because Michael told me that mental illness is partly genetic. Which kind of makes sense, actually. Because *you're* acting crazy about Karina."

I am crazy about Karina. On the verge of foolishly admitting it aloud, Reid frowned at his image in the mirror. Then, belatedly realizing this beard would be too much for any ordinary razor to tackle alone, he wiped off the lather again.

He reached for the scissors. First, a close trim.

"Aren't you supposed to be going to the Christmas parade?" Vanessa had promised him she'd take the girls. "From what I remember, it's quite a show. Everyone in town goes to it."

Unconvinced, Nicole sighed. "*You're* not going."

It would break my heart to go this year. "I've already been to the Christmas parade," Reid told her. "I've seen it."

"But doing it over and over and over again is part of the magic of Christmas!" Nicole gulped in a breath. "Michael told me that. He said people like traditions. *He* likes traditions."

"Honey . . ." Sadly, gently, Reid gazed at his daughter. He abandoned his scissors—just for the moment. "You're going to have to quit talking about Michael—about all the Barrett kids."

Nicole looked puzzled. "Why? I like them. They're nice."

"Because . . . They live in California. We don't."

"So?" His daughter wrinkled her nose. "We've lived all over the whole globe!" She stretched her arms wide, leaving her stuffed dingo to dangle from her hand. "Why not San Diego next?"

For a heartbeat, Reid gave in to that idea. He imagined them in a sunny beachside home. All seven of them. Together.

"I haven't decided what to do next," Reid said truthfully.

"Well, *I* vote for California!" Nicole said. "It would be *so* cool to go to Olivia's school! We could see *Twilight* movies together, and visit the mall, and have slumber parties."

Alexis arrived, pushing her way into the bathroom doorway. She slumped next to her sister, then glumly started picking at her fingernails. "Don't be dumb, Nicole. Dad is *totally* going to hide out someplace more remote than ever now. We'll probably wind up in some backwater country we've never even heard of."

With his scissors just a few millimeters from his beard, Reid paused. Sternly, he arched his brow. "'Hide out'?"

"Well, that's what you do, isn't it? Hide out?" Seeming too annoyed to be circumspect, Alexis crossed her skinny arms over her chest. "That's what you did when you and Mom split up."

It was. Sort of, Reid realized. Filled with hurt feelings and pigheaded pride, he'd been determined to show the world that he didn't need Gabby to make his family complete. He didn't need help to raise his daughters. All he needed was himself. Period.

But the realization was fleeting. Reid hadn't lined up his shaving soap and razor just so he could be psychoanalyzed by his own pint-size headshrinker. He was fine, just the way he was.

His daughters were fine too, world travels and all.

"And *that's* what you're doing now, with Karina," Alexis went on, still sounding upset. "You're running away from her."

How could his daughters have any inkling about Karina?

They couldn't, Reid decided. They were just bored. Probably, they wanted to blow this burg and catch a plane.

"Ha. If I'm running away from anything," Reid joked, winking as he hoisted his scissors again, "it's Christmas. I can't wait for this stupid holiday to be over and done with."

Now Nicole crossed her arms too, her brow furrowed. Alexis—wearing a Rudolph sweater, he noticed—actually growled.

Damn. Didn't anybody have a sense of humor anymore?

Apparently not. Both his daughters glared daggers at him.

"I don't want to go to a no-name remote country!" Nicole cried. "Those kinds of countries don't even have normal toilets. You have to squat over a stupid hole in the floor to pee."

"And eat with your hands." Alexis glowered, her expression reminiscent of the one Reid had been confronting in the mirror since yesterday. "I want a *fork,* Dad! Not chopsticks, a piece of *injera,* or a spork! For once I just want to have a normal life."

Pulled in multiple directions at once, Reid stared at the ceiling. He still wanted to get away. He still wanted to lose his troubles in cliff diving or bungee jumping or crawling through a dangerous underground chasm someplace. But for the first time (and after following some of that well-intentioned "just wait it out" advice he'd given to Josh), Reid recognized that impulse for what it was.

Running away. Because Alexis had been right.

Ever since Gabby had ended their marriage, Reid had been running away, in one form or another. He'd been determined never to feel that breakable ever again. It had taken Christmas—and Karina—to make him see that unless he stayed put, he'd never feel loved again, either. Not the way he wanted to be.

Not the way he *needed* to be.

Muttering a Dutch swearword, Reid gazed at his daughters via the vanity mirror. "A spork isn't that bad, is it?"

"Dad," Alexis said, "a spork isn't a fork."

"And it's not a spoon, either," Nicole added. "It's just stuck in between, wanting to scoop *and* poke. It's bad at both."

His daughters had a point. "I'm stuck in between too," Reid mused. "I'm not in the wilderness, but I'm not all the way here, either. I almost was here, all the way"—*when Karina was here with me*—"but now . . . I'm a spork. *I'm* a spork!" Recognizing the truth, he smacked his head. He groaned. "How did this happen?"

Alexis shrugged. "Don't be too hard on yourself, Dad."

"You're the *best* spork-dad," Nicole said loyally.

"I can't keep doing this." Slowly, Reid put down his scissors. "I have to settle down, girls. For all our sakes."

"In San Diego?" Nicole hinted. "You'd like it there."

"With Karina and her kids," Alexis said bluntly. "You should do it, Dad. You should forgive her and sweep her off her feet!"

At his elder daughter's surprisingly dramatic suggestion, Reid glanced at her. Questioningly, he raised his eyebrows.

Alexis grinned. "Blame that *Twilight* book." She shrugged. "It's a pretty romantic story. I borrowed Olivia's copy."

"Aha." Filled with revelation, Reid considered his daughter's suggestion—to forgive Karina and sweep her off her feet. But it wasn't Karina he had to forgive, he realized. It was himself. He had to forgive himself for not helping his grandparents—for not being the nearly superhuman dad (and man) he wanted to be.

No wonder he'd been so touchy when everyone had suggested Alexis and Nicole needed something more than a nomadic life. Giving up on globe-trotting had meant admitting defeat.

But not anymore. "Sweep her off her feet, huh?" he asked.

"Yes!" Alexis and Nicole jumped up and down. "Do it!"

That proved it. "Well, I guess I was wrong," Reid mused. "I guess you girls *do* need a feminine influence in your lives."

"Dad! Duh!" Alexis shook her head, looking exasperated. "We don't want to be around Karina because she's a *woman*."

Nicole nodded. "It's because she's her! She's Karina!"

"And she's awesome. We really, really like her."

Feeling a tiny glimmer of hope, Reid met their excited gazes. "I do too," he admitted. "I really, really like Karina."

"Again, *duh!*" his daughters said in unison. They looked as though they wanted to shove him out the door. "So what are you waiting for?" Alexis asked. "You know where Karina is."

"I *did* book her and the kids that hotel room downtown. . . ." Newly decisive, Reid abandoned his shaving accoutrements. He charged into his room, his path cleared by his eager-to-help daughters, then grabbed his coat. He slung it on. He shoved his feet into a pair of boots. He grabbed his scarf. "Okay. Here I—"

Turning around, Reid confronted Alexis's and Nicole's jointly appalled expressions. Confused, he quit talking.

"Dad, *stop*." Alexis swiped her hand across her throat, mimicking a director's "cut" sign. Her gaze slid past Reid's coat and scarf, all the way to his hastily pulled-on winter boots. "You're wearing *pajamas*," she hissed. Nicole nodded.

Oh. Yeah. "So? Only the bottoms, that's all." Reid gestured at his perfectly acceptable thermal T-shirt. "Time's wasting."

His daughters delivered him indomitable looks. They weren't going to back down on this, Reid realized. "Fine. I'll change into some pants." He toed off his boots, then dropped his scarf. He shucked off his coat. "But then we're going to get Karina."

"And bring her back here for Christmas?"

For the first time, Reid felt nervous. "Yes. I hope so."

"My goodness, Robert!" someone said from the doorway. "It sounds as though we've missed quite a lot around here!"

Reid turned. His grandparents stood there, wearing identical *Arizona* logoed golf visors and matching smiles. They didn't *look* like people whose retirement dreams had been crushed. But then, appearances could be deceiving.

After all, Reid looked like a man who didn't own pants.

"Great Grammy Sullivan!" Nicole yelled, running to hug her.

Robert chuckled. "What, I don't rate a hello around here?"

"And Great Grandpa Sullivan!" Alexis added at a shout, coming in for a boisterous tackle hug. "We missed you *so* much!"

There were hugs all around. Baffled, Reid stared at his grandparents. "But . . . How did you get home?" he asked. "I know for a fact all the flights are booked solid right now."

All four of them stared curiously at him.

"How do you know that?" Robert asked. "Planning a getaway?"

"For once, no!" Nicole said gleefully. "We're staying!"

Alexis nodded in confirmation, doing a gangly happy dance.

Ignoring his grandparents' delighted expressions at that news, Reid raised his chin. "I might have been . . . keeping tabs on available flight statuses." Just because he'd left Kismet years ago didn't mean he didn't still have friends who could keep him updated on the status of one particular curly-haired blonde and her adorable children. "The point is, how did you get here?"

"Oh, they always had today as their return date," Alexis said with an offhanded wave. "That's how the flights were booked."

"They wanted to be at home for Christmas," Nicole added.

Still confused, Reid shook his head. How did Alexis and Nicole know so much about their great-grandparents' plans? He'd assumed that Betty and Robert had gotten the bad news about Edgware and flown home on an emergency basis. On one of those supposedly fully booked flights. Maybe to start trying to sell The Christmas House to another hospitality company, so they could still salvage their Arizona retirement dreams. But how could Alexis and Nicole have known about any of that?

Sure, his daughters had been talking with their great-grandparents on the phone, Reid knew. They'd been e-mailing them. They'd even become buddies on an online social networking site—all things he'd encouraged them to do, as a way for Alexis and Nicole to stay connected with their relatives, no matter where they lived. But that didn't explain any of *this*.

"Oh dear." Betty Sullivan smiled at him. "I'm afraid you girls did your job too well. Your dad seems bewildered."

"Only because I am," Reid said. "What's going on?"

"We've been conspiring!" Nicole blurted. "Together!"

"Let's not baffle your father any further." Betty came closer, then gently took Reid's arm. "Why don't we all go downstairs and have a nice cup of cocoa and explain everything?"

Feeling dazed, Reid nodded. "But we'll have to do it on the run. There's something important I have to do." He glanced at his grandparents, then at his daughters. "Can we do this in one of the B&B's transport vans on the way downtown?"

"Of course!" Jovially, Robert slapped him on the back. "I'll drive. I've been wanting to get behind the wheel of something bigger than a damn golf cart, anyway."

The plan was set. Hoping he wasn't too late, Reid grabbed his boots and coat again, then led the way downstairs.

Arriving on the landing, he glimpsed the personalized stockings lined up on the B&B's fireplace mantel—in particular, the four stockings whose cuffs were embroidered with the names *Karina, Josh, Olivia,* and *Michael.* Someone on staff at The Christmas House was supposed to have taken down those stockings when Karina had left.

Now, Reid smiled at the sight of them. With a little luck, they would need those stockings on Christmas morning . . . when Karina came back to him, and the future looked truly merry.

"Let's go!" he said, ready to lead the charge to that future.

At Reid's signal, the whole lot of them trundled to the door, ready to commandeer a van, confess a conspiracy, and find a true love—probably in that order, probably awkwardly, and probably far more slowly than Reid would like . . . but with a whole lot of Christmas cheer on the part of everyone involved.

Chapter Twenty-One

December 24th
Riverfront Hotel
Kismet, Michigan

Curled up in a blanket atop her hotel room's double bed, Karina put the finishing touches on a text message to Chelsea.

I HOPE WE CAN ALWAYS BE FRIENDS, C., she typed. LOVE, K.

There. That should do it. With her heart pounding, Karina sent the message. At the resulting confirmation from her cell phone, Olivia glanced up. She thumbed the TV remote, muting the *A Charlie Brown Christmas* cartoon they'd ordered on pay-per-view.

"What's that, Mom? Are you still texting Dad?"

"Nope." Fondly, Karina pulled her daughter closer for a hug. She kissed the top of her blond-haired head. "Dad and I quit texting a while ago. That was a message for Chelsea."

"Oh." Olivia snuggled closer. "What did you say?"

"Well, that we'll be home soon. And . . . some other things."

"I hope you told her to take us surfing when we get back!" Across the room, Josh glanced up. He'd twisted sideways in his chair with his feet slung over the arms. "I told Reid that we go surfing sometimes, and he said he'd like to try it."

"Cool!" Michael chimed in, temporarily abandoning his efforts to surreptitiously weigh the Christmas gifts on the hotel room's bathroom scale. "It would be so awesome if Reid visited us in San Diego! We could hike by the ocean, go parasailing at Torrey Pines, visit SeaWorld—lots of stuff!"

"You guys." Regretfully, Karina wrangled their attention, then snuggled into her pajamas. Since they'd decided not to attend the annual Kismet Christmas parade, she'd reasoned there was no rush to get dressed. Not today. "You're going to have to quit talking about Reid—about all the Sullivans, actually."

Josh looked puzzled. "Why? I like them. They're nice."

"Because . . . We live in California. They don't."

"So?" Olivia wrinkled her nose. "They've lived all over the whole globe!" She stretched her arms wide, nearly smacking Karina in the nose with the remote. "Why not San Diego next?"

For a single heartbeat, Karina surrendered to that idea. She imagined Reid, Alexis, and Nicole coming to the Sunshine State—deciding to stay with them. All seven of them. Together.

"I don't think that will happen," Karina said truthfully.

"Well, it ought to!" Michael said. "And since it's Christmas, maybe it will," he insisted. "Christmas is magic."

Karina knew she should correct that idea. Obviously, her disastrous holiday affair with Reid was proof that Christmas *wasn't* magic, no matter how ardently she'd hoped it might be. But just as she sucked in a breath, preparing to speak, someone knocked on their hotel room door. Startled, she glanced up.

Oddly enough, none of her children did.

"Karina!" Vanessa shouted through the door. "It's me!"

"Vanessa?" At the sound of her friend's voice, Karina flung

off her blanket. She padded to the door, then opened it to see Reid's cousin standing in the wide hotel hallway. "Um, hi!"

Self-consciously, Karina poked at her unruly hair. Because, she realized belatedly, it wasn't just Vanessa who'd come for a visit. It was Suzanne. Rocky. Neil. Amanda. Rodrigo. At least two of the maids. And both of the B&B's chefs. Each chef toted a covered wicker basket. They offered them to her with smiles.

"Merry Christmas!" they said. "We brought the food."

"And we brought the music." Rocky hoisted a portable stereo. Beside him, Neil and Suzanne waved hello, also smiling.

"And *we* brought the stockings!" Amanda and Rodrigo said in unison. Then, empty handed, they glanced at each other. "I thought you got the stockings from the mantel," Amanda said.

"I'm sorry, *cariño.* I thought you got them."

"Whoops. I guess we got . . . distracted," Amanda told Karina.

"That's all right!" Karina stepped back, inviting them all inside. "Come on in! I'm so surprised"—*and mystified*—"to see you! Look, kids!" She turned, waving her hand. "We have company."

"Hi," her children said simultaneously, still unsurprised.

It was almost as if Olivia, Josh, and Michael had been *expecting* half of The Christmas House inhabitants to visit. That was . . . weird. What, exactly, was going on here? Karina wondered.

"We couldn't stand the thought of you and the kids spending Christmas Eve here all by yourselves." Cheerfully, Vanessa took off her coat, then flung it on a chair. Everyone else also got situated, littering the room with coats and hats and gloves and scarves. "So we hijacked the B&B's transport vans and came to get you!"

"To get me?" Karina frowned. "For what?"

"To make sure you wouldn't be all alone today!" one of the maids said. "To make sure you had a *good* Kismet Christmas."

Everyone nodded. Karina couldn't help staring in surprise. And gratitude. "You came all this way across town, just for us?"

"Of course!" Vanessa said. "So get dressed. The Kismet Christmas parade is about to start. You don't want to miss it."

"Actually, our room overlooks Main Street," Karina said, gesturing to their hotel room window, "which is right on the parade route. So we won't miss a thing! All we have to do is look outside. And I can do that in my pajamas."

Appearing flustered, Vanessa glanced at the window. "Well, seeing the parade that way is one thing," she hedged, "but for the very best experience, you really need to go outside. All the rest of the B&B guests are waiting for us downstairs."

"All the rest of the—" Perplexed by Vanessa's insistence—and not wanting to delay any of the other guests' holiday fun—Karina shook her head. "I'm sorry. You go ahead, okay? I just don't feel up to all the merriment out there."

"But it will be *fun!*" Vanessa urged. "Come on!"

Amanda and Rodrigo, the maids, the chefs, Rocky and Neil, and Suzanne added their voices to the chorus. "Let's go!"

Silence fell while Karina deliberated their offer.

"Nice try, everyone," Olivia said in a dour tone. "But you might as well save your breath. She won't go. It's too late."

"Yeah," Josh agreed, equally sullenly. "You shouldn't have bothered. *None* of us should have bothered."

"Bothered with what?" Baffled, Karina stared at them.

So did Vanessa. "What are you kids talking about?"

"They're talking about the fact that it's no good trying to get my mom to leave here," Michael said. He'd never sounded more grown up—or more disappointed—than he did just then. Mumbling, he added, "Sorry we couldn't call you sooner, Vanessa."

"Our mom was using the phone the whole time," Josh said.

"Call me?" Vanessa said. "Call me to tell me what?" She gestured at Karina's PJs. "I can see things are pretty dire—"

"Hey!" Karina protested, defensively smoothing her flannel pajama pants. "Give a girl a break. I'm brokenhearted!"

"—but I'm not ready to give up," Vanessa went on, "so—"

"So you might as well get ready to give up," Olivia said, appearing just as let down as Michael did. "Because about half an hour ago, my mom agreed to get back together with my dad."

The B&B's transport vans were nowhere to be found. Neither was Reid's rented Subaru or any of the other vehicles he'd expected to find.

Standing near the snow-filled driveway of The Christmas House, Reid scratched his head in puzzlement. Come to think of it, he realized, the entire B&B had been curiously empty as they'd come downstairs. He hadn't seen any guests. The staff hadn't been hanging holiday light strings or serving eggnog. Even his busybody cousin hadn't been manning the front desk.

Beside him, his grandparents and daughters came to a stop.

"We didn't like Arizona much anyway," his grandfather was saying. "The weather's too same-y. Never changes. Always sunny."

His grandmother nodded. "They put Christmas lights on the *cactus* and call it festive! It's better that we're back here. Kismet is where we belong." She stopped, as though realizing they weren't all piling into a van and speeding toward downtown Kismet. "What's the matter, Reid? Don't say you *like* cactus with Christmas lights on them. They're practically sacrilegious!"

"No, it's not that." Reid shook his head. He pointed at the empty driveway. Only tire tracks and a few oily spots in the snow marked the places where the gift-wrapped transport van should have been. "The vans are gone. We're not going anyplace."

The five of them scoured the driveway with squinty gazes. Then they examined the newly plowed street. Nada. What the hell?

"My rental car is gone too." Undaunted, Reid turned. "I'll call a taxi."

"On Christmas Eve?" Robert said. "You'll never get one."

"Especially with the Christmas parade going on," Betty agreed, adjusting her golf visor. "It'll be crazy downtown."

"Getting to Karina's hotel will be tough," Nicole said. "Even for an adventure travel guide like you, Dad." Sadly, she adjusted her mittens. "We sure can't *walk* that far in the snow."

Alexis scoffed. "Yes, we can! We can't give up now. I didn't put that GPS tracker in Karina's purse for nothing!"

Silence fell. Reid frowned at her. "The what?"

Defiantly, his daughter faced him. "The GPS tracker. I put one in Karina's purse, just in case we all got separated. When Josh realized he'd accidentally stolen his mom's purse, I took it and rigged it." She put her hands on her hips, chin jutting with pride. "It was a stroke of luck, really. Not like when I—"

Abruptly, Alexis snapped her mouth shut.

"Not like when you . . . ?" Reid nudged in his sternest voice.

"Not like when she fixed Karina's phone so the college students she advises would quit bugging her on vacation," Nicole volunteered, ignoring her sister's killing look. "Olivia asked her to do that. Also, probably not like when she had the idea to scheme with Great Grammy and Great Grandpa Sullivan in the first place. I mean, how else were we going to get out of Australia?"

Scheme? Astonished, Reid glanced from Nicole to Alexis.

Belatedly, he remembered Nicole's earlier confession.

We've been conspiring! Together!

"Argh! Geez, Nicole!" Looking aggravated, Alexis rounded on her sister. "If we got caught, you were *supposed* to put a good spin on all this! That's your specialty! Sweet talking people into going along with you." She smacked her head. "Duh!"

After a moment's thought, it all seemed clear to Reid. His daughters had concocted some sort of plan with his grandparents. If he didn't miss his guess, that plan had been designed to bring him home for the holidays . . . and get his kids out of Oz.

He turned. His grandparents were examining the Christmas yard decorations, ostensibly unaware of what was going on.

"What scheme?" Reid asked them. "You never did explain exactly what kind of 'conspiring' you four were doing together."

His grandfather whistled, peering at an icicle on the eaves. His grandmother plucked a handwritten card from one of the porch pillars, where it had been pinned with a thumbtack.

"Oh look!" Cheerfully, Betty waved it. "Vanessa left a note to say that she'd borrowed the vans—and your rental car— and would be back later!"

"Scheme?" Reid repeated, advancing on them. "Conspiracy?"

"All right. Fine." His grandparents exchanged abashed looks. "I guess we'd better tell you all the details."

"I guess you'd better." Reid nodded. If this was going to delay him a moment longer from getting to Karina, it had damn well better be good, too. "From the beginning. I'm all ears."

At Olivia's revelation, Vanessa gasped. She turned to Karina, her face stricken. "You're getting back together with your ex-husband?" she wailed. "Since when? Why? How?"

"Since today," Michael said, ticking off answers on his fingers. "Because . . . I don't know. And over videoconference."

"Thanks, Michael." Vanessa gave him a hasty smile of acknowledgment. Then her attention returned to Karina. "I can't believe it. I honestly thought you and Reid would work things out. I thought if I took *you* to Reid, you'd kiss and make up. I mean, I might have failed at getting *him* here today, but I still had hope. I still wasn't ready to give up on you two."

Aha. "That explains why you wanted me to get dressed and leave the hotel," Karina said. "You're still matchmaking."

No matter how hopeless those efforts might be.

So were her children, she realized in surprise. They were matchmaking too! Suddenly, their earlier conversation—about calling Vanessa (undoubtedly to conspire and coordinate plans with her)—made a lot more sense.

"I was fully prepared to kidnap you to do it, too." Vanessa grinned, gesturing at the group gathered there. "We all were."

There were nods all around. Except from one person.

"Well, this is great. Just great!" Neil interrupted in a tone laden with sarcasm. He stood, throwing his arms in the air with clear exasperation. "I jeopardize my job for the sake of helping put Karina and Reid together, and what do I get as a thank-you? A big, fat 'don't bother'! That's just great."

"Come on now, Neil," Rocky soothed. "You don't mean that."

"The hell I don't!" Neil fixed Karina with a frustrated look. "Ten years at Edgware, straight down the drain. And all because I couldn't stand the thought that *my* evaluation might have contributed to your split with Reid." He shook his head. "Your kids were right. I should have saved my breath. But instead, I stupidly blew my cover and told Vanessa who I was."

"I'm still glad you did," Vanessa assured him. "When I tell Reid and my grandparents, they'll be glad you did, too. We needed to know the whole story about the evaluation."

"I'm not glad!" Neil sighed. "I'll be lucky if I ever get another assignment. If any of you reveal my job, I'm toast."

Thoroughly confused now, Karina frowned. She glanced at Vanessa. Helpfully, her friend summed up the situation.

"It turns out, Neil is an Edgware evaluator too," Vanessa said. "There was some kind of mix-up. Neil was assigned to assess The Christmas House, just like your sister was. He didn't realize the two of you were filing duplicate reports until the news broke about what you were really doing at the B&B—when we found out that you and Reid had split up over it."

Everyone in the room nodded. Taken aback, Karina gazed at them. Then she realized the truth. Of course word had spread about her falling-out with Reid—and the reasons for it.

"The duplicate reports were the real basis for Edgware putting the kibosh on the deal," Rocky explained, casting a commiserating look at his partner. "It was all automatic. Neil's boss told him the computer system flagged the duplicates and put the whole thing on hold." He hugged Neil. "Please don't worry about your job, though. Nobody here is going to tattle on you, I promise."

A chorus of avowals rang out to reassure Neil. Grudgingly, the (other) undercover evaluator nodded. "Thanks, everyone."

Tentatively, Karina glanced at Neil. "Does this mean The Christmas House *didn't* fail the Edgware evaluation?"

"Officially? No," Neil said. "It will be rescheduled."

"So that means I *didn't* bankrupt your grandparents and ruin their retirement dreams!" Karina told Vanessa, feeling a sense of relief overtake her. Apparently, she'd been more worried about that issue than she'd realized. "That means there's still a chance the B&B sale could go through! Right? Eventually?"

"Well . . ." Vanessa pulled a face. Hesitantly, she nodded. "Yes, that's true. Technically, the sale of The Christmas House could still go through. Not that any of us want it to."

Karina didn't understand. "But your grandparents—"

"Agree. They were in on the whole thing, all along," Vanessa told her. Beside her, Olivia, Michael, and Josh nodded, well versed in whatever was going on. "Let me explain. . . ."

With his mind whirling, Reid stared at his grandparents.

"Let me get this straight," he said. "You never wanted The Christmas House sale to go through at all? You set up the whole deal with Edgware as an excuse to bring me home again?"

"*And* get us out of the Outback," Alexis put in. "That too."

Betty nodded. "We missed you, Reid! We missed the girls! Once your grandfather and I realized Nicole and Alexis wanted to live in the states again, we had to help them get here."

"And *we* had to make sure we stayed here," Nicole said.

"That SpaceFace thing was a big help," Robert agreed. "We just went online, had a few secret chats, and bam! Done."

Guiltily, his daughters nodded. "You were always pretty busy, Dad," Nicole explained. "You never noticed a thing."

"Not even when I sneaked away at the airport to log on at a public Internet terminal and send Great Grammy Sullivan a message. You thought I was getting Minibons for forty-five minutes?" Jadedly, Alexis shook her head. "Get real, Dad."

Too late, Reid remembered Alexis's temporary disappearance at the Grand Rapids airport . . . and the way she'd dodged his questions by offering him mini cinnamon rolls afterward.

"But . . . the evaluation. The B&B!" Reid protested. "This was a pretty elaborate scheme, just to bring us home again."

"Well, you're you!" His grandfather smiled. "We couldn't

make it *too* easy. You would have guessed our plan right away."

"Besides," his grandmother added, "we wanted to make sure you had a chance to feel needed—to fix things and help out around here. We wanted to make sure you felt you *belonged*."

"You nailed that one," Reid agreed dispiritedly. He *had* felt he belonged at The Christmas House again. He'd felt that old Christmas magic. He'd felt *loved*. "But what about the Edgware evaluation?" he asked, pondering all the details. "You couldn't have known the B&B would fail. That's not possible."

"Well . . ." His grandparents exchanged a conspiratorial look with his daughters. "Actually, it *is* possible. . . ."

"I don't believe it." Shaking her head, Karina sat on her hotel room's bed. "All of you *sabotaged* the B&B's evaluation?"

The eager group in her room nodded, headed up by Vanessa.

"Not as part of the plan to bring Reid, Nicole, and Alexis back home," she explained hastily. "The sabotage part was extra. It happened sort of . . . organically. One by one, we all took turns introducing little *glitches* into The Christmas House's usually flawless holiday routine—just to make sure the sale wouldn't actually go through." Vanessa chuckled. "It wasn't until pretty far into the process that we realized we were overdoing it."

Suzanne waved. "Sorry about the power outage!"

Karina gaped at her in astonishment.

"Sorry about the spiked cider!" one of the cooks said.

More confessions came, fast and furious. Laughing, Vanessa held up her palms to stop them. She turned to Karina again.

"So Lagniappe at the Lakeshore was never sabotaging The Christmas House at all?" Karina asked. "It wasn't them?"

"No. It was us," Vanessa said. "I can see you're confused, but it all makes sense—honestly, it does. Because The Christmas House is part of Kismet. It's part of the community. It's part of the *family!*" Vanessa gestured wildly, emphasizing the point. "No one wanted to see the B&B change hands. Not really."

"Someone should have told your grandparents that," Karina pointed out, her head swimming with all she'd been told. "Before they plunked down a bunch of money on their retirement home."

Michael gave a nonchalant wave. "Oh, that was a rental."

"Yeah," Olivia agreed. "We *all* knew that."

"Except Reid," Josh mused thoughtfully. "Nobody told *him.*"

At that, everyone appeared stricken . . . including Vanessa.

"I forgot about that!" she said. "I was so focused on making sure Reid and Karina got back together again that I forgot to fill him in on all this planning and scheming!"

"Don't worry." Olivia glanced at the clock. "By now, your grandparents are probably here. They're probably telling him."

Josh and Michael nodded. So did Amanda and Rodrigo.

Apparently, Karina realized, *everyone* was in on this.

Everyone, that is, except her . . . and Reid.

"We have to make sure!" Karina jumped to her feet, looking for her borrowed winter boots. She found them, then stuffed her stockinged feet into them. "We have to tell Reid everything!"

She turned. Everyone in the room stared balefully at her.

Karina looked down. "If this is about my pajamas again," she said defensively, "I swear I'm boycotting pants altogether."

But Vanessa only folded her arms. "Why do *you* care about what Reid knows? You're reuniting with your ex-husband."

Yeah! said the combined, betrayal-filled gazes aimed at

her—including those belonging to her children. Discomfited, Karina made herself quit searching for a sweater and scarf.

Somberly, she looked at her children. Their expressions made their feelings pretty plain. But just to make sure . . .

"You three think I've made a huge mistake, don't you?"

As though they'd been on mute until now, Olivia, Michael, and Josh spoke up at once, not caring who else heard them.

"I used to want you and Dad to be together again," Olivia admitted in an urgent voice, "but not anymore! Not since Reid."

"I just like it better when you're both happier," Josh said. "There's less crying. And more boogie-board riding."

"I prefer having two bedrooms, twice as many toys, and all the Flamin' Hot Doritos I can eat at Dad and Chelsea's condo!" Michael said, rubbing his belly. "Don't worry about me, Mom!"

Awed, Karina gazed back at them. "Well, I guess that's a good thing, then," she said, feeling another overwhelming surge of relief. "Because I *didn't* get back together with your dad."

Olivia widened her eyes. "You didn't? Really?"

"Nope." Karina shook her head. "I was tempted, for your sakes. But then I realized that I wanted *me* to be happy too. And being with your dad wasn't going to make me happy."

In a singsong voice, Vanessa hinted, "I know who would. . . ."

Grinning at her friend's unstoppable matchmaking, Karina opened her arms. Michael was first to run into them. Olivia and Josh weren't far behind, piling on for hugs. "I'm sorry about the divorce, you guys. But we're making this work, right?"

All three of them nodded. "Don't worry, Mom," Olivia said.

Touched by her daughter's reassurance, Karina hugged them all more tightly. "I love you. You're the best kids ever."

"We love you, too, Mom," they chimed in heartfelt unison.

At that, Karina would swear everyone in the room awwed.

Olivia gave her an inquisitive look. "But, Mom, what about that text message you sent to Chelsea? You said, 'I hope we can always be friends.' I thought you were apologizing because of their breakup—because you were taking Dad away from her."

Michael and Josh nodded. They must have discussed this.

At that imaginative interpretation, Karina smiled. Her children might be smart, but they were still children. "I was apologizing for accidentally getting a snag in one of the sweaters Chelsea lent me." *When I was jumping on top of Reid.* "That's all. And I was telling Chelsea that, even if she and your dad *didn't* work things out—but I think they will—I want to stay friends with her. It turns out, 'C' is all right."

"Oh." Josh smiled. "I'm glad you're friends now."

"Me too. So, you see? I'm still pretty helpful sometimes, to some people," Karina said. "Even if the college students I advise don't need me quite as much between semesters this year—as evidenced by all the student phone calls I'm *not* getting."

"Um, Mom?" Wearing a guilty expression, Olivia cut her off. She traded glances with her siblings. "About those phone calls from your students . . . There's something we have to tell you."

"So," Betty Sullivan said, "everything is all right now." She clapped her gloved hands with an air of satisfaction, surveying the festive B&B with evident pride. "We'll keep on running this place ourselves, just the way we love to do—"

"Although you don't seem to have done *such* a bad job of things," Robert put in, slapping his hand on one of the garland-wrapped porch pillars, "during our brief absence."

"—you and the girls will move back here to the states—"

At that, Nicole and Alexis beamed, high-fiving each other.

"—and everyone will live happily ever after," Reid's grandmother concluded. Her eyes sparkled. "I'm so happy for you, Reid. The minute you told us what happened while we were gone, I *knew* we'd been completely right to conspire behind your back."

Betty said it so sweetly, so innocently, that Reid could hardly find it in his heart to be angry with her for doing it. In fact, he wasn't angry with anyone. If there was one thing the Sullivans were good at, it was being loyal . . . and being loving.

Besides, given the way his grandparents had reacted to *his* one small confession, he couldn't be anything except happy.

Grammy, Grandpa, he'd said after their multigenerational conspiracies were revealed, *I fell in love. I fell in love at Christmastime, with a wonderful woman—and her three children.*

Betty and Robert Sullivan *hadn't* laughed themselves silly at the idea, the way Reid had feared. Instead, they'd stood there in the fluffy Kismet snowfall that had begun drifting down, and they'd listened raptly as he'd told them about meeting Karina. About falling for her. About getting to know Olivia, Josh, and Michael, and loving them a little too.

"So what are you waiting for?" His grandfather startled him by asking, his voice booming into the frosty air. "Get going!"

"Yes!" his grandmother urged. "Go get Karina! Hurry up!"

They both appeared more than eager to meet her. And Reid was definitely eager to get her. To find her. To apologize to her. To beg her, if necessary, to forgive him for making her leave—for not trusting her, most of all, to love him back.

"I'd love to," Reid said. "But there are still a few obstacles here. The B&B's transport vans are still gone. The Kismet taxis still aren't running. The Riverfront Hotel is still a long way away. And we don't have any transportation."

"Bah. A Sullivan never quits, Dad!" Nicole said. "Not

when climbing a mountain, and not when doing anything else either."

"That's right!" Alexis proclaimed. "Where do you think we learned to be so good at getting what we want, huh, Dad?"

Before Reid could guess, his grandfather answered that question himself. "They learned it from *you,* Reid. So go on—go get that girl of yours! Don't let anything stop you!"

Newly fired up now, Reid scanned The Christmas House and its grounds. Surely there was some way he could get to Karina. If he had to, he'd walk every icy step of the way. He'd crawl. He'd put on snowshoes, ice skates, cross-country skis. . . . He'd do whatever it took. Because that's how much she meant to him.

Suddenly, Alexis took out a GPS device from her pocket. She showed it to Reid. "Uh-oh, Dad. Look! Karina is on the move!"

That did it. With one last glance, Reid made up his mind. "I have an idea," he said, motioning them onward. "Let's go!"

Chapter Twenty-Two

December 24th
Riverfront Hotel
Kismet, Michigan

Wearing a coat, a scarf, two sweaters, a T-shirt, a silky camisole, two pairs of wooly socks, warm boots, gloves, thermal underwear, holiday-print pajama pants, and a hat, Karina led the way out of her room at the Riverfront Hotel. Everyone else thundered behind her down the hall. Her children took the forefront, scampering like eager puppies, elated by the prospect of having another mission.

Not a *secret* mission this time . . . just a mission. A mission Karina devoutly hoped they succeeded at. So much was counting on this. Her heart. Her soul. Her notion of a happy holiday for Olivia, Josh, and Michael. Even, if she was lucky, her future.

They rounded the corner and approached the elevator bank. One of the cars was out of order; the other appeared to be stuck on a lower floor. With a groan of urgency, Karina wheeled around, almost colliding with Vanessa, Rocky, and Neil, who'd been hard on her heels. Almost crashing into them were the maids, the two chefs, and Suzanne. Karina didn't want to think about what a Benny Hill–style comedy routine this would have turned into had all the guests still waiting downstairs joined them already.

Filled with a sense of purpose, she raised her arm, signaling everyone to stop. She motioned to a door.

"Let's take the stairs!" Karina said. "It'll be faster."

As she wrenched open the stairwell access door, the first sounds of the annual Kismet Christmas parade reached her. Strong enough to filter through the hotel's walls, a flourish of joyous holiday music could be heard—a marching band, if she didn't miss her guess. Parades always had marching bands—even, apparently, if they had to do their marching through snowdrifts.

Newly urgent, Karina hurried downstairs. Her footsteps (and the parade music) were almost immediately drowned out by all the other footsteps following behind her. Olivia laughed and went faster, racing with her brothers. Vanessa pursued Karina along with the staff and guests, probably still hoping her vaunted matchmaking skills would prove unassailable, once again.

"I'll expect an invitation to the wedding," Vanessa panted, as though reading Karina's mind. "Be sure to tell Reid!"

"All I'm going to tell him," Karina insisted, "is that trusting me *didn't* wreck his grandparents' dream retirement." That's why she'd left her room in such a rush. That's why she intended to leave the hotel and get back to The Christmas House as fast as she could—whether by gift-wrapped transport van or some other means. "Reid needs to know that he did a good job at the B&B. That all the people he loves are going to be okay."

"Seriously." Vanessa still jogged along with her, neck and neck down the stairs, scarf flying. "My grandparents planned to be here by now. They've probably already told Reid everything. What *you* should be telling him is how you feel about him!"

"That's sweet, Vanessa." Karina read a sign as it flashed by in her peripheral vision. Two floors to go. Her retinue's pounding footsteps still hammered the stairs. "But Reid made it pretty clear that we're over with. I can't hope for more."

Even though, foolishly, I still do. . . .

"But you *could* have more!" Urgently, Vanessa kept pace with her. "If you would only tell Reid how you feel, I *know* things would work out between you two. After all, it's Christmas!"

"Christmas is magic, Mom!" Michael piped up from nearby.

Argh. Driven to distraction by all the events of the day— and yesterday—Karina shook her head. "How can you still believe that, Michael?" she demanded. "Does *this* really feel magical to you?" She gestured. "Racing down a dingy hotel stairwell?"

Her younger son only nodded. "Yep. It's fun!"

"We're all together, Mom," Josh said. "That's what counts."

"I don't know why you're wasting time talking," Olivia put in. "*Run,* why don't you? Bella would run for Edward!"

Laughing, Karina felt spurred onward. She did descend the final few steps at a run, followed by everyone else. At the landing, the parade music grew louder, accompanied by cheering and the muted conversations of passersby. The parade must be happening just on the other side of the access door.

Vanessa grabbed her arm, her expression grave. "Just consider it, okay?" she begged. "Just consider telling Reid how you really feel. For me? No, wait. Do it for yourself. Okay?"

Struck by her new friend's sincerity, Karina couldn't turn her down just like that. But with no reason to believe things had truly changed between her and Reid, she couldn't offer Vanessa much hope, either. Torn, she decided to hedge her bets.

"If Reid still has his 'nookie beard,' I'll tell him how I really feel about him," Karina promised. Because, after all, what were the odds he hadn't already shaved it off, thereby proving to himself (and the world) he was over her? "And if he's clean shaven, I'll stick to the facts about Edgware. Deal?"

Feeling certain there was no risk involved—except to her poor beleaguered heart—Karina stuck out her hand.

Vanessa eyed it. She quirked her mouth. "You should know that my track record of fix-ups is unbeatable."

"I'll take my chances," Karina deadpanned.

"Also, Reid was in the process of shaving when I left."

At that, Karina quailed. "Do we have a deal or not?"

Firmly, Vanessa clasped her hand. "We do. Let's go!"

Then Karina pushed open the hotel's access door, the frigid December air rushed in the stairwell, and their entire entourage stepped onto the sidewalk, nearly in the midst of the parade.

The first things Karina saw were the two gift-wrapped B&B transport vans, handily parked close by. At least she had transportation! She could put Reid's mind at ease about his grandparents and their retirement without delay. Then she headed nearer, saw the throngs of fellow B&B guests standing by the vans to enjoy the parade, and realized she had a problem.

The parade flowed past on both sides. Jolly-looking Kismet residents and tourists were packed in tightly nearby, currently watching a red and green float drive past, gaily decorated with streamers. The transport vans were completely hemmed in.

Karina wasn't going anywhere. Not until after the parade.

It took Reid much longer than he expected to reach the Kismet city limits. Skirting the frozen pathway between the lakeshore and riverfront, he watched his breath puff into the frosty air and wondered what would come first: frostbite or more heartbreak? Because there was every chance Karina didn't want to see him—much less see him the way he was about to arrive.

After all, he *had* been extraordinarily mean to her. He'd demeaned her career expertise—that had to hurt. He'd laughed off her attempts to help him. And then he'd turned his back on her.

If their roles were reversed, Reid didn't know if he'd have the strength to forgive. Forgiveness wasn't like leading a pack of newbie adventure travelers. That mission was easily accomplished by anyone with the proper training and experience.

Forgiveness was more like scaling an icebound mountain. To do that, a person had to work hard at it. The person had to be careful and diligent. Sometimes the person had to drive in a pickaxe and just hang on, doing his or her best not to tempt failure by looking down.

A person trying to forgive had to look up. Up up up.

He hoped like hell Karina would look up.

As though sensing his trepidation, Nicole took his hand. She squeezed it in her smaller, mittened hand. "Don't look so worried, Dad. Chances are, Karina *probably* still likes you."

"Yeah," Alexis agreed from his other side. "And even if you blow it and *don't* get Karina back, we'll still love you!"

"That's . . . very reassuring, girls. Thanks."

He kept going. Near downtown, though, Reid was forced to stop. As his grandparents had predicted—and reiterated just then from their positions near him—the streets were choked with parade traffic, pedestrians, or both. A light snow drifted down on all of it, partly obscuring Reid's path—not to mention the town's old-fashioned wrought iron street lamps, sparkling lights, and Christmas decorations. Far in the distance, the Riverside Hotel loomed, several stories high, taunting him with its inaccessibility.

"I'm afraid this is the end of the line," Robert said.

"I don't know how we can get through this," Betty added.

But Reid knew. He'd get through it the same way he got

through everything in his life. With grit. Determination. And a big, ass-kicking helping of *just keep going.* He set his jaw.

"I didn't come this far to turn back now," he said. "I'm going. But if you all want to stay here and wait . . . go ahead."

For a heartbeat, Reid paused. No one moved a muscle.

"Okay." For the first time that day, Reid grinned whole-heartedly, warmed by his family's devotion. "Here we go!"

Standing on tiptoes, flanked by her children, Vanessa, and most of the guests and staff at The Christmas House, Karina peered over the heads of the paradegoers. Far down Main Street, more floats snaked their way forward, moving at a snail's pace. Clowns in Santa hats meandered down the snow-covered street, reaching into their Santa bags for candy. They flung it to the eager children on the sidelines, who thronged to catch it.

In front of her, yet another marching band passed by, playing a rollicking rendition of "Jingle Bell Rock." It sounded wonderful . . . but in this din, it wouldn't even be possible to call Reid on her cell phone. Karina had no choice but to wait it out. The only trouble was . . . did Reid still want to see her? And if he did, would she still have the courage, twenty or thirty minutes from now, to face him?

If he gave her another stony I-don't-know-you look, she didn't know if she could endure it. But for now, Karina felt strong. Bolstered by her new friends, encouraged by her children, and heartened by the knowledge that she *didn't* have to be endlessly helpful to everyone around her or risk being abandoned by them, Karina held her ground. Surely the parade couldn't last too much longer. Could it?

Impatiently, she watched another float pass by. She stamped her feet for warmth, then traded a smile with Suzanne. But there were no two ways around it: This parade was killing her! Karina needed it to end. She needed to get to

Reid, to make sure he didn't blame himself for the crazy mess of this year's holiday season at The Christmas House. Knowing Reid, he'd taken all the accidental mishaps to heart, when he wasn't responsible at all.

Watching one of the Santa clowns, Karina realized she could use this delay to rehearse. That way, she'd know exactly what to say when she finally caught up with Reid at the B&B.

Reid, I love you, she practiced, then shook her head.

That wasn't what she would say. She had to focus!

She had to concentrate on the issue at hand: Reid's feelings. His feelings of failure, vulnerability, and (probable) culpability.

Karina wanted to ease those feelings . . . to make sure Reid was happy. Sure, a part of her still hoped he had room for forgiveness . . . and maybe a little room for something more. But she couldn't count on that, Karina reminded herself—no matter how assured Vanessa had seemed. After all, according to Reid, his cousin's matchmaking track record was notoriously awful—even if no one wanted to hurt Vanessa's feelings by telling her so.

"Come on. Hurry up!" Karina muttered to herself as the next float passed by in a glittery spectacle of tinsel and lights. She craned her neck, trying to gauge how many more floats might remain in the lineup . . . and caught sight of something strange.

A horse-drawn sleigh. A very *familiar* horse-drawn sleigh. A horse-drawn sleigh pulled by two massive Clydesdales and emblazoned with the recognizable, holly-wreathed logo of one very popular, very beloved Kismet B&B: The Christmas House.

Vanessa saw it too. She blinked. "Is that . . . ?"

"It is." Karina nodded, hardly able to believe her eyes. As she watched, the sleigh's determined-looking driver veered his rig into the parade traffic, sliding into position as though he'd been meant to be there all along. *Reid,* she recognized.

Reid was driving the sleigh. Alexis and Nicole were with him, too, along with a pair of golf-visor-wearing, parade-waving seniors. "It's The Christmas House's sleigh!" Karina turned to Vanessa. "I didn't know the B&B was part of the parade!"

"It's *not* part of the parade." Frowning in perplexity, her friend stared down Main Street. "I'm pretty sure Reid just party crashed the parade. And he's coming this way, too. Look!"

Karina did look, her heart in her throat. So did the rest of her retinue: the B&B's guests, the staff, Amanda and Rodrigo, and her children. Chattering excitedly, Olivia, Josh, and Michael pointed to the horse-drawn sleigh.

"Mom, look!" Michael shouted. "It's them!"

"Go get Reid!" Olivia added. "Now's your chance!"

Suddenly torn with indecision, Karina gazed down the street. Seeing Reid was like seeing her future coming nearer—a grim-faced, determined future that was moving at a snail's pace.

"Why does he look so mad?" Karina asked Vanessa.

"Probably because he misses you," Vanessa said with typical confidence and ridiculous optimism. She nudged her. "Go!"

"I—" Karina bit her lip. Wildly, she said, "I'm going!"

With her heart pounding madly, she ducked a couple of parade watchers, then headed down the street. Was she really going to party crash the parade herself? she wondered. Was she really going to . . . to do what, exactly? Flag down the sleigh? Jump onto it, hobo style? Jog alongside, trying to talk to Reid?

Karina didn't know. All she knew was that she was doing it.

For the first time in a long time, she was truly going for it. For herself and no one else.

Oddly enough, the realization was exhilarating. Feeling herself break into a smile, she ran faster. The crowds parted. Karina reached the edge of the street. But somehow, incredibly, she couldn't see The Christmas House's horse-drawn sleigh anymore. She turned in a circle, looking. Where had it gone?

"Quit it with the intimidation face, Dad!" Nicole gave him a ferocious poke. "You're going to scare away Karina!"

"Yeah, Dad," Alexis urged. "Try to look nice!"

"I *do* look nice!" Reid argued, frustrated with the floats and clowns and marchers that were keeping him from Karina. He scowled at them, fervently wishing they'd vanish. Still holding the reins, he worked at controlling Holly and Ivy while simultaneously keeping his eye on the Riverfront Hotel.

If he could only get there in time. *Come on, parade!*

"I don't know. You probably shouldn't have entered the Christmas parade by force, Reid," his grandmother admonished from the backseat. "The city fathers are going to be very unhappy about this. You're supposed to have a permit."

Parade events and snow swirled crazily around them.

"He's going to get his girl!" his grandfather piped up, giving Betty a reproachful look. "Don't you have any romance in your soul, woman?" Impatiently, Robert slid across the front seat. He gestured at Reid. "Here. Give me the reins."

"I'm almost there." Reid kept driving. "Just a few blocks farther."

"Dad!" Alexis eyed her GPS device, then waved her arm urgently. "Hurry up! Karina is on the move again."

At that, Reid did surrender the reins. He didn't have time to follow the prescribed parade route. He had to get to—

Karina. All at once, Reid saw her, wearing a pompom hat and a coat and a scarf and probably six sweaters, weaving her way through the crowd. At the sight of the woman he'd been looking for, Reid felt himself go still all over. As though time slowed, he glimpsed Karina's insistent expression, her hasty movements, her curly blond hair. She turned her head, searching the crowd.

Then she turned away, headed in the wrong direction.

She was leaving, he knew then. She wanted to get away from Kismet so much that—apparently—she was willing to walk out of town in the middle of a parade . . . walk away from Christmas and walk away from him.

No. He couldn't let that happen. Not now.

With a yell, Reid leaped from the sleigh. *"Karina!"*

His earsplitting bellow caught the attention of . . . all the people around him. But not the woman he wanted. Landing upright on the icy packed snow, Reid gestured to his grandfather.

"Keep driving!" he called. "I'm going to get Karina!"

"Just *go!*" all the sleigh inhabitants yelled in unison.

So Reid just went. He careened through the crowd, even as the parade went on and the marching band continued to play Christmas carols and everyone who already had someone to love held that person close and laughed at all the holiday antics.

"Karina!" Reid yelled again . . . and then he saw her again.

She turned around. Her eyes widened. A smile broke on her face, making her appear even more beautiful than he remembered.

Her gaze shifted to his beard. Her mouth turned into an O of surprise. Karina stopped in place, her attention fixed.

Within seconds—far too long to wait—Reid reached her. He stopped with his hands fisted at his sides, forcing himself not to touch her. Not yet. He couldn't risk scaring her away.

Quit it with the intimidation face, Dad! You're going to scare away Karina! He'd already done that once. Never again.

"Please don't go!" Reid said, his voice a husky plea he could neither stop nor deny. "Not yet. Not until you know—"

"Your beard." Karina pointed. "You kept it."

"—that I'm sorry. I'm so, so sorry, Karina!" Reid went on. Heedless of the nearby crowd, not caring who heard, he moved a little closer. "I never meant to doubt you. I *do* know who you are. I do." Finally trusting himself, he raised his hand to her cheek. He gazed into her eyes. "You're the woman I love, Karina. I love you with everything inside me—with everything I am right now, and everything I'll ever be. You make the sun rise! You make me feel . . . *everything*." Feeling his breath hitch, Reid made himself keep going. "I've done a lot of things. I've traveled a lot of miles, and I've experienced a whole world of adventures. But all of them pale beside you. None of them matters as much as *you* do, right now. Please, *please* say you'll give us another try. Because I swear to you, if it takes me the rest of my life, I'll make you the happiest person in the world."

Appearing awestruck, Karina shook her head. At the gesture, Reid's heart plummeted. She didn't want him? He was too late?

But then she smiled, and he saw there were tears shimmering in her eyes, and even as he held his breath, Karina took a brave step closer to him. If he was fearsome, Reid realized with pure thankfulness, then Karina was at least equally courageous.

She stroked his jaw . . . his beard. "You didn't shave," she said in a voice choked with emotion. Then, stroking him again, she laughed with evident relief. "I'm glad you didn't shave."

"It would have been a lie," Reid told her, covering her hands with his. "Because I never gave up hope. Not on us."

No wonder he'd had so much trouble shaving today, he realized. The problem hadn't been the Christmassy atmosphere, the interruptions, or the implements. The problem had been a lack of will. Reid simply hadn't had the will, deep inside, to rid himself of his good-luck nookie beard and admit defeat.

"I'm glad," Karina said, "because I love you, too, Reid.

I'm so sorry I didn't say so before! I'm sorry I hurt you—
sorry I lied to you. I never meant to." Fervently, she shook
her head. "I swear, I never will again. Never! And if you say
you can't believe me . . . well, I guess I'll have to live with
that." Her gaze met his, nakedly hopeful but willfully strong.
Tearfully, she gulped back a sob. "But please don't say that!
You don't know how much you mean to me, Reid. I'd given
up on finding someone. I'd given up on myself! I was so
scared . . . of not being needed. Of not being wanted. Of not
being *loved*."

"I love you." Reid squeezed her hands. "I do."

"But what I should have been scared of is not taking a
chance." Karina shook her head, her chin quivering. "I should
have been scared of losing you. I almost did lose you! And
now—" She broke off, her gaze searching his. "Now, I can't
believe you're here. Here in time to know that I love you, and
I need you, and I missed you—so much!—and I love you—"

"You already said that one," Reid told her, "but I'll never
get tired of hearing it." Unable to resist, he kissed her.

At the first touch of their lips, Karina melted into his arms.
Making a thankful sound, she kissed him back. As one, their
bodies slammed together, equally ardent and equally bundled
up . . . all except for one crucial area. Wearing a beaming
smile, Karina leaned back. Even as Reid went on holding her,
she aimed her gaze lower . . . all the way to the flannel pajama
pants he'd inadvertently forgotten to change out of, after all.

Then she nodded at her own PJ pants, also made of flannel
but printed with girly-looking bows and Christmas ornaments.

"Hmmm. Something tells me," Karina said as her smile
widened, "that we're perfect for each other."

Reid kissed her again. "You're only just realizing that?"

"Well . . . sometimes I'm a slow learner. For instance, it took
me a while to come around to the real magic of Christmas."

"Me too," Reid admitted. "But now I'm a Scrooge no
longer. Thanks to you," he said, "I feel Christmas here"—

he touched his fist to his heart—"in a way that's never going to leave."

With a heartfelt sigh, Karina hugged him closer. "You feel so good! Even with all this cold-weather gear on. I can't wait to find out what you feel like with nothing but beachwear on."

At her saucy eyebrow waggle, Reid grinned. "Beachwear?"

"Preferably tiny board shorts," Karina specified with a lascivious, loving gleam in her eye. "That's what men wear on the California beaches these days. *You'd* make them look good."

"I'd make them—" Newly elated, Reid raised his eyebrows. "You're damn right, I'd make them look good." He couldn't wait to see Karina in a bikini, either. "Does this mean . . . ?"

A nod. "I want you to come to San Diego with us. You can check out the ocean, experience the sunshine, find out if—"

"I'm in," Reid promised hastily. "I'm in all the way."

Karina laughed. "You didn't even let me finish inviting you! You must really mean it."

"I do," Reid swore, kissing her again as another holiday float passed by, blaring Christmas music. "I really mean it."

"There are practical considerations, you know," Karina demurred. "For instance, there's probably not a lot of hard-core adventure travel guiding going on in the suburbs these days."

"Probably not." Unconcerned, Reid smiled at her. He squeezed her hand. "But I have more skills than you know about. Photojournalism, diving, rock climbing, orienteering—I could probably make a living at one or two of those things."

"Or at teaching them to other people," Karina agreed. Appearing dazed but content, she smiled back at him. "We're really doing this! We're really going to be together."

"For Christmas and for always." Reid motioned to his own flannel pajama pants. "The PJs decree it. We're a team now."

"Oh no!" someone groaned from nearby. "This is awful! They're going to be the pajama pants–wearing team!"

Olivia. Reid turned to see Karina's daughter shaking her head. Beside her, his daughters did the same. So did Josh.

"We'll *never* get them out of their pajama pants now!"

"What have we *done?*" Michael asked with a hilariously dramatic waggle of his hands. "We're doomed!"

Vanessa looked on with clear satisfaction, arms crossed over her chest. "Quiet, kids," she shushed. "In the matchmaking game, you have to take the wins where you find them."

"I think the PJ pants are cute," Betty volunteered.

"*I* think the girl is cute!" Robert stepped forward, holding out his hand. "I'm Robert Sullivan. You must be Karina."

Blushing, Karina took his hand. "Pleased to meet you."

As though Reid's grandfather had issued a signal, everyone else surged forward too. Reid's B&B guests. His staff. All the chattering kids. Suzanne, Neil, and Rocky. Amanda and Rodrigo. Even a few good-natured Kismet residents, who'd apparently been following along with the action, having decided that Karina's and Reid's declaration of love beat a Christmas parade any day.

Close by, one of the Clydesdales whinnied. Reid looked in the direction of the sound and glimpsed The Christmas House's horse-drawn sleigh, parked just off the parade route in front of the Riverside Hotel, where his grandfather had apparently left it.

It seemed he'd left it in capable hands. Because his hulking, always cheerful neighbor Nate Kelly stood beside it with his wife, Angela, and stepdaughter, Kayla. Catching Reid looking, Nate gave him a thumbs-up sign.

"All's well that ends well, eh?" Nate nodded toward the sleigh. "Want me to take this back to the B&B for you?"

Hugging Karina to his side, Reid shook his head. "I'll take it. I think we're all going that way soon. But you're welcome to come too, Nate! You and your family." He smiled at them.

"We're here with our friends, Rachel and Reno." Nate's nod indicated a hand-holding couple nearby. The woman stood dressed in conspicuously fashionable clothes, and the man—well, Reid recognized former NFL kicker Reno Wright. Everyone knew Kismet's very own BMOC. "Is it okay if they come along too?"

"Sure!" Karina called. "The more the merrier, right?"

"That's exactly what I was thinking," Reid agreed.

"No wonder we're perfect for each other," Karina told him.

They beamed at each other, relieved and confident and more than ready to get their future started. Then Vanessa elbowed her way forward, put her hands on her hips, and shook her head.

"Okay, okay. That's enough," his cousin said as the parade began to break up behind her. "No need to rub it in, you two."

Surprised, Reid gazed at Vanessa's disgruntled face.

So did Karina. "Why, Vanessa . . . You sound a little peevish about something." Karina traded a knowing glance with Reid. "Could it be that *you* need a matchmaker of your own?"

Reid's cousin blinked, seeming on the verge of . . . denying the very idea. She scoffed, adopting her trademark stance. "No way. I'm all about the fix-up, not *being* fixed up. Besides, it's Christmas Eve. Let's get this party started already!"

Reid didn't need to be told twice. Grabbing Karina, he herded together all their children, then conferred with his grandparents and cousin. Together, they made plans to get everyone safely and promptly back to The Christmas House.

They had a damn holiday to celebrate, Reid knew. A holiday full of laughter and good cheer and Christmas merriment. There was no way he meant to delay any of that any longer.

He'd already spent nearly twenty years missing out on Christmas. This year, with Karina by his side and all their children gathered around, Reid intended to savor every moment. Because now that he'd given in to the sentimentality of the season, he didn't want to go back to anything less. This year, Reid wanted carols and gifts, tinsel and gingerbread, eggnog and blinking lights and even that ridiculous dancing Santa figurine.

He wanted all of Christmas, all the time. He wanted it all.

Glancing up at Karina as he helped her into the B&B's horse-drawn sleigh, Reid realized that he already had it all. He had everything he could have asked for and more. He had a new love, a new family, and a whole new future with his daughters to look forward to. If that wasn't some kind of Christmas miracle, Reid didn't know what was. He couldn't believe he'd doubted it.

"This year, I hardly need Christmas and stockings and gifts to unwrap," Karina said as Reid settled beside her and took up the reins. "I already have everything I ever wanted. Because now I have you." She smiled at him. "I love you so much, Reid."

"I love you, too." Reid smiled back, then set the sleigh in motion, charting a course around Kismet's scenic frozen lake. "But I wouldn't be too sure about that 'already have everything you want' idea," he told Karina. "There might be a few more surprises in store for you yet. Just wait and see. . . ."

Chapter Twenty-Three

December 25th
The Christmas House
Kismet, Michigan

"Mom! Mom! Wake up!" Michael yelled, bursting into Karina's peaceful, gingerbread-scented dreams with his usual Christmas morning holler. "It's Christmas. Right now! Wake up!"

Her younger son bounded onto the bed in Karina's snug attic room at The Christmas House. Tousle haired and full of energy, Michael clambered nearer, making the mattress dip and sway.

"Wake up, Mom! We're going to miss *everything!*"

Blearily, Karina yawned. "What time is it?"

"The sun came up five minutes ago," Josh said. "Let's go!"

Well, that *was* their traditional agreement, Karina remembered. No Christmas-morning wake-ups until at least dawn.

"Hurry up, Mom," Olivia said. "Michael is ready to chew through the gift wrap with his teeth to get to his presents."

"Well, paper isn't very nutritious." Karina yawned again, feeling—despite her tiredness—an undeniable tingle of anticipation too. "I guess I'd better get moving then."

"Come *on!*" Michael urged. "We're missing Christmas!"

"Honey, we can't miss Christmas." Groggily, Karina sat up. Her hair stood out in crazy ringlets, her pajamas were wrinkly, and her breath . . . Well, it could knock out Rudolph. But there was no refuting the truth: This year, she was doubly excited about the holiday festivities. She and Reid had stayed up till all hours though, talking and planning, and she was beat. "We can't miss Christmas, because *we're* Christmas," Karina explained to her anxiously waiting children. "It only happens if we're there to make it happen, with love and to-getherness."

Serenely, she smiled at them, pleased with herself for having come up with that original bit of parental wisdom. It was downright poetic. It ranked right up there with her combined philosophies that cheaters never prospered, that love conquered all, and that the child who divided a piece of cake could never be the first to choose his or her portion of said cake.

Feeling very Solomon-like, Karina nudged at her hair.

"Hmmm. What's that about love and togetherness?" someone asked from the other side of the room.

At the sound of that deep, masculine, irrefutably jolly voice, Karina started. She looked in that direction.

Reid stood there, tall and broad shouldered and smiling. "That sounds promising. I'd like to explore that idea in a little more detail," he said. "Right after you open this."

Reid came closer, then handed her a gift-wrapped package. Taken aback, Karina gazed at the paper and crookedly tied bow.

"We let him sneak in earlier, while you were asleep," Michael explained with his usual ebullience. He cast Reid a chary look. "But he didn't say he was bringing a gift. I didn't even have a chance to guess what it was first!"

"Maybe next time, buddy." Reid ruffled his hair.

That's when Karina realized that, although she hadn't

noticed it in her muzzy, newly awakened state, Alexis and Nicole were there too. They sat together on Olivia's bed, wearing identical glitter-covered, felt reindeer-antler head-bands. On the floor beside them, Josh sat cross-legged with an oversize sweater pulled over his pajamas. Michael skipped into the picture and then plunked down too, making their merger complete.

They really *were* becoming a new blended family, Karina thought as she looked at them. She and Reid and their com-bined children were starting their futures together, now, on Christmas morning, with the scent of perking coffee float-ing into the air from the B&B's kitchen downstairs and the first faint stirrings of joyful Christmas carols drifting over the sound system.

Feeling her heart swell with happiness, Karina glanced at the frosty window, hoping to catch her emotions before they ran away with her completely. Instead, she glimpsed an idyl-lic wintery snowfall floating past her room's window and knew she didn't have a chance at keeping her equanimity intact.

This Christmas *was* the perfect holiday for her children. She'd finally given it to them, Karina realized, just the way she'd dreamed. All because she'd dared to reach out for a love that should have been impossible . . . and was all the more precious because of it. She was so lucky to have found Reid.

So lucky to have found the Christmas inside both of them.

"Go ahead." Wearing a warm smile—and another pair of flannel PJ pants, thereby sealing their bond forever—Reid sat on the bed near her. He nodded at his gift. "Open it."

Holding her breath, Karina did. She undid the bow, took off the ribbon, lifted off the box lid, and revealed . . .

"A compass?" Perplexed, she gazed at the small metal in-strument, nestled carefully on a bed of ethereal tissue paper. She wasn't sure what to make of it. Nevertheless, she pre-pared her finest smile. She didn't want to hurt Reid's feelings.

"It's so you never get lost again!" he told her.

Aww. He'd tried to turn a last-minute sporting-goods-store gift into a romantic gesture. That was sweet. All men couldn't be expert gift givers, Karina knew. She broadened her smile.

"I could rig it with a GPS device," Alexis offered, "if you want me to. Then you'd *really* never get lost again."

"Well . . . Thank you!" Karina boomed. "It's *wonderful!*"

With her smile wobbling, she glanced up . . . all the way into Reid's sparkling eyes. He laughed. "Nice try. *Very* convincing."

"What do you mean?" Rats. Desperately, she tried to feel thrilled about her new compass. Karina grabbed it. "It's great!"

"It's only part of your gift." Reid raised his cupped hand. "This is the other part." He spread his fingers, revealing the modest gold and sapphire ring nestled in his palm. "If you want it. It's not fancy, but it's a family heirloom. I want you to have it."

Karina gasped. She gazed into his face. "Is this . . . ?"

Patiently, he waited for her to finish. Of all the times when Reid might have agreeably interrupted, this was one of them.

Excitedly and nervously, Karina tried again. "Is this"—another tentative glance—"an engagement ring?"

"Only if you take it." Reid held it closer. "But I have it on good authority that when it's right, it's right. And that sometimes you just have to follow your heart."

Belatedly, Karina recognized Amanda's impassioned arguments in favor of her and Rodrigo's whirlwind romance.

"I love you, Karina," Reid said. "Will you marry me?"

She didn't waste an instant. "Of course I will!"

Laughing, Karina flung herself across the bed and into his arms. Reid collapsed beneath her onslaught, holding her to him, laughing too. When Karina finally looked down at him, then framed his face in her hands and kissed him, she knew exactly how right she'd been to come to Kismet for Christmas this year.

The Christmas House had definitely made all *her* holiday dreams come true. That was why she could honestly say, "We can't let Amanda and Rodrigo have all the fun, can we?"

With her Rudolph-knockout breath and all, she kissed him. It was only a small kiss—a sensibly closed-mouth kiss, the only kind even remotely suitable for a postdawn lip smack—but it was a celebratory kiss, all the same. Joyfully, Karina smiled.

"I love you, too, Reid. Merry Christmas!"

"Merry Christmas!" Looking dazzled, Reid shook his head. "You know what? I've never been happier to say those two words. I thought they were lost to me forever." He brought his forehead close to hers, then smiled at her. "But you brought Christmas back to me, Karina. If not for our holiday affair—"

"Holiday *love*," she corrected.

"—then I wouldn't have found any of this."

Reid spread his arms, indicating their togetherness, their cozy B&B room, their close-knit, laughter-filled Christmas morning . . . and their children, all of whom sat waiting, with palpable impatience, for them to be finished canoodling.

Olivia crossed her arms. "Are you guys *done* yet?"

"Yeah." Josh made a face. "We're *still* missing Christmas!"

"Don't mind us." Michael waved them off. "I can wait after all. I'm pretty sure I already guessed all my gifts, anyway."

At his cocksure tone, Karina laughed. So did Reid.

"Oh yeah?" Reid asked, getting to his feet. He extended a hand to Karina, helping her get up too. "We'll see about that."

"Does that mean we're going downstairs?" Nicole asked.

"You've been telling us that Christmas Day at The Christmas House is *awesome* ever since we got on the plane to come here," Alexis added. "It's about time we found out if you were right."

Wearing a heartfelt smile, Reid examined them all. He nodded. "Oh, I'm right. No doubt about it. Christmas Day at The Christmas House really *is* awesome."

At his wave of permission, all the children raced for the door. Alexis took the lead, followed by Olivia and Nicole. They were pursued by Josh, then by a barking, sweater-wearing Digby the dachshund, and then (laggardly) by a nonchalant Michael.

"I'm pretty sure I'm getting that Transformers toy I asked Santa for," he informed Karina and Reid as he passed them. "It weighs two-point-one pounds, and so did one of the packages I found."

"One of the packages you—" On the verge of offhandedly dismissing her son's boast, Karina realized what he'd said. *"Found?"* she repeated. "You *found* the gifts I hid?"

"Mom." Wearily, Michael shook his head. "I *am* me, you know. Of course I found them." In the doorway, he tossed her a grin. Then something else seemed to occur to him. "Next time, though, you should let *Santa* have some of the glory, okay?" Michael shook his head. "You don't have to steal Santa's thunder *every* year by getting the best gift for me yourself."

Duly chastened, Karina nodded. "I'm sorry. I'll try."

"If it's not you doing it," Michael elaborated with a trace of chagrin, "it's Dad. You guys have got to stop. Poor Santa!"

Beside her, Reid agreed. "We don't want to upset Santa."

"Okay. Good." Michael nodded, then left.

As her younger son followed the others downstairs, Reid smiled at Karina. She smiled at him. In mutual accord, they linked hands, then headed downstairs too, ready to embark on the first of many Christmases they'd spend together—trying not to upstage Santa, taking sleigh rides, baking pfeffernüsse, singing Christmas carols . . . and figuring out where all the best gifts were hidden.

Sometimes finding the true gifts in life wasn't easy, Karina thought as she trundled to the upstairs landing with Reid. Finding and keeping love wasn't always easy either; she and Reid both knew that. But with a little diligence—and a lot of love—she expected the effort of doing so to keep them happily engaged for years to come . . . and a lifetime of Christmases too.

Gazing down as their children ran pell-mell to the piles of gifts under the sparkling, fully lit, popcorn-and-cranberry-garland-embellished trees, Karina drew in a deep breath.

"Here we go," she told Reid. "Are you ready for this?"

"Absolutely," he said. "As long as you're by my side."

"Forever," she promised. Then, with Christmas carols and gleeful children's shouts ringing in their ears, Karina and Reid went to start their lives together—for this Christmas, for next Christmas, and for every day in between . . . now and forever after.

Dear Reader,

Thank you for reading *Holiday Affair*.

As you might have guessed already, I truly love this time of year. The Christmas carols, the sparkling lights, the gingerbread, the togetherness, the traditions, the surprises—they all mean so much to me . . . as do *you,* for allowing me to be a part of your holiday season! I hope you enjoyed Karina's and Reid's story. I was delighted to return to Kismet, and I did my very best to bring you another fun read. If this was your first visit to Kismet, you can find out more about the "merriest town in Michigan," Nate and Angela, and Reno and Rachel, in my previous book, *Home for the Holidays.* I hope you'll check it out soon.

In the meantime, please drop by my Web site at www.lisaplumley.com, where you can read free first-chapter excerpts from all my books, sign up for my reader newsletter or new-book reminder service, catch sneak previews of my upcoming books, request special reader freebies, and more. Or visit me on Facebook, Twitter, or MySpace, and "friend" me on the service of your choice! The links are available on lisaplumley.com.

As always, I'd love to hear from you! You can send e-mail to lisa@lisaplumley.com or write to me c/o P.O. Box 7105, Chandler, AZ 85246-7105.

By the time you read this, I'll be hard at work on my next Zebra Books contemporary romance. I hope you'll be on the lookout for it. Until we meet again . . . Merry Christmas!

Lisa Plumley

More by Bestselling Author
Hannah Howell

__Highland Angel	978-1-4201-0864-4	$6.99US/$8.99CAN
__If He's Sinful	978-1-4201-0461-5	$6.99US/$8.99CAN
__Wild Conquest	978-1-4201-0464-6	$6.99US/$8.99CAN
__If He's Wicked	978-1-4201-0460-8	$6.99US/$8.49CAN
__My Lady Captor	978-0-8217-7430-4	$6.99US/$8.49CAN
__Highland Sinner	978-0-8217-8001-5	$6.99US/$8.49CAN
__Highland Captive	978-0-8217-8003-9	$6.99US/$8.49CAN
__Nature of the Beast	978-1-4201-0435-6	$6.99US/$8.49CAN
__Highland Fire	978-0-8217-7429-8	$6.99US/$8.49CAN
__Silver Flame	978-1-4201-0107-2	$6.99US/$8.49CAN
__Highland Wolf	978-0-8217-8000-8	$6.99US/$9.99CAN
__Highland Wedding	978-0-8217-8002-2	$4.99US/$6.99CAN
__Highland Destiny	978-1-4201-0259-8	$4.99US/$6.99CAN
__Only for You	978-0-8217-8151-7	$6.99US/$8.99CAN
__Highland Promise	978-1-4201-0261-1	$4.99US/$6.99CAN
__Highland Vow	978-1-4201-0260-4	$4.99US/$6.99CAN
__Highland Savage	978-0-8217-7999-6	$6.99US/$9.99CAN
__Beauty and the Beast	978-0-8217-8004-6	$4.99US/$6.99CAN
__Unconquered	978-0-8217-8088-6	$4.99US/$6.99CAN
__Highland Barbarian	978-0-8217-7998-9	$6.99US/$9.99CAN
__Highland Conqueror	978-0-8217-8148-7	$6.99US/$9.99CAN
__Conqueror's Kiss	978-0-8217-8005-3	$4.99US/$6.99CAN
__A Stockingful of Joy	978-1-4201-0018-1	$4.99US/$6.99CAN
__Highland Bride	978-0-8217-7995-8	$4.99US/$6.99CAN
__Highland Lover	978-0-8217-7759-6	$6.99US/$9.99CAN

Available Wherever Books Are Sold!

Check out our website at
http://www.kensingtonbooks.com

3 1901 04941 8330